Praise for
Sloan Parker's Other Books

"Sloan Parker is an amazing writer. Her work is beautiful and touching and emotional. If you haven't read any of her books, I suggest you run out and do so!"

—Sadonna at The Armchair Reader

"...I have loved every one of Sloan Parker's books and this one is no different. ...exciting, suspenseful and most importantly, romantic. The love story between Walter and Kevin is so sweet and real. They have a connection that can't be denied by either one of them."

—Literary Nook on HOW TO SAVE A LIFE

"...a smoothly flowing plot that has enough angst, obstacles, and mystery to keep you glued from the first page to the last... I thoroughly enjoyed reading this fascinating and enthralling book and would definitely recommend it to anyone looking for a fantastic read that is worth every minute spent on it."

— Trish at Mrs. Condit Reads Books on HOW TO SAVE A LIFE

"...an emotional and sensual blockbuster."

—Joyfully Reviewed on MORE

"I loved both of the heroes... and found myself easily rallying for their relationship to grow from being best friends to developing a loving, romantic relationship together that lived long within my heart long after the story was over."

—Night Owl Reviews on TAKE ME HOME

"So sweet and romantic and incredibly well done in such a short format."

—Joyfully Jay on SOMETHING TO BELIEVE IN

OTHER TITLES BY SLOAN PARKER

More
Take Me Home
How to Save a Life (The Haven #1)
More Than Just a Good Book
The Break-In
Swept Away
Something to Believe In
I Swear to You

Breathe

SLOAN PARKER

DEDICATION

To Mom and Dad. Thank you for all the love and support.

Chapter One

Hope you found some peace in jail. You never will again.

Lincoln McCaw read the note one last time and crushed the paper in his fist. The bus jerked forward as it came to a stop. No need to check. He was home. The smell of hog manure from the surrounding farmlands and the burning steel of his hometown's only manufacturing plant filtered in through the crack in the window one seat over. Funny how he couldn't feel the coolness of the winter air hissing in through that crack.

Maybe he never would again.

He stuffed the wadded-up note into his duffel bag, stood, and headed to the front of the bus. The jail wasn't far from Edgefield, but he hadn't wanted Nancy waiting for him outside. Who knew what sort of people lurked outside a jailhouse.

He laughed at that. Who was he afraid of? Men like him?

Six months in the county jail. His fellow inmates and the deputies probably thought he was the worst of the lot. He'd spent more days there than most of the guys who came and went. Some spent less time at the state pen.

But the jail was behind him now. It was over. Wasn't it?

Not according to the latest "love letter" he had tucked in his bag.

He stepped off the bus. The driver shut the door and pulled away as soon as Lincoln's boots hit the pavement. Not surprising. Most didn't want to stick around the three-stoplight town. But Lincoln did. He had a lot of reasons to be there. A lot of reasons he'd never leave.

Clear plastic walls surrounded the bus stop bench, cracked on all three sides and coated in a slime no amount of scrubbing with the industrial strength cleaner they'd used at the jail would remove. No one would wait inside the enclosure, no matter how desperate they were for a bus out of Edgefield.

He checked anyway. Splinters covered the faded wood of the

bench. If anyone sat there, they'd get an ass full of tiny wooden daggers. Not the best way to ride the bus. Edgefield was so damn inconsequential nobody at the Metro Transit Authority probably gave a shit about the upkeep on the small-town stop that made up the farthest point of the outlying community bus route.

Home sweet home.

"Lincoln!" Nancy crossed the parking lot behind the bench, waving her arms through the air, a smile spread across her face. She quickened her stride. He did the same and hugged her when they met. The warm embrace reminded him of their mom, reminded him one person in the world loved him. She squeezed tighter.

"Nance, I can't breathe."

"Oh sorry." She released him and stepped back. She wore a brown and orange waitress uniform and those heavy-duty shoes nurses wore, designed for support and long-wearing comfort. Hers were dingy, nowhere close to the white they must've started out as, and were on their last leg. They wouldn't provide much support or comfort. Her disheveled dark hair fell from the ponytail in several places, and she had a hint of makeup smudged under and over her eyes. Exhausted. His baby sister was working herself to death.

Despite that, her eyes shone at him. The smile was also a reminder of their mom. Nancy had always taken after their mother in a physical way. Whereas he looked more like their dad with skin tone and features that gave a nod to their Iroquois heritage.

"Just missed you," she said.

"Missed you too."

"I wish you would've let me visit. Was it bad?"

"Nah. It was okay." No need to tell her about the gray food that smelled of dish soap, the foul stench from the unwashed inmates he shared space with, the lack of privacy, the endless hard surfaces of metal bars and concrete floors, or the countless cracks about his short-lived racing career from the two good ol' boys who'd recognized him.

He'd hated every minute of his time there.

And he deserved far worse.

"Come on. I parked over here." She tilted her head to the left and pointed to the vehicle she'd driven. His black pickup. The damn thing looked huge in the empty lot.

He missed the truck. He also hated the hell out of it. Like it was the truck's fault.

Nancy had parked next to the County Cooler, an ice-cream stand run by the Drakes, the elderly couple who'd owned the place since Lincoln had been a kid. Every winter they boarded up the stand and headed south to visit their grandkids in Texas. When the place closed, it always had the look of a shack you'd see Bo and Luke Duke plow the General Lee through as Rosco P. Coltrane chased them down. In Lincoln's day, local teens needing a dry place to hold their beerfest orgy sneaked in during the long winter months while the Drakes were out of town.

An open window near the garbage bin was missing several slats of wood. Lincoln smirked. Same window he'd used when he first had sex with Tommy Vanderline during their sophomore year of high school. Nice to know some things never changed.

"You wanna drive?" Nancy asked.

His smirk vanished. "No." He yanked open the passenger-side door, tossed in his bag, and sat.

Then again—sometimes everything changed.

Nancy slid into the driver's side and wrenched the seat forward until her feet touched the pedals. "Sorry. I thought you might want to. You haven't tried it out since it came back from the body shop."

He leaned his elbow on the armrest of the door and stared out the side window. "Can't. Restricted to work privileges. There and back. That's it."

They drove in silence, the darkness surrounding them in the cab, the sound of the truck's heater filling the void of unasked questions until he couldn't stand not knowing.

"Did he hit you again?"

He would've missed her slight nod if it weren't for the dim display of the dashboard. She turned away from him as though checking the side street traffic at the next intersection.

"You didn't call the cops?"

"I should have," she said.

"Fuck, yes, you should have." Lincoln stabbed at the door lock with two fingers. Lock. Unlock. Lock. Unlock. He took a deep breath and let off on the button. She didn't need him being an ass. "When did he come back?"

"The Friday after you left."

"How long did he stay?"

"Until a couple of weeks ago."

"Jesus, Nance!"

"I needed—I couldn't afford the hospital bills without him, or her medicine without his insurance."

"Well, now you can. Soon as I get a new job." He'd take care of her like he should've been doing for the past six months. If he had been there, Mel wouldn't have had a chance to hurt her again. "Is he gone for good?"

She didn't answer.

"Why not?"

"He left some of his stuff."

"You let me know the minute he shows up." He'd remind the asshole that family looks after their own. "The kids okay? Did he—"

"No!" Her tone was defensive, and she threw him an angry look before she focused on the deserted street ahead. He shouldn't have asked. She wouldn't let anyone hurt her kids.

When she spoke again, her voice was under control, more conversational. "Could you stay with Davy and Jessica tomorrow after school? Adam has basketball practice." Softer she added, "They've been home alone a lot lately."

He stared out the window into the darkness and said, "I'll be there."

A block from Nancy's, they pulled up to a stop sign next to the Late Night Paradise Plaza—home to the only all-night gas station and carryout in town, a movie rental shop, and Sonny's Tavern.

Lincoln sat taller. "Can we make a stop? I need smokes."

"Lincoln…"

"I'll quit again. Just need a pack to get me through the transition."

She sighed and turned into the plaza's drive.

The neon signs advertising an ATM machine, lottery tickets, and beer had him shielding his eyes with the back of his hand. There were no neon lights in jail. Sounded like the title of a country music song. Something his fans would have blasted from their car stereos as they drove in on race night. He reached for the truck's door handle, but her voice stopped him.

"No smoking around the kids, okay?"

He opened the door and said, "You know I won't."

"Or in the house," Nancy called through the side window as he strode for the store.

Lincoln waved an okay sign her way and opened the door to the carryout. A young man passed by the front of the store, hands shoved inside his pockets, head down as if he had to watch his every step. Lincoln froze in the doorway.

Great-looking guy. Nice body.

The kid headed for Sonny's Tavern.

Great ass too.

Fuck. Lincoln had been away too long. Not a good idea—gawking at straight guys on the streets of Edgefield. But…the kid had stopped, hand on Sonny's front door, replicating Lincoln's frozen stance. He was staring at Lincoln, his mouth parted, his eyes conveying a hunger Lincoln knew all too well.

The door to Sonny's burst outward, almost smacking the kid in the forehead, and two guys exited. The kid moved out of their way, then slipped inside, his gaze on his feet again.

Lincoln's body screamed at him to follow. He ignored it and entered the carryout.

What was that look? Something?

It didn't matter.

He passed by the front counter with the smokes and found what he'd really wanted—a bottle of Jack Daniel's. He grabbed two for good measure.

* * * *

"Jay, did you hear me?"

The front door of Sonny's Tavern flew open, and cold winter air blasted in.

Another man might have chosen a stool farther from the entrance. Not Jay Miller. The cold didn't bother him. Why would it? He was already numb.

"They let the bastard out today." His dad's voice cut through the haze of alcohol. "Six months and now he's…" He trailed off.

Jay dropped the beer he'd been nursing for the last fifteen minutes onto the bar. The bottle clanked and rocked, foam building, drops of the precious liquid spilling. He didn't bother rescuing it. He'd just order another as soon as his dad left, like he planned to do for the next couple of hours.

"Your mother's still going on about frying his ass, and he gets out the day before…" His dad cut off midsentence again. Maybe he always did that. Usually Jay's mom was there to continue on.

"Today?" Jay asked.

The look his dad gave him was comical—if anything could make him laugh again—as if his dad thought he was mentally deficient in some way. Maybe he was. How much did you have to drink before the brain cells died off?

"He's probably already back in town."

In Edgefield? How long until Jay found himself face-to-face with the man? He nodded. That was all he could manage. Six months in jail and the man who killed his wife was getting his life back. He'd be working and living and loving. And Katie was turning to dust in the ground. Jay would never have his life back. He'd never have anything.

The door swung open again, and a pair of giggles floated in with whoever entered the bar. What the hell were they so happy about?

He had to get out of there. Get away. Escape all of it.

"Why don't you come stay at our place tonight?" his dad said. "You can sleep in your old room. Then we'll all visit the cemetery tomorrow."

The restroom. Maybe if he didn't come out right away his dad would get a clue.

Jay stood, and the weight of his body proved too much for his unsure legs. He sank onto the bar stool. The beers—which he drank fast and barely tasted—had hit him hard, but news of Lincoln McCaw's fate had finished the job. It was over.

Except it wasn't. It never would be.

His dad put a hand on his back. "Hey, Sonny, get us a cup of coffee?"

"Sure," the bartender said. When he returned with the coffee mug, he added, "He's had a few."

"I imagine so." Jay's dad pushed the coffee closer.

The smell of it churned Jay's stomach. Nothing smelled good anymore. Nothing tasted good either. What had he last eaten? And when? Probably why the beer wasn't settling too good.

His dad was talking again. Didn't he get it? The last thing in the world Jay wanted to do was give up the beer and face that McCaw was done with his punishment.

"You should come tomorrow," his dad said. "It might give you closure."

Closure? There wasn't enough beer for that.

There was one thing that would give Jay closure. Finally confronting McCaw, looking the man in the eyes, making him understand how much he took from the world, making Lincoln McCaw suffer.

That'd be closure.

Chapter Two

The house was dark when they pulled into Nancy's driveway, and Lincoln said, "Guess I missed the kids." *Damn*. Hearing their voices on the phone hadn't been the same.

"I told them to go on to bed. They'll see you tomorrow." She cut the engine, and they walked to the house in silence.

Nancy opened the front door, and Sparky barreled into them. The large black mutt didn't bark, but he rammed his paws into Lincoln's abdomen in greeting.

"He gain more weight?"

"I think the kids have been feeding him junk food while I'm at work." She smiled, but her eyes didn't join in on the expression. A working mom with two jobs meant a lot of nights home alone for her kids.

Lincoln patted Sparky's head and sighed as the dog ran off down the hall. He stepped to the couch in the living room. Same couch he'd slept on during the long months between the accident and the start of his time at the Grant County Justice Center. The secondhand piece of furniture had been uncomfortable back then. After months on what could only be described as a metal slab with a mattress the thickness of a blanket, the couch was a welcome sight. The exhaustion of the long day slammed into him. Waiting for your freedom took a lot out of a man. They had released him late in the day, and by the time he'd signed his paperwork and made it to the bus stop, he had to wait for the last bus, which worked out since Nancy had been on the late shift.

He dropped his duffel bag and the paper sack with the smokes and whiskey onto the couch.

Nancy shook her head from where she had stopped at the hall doorway that led to the bedrooms. "I've got you set up in Davy's room."

"I was fine on the couch."

"That was only for a couple of months. I was hoping… I thought you said you'd stay with us."

He picked up his bags. "I will." He followed her and said, "Just don't want to put anyone out."

"Davy's fine with his brother." She opened the last door on the left, and Lincoln entered the small bedroom. A child's room. A twin bed. A kid's desk he'd never be able to fit his knees under. A dresser that had machine screws sticking out where the knobs should have been. Action figures and half-constructed LEGO sets piled beside the desk as if someone had swept the treasures there with a broom to clear a path to the bed. A green beanbag chair in the corner surrounded by toy cars, fire trucks, and army tanks, each vehicle neatly lined to form an arch around the giant cloth ball, pointed outward as if to protect the chair from unwanted visitors. Lincoln smirked. He'd never sit in the chair. It'd be hell getting up. But it did seem like a comfy place to get drunk and pass out.

He shrugged off his coat and draped it over the back of the desk chair. The chair teetered, rocking in indecision if it could hold the weight of the leather jacket.

For the first time since Lincoln left the jailhouse, the cool air reached him, and he shivered. "Is the heat on?"

Nancy stood in the doorway. "The thermostat isn't right. I keep having to turn it up to eighty-five to get any heat."

"I'll look at it tomorrow." He'd also look at the sliding door on the laundry closet they'd passed in the hall. It was off the track, the plastic hinge snapped in two.

"Thanks." She stayed at the door as if she shouldn't step inside the room. Which was bullshit. This was her house, not his. He'd left his house the day he was arrested and hadn't stepped so much as one foot inside since.

It hit him then. How different his life was going to be now. He'd never sit in his recliner again. Never watch his big-screen TV. Never drive another race. Never make love in his bed.

There were a lot of things he'd never do.

He was staying in an eight-by-eight-foot room he'd commandeered from his ten-year-old nephew. He sat on the edge of the bed and laughed when he pulled back the blankets and found sheets and a pillowcase covered in metal robots from the movie *Transformers*.

Nancy didn't laugh with him. Probably had more to do with what she tugged out of her pocket than her lack of humor over the bedcovers. She unfolded the papers and stared at them for a moment before she handed them to him. "The insurance I mentioned."

He snorted as he looked it over. "Ain't cheap."

"It was the only one that—"

"Would take on a man who killed someone?"

"Don't say that." She brushed aside the dark bangs that were stuck to her forehead. "They said they'd insure you for any vehicle except your race—"

Lincoln held up a hand. "Yeah. I get it."

"If you want to sign, I'll fax them at work. They said the coverage can start tomorrow."

He took the pen from Nancy and signed the contract. "Am I going somewhere?"

"I talked to Mitch like you asked."

He handed the papers to her. "And?"

"He said to come by tomorrow after lunch. You can't so much as drive a forklift, but they've got some manual work in the warehouse. He might be able to get you on the payroll in the next week or two."

"Thanks."

"Will you make good money there?"

"Mitch does okay." Lincoln tried to meet her gaze, but she wouldn't look at him. "Nancy, are you in trouble?"

"I'm behind on the utilities." She swiped at the stubborn pieces of hair again. "They're threatening to shut off the phone. And the electric."

"It's the middle of fucking winter. And you've got kids living here. Did you tell them that?"

She shrugged as if it wasn't bothering her. Right. He *had* to land the job with Mitch.

He stood and went to her, wrapping his arms around her shoulders. She dropped her head to his chest. If he had been home, he would've seen how much trouble she was in. He would've been able to stop his asshole brother-in-law from laying another hand on her.

"I'll help out," he said. "Don't worry about it."

"I'm glad you're home. And it's not the money." She breathed deep, then spoke softer. "I missed you. I'm glad you're staying."

He tickled her sides. "You won't kick me out when I get in the way?" He'd leave in a heartbeat if she wanted him to go. He wouldn't be a burden on her.

She giggled and pulled away from his tickling. The smile on her face brought out his own. He could've sworn his cheeks creaked with the expression. He hadn't cracked a smile since the life he'd known had ended one year ago.

His last smile had been the morning of the accident, in the shower as he looked down at Paul on his knees before him. Paul had made a lame joke, and the mischievous look in his eyes teased Lincoln, as did the man's tongue swirling over the crown of his dick. He caressed Paul's cheek with his thumb as the man set to giving him a blowjob—the last blowjob he'd had since then.

Lincoln drove the image away.

He should get laid. Someone like the guy he'd seen outside Sonny's.

No. Edgefield wasn't the place to cruise for a simple fuck or blowjob. He'd wait till he could make the fifty-minute trip to Fort Wayne.

Or maybe he'd wait a little longer. He wasn't up to feeling that good. Not yet.

He spotted three boxes stacked in front of the closet. He walked to them and kicked the bottom box. "My stuff?"

Nancy nodded. "He brought them by a couple of weeks ago. There's more in the garage."

Lincoln grunted.

"He asked about you. Wanted to know how you're doing."

"Don't want to talk about him."

"He wanted to be there for you—for the arraignment, the sentencing, all of it. You pushed him away and that wasn't fair."

"He's moved on."

"But he hasn't forgotten. You never gave that man closure."

"He's got his dick in someone else." Lincoln dropped to the bed. "I'd say he's over it."

Nancy shifted on her feet, her attention on her shoes until she spoke. "You've got to let it go, Linc. Give yourself permission to forget what happened. Move on."

"I'm trying to."

"Forgive yourself."

That, he couldn't do.

Nancy was quiet again until he looked her way. She said, "You have a chance to start over."

"But do I deserve it?"

She came to the bed and placed a kiss on the top of his head. "You do. And someday you'll be able to accept that." She shut the door behind her before he could argue.

He shouldn't have said anything about what he deserved or didn't deserve. Nancy didn't need to deal with his guilt on top of everything else. He toed off his boots and stretched out on the bed. His feet hung off the end, the backs of his ankles digging into the edge of the mattress. He sat up and leaned against the headboard, then grabbed the brown sack and pulled out a bottle of whiskey.

Maybe with enough, he could close his eyes and not see the woman with red hair lying broken on the pavement of State Road 91, her green sweater soaked with blood, her body perfectly still—too still.

Maybe he could forget the biggest mistake of his life.

Chapter Three

Jay punched at the doorbell with his fist. What were they thinking? In the middle of the goddamn day? Couldn't they have waited until after dinner?

His boss was none too pleased when he'd said he needed to take the afternoon off. It wasn't like he'd had the job all that long. He might not be able to forgive himself if he lost another.

He also might not forgive his parents or the Shaws. Did they need to go there again? So much for the promise he'd made his wife at the funeral. How could he celebrate her life standing over her—

The door swung open. "You're late." His mom grasped his arm and hauled him inside. The force of her action didn't fit her small stature or her matching pink skirt and jacket. Her manicured fingernails dug into his sleeve as she shoved the door closed. What was she doing opening the door anyway? It wasn't her house.

He shrugged her off his arm. "Good to see you too, Mom."

She straightened the collar of his dress shirt and smoothed the fabric over his shoulders. Her pursed lips proved she wasn't pleased with his selection. "Your brother's even here already." She hauled Jay into a fierce hug, holding on as she said, "You didn't have time to get your hair cut? What will the Shaws think?"

Jay jerked away from her. He had only agreed to go to the cemetery with them because they had all loved Katie, and the anniversary of the day she died couldn't possibly hurt any worse than every other day without her. Could it?

Maybe. Since he had to spend it with his family.

He entered his in-laws' living room, hoping to work his way to a seat beside his brother. Todd was nowhere in sight. *Great.* Jay hated this part—being alone with them.

Emily and Stuart Shaw sat on a love seat to his right. Emily smiled in greeting, but the expression didn't reach her eyes. He hated looking at her. She was as beautiful as her daughter had been, despite their differences in personality and available money to spend on clothes and accessories.

Stuart Shaw was also beautiful, if a man his size could be called such a thing. He was as into his looks as any woman Jay had known. Never a gray hair in sight, not a bit of stubble on his face, nor a single hair between his eyebrows. Katie had teased that the man spent more time preening than either her mother or she. Jay almost laughed at that as he gave the man a nod, but he held back. There'd be no explanations for laughter...not today.

Stuart grunted his hello from the sofa.

Standing near the man, Jay always felt insignificant, unimportant, even with Stuart still seated. As a former defensive lineman for the Indianapolis Colts, Jay's father-in-law was the first person most noticed in a room. No matter where. No matter when. He trumped everyone else.

Jay's dad stood and stepped forward. He shouldn't have looked so small, but he did, whenever they were in the Shaws' house. His dad didn't speak as he gave Jay's shoulder a double pat before returning to his seat. How many people had given Jay that same reception in the past year? Too many. Although the double pat was more than most did.

Was it because no one knew what to say? Jay couldn't help them with that. Anything they'd likely say he didn't want to hear. Funny how similar he had become to his father since the funeral. Detached. Uninterested. As if he was sleepwalking through life. Jay had always hated that about his dad. The only time he'd seen the man full of life in any way was when Jay was in high school and he'd woken up at four thirty in the morning to find his dad in the kitchen filling a travel thermos full of coffee. The man was headed for his annual fishing and hunting trip. The animated way he talked about his plans as he poured the coffee was like nothing Jay had ever seen from the man. Hadn't since.

Jay also hated sitting in the Shaws' living room. No matter what he wore, he figured he'd soil the pristine, off-white furniture when he sat. The room smelled of lemon furniture polish, like it always did. There was no clutter, no day-old newspaper on the coffee table, no stacks of magazines or catalogs, no knickknacks or mementos— nothing that signified life happened there, like a painted replica of the upper-middle class. The worst part...there was not one sign Katie had ever existed. No photos. No hand-painted gifts from her school years. Not even the framed poem she'd given her parents when she'd graduated high school. Like she had never existed. Or they'd erased her from their lives.

Emily offered a cup of coffee to Jay and said, "I'm glad you decided to come."

"Of course he wanted to come with us," his mom said as she took a seat on the couch beside his dad.

Jay gave Emily the most polite smile he could manage and shook his head about the coffee. Better not to chance anything in his stomach. He chose the antique wooden rocker several feet away from both sets of parents. The rocker creaked as he sat. Emily jumped with the sound, and Stuart glared at him. What was he supposed to do? Apologize for sitting? Stand still? Not breathe? Not live?

No one in the room said a word.

The Shaws didn't move again, their faces as stern as their postures. Where had Katie gotten the light and laughter she lived with every day?

The silence stretched on as if none of them spoke the same language, and they knew it was easier not to speak at all. The sharp grind of a snowplow passing by outside startled Jay.

What was he doing there? Surrounding himself with their anger and grief. He'd been treading in the water of despair so long, the exhaustion a part of his every molecule, it wouldn't take much for them to pull him under the surface where he'd never be able to breathe—where he'd never be alive again the way Katie would want him to.

His mom dug into her purse as if she just remembered something. She removed a photo and handed it to Emily. "It's the same as the one in our living room. I've been meaning to get a copy made for you."

"Oh," Emily said, the sound more of a gasp than a word. "It's…" She bit her bottom lip, and it quivered when she let go. "It's lovely. Thank you." She held the photo out for her husband. Stuart leaned to look but didn't touch it. When he sat back, Emily rested the photo in her hands on her lap. Tears filled her eyes as she stared at it, and then she set the picture on the coffee table in front of her as if she couldn't hold it for another second.

Jay didn't want to see it. He jumped out of the chair and went to stand at the large picture window. Fresh snow coated the ground. It sparkled and glinted the way new snow did when it hadn't been disturbed by any part of the world. Almost beautiful.

Almost.

The snow blanketed every surface: the lawn, the porch railing, the neighbor's roof across the street, his wife's grave they'd be visiting shortly. Cold, heavy snow covered her dead, lifeless body. Jay didn't want to see that. But he had no choice. Did he? He always went with his parents and the Shaws. On Katie's birthday. On his wedding anniversary. On every Sunday for the first three months after the accident. Until his dad had spoken up, saying Jay needed to get distance from it all. Funny how his dad had done that. The man never talked against his wife's wishes. Hadn't since, come to think of it. Was there anything that would make him do it again?

Probably not. Because here they were again. "Something to mark the day," his mom had said. Like there'd be any forgetting.

Falling snow piled on top of the four inches from overnight. Drifts still covered the sidewalks lining the street, but not the Shaws' walkway or their driveway. Jay couldn't picture Stuart out hefting shovel loads of snow. The man had the body for physical labor; he just didn't have the demeanor for it. They'd have a service that came first thing after every snowfall. That's how people like the Shaws did things. By not doing anything at all.

The silence unnerved Jay. Any minute they'd start up. He almost counted off the seconds. He wouldn't have gotten far.

The winner…Stuart Shaw.

"One year. One goddamn year, and that man is walking around like nothing happened."

Jay squeezed his eyes shut, closing off the picturesque winter scene before him.

The words "vehicular manslaughter" rang in his ears as the foursome at his back addressed the charges, the plea agreement, and the sentencing of the one man Jay didn't want to think about. Didn't they realize talking about it couldn't change the past?

He crept out of the room and headed for the Shaws' kitchen. He'd dated Katie since they were fifteen, had known her since her family had moved to town when she was seven. He was as familiar with the Shaws' place as his own parents' house. He opened the fridge and pushed aside the cage-free eggs and package of Brie to rescue a Heineken hidden in the back. He tossed the bottle cap onto the table and sat, downing the beer in a series of long gulps. And since no one had come for him, he helped himself to another.

He opened the cabinet door under the sink to toss the empty bottle into the recycling bin and stopped short. The polished, stainless steel garbage pail contained only a clean, white trash bag that smelled of citrus fruit. Not a scrap of food or piece of junk mail. Not one empty box of macaroni and cheese or wad of used tissues.

Nothing.

Like the first time.

Katie had laughed for ten minutes before she calmed enough to tell him about her mother's obsessive need to have all the trash receptacles in the house fresh and clean whenever guests arrived. It didn't matter Jay was a fifteen-year-old who was only there for dinner because that's what the Shaws demanded before he and Katie could go on a date. Like any teenage boy trying to get to third base cared whether the trash smelled like lemons or coffee grounds or dirty gym socks.

Sitting in the Shaws' kitchen, nursing the beer, Katie's laugh was as real to him as it had been that day. Her voice as warm as she said, "That's my mother. Nothing messy in her house." She wrinkled her nose, forcing the freckles together in a cute cluster that always had him smiling.

If only that face, that voice, the laughter, the memories would consume him until he resurfaced to a better time—where he'd never know the bad that would follow.

He swallowed the last of his beer and whispered, "I miss you."

"I missed you too." Todd bumped Jay's shoulder with a fist on his way by the table and sat across from him. "But we've got to stop meeting like this."

"Tell me about it."

Todd tilted his head toward the empty Heineken. "You really should quit drinking when you get to the part where you're talking to your beer before lunch."

"Maybe if you said something to Mom, told her it wasn't how we wanted to remember—"

"Uh-uh. No can do. You know when Mom gets an idea in her head, there's no changing her mind." Todd stood and picked up Jay's empty beer bottle. He opened the same cabinet Jay had and tossed the bottle into the trash instead of the recycling bin next to it. The residual drops of beer splattered the top of the pristine bag as the bottle bounced off the edges and made its way down. Katie would love that. The stench of beer fouling the fresh citrus bag for her mother to experience later.

Todd swung the cabinet door shut and returned to the table.

"Marge come with you?" Jay asked.

"Not today."

"She still working?"

"Yeah. She says she's fine since she sits behind a desk all day. She doesn't want to quit until…you know."

Jay nodded. "Everything going okay?"

"Yep." Todd was always curt whenever they talked about Marge's pregnancy. Jay wished he could tell him it was okay, but it really wasn't. And they both knew it. Jay didn't want to hear about due dates, doctors' appointments, or ultrasounds. He didn't want to think about babies at all.

Both sets of parents had been pissed when he and Katie had eloped six months after high school. For two years, they kept that anger going. Until the day of the accident—when he and Katie had announced they were about to start trying for a baby.

Who knew eight hours later that dream would be crushed with the smash of her car.

"So," Todd said, "you doing okay?" His brother gave him the all too familiar look of pity everyone else did. Jay hated that look. He preferred it when Todd offered suggestions about getting out and dating. That at least sounded more normal than conversations the Shaws and his parents had.

"I'm all right." He shrugged. "I didn't get fired."

"There's an accomplishment."

Jay laughed and tried to make a joke of it, but there was no joke to be found. They both stared at the table between them. Would there always be topics he and Todd avoided? Always be a distance between Jay and everyone else in his life?

Todd scratched the paunch of a belly that had been forming alongside his wife's rounded midsection. "Mom said you might be heading back to school."

Jay snorted. "Nah."

"Ah. Wishful thinking. It might do you good to get back to it."

"I need to work."

"No." Todd leaned forward and pointed a finger at him. "You need to get laid, little brother."

Playful suggestions about dating were one thing. Those made him feel normal, a part of the world. And they could be ignored. Sex? That was a different story. Mournfully missing your wife and a hard-on that was sick of your own hand didn't mesh. Jay's libido was pissed. He'd been having dreams. Long, detailed, erotic dreams.

If Todd knew who was featured in those dreams, would he have suggested sex? Would he want to know his little brother dreamed about another man on his knees sucking him off? Another man like the stranger Jay had seen outside Sonny's Tavern the night before?

Jay's real-life experience with men was limited to the time he was nineteen and he'd driven fifty minutes to the Forge, a gay bar in Fort Wayne where no one knew him, where he could figure out what he wanted after the month of jerk-off sessions starring Michael Malloy, captain of his high school track team. Jay had walked into the bar, the wedding ring for Katie in his pocket, determined to prove himself wrong. The night was uneventful, but it confirmed what he'd long suspected. It didn't stop him from proposing to Katie, though. He was more attracted to her than to any of the men in the bar. He marked off the mental checkbox for bisexual and continued on with the proposal. He'd made her a silent promise on the drive home. He'd be faithful to her for the rest of their marriage—the rest of her life.

He had expected that to be longer than two years.

And now that she was gone…he couldn't go there.

Could he?

"You're too quiet," Todd said. "You used to talk all the time. Ask all those incessant questions. Now, nothing."

"Sorry."

"Nah. Used to drive me nuts how much you talked." Todd laughed. He leaned his elbows on the table, and his expression grew grim. "You having trouble with your bills?"

"Some." Todd was the only person Jay would admit that to. "Almost missed the mortgage last month." He'd never forgive himself if he lost the house.

"You've got the money from—"

"No! I told you, no."

Todd held up his hand. "Okay. Let me loan you—"

"No." Softer, Jay added, "I've got to get my shit together."

"And how do you plan to do that?"

Jay let a smirk build. "Find the son of a bitch and punch his lights out."

"Now you sound like Mom."

Great. That was just what Jay needed. When she talked about McCaw she sounded crazy.

"I doubt he'll stick around here," Todd added.

"How do you mean?"

"The entire community knows what happened. No way a man is going to stick around for the abuse he's in for."

The parents in the next room had finally quieted. The tirade over McCaw's part in their turmoil had lasted longer than usual. A strange voice filtered into the kitchen.

"…*survived by husband Jacob Miller.*"

"What the hell?" Todd jumped up, the chair scraping the floor as the back of his legs smacked into it. "They're watching it again?"

"How?" That was all Jay could manage.

"Mom gave them a copy when it first aired."

Jay rose and shifted a couple of shaky steps away from the sound of the TV. "I'm going to the bathroom." He had never watched the news coverage of the sentencing. Hadn't been there that day either.

"Maybe you should go watch it," Todd said. "He said stuff to us that day, and you've never heard it."

Jay paused at the doorway. "I don't need to." He left the room and waited several minutes after finishing in the bathroom before heading to the living room. A story on the local news couldn't last that long. They'd only still have it on if they had replayed it several times. They weren't that obsessed. Were they?

The TV was on, but only a commercial filled the screen. Jay stood motionless as a can of dancing air freshener sang about spring while it squirted a spray made of flowers out its nose. He listened to his own breathing. It was slow and even. Maybe avoiding Lincoln McCaw was the best option.

Jay's parents and the Shaws still stared at the television and hadn't so much as flinched since he entered the room. They didn't appear to be breathing. They didn't appear to be anything. Was he the only one alive?

The air freshener can stopped singing. Stuart Shaw stood and walked heavily to the television set, turning it off with a slam. "Six fucking months."

"Stuart, please," Emily said.

His dad looked at Jay as if just noticing he had joined them. "At least they banned him from racing."

Was that supposed to comfort?

"Like that's enough," his mom said. "Thank goodness we challenged the plea agreement, or they might not have made him serve any time at all."

Jay moved past his brother to the picture window. He took in a deep breath, let it out, and repeated the process, waiting for it to feel natural. Everyone was talking at once, voices raised. Anger invaded Emily Shaw's sterile living room. Jay wasn't sure who said what, but their comments filled his head.

"Bastard probably always drove like that."

"He'll kill somebody else someday. You wait and see."

"A fine and six months in jail. That's it."

Wasn't this part over? Guess they wanted to make the day special.

He should leave, walk out the door and do anything else—be anywhere else. He clenched his hands into fists. He wanted them to stop talking about the accident, about McCaw, about all of it. Just to stop talking.

If he could see one sign of their love for Katie, from either set of parents, then he would've cared about their grief more than he did, but it'd go the way it always did. They'd carry on about the unfairness of the legal system and that the penalties in these cases were never strong enough, all the while their voices rising, the rage building. All the while his heart aching and not one of them noticing.

What were the stages of grief? And when would everyone move on to the next?

"Someone should kill him!"

Jay spun around. That was a new one.

His mom was standing, her entire body shaking. She pushed her husband away from her. "He needs to suffer and die like she did. He shouldn't be allowed to be getting his life back."

Had she lost her mind? Katie would hate her even thinking that.

His dad reached for his mom again. He put an arm around her shoulders and helped her to the couch.

She ignored him and said, "He's ruined Jay's life. Ruined all our lives. They were going to have a baby. He should be dead."

Dead? Was her grief that out of control?

"It was an accident," Jay whispered.

Five heads turned his way.

They stared at him like what he said was inconceivable, like what he said made no sense and his mom's words were the rational ones.

Why had he said anything at all? He was angry, grieving. Like the rest of them.

"An accident he caused." His mom jabbed a finger toward the TV. "No matter what that man said, he has no idea what he took from us."

She was right. How could anyone know Katie? Not the way Jay did.

"Susan, stop." His dad moved to stand between her and Jay. "Son, you need to deal with your loss, deal with what you're feeling— including your anger toward that man."

His mom shoved her husband aside. "Deal with it? Howard, this isn't going away. His wife died. He can't even raise their children. He can't ever get over that. Who could?"

Chapter Four

Lincoln lifted his ass and shifted on the bed before settling his weight. Did they give him a new mattress? The bunk had never been close to comfortable before. He opened his eyes and blinked until the sunlight seeping in through the half-closed curtains didn't blind him. A poster for a live-action *G.I. Joe* movie covered the opposite wall. A soldier wearing futuristic military garb made of a steel-like material, his face held in a constant scowl. He looked ready to lift the weapon he clutched and fire at Lincoln.

Right. Not the jail cell.

A ten-year-old boy's room.

Lincoln was lying on top of the blankets, still wearing his jeans. His shirt and socks were lost sometime between his first sip of whiskey and his last.

"Why you sleeping in Davy's room?"

The familiar, small voice floated up from the foot of the bed, comforting Lincoln, calling him home like the checkered flag on race night.

He sat up and leaned back against the headboard. "Got nowhere else to go."

Jessica stepped closer. Funny how you can't see kids aging when they're right in front of you, but stay away for six months and you miss a lot. Her pink flannel *Beauty and the Beast* nightgown no longer brushed the floor around her feet. The hem lay near her ankles. Her face was less round, her eyes more serious. Yet she still held the same ragged, purple stuffed animal that wasn't quite a bear and wasn't quite a dog. Lincoln had once asked her for clarification on the type of animal. All she said was his name, Mr. Wuzzie.

The specifics of the stuffed animal didn't matter to her. He was her favorite color, she got to name him, and he played whatever games she wanted, unlike her two brothers. The qualifications for the best friend of a five-year-old met. And despite Lincoln's absence, Jessica still looked like she loved Mr. Wuzzie.

"You slept a lot," she said.

Lincoln glanced at the clock. Almost noon. The longest night's sleep he'd had since he left for the Grant County Justice Center—hell, since a year ago to the day. Thanks to the whiskey.

As if to mock him, Jessica's tiny feet hit the paper sack as she came closer to the bed. The whiskey bottles clanked inside the bag. She glanced at what she had run into, but it didn't slow her down. She bounced onto the bed and sat beside him, her legs straight out in a replica of his posture, the soles of her feet lined up next to his legs midthigh.

She laid Mr. Wuzzie on her lap and pointed to the tattoo on Lincoln's left upper arm. "Your wolf was running while you slept."

"Yeah?"

"Your arms were all twitchy."

"Guess I was dreaming."

"Musta been a bad dream. You weren't smiling." She stared up at him with big, brown eyes. Nancy's eyes.

"How come you're not at school? I thought kindergarten was all day."

She wiggled her toes and watched them move. "I was sick."

"You don't look sick."

"I got better."

"Uh-huh."

He had to strain to hear her next words. "It was a bad night." She picked up Mr. Wuzzie and gave him a squeeze. Out of fear? Or thanks?

"But you're okay now?" he asked.

"Yep. Mom said you'd drive me to school if I got ready."

"She did?"

Jessica nodded, looking up at him again, her brown eyes wide. "She said you got a job interview after lunch, and my school's on your way. Is it lunchtime?"

"I guess. Go get ready."

She hopped off the bed. "Mom left the keys to your truck on the table." She spun around and ran out of the room, Mr. Wuzzie's head smacking the side of her leg as she went.

Lincoln let his head fall back to the headboard behind him. "Shit."

Not thinking about it was best. He'd wait to see what happened when he got behind the wheel again.

* * * *

"You know what irks me?"

Jay didn't want to encourage his mom. He kept his forehead plastered to the car window beside him and said nothing.

"What's that?" Todd asked.

Leave it to his brother.

She turned to face them in the backseat, her eyes squinted into slits like Todd was thirteen and had forgotten to take out the trash for the third week in a row. "They're letting him drive."

"The man has to work," Jay said. His mom ignored him or perhaps didn't hear. His voice had taken on that low whisper it did whenever he verbally disagreed with one of his parents.

She said, "It makes me want to follow him around with a warning sign. He should have to register like those sex offenders do. So everyone knows who's driving around their neighborhoods—around their children."

"We're here," his dad called out, his voice louder than usual. Maybe he was tired of listening to her too.

Jay blew out a huff of air that fogged the window, blocking the sea of headstones and monuments. Who knew he'd be relieved to arrive at the Pleasant Valley Cemetery—which was neither a valley nor pleasant. The foils of advertising.

Todd rolled his eyes after their mom exited the car. What would it be like to make the trip without his brother?

The Shaws pulled in behind them, and the group began their journey along the same path they always followed. Thirty-two headstones south. A few mentions of "that damn Lincoln McCaw" mixed in with the sound of crunching snow under their feet. Turn left at the stone marked *Victor Donnelly*, a WWII veteran *gone, but not forgotten* by his wife and three sons with the epitaph, *the acts of this life are the destiny of the next.* Five more stones east and stop under the thirty-foot-tall black oak tree. And just how did they keep from digging into the ruts each time they opened a new grave nearby? Jay never had the nerve to ask that question. His mom would faint at the mere mention of grave digging.

The large oak had provided welcome shade on the summer days when they'd made the trek. Now, the bare, lifeless branches taunted Jay, reminding him why they had come.

The choice of cemetery hadn't been a decision left to him. The Shaws granted him the uncomplicated ones like the shoes Katie should wear—and only after Emily had picked the dress, which left a single appropriate pair of shoes—and if he wanted his name as Jay or

Jacob in the obituary. He'd gone with Jacob, though he'd regretted it later. Katie had never called him that. Only his mom did.

The one decision he had spoken up on...the wedding ring. Her parents had wanted Katie buried with it. Jay had wanted it with him.

Standing in the cemetery one year later, he reached for the two simple gold bands—all he could afford at nineteen—hanging on a chain around his neck and slid them on and off the tip of his index finger, moving the bands as one.

He'd taken his own ring off and put it on the chain with Katie's the day they'd buried her. His mom had given him a look of horror when she saw he wasn't wearing it anymore. She hadn't bothered to ask him why. He hadn't done what she expected, and that was all that mattered to her.

The group stood in a semicircle around the grave. Jay kept to his usual distance—a step behind the parents—Todd at his side, and fidgeted with the collar of his shirt. Damn thing was too tight. His mom had bought it for him when he was sixteen. He'd have worn something else, but all he had were T-shirts and jeans. His mom never would've gone for that. The only suit, dress shirt, and tie he'd owned as an adult were the ones he'd worn a year ago for the funeral, and he'd thrown those in the trash the minute he'd gotten home.

Jay hadn't had so much as a sports coat before then. Todd had purchased the suit for him and brought it to Jay's house the morning of the visitation.

"So young," his mom said. She knelt on the ground and dropped a hand to the snow-covered grave. Why? It wasn't like Katie could feel her touch. "So unfair," she added. "What was she doing out so late all alone?" The same question she always asked.

Jay sucked in a deep breath and squeezed his eyes shut. Emily slipped her arm around his waist, but he pulled away from her and kept his back to his family. He pressed the palms of his hands to his eyes until he was certain he wouldn't cry. He would not shed one tear. Not in front of them.

* * * *

"Doesn't your truck wanna start?"

Jessica sat beside Lincoln in his pickup, her tiny form looking frail in the large cab. A pink and white Hello Kitty backpack was draped across her lap and her yellow winter boots dangled over the edge of the bench. The booster seat raised her several inches, but the seat belt still crossed her too close to her neck for his comfort.

When he didn't answer, she added, "Ain't you gonna try it?"

"I guess." He turned the ignition key, and the truck roared to life. Had the engine always sounded that loud? He gripped the top of the steering wheel with both hands. The custom wheel cover had cost a fortune, but at the time, it had mattered that his truck felt similar to his race car. The hubris of one who hadn't become a killer.

When his knuckles turned white, he eased up on the grip. The shaking in his hands had nothing to do with wanting a drink, but it—and the thirst—had a lot to do with the fear of "what ifs" a man like him could never escape.

He cut the engine and clicked the release on her seat belt. "We're walking."

Jessica smiled. "Okay." She tossed her backpack aside, opened her door, and disappeared behind the side of the vehicle. Her hand returned a moment later as she groped onto the seat for her backpack. Lincoln shoved it within her reach, and she lugged it out the open door.

He exited the truck and joined her on the sidewalk where she fumbled with a twisted strap. He helped her unwind it and slid the pack off her shoulders. "I'll carry it."

They walked two blocks in silence. As they rounded a corner, she slipped on an icy section of the walk, and he grasped her hand to steady her. When she was walking with a firm step, she made no attempt to remove her hand from his, and that suited him fine.

"Uncle Lincoln?"

"Yeah."

"Ain't you gonna live with Uncle Paul no more?"

"No."

"Can I still call him Uncle Paul?" She jumped to avoid a pile of snow, leaning her weight into his hand.

Lincoln stopped and looked down at her. "Didn't your mom—oh hell, you probably won't see him again."

"Oh." She breathed deep.

"Do you need me to carry you?"

"Nope. We're almost there." She tugged on his hand, and they walked side by side again.

"You got your inhaler with you?" What the hell was he thinking making her walk? Tomorrow he'd get behind the fucking wheel and actually drive. Of course he was limited to driving for work, and if the interview didn't go well today, he'd have nowhere to go.

"Yep," she said. "But it's almost empty."

He pulled her to a stop and knelt on one knee beside her, his skin growing cold under his jeans. "Did you tell your mom?"

"Uh-huh. I have to go to the doctor for more."

Doctors. Prescriptions. He *had* to get this job.

Jessica stared at him. "Your wolf might be running again. Your arms are all twitchy." She touched her hand to his leather jacket over the spot where the eagle feather and wolf tattoo decorated his biceps.

"He'll calm down."

"Probably just wants to run around now that he's free. I bet he didn't like the jail."

Lincoln chuckled. "Yeah, kid. He didn't." He stood and took her hand in his.

* * * *

Jay tilted his head back. He didn't want to see where he was anymore. Didn't want to see his family there with him.

A sparrow flew low and landed in the branches of the tree overhead. What had he heard about sparrows? Something about symbolizing true love and finding your way home. He watched the bird until it flew away, not missing the cosmic joke as the sparrow faded in the distance.

A sharp breeze shook the ice-covered branches of the oak tree above them. The creaking gave the impression that all the branches were headed for the gatherers below. *Mourning family impaled by icy tree limbs.* How often did someone die standing over another's grave?

The thought of Katie buried beneath all that earth, alone in her casket, sickened him. He wanted to remember her as she deserved him to. Remember the first time he'd met her. Their high school prom. Their wedding day. The last time he'd seen her... No. He never let himself think of that day. Not for any reason.

Stuart Shaw's words cut through the silence. "If they had charged him with vehicular homicide, he'd have done more time."

Here we go again.

"That's usually when the person's been drinking," Todd said.

Stuart threw him an incredulous look. "He murdered my daughter."

Emily Shaw let out a gasp. Jay's mom went to her, and the women hugged. Was the mutual comforting because of the reason they stood in the cemetery? Or the justice and vengeance the courts had robbed them of one year ago?

Jay focused on the tree branches, trying desperately to cling to something, anything other than the voices that surrounded him.

A half hour later, when the group finally separated, returning to their cars, he stayed behind and uttered the words, "I love you." A sweet, flowery scent filled the air. The only flowers nearby weren't growing in the ground. They were the attempts of the bereaved to bring life to the cemetery.

Jay turned away before a complete emotional meltdown kept him from leaving. He lingered during the solitary walk to his parents' car.

It was identical to every other time. No matter who spoke, no matter what was said, no one mentioned his wife's name.

"Ready?" his dad asked from where he leaned against the side of the car, his dress shoes covered in snow, his breath visible in the air. "The Shaws aren't coming to dinner this time, so it'll just be the four of us."

Perhaps the Shaws had grown tired of spending time with Jay's family. Too bad he'd missed their departure. Maybe he could've caught a ride.

Todd opened the door for Jay and whispered, "They really hate that man."

"Don't we all?"

Would they hate Jay as much if they knew the truth of that day? If they knew Jay's part in it?

Chapter Five

Jay parked his Jeep and got out. The door rattled as he slammed it shut. One of these days it was going to fall off the hinges, and he'd end up driving around with plastic sheeting and duct tape for a door.

The neon signs from the Late Night Paradise Plaza carryout nearly blinded him as he crossed the parking lot. He'd entered Sonny's Tavern a few times over the past year. A lot over the last six months. That's when the drinking had gone from a way to dull the pain to a way to get through each day. He couldn't face the empty house and the fading memories.

Most of the time, he walked to the bar and back. A necessity when you expect the bartender to keep the beers coming. Tonight he had some thinking to do before he fell into the bottle, so he'd made the stop off to Sonny's. He'd save the heavy drinking for when he got home. Time to figure out what he planned to do about Lincoln McCaw.

If Todd was right, and the man was leaving town, Jay didn't have a lot of time to make up his mind. This might be his last chance to face him—to get a look at the man who had taken Katie from him.

But what would he gain from finally seeing him? And was it worth tearing at old wounds when they hadn't even started to heal?

Jay shoved the bar's door in with his shoulder and welcomed the scent of beer and smoke that signaled the usual forthcoming alcohol stupor. The lighting in the bar was dim, and the brown wood paneling and hardwood floor added to the darkness. It took a minute for his eyes to adjust. Sonny was pouring a glass of whiskey behind the bar, and four men sat at a table nearby, celebrating a bowling league victory—unless they liked to dress in matching button-up shirts advertising the Edgefield Pizzeria across their backs. The group's laughter and the clink of their glasses drowned out the country music playing overhead. A young couple sat at a table along the back wall, paying attention only to each other. And the same old, weathered man who was always in Sonny's sat at his usual table near the restrooms, proximity obviously an issue for him. He was dressed in a dirty jean jacket worn to tatters at the seams and cuffs and sported a white and gray beard that he hadn't trimmed in years. The waitress on duty brought him another glass of whiskey. The old man gripped the glass and sucked in a long, slow sip before she retrieved his empties.

Jay ordered a beer and settled in at a table toward the back. He was nearing the bottom of the bottle and hadn't come up with a decision on whether to find McCaw when two men sat at a table next to him. One was short and sweaty. The other, tall, somewhat good-looking, but with a beer gut lounging out past the belt holding up his jeans. They made several lewd comments to the waitress and offered her a party at Short and Sweaty's place after her shift. Jay tried to tune them out until he heard the word he'd feared for a long time.

"He's a fag."

What? Jay stopped the bottle an inch from his mouth. How could they tell? Was there something in the way he had looked at them?

"Who?" Short and Sweaty asked.

"That guy. At the bar," the tall one said.

Someone else. Jay let a long breath into his lungs.

"The one in the leather?"

"Yeah," Tall and Gutty said. "Fucking fag."

"No shit?"

"Yep. Went to high school with him. Was a fag back then too."

Short and Sweaty shook his head, threw his arm over the back of an empty chair, and gave the man at the bar a disgusted look. "What the fuck's he still doing here?"

"Beats me," Tall and Gutty said. "Oughta head out to California or one of them pansy states that lets 'em get married."

"Maybe we should give him a clue." Short and Sweaty slid his chair away from the table without lifting his ass. The chair legs scraped the wood floor.

"My buddy Hal tried once. Three years ago. He and some of his guys went to the man's house. Fag was living with another guy. Can you believe that? Hal and his buddies beat the shit out of them. Cops came. Hal spent time in jail for it."

Short and Sweaty stood. "Ah, he ain't worth all that trouble. Let's head across town."

Tall and Gutty joined him, and they sauntered toward the door.

"Yeah. Don't wanna hang out in a fag bar." Tall and Gutty spat the last of his words toward the man in question, who ignored them.

Jay stared at the back of the man's leather jacket. A gay guy? In Edgefield? In Sonny's?

The dark-haired man lifted his head and took a long swig from his beer. *The guy from out front last night.*

Jay had no idea how to tell if someone was gay, but that long stare they'd exchanged had seemed like...something.

The man's shirt was untucked, hanging out past the bottom of his jacket. His ragged face sported several days' worth of stubble. His attention was focused on the beer in front of him, which he held on to with both hands. The expression on his face, his posture, the way he clung to his beer told of the despair. Lost. Broken.

Was Jay looking in a goddamn mirror?

* * * *

"You watching the game? Who do you think's going to win?"

Lincoln lit a smoke and ignored the questions. The kid had sat one stool away from him twenty minutes earlier and ordered a beer he'd downed in two gulps. Same guy Lincoln had seen outside the other night. Young. Gorgeous. With a sadness in his eyes a little too familiar. Probably a regular who had started coming in while he was at the jail. Lincoln had readied himself to find another seat if the kid talked too much. Damn regulars always felt the need to talk even when no one was listening.

Instead, the kid had ordered another beer and stared at the television set hanging over the bar, not even glancing away at the commercials, until he asked about the game. Lincoln didn't offer an opinion. It wasn't like he even knew who was playing.

The bartender stopped by, and Lincoln gestured for another beer. He gathered the new bottle in his hands and stared down the mouth at the liquid. He wanted a whiskey, but the beers would let him get his ass to Nancy's. He'd start in on the pint of Jack there.

The kid reached for a bowl of nuts in front of Lincoln, picked up a peanut, and took his time smashing it between his fingers, freeing the nuts from their shell. Lincoln silently cursed himself out as he watched the kid chew the nuts and lick the salt off his lips.

Damn. Maybe he should make a trip to the Forge sooner rather than later, find himself a nameless blowjob. If assholes like the ones from earlier caught him staring at good-looking straight guys in Sonny's, he'd get a pounding on the walk back.

Laughter erupted from the table of bowlers behind him, and they belted out a chorus of "We Are the Champions."

"Must have won the league championship."

Lincoln rolled his eyes and took another drink. Great. The kid was a talker after all. Lincoln grunted. There. He wasn't ignoring the man.

The bartender brought the kid a new beer and said, "Nope. Five years in a row they came in last place. Not this year. They were second to last."

"Oh." The kid turned on the stool and glanced at the men in bowling shirts. "Should I tell them champions doesn't mean 'we suck, but hey, at least we don't suck the most'?"

Lincoln huffed out a short laugh, almost choking on a mouthful of beer. He wiped his mouth with the back of his hand.

"Don't laugh while you're drinking," the kid said. "Beer up the nose burns like hell."

Good-looking and funny. At any other time in his life, Lincoln would have been seriously interested.

The kid slid onto the empty stool between them. "Can I bum a smoke?"

With the back of his hand Lincoln slid over his pack of Marlboros.

"Thanks." The kid picked up the smokes. He dug one out and placed the pack next to Lincoln's beer. "Uh, you got a light?"

The guy was really killing his buzz. Lincoln fished the lighter from his pocket and tossed it to the kid, who fumbled the catch but saved the lighter from hitting the wood floor. Good thing. Lincoln's grandpa had given it to him. He didn't need it scuffed up.

He also didn't need the kid sitting so damn close. He smelled clean, refreshing after time spent with the jailhouse inmates who weren't sure how to work the showers or the sinks. The kid held out the lighter, his eyes wide, his lips parted, his chest rising with each shallow breath as he stared at Lincoln.

Lincoln accepted the lighter, as well as the slight press of the kid's thumb to his palm.

Oh, hell. He'd never had someone come on to him in Sonny's, not in any local establishment for that matter. Public propositions for gay sex didn't go over well in a town the size of Edgefield.

Had the kid heard those fuckers from earlier?

Maybe he was toying with him. Maybe he was friends with those guys, and Lincoln was about to get his ass kicked out behind the bar. But it didn't feel like the kid was fooling. It felt good. To be touched. To be wanted again. His hand clenched as he set the lighter with his smokes.

The kid was staring at the TV again and made no attempt to move back to his previous stool. He played along the length of the cigarette with his fingers before he took another drag. His hands were a bit beat-up, rough, the hands of a man who worked for a living. Yet the kid treated the cigarette as if it were made of delicate tissue paper until his last puff. Only then did he crush the butt into the ashtray with the push of his thumb.

Would fucking the kid involve the same mix of tenderness and roughness?

Lincoln's dick had hardened more with each play of the long fingers over the roll of tobacco, with each drag between the kid's lips. *Damn.* He hadn't gotten hard that fast in a long time. Not from one look and a touch of hands. This twentysomething kid brought to life needs he'd learned to bury. Would it be so bad to just give in? To feel again?

He wanted a fuck, but could he let himself have even that much of a release?

No. Too soon to feel good. To feel anything.

At the next commercial, the kid said, "Did you know those guys from earlier?"

The man's low whisper had Lincoln's dick begging for a hand, a mouth, anything. Why couldn't his body listen to his head...or his heart? "If you came in here to talk, I suspect you sat by the wrong person."

Before the kid said anything more, Lincoln downed the last of his beer, grabbed his smokes, and headed for the door.

It didn't mean anything that the kid watched him go. Did it?

Chapter Six

"Uncle Lincoln!" Davy shouted as he sprinted out of the kitchen.

Lincoln held up a fist and the two tapped knuckles in greeting. "How you doing?"

"Okay," Davy said. "Just borrowed *Guitar Hero* from Richie. He said I could keep it until next week."

Mindless entertainment. Lincoln could go for that. He toed off his boots and draped his jacket over the back of the couch. "I'd like to try that one."

Davy walked backward in front of him as they moved toward the kitchen. "Yeah? I'll go set it up." He turned to run off, but Nancy's words stopped him short.

"Not now. Let your uncle have something to eat first. And you need to finish your homework." She wore hospital scrubs and the same worn orthopedic shoes she had on the night before. Did the patrons of the all-night diner on State Road 91 know she wore the same shoes to schlep their food around in the evenings that she wore to empty bedpans at the Fairlawn Retirement Home during the day? As soon as he had some cash for the bills, he'd talk her into quitting one of the jobs. He hated seeing her so tired, hated thinking how alone and scared she must've felt while he was gone.

Davy sank into a chair at the kitchen table and picked up an open math book. Jessica sat beside him coloring a pony in stripes the various colors of a rainbow. Lincoln laughed and ruffled her hair. A fluorescent purple crayon in her hand, she smiled up at him, then started coloring the horse's tail.

Nancy handed him a plate of meat loaf, mashed potatoes, and carrots. "Kept it warm for you."

"Thanks. I'll eat it in Davy's room so he can study."

"I put all your mail on the desk. Forgot to give it to you last night."

He said, "Thanks," and turned to leave.

She put a hand on his back. "Did you get the job?"

He faced her. "Yeah. Three weeks and I get my first check. I'll need a few bucks for spending money." No need to mention the smokes and whiskey. "But after that, it's all yours."

"I can't take all your money, Linc."

"I'm going to help pay for this place and the other bills." He forced her head up with a hand under her chin. "And that's final."

She bit her lip and nodded. The moisture in her eyes scattered with a blink of her eyelids. She sat at the table with the kids.

Lincoln stopped off in the hall to wave at Adam, who lay on his bed texting a message on his cell.

"Hey, Uncle Linc. Did you meet any drug dealers in prison?"

"Jail. Not prison. And we didn't talk about our crimes."

Adam waved an arm through the air and went back to typing with his thumbs. "Yeah. I get it."

Lincoln started down the hall and almost missed the "Glad you're home."

"Me too." He wanted to say more, but hearing about his stepdad being an asshole and how sorry Lincoln was that he and his siblings hadn't gotten a better deal in life would embarrass Adam. No need to remind the kid that the two men who should've cared about him the most hadn't bothered.

Davy's room had shrunk in size. Either that or Lincoln hadn't walked off the beers like he thought. He left the plate of food on the desk and collapsed onto the bed.

Crimes. Why had he used that word?

Because he was a criminal. He'd been arrested. Handcuffed. Charged. Sentenced. Sounded like the consequences due a criminal.

He breathed deep and closed his eyes. The small room filled with the scent of the charred edges on Nancy's meat loaf and the smoke from the bar. Burning rubber, gasoline, and blood replaced the smoke and meat loaf. Sounds invaded the room. Metal crunching against metal, plastic popping loose, glass sprinkling over the highway, and the sirens in the distance that would never arrive soon enough.

He swung off the bed and descended on the plate. He grabbed it and his duffel bag and charged across the hall into the bathroom. It took three flushes to get all the food down without a trace for Nancy or Sparky to find later. He showered, changed, and threw the smoke-covered clothes in with the dirty laundry.

Back in Davy's room, he was about to set the empty plate on the desk when he spotted the stack of mail. He'd gotten other envelopes like the one on top. He opened it and slid the two sheets of paper onto the desk. The first was a typed note, like all the rest.

Ever wonder if she cried out in pain? If she felt the
snap of bone? The crush of her chest?

I do. Every night.

Now I hope you will too.

The plate slipped from his hand and clanked onto the desk.

Lincoln seized the note. Underneath lay a photograph. He didn't reach for it. Touching it would make it real. If he didn't, maybe he'd wake in the morning and find out he'd had more to drink than he thought. He dropped the note and bent forward, resting his hands on his knees, keeping his face and body as far from the picture as he could, as if he were on a TV show, inspecting a dead body.

Which he was. A photo of Katie Miller. In the morgue from what it looked like. She certainly looked dead. Who the hell had taken a picture?

He flipped on the desk lamp and leaned closer. Every detail of the snapshot on Davy's desk stood out. The pale skin. The bare shoulders. The cut that ran the length of her right cheek. The shiny metal surface of the silver table visible behind her body.

He snatched the picture and backed up to the bed. His ass hit the mattress.

She was dead.

Because of him.

He removed the wallet from his back pocket. Tucked behind his driver's license was the newspaper clipping. He unfolded the paper, smoothing it over his thigh, moving his thumb in careful swipes.

He'd memorized every word of the newsprint and every inch of the photo above her obituary. The smile that never faded, the crinkle of the skin around her eyes, the birthday cake visible on the table over her shoulder, the hand she had on the knee of whoever sat beside her just outside the crop of the photo.

Why was she smiling and how long after that moment until she died?

"I'm sorry."

He ran a thumb over her hair. That hair had been what he was remembering when the kid sat at the bar next to him, distracting him.

The black-and-white newspaper print left the color of her hair to Lincoln's memory. Long and red, framing her face, fanning out over the highway where she lay contorted, the red hair with a deeper shade of red sticking to it, matting it to her face. He'd never forget how she looked in that moment.

The note sat across the room on the empty plate, mashed potato remnants seeping through to leave dark blotches here and there.

Seemed like someone wanted to make sure he never forgot.

He scoffed out loud. Fat chance.

But he had to forget. Didn't he? He had to stop reliving every detail. Nancy was counting on him. He couldn't keep a job if he couldn't stay sober.

He should take the notes and the photo to the cops. Nothing in the threats were specific, but it still had to be illegal—harassment if nothing else.

Hell, the cops would probably just laugh at his ass. It wasn't like anyone had come after Lincoln. They were only words. Sent by her husband, no doubt. Lincoln had already done enough to the man. He didn't need to send the cops to his house. He couldn't blame the man for hating him.

He tucked the obituary and the new photo into his wallet and hid the note in the nightstand drawer with the other letters. He stripped off his clothes, turned off the light, and crawled onto the bed, forcing himself to think of something else—anything else.

The kid from the bar. That'd work.

The light hair that looked like someone had run his fingers through it. The hint of toned muscles just starting to soften or fade, like a young man who had kept fit all his life but no longer bothered. The nervous eyes that confirmed the kid's touch. He was gay but new to the experience.

Lincoln took his dick in his hand and gave a few strokes to encourage his arousal. It didn't take much time. Not with the image of the kid kneeling before him, that tempting mouth on his dick.

He came, his body pulsating, his mind clearing of everything except the guy staring up at him, licking the cum off his lips.

If only that release lasted as long as the whiskey.

If only it were enough to chase away the question that lingered. Were the threats he'd received the empty words of a grieving husband—words Lincoln deserved—or was someone about to make him pay more than he already had?

* * * *

Jay opened the door and tripped over the stack of empty pizza boxes he'd left there the night before, a reminder to take them out with the rest of the garbage.

Too bad trash collection was three days earlier.

One year she'd been gone, and he still couldn't get the schedule right. How hard was it to remember one lousy day a week? Good thing he'd dropped out of college the week after the funeral. Apparently when your wife died, your brain cells died with her.

That was the only way to explain what he'd done at the bar. He'd been coming on to that guy. No doubt about that. Jay kicked the pizza boxes aside and staggered to the kitchen sink.

He couldn't deny his attraction to the dark-haired man. Was it because he was the first gay guy Jay had talked to? Or was it the serious eyes, the dark skin, the way the man's throat worked as he swallowed long gulps of the beer?

What must it be like for a gay man like Dark Eyes living in a small town? There were no gay bars for him to patronize. How did he find other men? Was he as lonely as Jay? And why did Jay care about the man's emotional or sexual state anyway?

He flipped on the light above the kitchen sink and squinted as he opened the cupboard. No glasses. He tried the next cabinet where they stored the plastic cups. Nothing. The top shelf with the coffee mugs? Nope.

Their house was turning to shit. It wasn't just the dirty dishes piled in the sink or the fast-food containers scattered throughout the kitchen and living room. It was the dozen broken things he didn't bother to repair. Like the doorknob to the bathroom that had loosened and finally fallen off, the torn shower curtain hooked on by four of the original twelve plastic rings, the shutters on the living room window that hung at odd angles and covered part of the window after they were knocked loose during the last storm.

Katie'd be mad at him for all of it.

This was their first home, the fixer-upper they were going to make special, where they had planned to raise their kids. She deserved better from him. Too bad he couldn't deliver.

He wanted to hate the place. He still owed the Shaws $8,572 from the down payment he and Katie had borrowed. But he couldn't leave. She was everywhere.

He couldn't walk away from that. He groped under the sink for the dishwasher detergent and found three bottles, all empty. He threw the last one into the sink. It bounced off the stack of dirty plates and whacked him in the forehead, then landed on the linoleum floor and skidded across the room to wedge under the refrigerator.

"Goddammit."

Oh well. *Getting by* was the theme of his life now. He turned on the faucet and bent to drink directly from it. The hair above his ear brushed the top plate with caked-on pizza bits and melted cheese. When he had enough water to keep from dehydrating in his sleep, he turned it off and brushed the side of his head. Crumbs fell to the plate in the sink.

That was the extent of his cleaning up before bed. He made his way to the couch in the living room and sprawled out on his stomach. He never slept there. Not since she died. The night of the funeral he dragged himself into the bedroom. He would not forget her or their nights together. He forced himself to lie in their bed where he hugged her pillow and remembered the last time they'd made love—every detail, every kiss, every breath—until exhaustion finally pulled him under.

But tonight…he couldn't lie where they'd made love so many times when he'd been in a bar not an hour earlier craving someone else. Could his life get more complicated?

He pictured the dark eyes with the haunted look so like his own, the way those eyes had looked at him, and how the man's hand felt pressed against his. The blood rushed to Jay's cock, and he ground his pelvis against the couch cushion.

Yep. More complicated was definitely possible.

He didn't want to do anything about the erection. But sex with another man had always been a kick-starter fantasy. Nothing got him off like that. Katie knew it and used the information on several occasions when she wanted to rile him up, telling him stories of what she'd like to watch him do with another guy.

A fantasy. Nothing more.

He'd loved her most in those moments. She hadn't gotten angry or jealous or defensive. She never questioned his faithfulness or his loyalty. She played with his desires and gave him all she could. She accepted all of him.

He eased his hand between himself and the couch. It was her touching him, her mouth on him.

But when he came with a grunt, it was a man with dark eyes who licked the cum from Jay's hand.

* * * *

"God, you sure are a cute one."

Jay cracked a smile as the woman at the far end of the bar flirted with the dark-haired man wearing a leather jacket. She had no clue she'd already lost the game. Not only was Dark Eyes gay, he also looked as lost as he had when Jay first saw him. No one stood a chance with someone who obviously wanted to be left alone the way he did.

She kept at it, though. "Come on. Buy me a drink." She ran her long, pink fingernails through the hair above his ear. Dark Eyes swatted her hand away and returned his attention to the glass that held something stronger than beer, gripping it with both hands.

Jay couldn't blame her for trying. Dark Eyes looked good in the black leather and faded jeans, his dark hair and skin a temptation for the fingers. Jay clutched his beer and took a swallow before setting it on the table he'd grabbed ten minutes earlier.

Sonny's Tavern was crowded, the eligible singles mixing with the heavy drinkers. Most—like the woman hitting on Dark Eyes—not knowing how to tell the difference between the two. The Friday night crowd was more animated than the last night Jay had been in. A group of couples danced near the back wall, creating a makeshift dance floor. There was a different bartender on duty, the television and music overhead were louder, but the same old man sat sipping whiskey near the restrooms.

Jay drank more of his beer and waited. It wouldn't take long.

By the time he finished the beer, the bar stool next to Dark Eyes was empty, the chatty blonde desperate for a free drink—and possibly more—had moved on. Jay waved for another beer, dropped onto the stool, and said, "Hey."

Dark Eyes ignored him and stood.

Apparently Jay sucked at the flirting thing. Which made sense. He hadn't dated many girls. The only one other than Katie had been a fellow classmate he'd agreed to go to the homecoming dance with his junior year during the five weeks he and Katie had their one breakup.

Dark Eyes removed his jacket, laid the leather over the bar, and sat again. The muscles of his arm flexed as he lifted the glass for a drink. The hint of a tattoo peeked out from under the T-shirt's sleeve. An outline of an eagle feather.

"Do I know you?" Dark Eyes asked.

He'd forgotten.

And here Jay was picturing what it would be like to blow the guy. He'd always wanted to know. Always imagined he'd like sucking cock and couldn't stop dreaming of doing it to Dark Eyes since the man had walked out of the bar the other night. Was it because Jay knew Dark Eyes was gay?

No. This guy was a total turn-on for him. He'd only been sitting next to the man long enough for one smoke, and already all Jay's fantasies were roaring to life.

"I uh…I was in here the other night."

"I remember," Dark Eyes said. "Saw you outside the night before that too. Thought maybe I'd seen you somewhere else, though." He slid the bowl of peanuts toward Jay.

Jay stilled the spinning bowl. "Don't think so. I'd remember meeting you." Heat rose in his cheeks. *Shut up!* But did he want to? He nodded to the TV. "You watching the game?"

"Nah. I gave up last half."

"Guess I didn't miss much excitement, then. I had to work late."

Dark Eyes removed one hand from his glass. He made like he was going to take a drink. "Where do you work?" The question came out in a rush before the glass hit his lips.

"Stacking loads at McNeil's Lumber Yard." Jay made eye contact with the man. Neither looked away. A nervous jolt shot from his gut to his groin. "It's a shit job, but I'm lucky to have it. I was going to college but, I…uh, I had to quit. And since they won't let you teach high school history without a college degree, or a teacher's license for that matter, I'm stuck with whatever pays the bills."

Dark Eyes let go of his drink and turned on the stool a fraction of an inch in Jay's direction. The slight curve of his lips wasn't as unnerving as the intense stare.

Jay kept talking. "History's always been my thing. Since I was a kid. Everyone thinks I'm crazy for wanting to teach high schoolers, but there's a lot we can learn from history." And why was he sharing any of this?

The grin on the other man's face grew. "You always talk this much?"

Jay shrugged and sipped the beer he'd forgotten he had. "I don't know." He laughed. That statement was worth a laugh—the first real one in over a year—considering Todd's recent comments about how he hadn't been talking much anymore.

"What's funny?" Dark Eyes asked.

"Nothing. What do you do?"

"Just started over at the steel plant. Used to drive loads for them years back." Dark Eyes gripped his glass again, clutching it in one hand. The other joined the first until he held on to it with both hands. What would those hands feel like when they touched Jay's body? His ass? His dick? What would those arms feel like wrapped around him? How would the skin of that neck taste? What would that dark hair feel like when he grasped the man's head in his hands while Dark Eyes blew him?

Jay breathed deep. Fantasies…just a fantasy. He wasn't ready for anything physical with anyone. Was he?

Before that week, he hadn't been ready for so much as a one-night stand. When he let himself get close to someone, all his thoughts would turn to Katie and every sexual moment they'd spent together. He hadn't wanted to go there, especially not for a quick fuck to please his cock.

Had that changed?

His body was ready, but was he?

Maybe someday…a roll in the hay with a woman. Maybe even with a guy. Might be nice to know if all those fantasies had been leading him on about what he wanted—or whom he wanted it with. But not yet. Not after only a year.

Then why had he sat next to the guy in the first place? Why had he looked for the man?

Dark Eyes leaned his upper body in close, almost touching Jay's arm. That rattled him out of his trance. Damn, he'd been staring at the man for too long. The husky whisper as Dark Eyes spoke did nothing to aid Jay in regaining his concentration.

"Quit looking at me like that, kid. Unless you're willing to back it up."

Oh God. Maybe the flirting had gone better than Jay thought.

The only sexual experience he had other than Katie was the ten-minute fuck in the back of Christy Harper's car on homecoming night. He'd gotten off, but it hadn't been anything special. He'd put every last minute of it out of his mind as soon as he and Katie had made up.

The weeks they'd spent apart were the worst weeks of his life until a year ago.

No. The worst part was telling Katie about what he'd done with Christy. Katie had gone on her own date, and Jay hated hearing about the kissing and groping she'd done. He could only imagine how much it hurt Katie to listen to his confession about his backseat "date." He made a promise to himself as he drove her home that night, both of them sitting in the front seat of the Jeep in silence. He'd never hurt her again. Never cheat again. Even though she said he hadn't technically cheated and she understood how it had happened, it sure had felt as though he'd been unfaithful. He never wanted to feel that way again. Never wanted any other person pleasuring him. Only her.

And now here he was hoping another guy was interested in him.

How had he given this guy the right signals? Or the wrong ones? And how was he supposed to respond?

Jay licked his dry lips and forced his attention on the TV above the bar. Commercials. Something with beer and babes in bikinis. How apropos.

"Kid." That one word in the low, deep voice had him facing Dark Eyes again. Jay barely heard the whispered command over the sound of the country music. "Give it a few minutes, then meet me out back." Dark Eyes stood, threw some wadded cash onto the bar, grabbed his coat, and exited out the back entrance that led to the rear parking lot. The music and crowd in Sonny's muffled the bang of the door closing behind Dark Eyes.

Jay turned to the bar. He needed to leave. Out the front entrance. Now.

Why wouldn't his legs help him out? He guzzled his beer in four tries, dropped the bottle onto the bar, and stood. What the hell?

He walked toward the back door at a quick clip, hoping no one knew where he was going.

Or why.

Chapter Seven

Jay pushed open Sonny's door and stepped outside. The crisp night air rushed toward him. Maybe it would cool him down.

Or maybe not.

Dark Eyes gripped his arm at the same time the country music cut off with the close of the door behind him. Jay tripped over his own feet but couldn't stop moving toward the other man even if he wanted to, and he didn't.

"Come here." Dark Eyes pulled at Jay until they stopped beside a wooden structure that jutted out the back of the bar.

The man's hand on Jay's arm was warm, even through his jacket, and had him forgetting the cold snow his tennis shoes burrowed into. The building blocked the wind, but the chill in the air should have cut through him. It didn't. Not with Dark Eyes touching him, staring at him. Heat built up everywhere. Jay's face, his hands, his cock.

He didn't flinch as the other man moved in to his space and kept coming at him until only an inch of air separated their chests, their lips, their groins.

"If I'm wrong here," Dark Eyes said, "tell me to fuck off. No trouble."

Words wouldn't come. Jay raised a hand, seized the man's right hip, and tugged him forward. Their groins mashed one against the other, and the pressure on his cock overcame any worry about what he was doing. Jay wanted the man's mouth on his.

Their lips joined, mouths opened, and the wet heat of their tongues combined. The smooth slide of that simple touch had another surge of lust flooding Jay's body. There was no denying the roughness of the kiss, the brush of facial hair on his chin, the pressure of strong lips covering his, the persistence of tongue that demanded a taste. Like no kiss he'd ever had, like no kiss with—

No. He had to live in the moment. Had to stay right where he was.

Looking back would end it. No way could he enjoy the man kissing him if he let anything else in.

So he didn't. He wrapped an arm around Dark Eyes and let the desire engulf him, let his tongue explore the other man's mouth.

A man. He could not believe he was doing this. But he didn't want it to end. He longed to grab hold of the other man and fuck him until the relief he craved overtook him and exhaustion settled in. And that scared the shit out of him. He shouldn't be so out of control.

Dark Eyes shifted. His erection pressed against Jay's own. Like nothing Jay had imagined. Better than all the fantasies, and they were fully clothed, standing in the damn snow plowed against the building. Dark Eyes came in closer. He clutched Jay's ass and massaged. It seemed like forever since Jay had been touched like that, since he'd been touched at all. Their bodies drove together. Their tongues worked in a caress that deepened with every second.

Jay tightened his grip, one hand on the man's hip, the other around his neck. He fell into the sensations, the thrust of hips, the slow slide of the man's hands running over his ass, the scent of beer and sweat and musky cologne. Nothing flowery or sweet. Strong. Masculine.

Dark Eyes pulled back and rested his forehead against Jay's temple. "This isn't the safest place to do this, but…Jesus, you can kiss. And it's been too damn long."

"For me too." Jay crushed his mouth over the other man's.

Their bodies moved with an urgency that spoke volumes about how long it had been. For both of them. Dark Eyes brushed a hand over Jay's aching cock and opened his jeans.

Jay grabbed the man's arms and shoved him backward. "Wait. Wait. Let me think for a minute." The muscles in those strong arms jumped under Jay's hands.

Dark Eyes searched his face in the low light of the streetlamp. "You've never been with a man."

Jay dropped his hands and wiped them on his jeans. "I was married at nineteen."

"Divorced?"

"No." He stared at their footprints in the snow. If anyone looked closely at the overlapping, muddled prints, they'd know what the two of them were doing. He whispered, "Cancer." He couldn't manage more than that. Why had he lied? Because it was easier than the truth. Saying how she had really left him was too real, too horrific to repeat. Or to remember.

"But I didn't read you wrong?" Dark Eyes asked.

Jay gave up on the snow and met the man's gaze. "Nah."

"Most guys who figure it out too late usually step out on their wives."

"I loved her."

Dark Eyes leaned against the brick wall perpendicular to Jay and watched him.

"She knew I was…" Words escaped Jay. Or maybe that one word. He'd never said it before. "She knew. But I never cheated. I just thought about stuff."

"Stuff?"

"Stuff I wanted to do."

"I see." Dark Eyes swept a hand through the hair at the nape of Jay's neck. He raised an eyebrow. "Want some of that stuff to come true? Want me to kiss you again?"

"Yes. Please." Begging? Jay's control was slipping away. But kissing the man, touching him, nothing had felt so right, not since—

Dark Eyes ran his hands lower, returning to the front of Jay's jeans.

"I don't know—" Jay licked his bottom lip and swallowed. "I don't know what I'm doing."

The other man laughed. His eyes softened with the smile. Not an expression he'd had yet. "You talk too much." Then he bent his head until they were eye to eye, a serious look on his face as he said, "Just 'cause you wanted to kiss me doesn't mean you're gay. Maybe you were just curious."

"Not just curious." Jay kissed him to prove his point. He didn't think he'd be able to move away if they stopped. He'd have to jerk off right there in the snow-covered parking lot, standing next to the bar's trash bins before attempting to get to his Jeep.

The kisses turned vigorous. Passionate. Sensual. Dark Eyes tasted like cigarettes and whiskey. So new. Heady and intense. Jay's pulse quickened, and Dark Eyes held him tighter. The man's body was tense, his muscles on alert. What was his deal? Wasn't he enjoying himself? What would it take to smooth away the tension?

"I'm gonna…" Dark Eyes tilted his head back, arched, and clutched Jay's hips. "Jesus. Been too long."

Jay pushed Dark Eyes to the brick wall beside them. He clasped the front of the man's jeans and tore them open. No thought required, he shoved the briefs out of the way and took another man's dick in his hand for the first time.

Larger than his own. Longer. Wider. Hotter. A few more strokes and Dark Eyes groaned. His hips jerked, and he clutched Jay's upper arm. Cum shot up, some landing on Jay's hand, more on the snow at their feet, the smell of it strong, the feel of it like his own but somehow so different.

Light and laughter spilled out the rear entrance of Sonny's as the door opened.

Jay stepped back, and Dark Eyes faced the wall while he closed his pants. Two couples staggered toward an SUV in the front row of the parking lot, laughing as they went. One pair climbed into the back of the vehicle, and the driver faced Jay as he held open the front door for a female passenger.

Dark Eyes reached into his leather jacket as he took two steps away. He removed his smokes, lit one, and leaned against the wall.

Sure. He could be casual. He'd gotten off.

A gust of crisp air rounded the corner of the bar and smacked into Jay. The sticky cum on his fingers cooled with the wind. His hand trembled as he wiped the remnants of another man's pleasure on his jeans.

What was he thinking? He wasn't ready for this.

"Don't go," Dark Eyes said.

With those two words Jay froze. He wanted more—more kissing, more touching, more everything. Just more.

After the SUV drove away, Jay slunk back to their previous location without another thought about right or wrong, guilt or loss— wanting something, anything to ease the ache. Dark Eyes leaned in. His warm breath hit Jay's cheek.

"Tell me more stuff you want to do. One thing you've dreamed about."

"A...a...blow—"

Dark Eyes brought their mouths together and gave Jay a long, slow kiss, then sank to his knees in the snow.

Oh, God. Was this really happening?

The man opened Jay's pants and lowered his briefs. The cool air reached his exposed flesh, but nothing diminished the hard-on. Dark Eyes kissed the skin of his hip, brushing cock and balls with his chin.

Yep. Not another dream. Real. So goddamn real.

The man's hand shook as he gripped Jay's cock. How long had it been for him? Dark Eyes slid his hot lips over the tip of Jay's dick, and Jay threw his head back and his hands out, holding the other man by the back of the head. The short hair felt odd. Why wouldn't it? It wasn't like he went around touching other men's hair.

He tightened his hold, giving in to the pure instinct to hang on to the man blowing him. Dark Eyes lowered his mouth over Jay's cock and lifted up. The drag of his lips sliding along Jay's length, the man's exploring hands on his balls, the intense suction that proved Dark Eyes had experience behind him—it all had Jay's body on fire, had him ready to explode.

The orgasm crashed through him, wave after wave. He wanted to keep it at bay for a few more moments of the amazing blowjob, but he had no warning. He grunted and hissed, "Shit. Oh shit."

Dark Eyes held him in the tight heat of his mouth until Jay's cock grew soft. The man pulled back, licked his lips, and smiled. He had swallowed Jay's cum.

No one had—

She didn't—

No.

No comparisons.

The guy looking blissed-out, on his knees, with a hand still touching Jay's cock did not remind him of her. They were nothing alike.

Dark Eyes looked up at him. "What's your name, kid?"

He swallowed and found his voice. "Jay. Yours?"

The man ran his tongue over the crown of his dick in another slow taste. Jay flinched and gripped the back of the man's head tighter. If Dark Eyes kept touching him, he'd be hard again in short order. He rolled his hips. More of the man's mouth wouldn't be a bad thing. Would it?

Dark Eyes sat back on his heels. "Lincoln."

What? Jay dropped his hand. "Wh-What?"

"Lincoln." The man smiled. "Weird, I know. My mom had a thing for history too."

"M-McCaw?"

"Yeah." McCaw stood, his eyebrows drawn in. Then his expression softened. "Hey, you seen me race?"

Oh God...No...No! Jay slid along the wall.

"Shit, kid. Don't freak on me." McCaw reached for him. "You okay?"

Jay backed up more, his pants still open, his dick sticking out. He fumbled to get himself in order. He pointed at McCaw. "This did not happen. Do you understand?"

McCaw closed his eyes for a moment, then looked at Jay and said, "No matter what anyone tells you around here, there's nothing wrong with being queer."

"No! It did not happen." Another gust of cold air whipped around the building. Jay's fingers were still sticky. He wiped them on his jeans again.

McCaw leaned back to the wall and crossed his arms over his chest. "Sure, kid."

Jay had to get away from what he'd just done. And whom he'd done it with. Without looking back, he dug into his pocket for his keys and headed toward the corner of the building. Even if he'd wanted to, he couldn't ignore the whispered words from behind him.

"Thanks, Jay."

He made it to his Jeep but couldn't get the door open. The piece of shit was always sticking in the winter months. The summer months too. He tugged and cursed until he fell to his knees, and his stomach gave up the beers to the snow-covered parking lot.

The retching ended, and he pressed the back of his shirtsleeve to his mouth until the threat of tears had passed.

What the hell had he done?

Chapter Eight

The screwdriver slipped from where Lincoln had it wedged between the top and bottom sections of the air purifier. He jammed his thumb and dropped the screwdriver. *Fuck.* He sucked on the tip of his throbbing thumb as the blood rushed to it.

He'd been working on the damn filter for an hour and still hadn't managed to get the lid off to see what was wrong underneath. Without it, Jessica couldn't breathe as easily at night. He should head out to get her a new one, but Nancy said the kind that helped with her allergies was expensive.

And of course, he couldn't drive anywhere.

He picked up the screwdriver and gave another try at prying open the filter. The tool slipped again and struck his leg. "Goddammit."

"Goddammit!" The younger-sounding echo of Lincoln's curse was followed by a door banging shut.

Lincoln stood and kneaded his thigh as he made his way into the hall.

Adam was wrenching off his shoes. He kicked one then the other down the hall without even looking where they went. "Shit."

"Hey. Your mom let you talk like that?"

"Oh. Uncle Linc. Forgot you were here. Sorry."

"No big. What's up with you?"

"Nothing."

The front door opened. Adam took off for his room as Nancy came into the house.

"Adam!" she hollered. "Come here."

He ducked into his room, and the hall wall shook with the slam of his door, rattling the one on the laundry closet next to the kid's room. At least the repair on the sliding doors held up.

Lincoln followed Nancy into the kitchen. She tossed her purse onto the table and rubbed her closed eyes with the heels of her hands.

"What's going on?"

She stripped off her coat, revealing the scrubs underneath. "He's suspended."

"What for?"

"Fighting."

"Not good."

"No. Where do you think he learned stuff like that? His no-good dad and his worse stepdad. Some track record, huh?" She dropped into a chair. The metal tips on each leg scraped along the floor and sounded oddly like the screech of tires. Lincoln flinched. It didn't faze Nancy.

"Why was he fighting?" he asked.

"I don't know. He wouldn't tell the principal, and he won't talk to me."

"Doesn't sound like Adam."

Her sad gaze met his. "You don't know. You haven't been here, haven't seen—"

Adam stomped into the kitchen and threw open the fridge door. He grabbed a bottle of soda. "I'm not apologizing. They can't make me."

Nancy bounded to her feet. "They can. And you will. Otherwise, they might not let you go back to school. They won't put up with violence. You're lucky it's only a suspension."

"Yeah?" Adam kicked the fridge door shut. "I was lucky Big Jim from the football team was on my side."

Lincoln couldn't hide the smirk. Nancy threw a scowl his way, and he backed off on the grin.

"I had a reason," Adam said. "There was—"

"I don't care about your reasons." Nancy pressed her hands to her hips.

"You're not listening to me." Adam waved the bottle of soda in the air as he spoke. He'd be lucky if it had fizz left when he was done.

"*You're* not listening. They were clear about what you have to do before you can return to school."

Adam jabbed the bottle of soda toward her. "Screw that."

"Watch it." Lincoln stepped forward. "Don't talk to your mom like that."

The kid turned the soda bottle on him. "I don't have to listen to you. You're not my father."

"I've got this." Nancy glared at Lincoln.

"I'm out of here." Adam spun around to leave.

"Nuh-uh," she said. "Get back here. I had to leave work early. We're talking about this now."

Adam kept going. Lincoln tried to stop the kid before he could get through the kitchen doorway. Adam tucked his arm to his chest and shrank sideways. His left side smacked into the doorjamb.

Lincoln moved toward him. "Jesus. You okay?"

"Just tripped," he muttered and left the room.

Lincoln spun around as soon as Adam's bedroom door closed. "Dammit, Nancy. Did he hit the kids?"

"I told you, no."

"Then what was that?" He pointed toward where Adam had flinched.

"I don't know. You're kinda scary." She tried for a smile, but it wasn't real. She couldn't fool him.

"He's never been scared of me." Lincoln glanced at the kitchen doorway. "Is it 'cause of the jail thing?"

"No." She slumped into the chair. "Before you, every guy who's lived here scared him." Lincoln sat next to her. He reached for her hand, but she pulled away from him. "I can take care of my kids. And myself."

"I know you can." He went for her hand again and didn't let her get away from him. "I want to help."

"I appreciate it. I do. I appreciate that he's got one man in his life who isn't a piece of shit. But I've got to fix things with him. It's part of the reason I wanted Mel to leave. I saw the signs. Adam was changing. The anger, the fights. Mel wasn't good for him."

"He wasn't good for any of you. Adam wasn't like this before I left." Somehow the asshole stepdad had managed to change Adam from a typical looking-for-fun teenager to a scared-in-his-own-home kid. If only Lincoln could show Adam... What? That life fucking sucked sometimes? Maybe moving in with them wasn't a great idea.

"I've made mistakes," Nancy said. "And I need to fix it." She patted Lincoln's hand. "And you can't spend all your time worrying about me, or my kids. You've got to get back to your life. See your friends. Meet someone new." She grinned. "Have some hot, kinky sex."

He snorted. The night before at Sonny's had been hot. A damn handjob had never had him so undone. If only the kid hadn't freaked. It wasn't easy figuring out you were gay in small-town America.

"You never had trouble finding guys," she said with a laugh. "Even in Edgefield."

He wanted to find the kid again. The one person who made him forget everything else. The one person who hadn't looked at him with contempt or pity.

The one person he'd connected with who knew nothing of what he'd done or where he'd spent the last six months.

"Mom!" Davy sprinted into the kitchen, a Hello Kitty backpack dangling from his right hand. "Jessica can't breathe."

Nancy jumped out of her chair. "Where is she?"

"Outside. We were just walking home like you said we could."

Lincoln headed for the open door. Jessica stood on the top rung of the porch steps, wheezing, a tiny black-and-white kitten in her hands.

"She ran." Davy sounded as if he was about to cry or scream or both. "I told her not to, but she wanted to catch it."

Shallow gasps punctuated Jessica's words. "She's...too small...to be...alone."

Lincoln scooped her up and carried her into the house. He lowered her feet to the floor and knelt next to her. "Breathe deep. Nancy!"

She frantically searched through the backpack. "It's not in here. Davy, go get the one by her bed."

Jessica's entire upper body heaved with each hitch of her breath. Lincoln rubbed her back, whispering in her ear. "Breathe. Slow. Easy. Just breathe." Her wide, brown eyes watched him, her tiny hands still clasping the kitten.

Davy returned in a hurry. "Not there."

The backpack hit the floor at Nancy's feet. "Not there?"

"We're taking her to the hospital." Lincoln didn't hesitate. He picked Jessica up, pried the kitten from her hands, and dropped it to the couch. "Your new friend stays here." The stupid little thing could fend for itself for now. Maybe Sparky wouldn't eat it before they got back.

Nancy followed him to the door. "She just needs her inhaler."

"We're not waiting. Get your keys."

"All right." Nancy called for Adam and asked him to stay with Davy. Despite their argument, the kid didn't complain once he took a look at his sister.

They were in Nancy's car in no time, Jessica on Lincoln's lap, her back to his chest, her every struggle for air obvious. A five-year-old should be able to do something as natural as breathing. Life fucking sucked sometimes.

Nancy seemed to agree. "I wish she hadn't lost her inhalers. I don't have the money for this."

He brushed a stray clump of hair behind Jessica's ear and kept stroking her head. "We'll work it out."

* * * *

"Susan! Turn that off. Jay doesn't want to see it."

Jay followed his dad into the living room where his mom sat in front of the television, a crushed tissue in her one hand, the TV remote clutched in the other. She stared up at them, tears on her cheeks, anger in her eyes. She didn't make a move to do as her husband had said.

On the television screen, a reporter stood outside a courthouse recapping the events of the fatal car crash on State Road 91 and said, *"Justice has finally been served for the family of Katherine Miller."*

Was this all she did? And why now? She knew Jay was on his way over for dinner.

"I said turn it off." Jay's dad tried to grab the remote from her.

She jerked her hand out of reach, playing keep-away from her husband. After a minute of their flailing arms, his dad gripped her wrist and wrenched the remote from her hand.

It was amusing until the reporter said the name, *"Lincoln McCaw."*

His dad was right. He didn't want to see this. Not after having met the man—not after what they'd done in the snow behind Sonny's Tavern.

The reporter continued. *"McCaw shed tears as he apologized to the family of Katherine Miller."*

Jay's dad pointed the remote toward the DVR.

"No," Jay said. "Leave it."

From where she sat, his mom reached for the remote, slipped it out of her husband's fingers, and held it to her chest as if it were a lifeline, as if it were all she had in the world to hold on to.

Jay moved the wooden chair from in front of the fireplace so he could sit near the TV and pretend his parents weren't behind him.

In a flash, there he was.

McCaw.

Looking so different from the man Jay had kissed—the man who had sucked him off in a back parking lot. A slight shiver worked its way through Jay. Goose bumps rose up with thoughts of Lincoln McCaw on his knees, but the images faded as Jay took in the televised pictures from six months earlier.

McCaw looked thinner than he did now. His dark hair contrasted with the paleness of his face. His eyes were bloodshot. The bags underneath gave him a look of intense despair. Tired. Broken. Destroyed. Worse than the first time Jay had seen him at the bar.

As the judge read the sentence, the camera tightened in on McCaw. A slow buildup of tears swelled into silent sobs. The newscast cut to McCaw addressing the court.

"I can't say I'm sorry enough. There...there aren't words." Tears

streamed down his face, and he batted at them with trembling fists. "*I will never forget that moment.*" He swatted away the last of his tears, struggling to say more. "*I want the family to know how sorry I am for their loss. How if I could go back and make things right, I would. I'd give anything to take back what I've done. I can only imagine the pain, the sorrow I've caused.*"

The television screen returned to the reporter who wrapped up the story with the standard "*Reporting live, this is…*" salutation. Jay's dad had the remote again, and the television went black.

But all Jay saw were those dark eyes filled with the same haunted look he saw in the mirror every morning.

* * * *

Jay cut the engine to his Jeep. If he left it running any longer, he wouldn't have enough gas to get home. He didn't want to end up stranded outside Lincoln McCaw's house. Especially since he hadn't made up his mind about knocking on the front door. What could he say to the man?

The truth.

He owed the guy that much. Jay didn't think he could stand in McCaw's presence for long without thinking about what they'd done behind Sonny's Tavern, but the man in the courtroom footage deserved closure. They all did.

Jay climbed out of the Jeep, headed for the porch, and took a deep breath as he rang the bell. The front door opened, and a huge German shepherd lunged at him.

"Duke!" A man grabbed the dog's collar and yanked him into the house. "Sorry. Duke, stay back." He released the dog, who went barreling into the house with a slight shove from his owner's hip. The man was in his thirties and stood a touch shorter than Jay. "Can I help you?"

"I'm looking for Lincoln McCaw." Why did that sound so odd? Right. No hint of the hatred or disgust usually surrounding that particular name.

The man let go of the door and crossed his arms over his chest. The smile faded. "He doesn't live here anymore."

"Do you know where I can find him?"

He searched Jay's face. "How do you know Lincoln?"

"We used to race in the series together." The lie slipped out easily. Did that bother him? Jay had always hated lies. They were the coward's way out. So why was he spreading so many lately? Did it matter? All he needed was an address. "Thought I'd look him up. See how he's doing."

"Why don't you come in."

The other man held the door open, and Jay entered the house. Had Lincoln McCaw come here that night? Had he walked through the front door and gone upstairs to his warm bed while her cold body lay in the morgue? Had he gotten any sleep?

"Said the name's Paul." The man had a hand out.

"Jay." They shook, and he followed Paul into a kitchen.

"Have a seat." Paul opened the refrigerator. "Want a beer?"

"Thanks." Jay sat at the kitchen table. The room was sleek, the appliances a matching silver, the countertops a marble he'd seen in more upscale homes like the Shaws'. Fancier than the exterior had suggested. And the exterior was the best of the block. The only sign of wear in the room was a scratch along the edge of the wooden kitchen table. Jay ran his thumb over the imperfection, mentally clinging to it as if it were all that grounded him to his own destroyed life— grounded him to the anger he hoped to hold on to. He couldn't forget who Lincoln McCaw was, couldn't let his desire get the better of him.

Paul disappeared behind the fridge door and rummaged around before he returned with two beers. "These are all I've got. Don't drink much anymore." He sat opposite Jay and slid a bottle across the table.

Jay reached for it, but Paul didn't let go. His gaze roamed all over Jay. "You raced with Lincoln?" he finally asked. "Friends?"

"Yeah."

He let go of the beer and sat back.

"I take it you know him," Jay said.

Paul took a long swallow from his beer, his stare never leaving Jay. The bottle clanked onto the table. "I knew him. Quite well."

Footsteps thudded outside the kitchen. "Hey, babe. Who was at the door?" A blond man stepped into the room wearing a pair of jeans and nothing else. He froze when he spotted Jay. "Sorry. Didn't mean to interrupt."

"Sam, this is a friend of Lincoln's. From his racing."

Sam gave a nod to Jay.

"I'm sorry to just show up like this," Jay said. "This was the only address I found."

Sam fixated on Paul, his eyes wide. Was he even listening? What was making them uncomfortable? Jay's visit? Or the mention of Lincoln McCaw? In either case, Sam was uneasy, and Paul knew it.

Jay rambled on. He had his own secrets to keep. "I wasn't sure if he'd moved or was still around. How long have you lived here?" he asked Sam.

"I don't. It's Paul's place. You've lived here what? Five years?"

Paul nodded.

The pieces were falling into place. "You lived with McCaw?"

"Yeah." Paul sized Jay up again as he drank more of the beer. "We were together. You got a problem with that?"

Jay didn't have to lie on that one, even if he was lying his ass off about everything else to these two.

Sam spoke before Jay could. "I'll let you two talk." He hesitated a moment, staring at Paul until he left the room.

Jay offered an answer. He couldn't afford to offend. "I don't have a problem with it. I know he's gay. Just didn't know he'd lived here with someone."

Silence followed. Paul looped his forefinger and thumb around the neck of the beer bottle and twisted it back and forth without lifting it off the table. The scrape of glass on wood didn't seem to bother him. "That's surprising," he said. "He's not ashamed of it, but around here, you don't advertise. Most people he raced with didn't have a clue." He stilled the bottle. "You know about the accident?"

Jay's breath hitched. He inhaled and tried to make it appear natural. "Yeah."

Paul leaned forward in a posture of pure warning. "If you're here because you're a friend, then I might tell you how to find him. If you're here 'cause you hate him for beating you on the track or something else he did to you back in the day and you're out to stick it to him, then fuck off." He paused and then added quietly, "He's in a bad way."

"You've seen him since he got out?"

"Nope." Paul seemed to have passed by some hidden barrier and couldn't stop himself. He assumed they shared a kinship in their affection for McCaw. "I tried to help him. I did. He broke it off and refused to see me. Our relationship died the day of that accident."

Paul's words penetrated Jay and plucked away at his resolve to hate and blame.

Was seeing Jay again, no matter what the reason, going to make things worse for McCaw? Worse for both of them?

The answers didn't matter. Something inside Jay told him he had to do this—had to let the tortured man from the courtroom recording off the hook. It's what Katie would want. "I need to find him."

"Sonny's Tavern. South side of town."

"I tried there. They said he hasn't been in for a few days."

"Before he left, he was there a lot. I imagine he'll pick up right where he left off." Paul took a long drink from his beer, then met Jay's stare. "Maybe you can help him. If you don't want to try, then don't bother, yeah?"

All Jay could manage was a nod. Maybe he had used up his allotment of verbal lies.

"He's staying with his sister. Nancy Connell." Paul wrote an address on a slip of paper and gave it to Jay.

"Thanks."

"Could you give him a letter for me?" Paul went into the hall and returned with an opened white envelope. "It came for him last week." He slid the envelope across the table. "There was no return address, so I opened it. I thought it might be important."

Jay nodded and picked up the envelope.

"It's some kind of hate mail. I guess about the accident."

Hate mail? "What?"

"It doesn't say who it's from. Maybe the guy whose wife died wants Lincoln to feel bad. I don't know. I tried to contact Lincoln, but he won't return my calls. He should know about this, though."

"I can…" Jay stared at the envelope in his hands. Who had sent it? And what did it say? "I can give it to him."

"Thanks."

Jay stood. He made it four steps toward the kitchen doorway then stopped, his back to Paul. "How long were you and Lincoln together?"

Paul didn't respond.

He should let it go. Keep walking. What did it matter anyway? But the silence disturbed Jay. He turned around.

Paul was staring sideways into the empty kitchen. When he finally looked at Jay, he said, "Seven years."

Longer than he and Katie, even counting the high school years between going steady and their first official date. "I'm sorry."

Paul got up from the table and walked to stand before a window across the room. "It wasn't his fault. It's just how it had to be for him. Looking back, I don't think we could've avoided it—other than the accident not having happened. Not that anyone can change that now. He needs to let go of the guilt. He needs to forgive himself."

Blame. It surrounded Jay. Every day for a year. And here was a man who placed none of it on McCaw.

What did it mean to be at fault? Was being sorry for your actions enough? It couldn't erase the pain, the despair, but what could be gained by hating a stranger?

Jay wasn't happy with the answers he was coming up with.

He thanked Paul, left the house, and climbed into his Jeep. Despite the budding need to give them all closure, he wasn't ready to let go. Not yet. The anger couldn't dissipate before he had another chance to look into the face of the man who'd taken his life from him.

If he let go before then, he might not be able to walk away from the first person who'd held him in a year.

And that would be bad. For everyone.

Chapter Nine

The dead don't cry at night. But I do. And someday
you will too.

The words sent a chill down Jay's spine. He started his Jeep and cranked up the heat. He had debated for several minutes on whether or not to look inside the envelope addressed to Lincoln McCaw, but the local postmark, the typed front, and Paul's words piqued his interest. If it was about the accident, had someone he knew sent it? He pulled out the lone piece of paper while he still sat parked at the curb in front of Lincoln's old home.

Where he still sat ten minutes later.

Both the note and envelope were printed, nothing handwritten. The envelope was plain white, the kind with privacy tinting to keep nosy neighbors and postal workers from stealing your credit card number or bank account information. Or from reading your creepy threats to an ex-race car driver.

The piece of paper was cream colored and thick, like something used for formal announcements or letters. It didn't match the stark white envelope. Jay held the paper over his steering wheel under the dim streetlights. There was a watermark. A circle with lettering around the outer edge. He couldn't make them out in the dim light. Four images or initials even harder to see occupied the center of the circle. Maybe in brighter light he'd have better luck. He folded the note and slipped it into his jacket pocket.

Who could've sent it to McCaw? Someone who wanted to scare the man. Someone who didn't want him to get comfortable in his life. Someone who wanted him to pay.

Who cared enough about the accident to want to torment and threaten Lincoln McCaw?

Everyone in Jay's life.

Jay shifted the Jeep into drive and pulled away from the curb.

He'd try Nancy Connell's place first. If Lincoln wasn't there, he'd hit Sonny's again. He had to find out if there'd been other notes. And if so, he had to know if they were empty threats or if someone he knew was planning to make good on them.

He wasn't about to let anyone he cared for get into trouble. Not over an accident.

* * * *

"Another beer?"

Lincoln almost laughed at that. Instead, he nodded and said, "Keep 'em coming." He lit a smoke and took a long drag. He needed to quit. His lungs were already protesting. The laundry alone was killing him. Every time he went back to Nancy's, he had to change. He couldn't risk the lingering smoke around Jessica. He tipped his head back and swallowed the new beer until it was half gone.

Sonny's Tavern was the kind of place he could sit and drink and forget the day—forget about hospital bills and sick kids, forget about the cost of prescriptions. And the cost of mistakes.

Perched on the same bar stool as the week before, he downed the beer as he waited. He wasn't waiting for the kid, though. Was he? He wanted to be alone.

Then why had he convinced himself to return to the bar? Because he wanted the kid again. He couldn't hide from that.

After Lincoln ordered his third beer, and after eight other people had walked through the front door, Jay entered Sonny's. Lincoln's breath caught in his chest. The reaction was more the lack of sex than anticipation over this particular guy, wasn't it? He turned back to his beer.

A moment later, Jay sat on the stool next to him.

Lincoln gave a curt nod. "Jay."

Their gazes met, and Lincoln held the stare longer than should've been natural for two men who barely knew each other, two men sitting in the middle of a straight bar like Sonny's.

Jay's gaze darted around the room as if he'd just realized what he was doing, and it disgusted him.

Closeted. Lincoln understood. But did he want to deal with a kid just figuring out he was gay? A guy who looked like he battled an inner war—like he wanted to hate Lincoln at the same time as wanting to fuck him?

Jay reached in front of him and grabbed Lincoln's pack of Marlboros. Lincoln's heartbeat pounded as Jay pulled out a cigarette using only his lips and tossed the pack onto the bar.

Had his heart been beating before? Or had it been lying in wait?

Jay wrapped two fingers around the cigarette and let it slip from between his lips. "Got your lighter?"

Those lips needed a warning label. They let a man forget where he was. Lincoln stood and whispered, "Come and get it." He strolled to the back of the bar and into the bathroom.

He shouldn't do this. Not in Sonny's. Not with a kid who was too young to be okay with gay life in Edgefield, too young to have learned what sucked about life.

Lincoln didn't need the complication.

It wasn't stopping him, though. He checked the stalls and found he was alone. Hopefully not for long. He waited in the last one.

His dick was already hard. He wasn't going to last. He faced the far wall and laid his hands flat against it, trying to ease his breathing. He needed to calm down. He'd made a fool of himself in the back parking lot. This time he hoped for more than the kid's hands. Maybe they could get off and then head somewhere else to really have fun.

The outer door opened a minute later. Jay slipped into the stall and without delay pressed his groin to Lincoln's ass, and ran his hands up the front of Lincoln's thighs.

Lincoln clutched the top of the stall. He hadn't been fucked in a damn long time. Paul preferred to bottom, but he'd fuck Lincoln once in a while. The last time had been a few weeks before the accident.

It wasn't the long wait, though, that was driving Lincoln crazy. No. It was the kid.

But they couldn't fuck in Sonny's. He just hoped for a quick grope, another one of the kid's kisses, and then he'd suggest they get out of the bar. But the pressure against his ass had him ready to go off, rather than calming him down.

Jay worked his hands over Lincoln's dick. "Found what I wanted."

"Jesus, kid. You talk too damn much. Gonna have me coming again before I get to kiss you."

"I doubt it's my words that have you ready." Jay squeezed his cock and glided a hand down, then back up, not missing one inch of Lincoln's dick through the jeans.

"You sure you've never done this before?"

Jay gripped Lincoln's arm and swung him around. Lincoln barely had time for a breath before Jay's mouth met his. The recent fantasies hadn't been wrong. The kid could kiss. Lincoln wanted more. A lot more.

Maybe Jay didn't. He froze, and then took a step back.

"Something wrong?"

"Hate this song. It was… She liked…"

Not now. Lincoln didn't need the kid shutting down. "If you can hear the music, I must be doing something wrong." He licked Jay's earlobe and proceeded lower, sliding his lips along the man's neck, taking in the faint scent of soap and cologne. Jay hadn't smelled like this before. Had the man spruced up to see him?

Jay jerked away and moved as far from Lincoln as he could get in the bathroom stall. "I can't do this."

What the hell? Lincoln let go of him and tried to calm his heavy breaths.

"I thought maybe I could take what I wanted. Use you. Forget who you are long enough to—"

"Who I am?"

Jay bit his bottom lip, then released it and inhaled an uneven breath. "My name's Jacob Miller."

No.

Lincoln shook his head. *No fucking way.*

He fumbled with the lock on the door. Jay interrupted his attempts and released the latch. Lincoln shoved the door open. It slammed against the wall with a *thud* that echoed in the small bathroom. He faced the row of sinks and the large mirror but couldn't look at himself, or the man behind him. "She was your wife?"

Jay didn't say anything. Lincoln met the man's stare in the mirror, and Jay nodded. The smudged mirror distorted his face to where he looked more like a mirage than a flesh-and-blood man.

"Jesus Christ." Lincoln ran a hand through his hair. His biceps jumped with the movement. The wolf and eagle feather tattoo danced in the mirror's reflection. "You knew who I was last time? When I told you my name?"

Jay nodded again. Maybe he'd said all he could.

"And you still came back here and hit on me? Let us get this fucking far?" Lincoln pointed at the stall they'd just vacated. How the hell could Jay have touched him again?

When Jay answered, he didn't look at Lincoln. "I wanted you. I won't lie about that. But now—"

Movement sounded outside the bathroom door, drawing Lincoln's attention.

After a minute of silence and no one had entered, Jay said, "I can't." His voice was low, his gaze on Lincoln's in the mirror again.

"No shit, you can't." Lincoln clutched the edges of the sink in both hands, keeping his back to Jay.

"I wanted to talk to you, wanted you to know she—" Jay stopped and stared at the ceiling.

Wanted to know she what? What couldn't he say?

When Jay finally lowered his head, he dug into his pocket and pulled out a piece of paper and an envelope. "Do you know who sent you this?"

Lincoln twisted around and snatched the familiar paper. He read the note, his stomach pitching with the threat. "Where'd you get this?"

"Paul."

Paul? His Paul? Well no, not his any longer. "When'd you talk to him?"

"Today."

"What the hell for?"

"I was trying to find you."

Lincoln held up the note. "He gave this to you?"

"He thought we were friends."

Friends? Lincoln laughed with a snort. "How'd you pull that off?"

"Are there more?" Jay asked.

Lincoln forced a swallow down his dry throat. "Yes."

"Do you know who sent them?'

"Thought I did. But since I blew him last week, I'm a little confused."

Jay ripped the note out of Lincoln's hand. "I did not send this to you."

Why was the kid pissed? Who wouldn't have assumed it was him? "I should take your word on that?"

"I have nothing else to give you. Did you show them to anyone? Tell the police?"

"No."

"I have to find out who they're from."

"*You* have to?" Why? To thank them? No. Jay didn't seem like the kind of man who'd want to torment anyone. Not even the person who'd destroyed his future. Although Lincoln had no idea how he'd come to that conclusion.

"I can't let anyone else get hurt over this."

"Over me?"

Jay folded the note and tucked it into the envelope. His hands moved slowly, the paper treated as if it contained secrets to winning the Mega Millions lottery. Like the kid needed more money.

"When did you start getting them?" Jay asked.

"The week after the accident. Who do you think is sending them?"

"I don't know. Obviously someone who knew my wife. Someone

who loved her. Maybe from her family." He drew in a deep breath. "Or maybe mine." Odd how easily Jay said it. Maybe he was telling the truth.

"Will they do anything to hurt my family?"

"No!" Quieter, Jay added, "I'm certain this is just to scare you, make you feel bad."

Was it? Or was Jay Miller trying to protect his own?

No way was Lincoln sticking around to find out. He left the bathroom and walked out of the bar without a glance back at the one man he'd hurt most in the world.

Chapter Ten

"Thanks for the ride," Lincoln said through the car's open window.

"Not a problem. See you tomorrow." Mitch put the car in reverse and backed out of the driveway.

Lincoln waved good-bye and trudged up the steps. The new job sucked. Not the job itself. Hard work never bothered Lincoln. It was the stares, the whispers, the lack of eye contact.

Mitch had gone out on a limb to get him the job. Lincoln had to give the man credit. People were going to talk, and it would've been easier to avoid the entire situation than back Lincoln with a job offer. The least he could do was not complain about some assholes.

The house was quiet as he stepped inside. Unease settled in his gut. The house was never this calm. Not with three kids. The words from the note Jay Miller had shown him in the bar's bathroom replayed in his head. He strode down the hall and stopped just short of slamming Jessica's door in when he heard her giggle.

He breathed deep and stepped back. He didn't need to scare the shit out of the kids. All for what? Typed lines of text meant to torment more than anything else?

Was that all it was? Should he call the police?

No. The look on Jay's face in the bar the other night said all he needed to know. The man didn't deserve the hassle of questions from the cops. And what if someone in Jay's family or his in-laws had sent the notes? They were people Lincoln had hurt. People who had been through enough pain.

He went to the kitchen and pulled out the fixings for a sandwich. He was slathering on the mayonnaise when he caught sight of the piece of paper taped to the front of the fridge. In the middle of coloring book pages, school spelling lists, and pizza joint magnets was another note, the front typed with one name: *McCaw.*

His hand shook as he reached for it. Nancy wouldn't just leave it hanging there for him. No envelope, no address. This one hadn't come in the mail.

Someone had been in the house.

He yanked the note off, the piece of tape giving way and ripping the corner of the pristine paper. He flipped it open.

> *You should keep a better eye on your family...and their medical necessities. She can't breathe all that well without her inhalers, huh? Such a shame. I hope more don't end up missing.*

Lincoln crushed the note in his fist and stormed toward the bedrooms. This time he didn't hesitate. He shoved in Jessica's door. She sat in a small plastic chair at a table no taller than his kneecaps, Davy opposite her. The boy's surprised, mortified expression could've been from the way Lincoln had busted into the room or because Davy wore a pink feathered scarf around his neck and an equally pink cowgirl hat. Mr. Wuzzie, dressed the same in purple, sat in a chair between the two kids. All had miniature yellow teacups and plates of chocolate brownies on the table in front of them—even the plush toy.

What mattered to Lincoln was the inhaler sitting on Jessica's bedside table. Right where it was supposed to be.

Davy's lips were smothered with chocolate. "I just wanted the brownies." He pointed at his sister. "She wouldn't let me have any unless I played her stupid games."

"I didn't use the kitchen oven," Jessica said. "Honest, Uncle Lincoln. We used my little oven this time."

Lincoln found his voice. "You been in here since school ended?"

"Mostly," Davy said. He unwrapped the scarf from around his neck.

"Anyone come by the house?"

Davy snatched Mr. Wuzzie's brownie and said, "Nope."

Lincoln wanted to rip the chocolate snack from the kid's hand and throw it across the room. He held back the instinct. This wasn't their fault. It was his. "You didn't answer the door or anything?"

Jessica shook her head.

Lincoln backed out the doorway. "Where's Adam?"

"In his room," she said. "Davy! You can't have no more unless you play right."

Davy wound the scarf around his neck again and took a bite of the brownie he'd confiscated.

Lincoln left them to their party and headed to the living room. He did a once-over on all the windows and doors, checking for signs someone had broken in, locking each one he found unlatched. Any number of them offered a way into the house.

He'd have to replace a couple of the windows or they'd never lock securely. He'd also install dead bolts on the front and back doors. First chance he got. He'd need to give Nancy a reason for messing with the locks. The truth would work best. He didn't want any uninvited guests. She'd assume he'd mean her asshole husband, Mel. He would. But he'd also mean whoever had taken the inhalers and left the damn note.

Once he had the place locked as tight as it was going to get for now, he went to Adam's room. He knocked and pushed in the door as soon as Adam hollered, "Yeah!"

The kid sat at a desk with open books before him, texting on his cell, earphones in his ears, bobbing his head to the *thump-thump* of whatever his generation called music. Explained the kid's scream for a hello. Didn't he understand how headphones worked? Lincoln could hear fine. It was he who needed to scream at the kid.

Adam made no move to remove the music from his ears. Lincoln pulled the earphones out with one tug on the cord that hung at Adam's chest.

"Hey, I was listening to that."

"You can listen later. I need to talk to you."

"Okay." Adam kept hitting buttons on his phone.

Lincoln gave his limited store of patience a reminder the kid was a teenager. Finally Adam hit the send button and gave Lincoln his attention.

"I need you to do as I say and not ask questions about it."

The phone beeped an alert for a new message. Adam read the text. If he pressed so much as one button, Lincoln was going to lose it. A total stranger had pissed him off. He didn't need the kid pushing his luck.

Maybe Adam got the message. He dropped the phone to the desk. "Okay."

"Stay inside the house with your brother and sister until I get back. Don't open the door for anyone. And don't let them out of your sight."

"Something wrong?"

Lincoln took a step closer and lowered his voice. "I'm taking care of it, but I don't want them scared. I need your help."

"All right." Adam stood. "I'm coming."

As he walked by, Lincoln bent his head until Adam met his gaze. "I'm counting on you."

Adam's wide eyes scanned Lincoln's for a minute. Then he said, "I'm on it."

Lincoln gave Adam's shoulder a pat. "I knew you would be. But first I need you to get online and look up an address for me."

* * * *

The banging on the front door jarred Jay out of the heavy sleep he'd drunk himself into. He rolled off the couch and onto his hands and knees on the living room floor. The pounding caused a reciprocal throb in his head.

Todd could be such an ass sometimes. He had called the morning before and left a message. He always worried whenever Jay didn't call him back right away.

"Hang on! I'm coming."

That didn't stop the banging.

Jay unlocked the door and turned the knob. The door busted in on him, shoving him backward. He stumbled, but caught himself before he ended up on the floor.

Lincoln McCaw barreled in, kicked the door shut with the heel of his boot, and hauled Jay up against the wall. The man growled, and the sound muted into words. On every other one, he thrust Jay's shoulders against the wall. The house wasn't built for such abuse. "I know what I've done to her. To you. To your family. But I swear to fuck if anyone hurts my sister and her kids—"

Jay shoved at Lincoln's chest. "What are you talking about?"

Lincoln gripped his biceps tighter and slammed him against the wall. "Someone left another note. Inside the house. They stole her inhalers. She couldn't fucking breathe. This has nothing to do with her."

"Who?"

"My niece. She's five years old."

"Oh God." Who would take things that far? It couldn't be someone Jay loved. "Is she okay?"

"For now. I don't care what I've done or how much you all hate me. No one is hurting them. *No one.* Not your family. Not her family." He released one of Jay's arms and jabbed a finger at his face. "Not you."

Jay searched Lincoln's eyes. The anger leaped out like a flame and burned him. "You think I'm the one doing this?"

"The thought had crossed my mind."

He swatted the finger away and shoved Lincoln again. "Fuck you. And to think I felt sorry for what you're going through."

Lincoln staggered back a couple of steps, his eyes wide and focused on Jay's.

"I wouldn't hurt a little kid," Jay said, then quietly added, "I wouldn't hurt anyone."

Lincoln charged forward and crowded Jay against the wall. Before Jay could stop him, Lincoln crushed their lips together.

It was the harshest kiss Jay had ever had. Lips, teeth, tongue, the scrape of male facial stubble against his chin. Damn, he wanted more. He clasped Lincoln's neck and tugged the man closer. He opened his mouth wider, taking in more of Lincoln's tongue.

It seemed Lincoln liked that. He pressed his groin against Jay's hip. The man was hardening right there, touching him. Jay slunk a hand between them and squeezed Lincoln's dick. That brought out a moan, and Jay's own cock firmed inside his jeans. God, he wanted to know. Needed to know. He slid down the wall to his knees.

Lincoln dropped a hand to his head. "You shouldn't... We shouldn't..."

Jay ignored him, got the man's jeans open, and lowered his underwear. Lincoln's cock looked larger than it had felt in his hands at Sonny's. He wrapped a hand around it and stroked as he pushed the briefs farther down. He leaned in and ran his tongue over Lincoln's balls. The heated flesh, the salty taste. So damn good. He opened wider and sucked a ball into his mouth, letting it fill him.

Lincoln worked the fingers of one hand through Jay's hair and stroked the back of his head. Not rough. A caress. A promise.

With that soft touch, all denials, all arguments, all hope of fending off what might be, were gone. Jay would not deny himself this. This—he had waited too long for. He grazed his fingers over the length of Lincoln's cock and palmed the base. What did other guys like? What did other people do? He'd only known the touch of one person's mouth on his dick.

No—that was no longer true, was it?

Lincoln had tasted him. The man had been damn talented at it too.

Could he translate the sensations to actions?

"You don't have to." Lincoln's voice was husky, deeper than a moment before.

Jay almost laughed at the words, but he had other priorities. He parted his lips and gave an openmouthed kiss to the tip of Lincoln's cock, tonguing his way to the bottom ridge of the crown. He couldn't stop himself. He opened wider and sucked in more, moistening the head, taking a deeper taste with his tongue, savoring the feel of another man inside him.

"Don't tease."

He pulled off. "Not teasing. Feels good." He knew he'd like it—like having a man's dick in his mouth.

"I knew that mouth would be great at this."

The words spurred him on. He took in more of Lincoln's cock. He wanted to go all the way down but his natural instincts kept it a remote wish. Another time. With more practice.

But there couldn't be more. Just this. Just now. Nothing more. He'd take as much as he could. He'd enjoy each moment, each sensation until it was over.

He dragged his moist lips up and down the length of Lincoln's dick, learning every inch of flesh. His own cock throbbed in his pants, blood thundering to it in a rush like it hadn't in a long time. Pleasure, like the caress of a palm, surged through his balls. He sucked harder, moved his head faster, all while he sped his hand over the base of Lincoln's cock.

Lincoln grunted with the changes. He snapped his hips and gripped Jay's shoulder, his fingers digging in. "Christ."

A burst of warm cum hit the back of Jay's throat. He breathed deep through his nose to keep from gagging, pulled to the tip, and swallowed. Lincoln shot more. It was sharp, bitter, stronger than the tastes Jay'd had of his own cum. He craved more for the comparison, but Lincoln was growing soft, the man's breath coming in heavy pants above him. Lincoln grasped his dick and withdrew.

A heady dizziness overwhelmed Jay. He drew in another long breath and rose to his feet, licking his lips.

Lincoln had one hand on the wall next to Jay, the other still on his dick. He stared at Jay's chest, and his face grew pale.

Jay followed the man's gaze. There over his T-shirt lay the two simple gold bands. They must have slipped in front of the shirt when he and Lincoln shoved at each other—or when he'd given the man a blowjob. Jay clenched the rings in his palm.

"Fuck." Lincoln backed up and zipped his pants shut. "We can't—"

"I know." Jay couldn't look away from his own hand covering the rings on his chest. "I just... I wanted to." He raised his head. "Wanted to taste you."

Lincoln ran a shaking hand through his hair. "I've got to get back to the kids." He went for the door and stopped with his hand on the doorknob. "I had to protect her. Had to keep her safe."

"Who?"

The tension in his broad shoulders was unmistakable. Lincoln drew in a long breath but didn't face Jay. "My sister's husband was beating her. She called me for help that night." He twisted the doorknob. "It's not an excuse. It's just where my head was then. I was trying to save her, and I ended up—" He rested his forehead on the door. "I'm sorry."

Jay's mouth dried. He couldn't swallow.

Lincoln opened the door. "I don't want anyone else to get hurt. Meet me at Sonny's. Tomorrow at five. You're going to help me find out who stole Jessica's inhalers, who's leaving the notes, or I'm going to the cops."

"Okay," Jay said.

The other man didn't glance back as he left.

Jay slid down the wall and landed on his ass. He lowered his head to his knees, the gold bands still in his grip. The shrill ring of the phone in the kitchen startled him.

Oh God. Todd could have walked in at any moment and seen him in Lincoln McCaw's arms, seen Lincoln's dick in his mouth. No one would forgive him for that.

What was he doing? And how the hell could he make himself stop?

Chapter Eleven

"Jesus, kid."

"What?" On unsteady legs, Jay stood beside Lincoln's table at Sonny's Tavern. They were about to go after whoever was threatening Lincoln—go after someone Jay cared about. That had to be what was getting to him. It had nothing to do with seeing the only man to whom he'd ever given a blowjob.

"Do you have to look so damn good?" Lincoln whispered.

Jay sank into a chair. "You said you wanted to talk about—"

"I know." Lincoln's voice lowered more. "Doesn't mean I still don't want to fuck you."

Jay stared at Lincoln, mouth hanging open until he realized what he was doing and forced himself to glance away. He licked his lips and said, "We can't."

"Right." Lincoln straightened in the chair. "But I need to figure out who's sending me this shit, who broke into my sister's. You think it's someone in your family? Hers?"

His mom, Stuart Shaw—maybe. But Emily? His dad? "They wouldn't hurt a little kid. There has to be an explanation. Even if one of them sent you—"

"How do we find out?"

"It can't be…" They wouldn't hurt anyone. Would they? They all despised Lincoln, but they had their limits. Even Stuart Shaw. Keeping medication from a five-year-old girl had to qualify. "They wouldn't go that far."

"Really?"

Jay stared at Lincoln, then dropped his gaze to the tabletop. He had to quit gawking at the man. Especially when Lincoln looked so damn sexy all Jay could think of was kissing those lips again. Better to stay focused on why they were there. Better to stay focused on who Lincoln was.

"I guess… I don't know. My parents, her parents—they all…"

"Hate me?"

Jay nodded.

"Okay," Lincoln said. "Let's not rule them out. Who else? Anyone else care about your wife enough to want to hurt me?"

"A lot of people cared for her. She was easy to love." Whoever had taken that love and turned it into vengeance hadn't really known his wife, or they'd know she'd never want this.

Lincoln rubbed his chin with the back of his hand. The slight shake was hard to miss. He reached for his beer and took a long swallow. "Besides her parents, is there anyone else from her family in the area?"

Family? Jay was her family. Even before they were married. "No. They moved here for a coaching job after Stuart retired from pro ball."

"You got family? Other than your parents?"

"My brother. And his wife."

"What about him?"

Jay shook his head as a waitress stopped by the table. He ordered a draft and tried to pretend they weren't running through a list of the people in his life like they were suspects in a murder mystery novel.

After the waitress brought the beer, Lincoln asked, "Why not?"

"He's my brother."

"So your mom and dad go on the list but not your brother?"

This was crazy. Todd was an EMT. He wouldn't fuck with a little girl's medicine. But he'd loved Katie too. He had as much motive as anyone else. He also spent a lot of time trying to please their mom. He'd do almost anything she asked. Was Todd carrying out her wishes? "Okay, my brother too." Jay downed a gulp of the beer and sat back heavy in his chair. "I can't believe we're having this discussion."

Lincoln's eyes narrowed. "Told you, I can have it with the cops if you prefer."

You'd think the man would be in a better mood when the day before he'd had what was probably his first blowjob in months. Was Jay no good at giving head? No. The noises Lincoln had made when he came proved Jay had done a damn fine job. And it had felt fine for Jay too. So much so his cock was excited at the possibility of another round.

But he couldn't go there. Not again.

Instead he asked, "Why didn't you go to the cops when you got the first letter?"

"I thought they were from you. That it was a grieving widower getting a little payback." Lincoln raised his bottle for another drink and added, "I figured I deserved at least that much."

"It was an accident."

Lincoln was quiet as he set the beer on the table and rotated the bottle in his hand. "It was. One I'll regret for the rest of my life."

Jay wanted to tell him the truth. That she was only out driving that night because of him. That maybe Lincoln didn't need to carry the burden alone. But all he could do was stare at the man.

"Stop looking at me like that," Lincoln said.

"Like what?"

"Like you understand me."

"Maybe I do."

"You're not supposed to. You're supposed to hate me."

"I suppose. But I don't."

Lincoln's throat muscles worked as he swallowed. The man's Adam's apple bobbed. Jay wanted to suck on it, wanted to taste the man's skin.

"Don't look at me like that either."

"Okay." Without another word Jay stood, walked to the other side of the bar, and slipped into the bathroom. He needed a minute away from the man to clear his head, to convince his dick this was a bad idea. The worst of his life.

The sight of the old whiskey-sipping man draining the last of his piss into a urinal helped calm Jay down. Sonny's wasn't the place to get caught up in some fantasy. Not a gay sexual fantasy. And not with Lincoln McCaw.

The old man shuffled his way to the door. *Back to the glass of booze.*

Why couldn't Jay's life be that simple?

He washed his hands, the cool water spilling over his heated flesh. The door opened again. Three large strides and Lincoln was behind Jay, crowding him against the sink, pinning his half-hard dick to the porcelain. He said, "I haven't fucked in over a year so you better quit teasing me."

No matter what Jay's brain was telling him about what a fucked-up idea this was, he could not ignore the solid cock wedged against his ass cheek. *No more thinking.* He turned and gripped Lincoln's neck. He drew the man to him. The kiss was slow and sensual, but tinged with desperate need, a longing months alone created in a man. Lincoln drove their mouths, their tongues, their bodies together, over and over. He consumed Jay with the kiss as they rocked and clutched. The taste of Lincoln, his smell, his touch was everywhere, all over Jay at once, and he didn't want it to end. He wanted to let Lincoln overwhelm him, let them both fall into an abyss of pleasure and satiation until neither man needed another drink to forget how he had gotten to that moment.

The bathroom door swung open and loud music poured in.

Lincoln twisted away from the embrace and stepped to a urinal. A bulky guy in a flannel shirt entered, laughing at something or someone out in the bar, his back to them. Jay returned his shaking hands to the faucet's spray.

The burly man kept chuckling as he staggered to a stall and shut the door behind him.

Lincoln moved past Jay, the length of his arm rubbing along Jay's back. "We've got to stop doing this here," he said in a low whisper as he cranked on the faucet a couple of sinks down.

"No shit." Jay reached for a hand towel. He tossed the towel in the trash and went out to their table.

Lincoln joined him but didn't sit. "We could go to your place."

"No." Jay glanced around the room. No one was paying attention to them.

"Right." Lincoln took a step back and made like he was going to sit.

"I meant, not my house." Jay stood. "Can we make it your place?" He fumbled into his pocket for his keys, hoping Lincoln said yes before either of them changed their minds.

"Yeah," Lincoln said. "That'll work. But no laughing at me."

* * * *

"How am I not supposed to laugh? You've got Transformers on your bed. And it's a *twin* bed." Jay did laugh then. It was all too goddamn unbelievable. He stood in Lincoln McCaw's bedroom—or what had become the man's room—about to do something he'd only dreamed of, with a man he shouldn't be talking with, much less anything else with.

Lincoln threw his jacket at the desk. The chair fell over with the weight of the leather, but it didn't stop him. He crowded Jay against the closed door. "It's my nephew's room. I told you not to laugh." He covered Jay's lips with his.

The kiss had Jay right back to where they'd left things at the bar.

Kissing another man—this man—was as hot and exciting as the first time, standing in the snow behind Sonny's. Lincoln ripped open the front of Jay's jeans and thrust a hand inside his briefs, all without breaking the intense kiss.

Jay had to break it off, though. He needed to breathe. Lincoln's hand touched his dick, and Jay arched his back. He held on to Lincoln's upper arms. The hint of the man's tattoo stuck out past the edge of the T-shirt. Jay would've asked to see it, but he was a little distracted. He thrust his hips with each stroke.

It was too easy to give in, to feel instead of think. He jerked back. "Wait. Nephew? Is anyone else home?"

"Nope," Lincoln said. "So you can come up with another reason to back out of this if you want."

"Back out?"

Lincoln cocked his head to the side and squinted. "You sure you're gay?"

"What?"

"I don't have an issue with liking to fuck guys. Don't want to be with someone who's going to freak halfway through this." Lincoln's gaze fell. He stroked Jay's cock again and said, "Been too long."

"I'm not going to freak. I wanted to kiss you." He rocked more as Lincoln jerked him faster. "Wanted to suck you."

"Doesn't mean you want to fuck me." Lincoln shook his head, still not meeting Jay's gaze. "Not me."

"Oh." Jay dropped his hands to his sides. "I don't know"—he breathed deep—"I don't know what I'm doing here."

"That's what I thought." Lincoln slid his hand out of Jay's pants.

"Wait." Jay's head spun at the loss of heat around his dick. "I didn't mean I don't know what I want. I want this, want you. It's confusing." Surprising. Astounding. Impossible. "But not..." He lowered his head. "It's just...I've never done this before. I mean..." Heat rose in his face.

Lincoln slipped a hand inside Jay's pants again and smiled. "Your body knows what it wants. So I'm thinking you not only talk too much, you think too much."

"No more talking. No more thinking. Got it."

Lincoln kissed him and continued lower, mouth to skin until his lips met the base of Jay's neck. His breath brushed skin as he spoke. "I don't mind the talking so much." He sucked on Jay's flesh. He had to be leaving marks.

"Okay," Jay said. "You sure about this?"

"Me? Did you miss the part where I haven't gotten laid in months?"

"But should it be with me?"

"I don't know why, but yeah. This is weird. And stupid. And

possibly the worst idea my cock's ever had." He flattened the palm of his free hand to the door beside Jay's head and leaned in. "But this has got to be harder on you than me. So I figure it's either one of two things." He ran his tongue up Jay's neck, this time adding teeth to the mix, his hand gliding over Jay's cock. Then he pulled back. "You're either fucking with me to get back at me. Or you really want me. I can't blame you for the first, so I won't complain as long as you aren't the one threatening my family. And..." He was back to working up marks on Jay's neck, his voice throaty as he said, "I want you to fuck me, so I'm willing to take the risk."

"You sure—"

"Stop thinking. No strings. A fuck. Nothing more. Nothing to feel guilty about."

"No. You sure no one's home?"

A grin hit Lincoln's mouth. "They went to a basketball game, but they'll be home later so we better not waste time."

"Okay." What the hell was he doing? And why couldn't he stop himself? Jay drew Lincoln to him, grinding his hard cock on the other man's hip, and shed his coat. He needed to feel Lincoln's skin on him, wanted to feel the contact of a man's chest against his. Who was he kidding? He wanted to know what *Lincoln's* chest felt like against his and what the man's body felt like pressed on top of him. Jay raised his shirt over his head.

The smirk on Lincoln's lips disappeared. He stilled the hand on Jay's dick and stared at the two rings dangling from the chain.

Jay would not take them off. He hadn't at any time during the past year. He wouldn't hide who he was. Not even to make this easier. For either of them.

Lincoln almost touched the tips of his fingers to the bands but stopped short. "There's been no one since?"

"No one."

All the desire had left Lincoln's eyes, his face grim.

Jay squeezed his eyes shut. Maybe he should take the rings off. He couldn't do this and think about her. She'd never blame anyone for an accident. Yet what would she think of where Jay was and what he was doing?

Lincoln lifted Jay's head with a push of one finger to his chin. "You want this?"

"Yeah...want to feel again." Jay's breath caught in his chest.

"You'll feel it." Lincoln leaned in and whispered in Jay's ear. "Just breathe." He slowly lowered Jay's pants and briefs, crouched to get them off, and stood.

Jay shivered with need, his cock hard, his skin heated, his body focused on one outcome. He joined it. All thoughts of anything else gone, he gripped Lincoln's shirt in both fists and tugged it over the man's head. He left getting the shirt the rest of the way off to Lincoln while he attacked the man's pants. Lincoln groaned as Jay's knuckles brushed his cock.

Pants and underwear off, they stood bare before each other. The hard, muscular flesh captivated Jay. The muscles of Lincoln's chest were well-defined, smooth, with little chest hair to obstruct the view. Jay placed his palms over the pectoral muscles and let his fingers explore. He flicked a nipple, ran his hands south over the taut stomach muscles, and then lower to the man's hips. The thick cock seemed too large to have been in Jay's mouth. And impossibly too large to fit in his ass. Jay shuddered, and couldn't pretend it had anything to do with fear, or denial, or guilt. It was pure anticipation at the idea of Lincoln fucking him.

"Touch me," Lincoln said.

Jay had been standing there, staring at Lincoln, the three fingers of one hand holding on to the man's hip, with no other part of them touching.

"Sorry," he said. "You're beautiful."

Lincoln scoffed. "Stop talking." He reached for Jay and pulled them together again. The press of chest to chest and the deep, exploring kiss had Jay ready to pop. One touch of Lincoln's hand to his dick, and he'd explode.

He wanted nothing more than the man's slick mouth on his shaft again. That was until Lincoln shifted, and their cocks slid against one another with each thrust of their bodies. *Better—it keeps getting better.* Jay never wanted it to end. But he also wanted to chase down his orgasm and ride it till morning.

Lincoln obviously had other ideas. He took a step back.

Jay whimpered. He actually whimpered out loud.

With a slight shake of his head, Lincoln said, "Gotta slow this down, or I'm gonna come. Get on the bed."

One unsteady step after another and Jay stood next to the bed. He didn't move.

"You okay?" Lincoln asked as he pressed against Jay's back.

"Yeah."

"Then what the hell are you doing?"

"Trying to remember the names of these Autobots"—he pointed to the bed—"on the sheets."

"What?"

"Just calming down like you said." Jay hoped to last, wanted his first time inside another man—inside *this man*—to be more than a couple of awkward thrusts. He wanted to savor everything. And for Lincoln to enjoy it too.

Lincoln chuckled and spun him around. Jay wanted another kiss. He didn't have time to get one. Lincoln shoved him to the bed and climbed on top of him. He bent over Jay's groin, his dark hair and skin a contrast to Jay's lighter skin, to the lighter patch of hair above Jay's cock. Lincoln settled on his knees, one on each side of Jay's calves. He hunched over and stared at Jay's dick and balls. He looked like a starving dog about to attack the only bone he'd seen in weeks. It was a little unnerving. Jay rose onto his elbows to get a better look as Lincoln parted his lips and ran his tongue over the tip of Jay's cock.

Jay couldn't help himself; he whimpered again, dropped to the bed, and bucked his hips. He clenched the bedsheet on each side of him, crinkling two images of the alien Autobots. Funny how his resolve to hate Lincoln McCaw had been as easy to destroy as the representation of the metal robots.

Also funny how he didn't care right then. Not with Lincoln's mouth dropping over the crown of his dick. "Jesus," he hissed. The man could suck. Lincoln wrapped a hand around the base of Jay's dick and set to a rhythm of pull and suck, squeeze and swirl that had Jay's head thrown back and his hands wrenched into the sheets more, bruising the skin on his fingers. Lincoln's sucking, his deep lunges, his every touch was passionate, powerful, unpredictable.

"Shit!" Jay cried out. "Gonna come."

Lincoln withdrew and sat back until his ass rested on Jay's lower legs. The man's heated balls grazed his flesh.

"Why'd you stop?"

"Almost couldn't." Lincoln licked his lower lip, the look on his face part hungry, part intoxicated. "You feel too damn good in my mouth. But you're going to fuck me. I'm not taking a chance you won't be able to get it up twice."

Jay sat up on his elbows. "I'll get it up again."

"That's what they all say. Anything to get my mouth back on your dick."

"I wouldn't do that."

Lincoln leaned forward and pressed himself against Jay's groin and chest, trapping their cocks between them.

Jay's breath hitched. God, he had missed this. The contact. The intimacy. Although having his dick rub against another man's wasn't anything he'd experienced before. Had never imagined it would have his body so on fire, his every nerve ending buzzing with sensation. Lincoln kissed him, a deep, slow kiss that curled Jay's toes with the intensity.

"Are you telling me you don't want to fuck me?" Lincoln asked. He ground his pelvis against Jay's, gliding their dicks together.

How could such simple rubbing, the slide of his cock against another feel so good? "I do. I want that." He wanted to know. He'd never done it. With anyone.

They stared at each other, their eyes and lips mere inches apart. Lincoln shot off the bed and went for his coat. He left the chair on the floor and removed several items from the leather's inner pocket. He held them in the air. A condom and a small bottle of lube. "You're lucky I'm always prepared. Only the one, though."

Oh God. They were really going to do this.

Lincoln tossed the condom and lube on the bed and climbed on top of Jay, straddling his thighs again. A tattoo covered a two-inch-high strip of Lincoln's upper arm. The outline of an eagle feather. Tribal. With a lone wolf depicted in midrun on the interior of the feather. Jay didn't think. He leaned forward and ran the tip of his tongue over the feather's edge, then the wolf.

"Fuck." Lincoln gripped the back of Jay's head, his fingers burrowing through his hair. "Love your mouth, that tongue."

The words spurred Jay on. He traced the feather again, loving the taste of salty skin, the scent of musk and sweat, the taste and smell of this man. Dizzy with lust, he fell back to the bed, wanting more—so much more.

And Lincoln gave him more. He bent forward and pressed another long kiss on Jay's lips before pulling back. He had the condom in his hand, the package already open. He removed the rubber, shimmied backward, and took Jay's cock in his hand. He rolled the condom on Jay, his big fingers moving slowly, carefully sliding the rubber on. Was that how his touch always was? Or were his careful movements an attempt at not breaking their lone condom, the only thing that could stop the moment?

Because apparently, nothing else could stop them.

The bottle of lubricant in Lincoln's hand, he squeezed a glob onto his palm and slicked Jay's cock, working the sensitive organ a little too long.

"Wait," Jay said. "You'll make me come."

"Don't you dare." Lincoln drew his hand away as if Jay's cock had caught fire. "Didn't you hear me? One goddamn rubber."

There couldn't possibly be any way for Jay to be more turned on than he was. Until Lincoln spread more lube onto his fingers and reached around to his own ass.

Watching Lincoln touch himself, getting ready for him was about to make Jay come faster than the friction of a moment before.

With his other hand, Lincoln grabbed Jay's and brought it to his ass. Jay felt Lincoln's fingers buried inside the man's own body, then Lincoln slipped his fingers free and slid Jay's inside him. Hot. Tight. Too tight for his dick. Jay's breath quickened.

"I—" He wasn't sure what to say.

Then no words were needed. Lincoln rocked his body, forcing Jay's fingers in and out. Jay got the hint and pumped his hand, and Lincoln moaned; his head tilted back. So sexy. Beautiful.

They stayed like that for several breaths, Jay fucking Lincoln with his fingers. The pose so hot, so erotic. Like nothing he'd ever done. Lincoln pitched forward, his hands on the bed on either side of Jay, his body still shifting as they kissed.

Jay raised his head to deepen the kiss, wanting more of Lincoln's tongue in his mouth, but Lincoln pulled back and kept retreating until they sat upright, Jay's chest and abs tight against Lincoln's body.

He lifted a leg and slid off Jay, his voice husky as he said, "Move aside."

They rolled together, Jay giving over as much bed as he could manage. Lincoln got on his knees and lowered his upper body to the bed. He pressed his forehead to the mattress, raised his arms over his head, and gripped the headboard in both hands. A sexy-assed, wanton, desperate move.

Jay froze. He'd never seen a guy bare himself in such a way.

Lincoln turned his head to the side. "Fuck me, Jay. Or I'm jerking off like this, 'cause I'm not moving."

Jerking off sounded good. But so did a lot of other things. Things he'd always wanted to try. Jay ran a hand over the man's ass. He couldn't help himself. He leaned forward and kissed Lincoln's lower back, putting tongue into it, tasting the flesh.

Lincoln moaned again, rocking back to him, and Jay straightened. Pure need driving him on, he spread Lincoln's ass cheeks and brought his dick to the other man's body. He breathed deep and surged forward, pushing the tip of his cock inside Lincoln, the pressure so intense Jay squeezed his eyes shut and had to force himself to stop. He gulped in another deep breath.

He wanted to give in, shove into the man. But it had been a while for Lincoln. "Am I hurting you?"

"No." The word was barely audible, the man's forehead plastered to the bed. "Just give me a sec."

Jay moved his hand over Lincoln's hip, rubbing in circles.

"Okay," Lincoln said. "Didn't want to come yet." He shifted beneath Jay, the action sliding his ass along Jay's cock. "Fuck me, Jay. It's okay."

Thank God he had Lincoln's go-ahead. Jay was ready to explode, and he wanted to pump inside Lincoln a few times before he lost control, wanted the moment—this first time—to last. He gripped Lincoln's hips in his hands again and buried his dick inside the man. He groaned with Lincoln that time.

"Yes!" Lincoln shouted. He pressed his forehead to the sheets and moaned louder, despite the muffle.

Jay didn't wait, couldn't wait for more. He drew back and thrust in, starting a rhythm that had his balls tingling, his cock on fire, his whole body alive. The most alive he'd felt in months.

Lincoln reached for Jay's hand, and he guided it to his own dick. Jay grasped the base and dragged his palm over the flesh to the head, matching his strokes with the drive of his hips. Lincoln held Jay's hand, gripping his fingers as they worked his cock together. So sensual—the way Lincoln touched him. Hard or soft, slow or fast—the man's hands on Jay felt passionate, erotic, like nothing he'd expected.

He rocked again, burying balls to ass and bent forward. He clutched the bedsheet beside Lincoln in his free hand as an explosion erupted inside him. The sounds that poured out of his chest were unlike any he'd let out in a long time. A freedom he'd been missing overcame him, and he shuddered, the intensity burning through him until every muscle in his body went slack. He wanted to lie on top of Lincoln and sleep for three days. Good thing he still had Lincoln's cock to distract him. He quickened the pump of his hand over the sleek shaft, precum aiding the glide, slipping between his fingers.

"Oh, fuck." Lincoln bucked beneath him. "Fuck yes!"

Jay spread the warm cum over Lincoln's dick, loving the feel and smell of the man. He collapsed onto Lincoln, his chest pressing along the heat of the man's back.

The wedding bands dug into Jay's flesh. "Damn." He lifted up and got the condom off. He dropped to the bed, his ass hanging off the side, his legs tangled with Lincoln's. There was not one inch of free space. A twin bed was not designed for two grown men to lie side by side. But he didn't care. About anything. He hadn't felt this light and free in weeks. "We are doing that again." He hadn't meant to say it aloud, but he wouldn't take the words back, wouldn't hide what he felt.

Lincoln hadn't moved. His ass was still in the air, his forehead plastered to the mattress, his body moving up and down with each gulp of air.

It went on for several minutes.

"You okay?" Jay finally asked when his own breathing had slowed.

Lincoln eased his body flat to the bed and rolled his head to the side. "Hell, yes. I haven't felt this great in a long time."

Jay couldn't stop the smile that spread over his lips.

"Except," Lincoln added, "there's no escaping the wet spot in this bed."

Jay laughed—a genuine, carefree sound. A tightness he hadn't noticed before eased in his chest. His eyes grew heavy.

"You look tired." Lincoln touched Jay's forehead with his thumb and followed an invisible path down his nose, over his lips, along his neck to his chest. Lincoln settled his palm below the rings. "Sleep."

No. He couldn't stay. He never slept well. Lincoln wouldn't get any sleep sharing the small bed with him. Never mind that Jay would never forgive himself for spending the entire night with someone else—she'd been the only one.

He didn't make a move to get off the bed or get dressed. *In a minute.* The warmth beside him was too good. He liked the easy way his breaths came to him.

That slow, soft caress Lincoln had given him had been what was missing in his life for the past year.

He let his eyes fall shut. *Just for a minute.*

Chapter Twelve

Jay awoke slowly, his eyes still closed, his body relaxed like he hadn't been in a long time. He savored the sensation until realization sank in...he wasn't in his own bed. Why had he slept on the couch? He was breaking so many promises lately.

He rolled to his side, and his ass slipped off the edge of the cushion. He tumbled toward the floor, flailing his arms and legs, trying to latch on to something until he smacked his left arm on the top of a small table. A lamp teetered and fell to its side, the lampshade crushing in on impact. He landed on his ass, his feet wrapped in a sheet, his left hand still clutching the table, his other gripping the fitted sheet that covered the mattress. The eyes of a metal robot stared back at him.

Right. Not the couch.

He and Lincoln McCaw had spent the night together. They'd had sex and slept in the same bed.

"You okay?" Lincoln leaned over the edge of the bed and peered down, a huge grin plastered on his face.

"This bed is ridiculous."

Lincoln laughed. "Sure it is. Try to tell me it wasn't worth it."

What could Jay say? It had been an intense night. One worth sleeping in a small bed, but was it worth the guilt?

Only there wasn't any of that. Hard to accept, but Jay wouldn't lie to himself, or to Lincoln. He felt nothing but an overwhelming peace.

Lincoln's smile faded. His eyebrows drew in.

"Yeah," Jay said. "It was worth it."

The other man's tight expression eased. Music and high-pitched voices of a kid's TV show filtered in through the closed bedroom door. Someone had either turned on a television or increased the volume. Along with the cartoonlike voices came the laughter of young children.

"You want to go watch?" Jay asked. "Maybe the *Transformers* cartoon is on."

"Fuck you." Lincoln smiled again. "Get back up here." He gripped Jay's forearm and yanked him onto the bed. Jay sprawled half on Lincoln. No room to do much else. Did he want to do anything else? Touching the man was like downing a tall glass of water after months spent in the desert with miles and miles of heat and sand.

Lincoln lifted his head and kissed Jay. Over and over. On his lips, his chin, his earlobes, his neck.

No more sand and all the water Jay wanted.

Quick steps padded in the hall outside the door and more giggling followed.

"Shit." Lincoln wrenched out from under Jay, crept to the door, and pressed in the lock. "Can't believe I left the door unlocked last night."

"You were somewhat distracted." The firm muscles of Lincoln's ass captivated Jay. He'd had that ass in his hands last night. Lincoln faced him. He'd also had that dick in his hands, his own inside Lincoln. And Jay had loved every minute of it, loved how the man made him lose focus, lose control, and how easy it had been to give in and feel again.

Lincoln smiled and got on the bed. "You liked it, huh?" He draped his body over Jay's. Was Lincoln touching him on purpose or was it just the lack of space?

It didn't matter. Jay pulled him closer, rubbing his groin against Lincoln's, touching the man's flesh wherever he could reach. He wanted to take all he could get before whatever they were doing ended. Because it would end. It had to.

And yet...it felt so damn good. The contact, the connection, to lie next to someone. To have a man's hands on him—finally. Hands that were large, rough from work, strong. Hands that—

Drove a pickup truck into his wife's car.

What the fuck was he doing? Allowing lust to give him a reason to forget.

Lincoln raised his head. "You okay?"

"Sure. Those are your sister's kids?"

"Yeah."

"You live here with them?"

"I do now."

"How come?" Jay shouldn't ask. He shouldn't be interested in the man's life at all. But he was. "The lovely decor aside, shouldn't you get your own place?"

"Nah. This'll do for now." Lincoln threw him a serious look. "Except, I'm going to be in a shitload of trouble."

"Because of me?"

"Nancy won't like this."

"That's gotta suck."

"It's not 'cause you're a guy. She's great about me being gay." He moved off Jay and looked toward the door. "It's hard to tell kids not to have sex with someone they barely know when the adults in their lives can't follow that rule."

Jay rolled to his side and faced Lincoln. "I shouldn't have stayed."

"It's fine. I don't hide who I am. Nancy'll get over it."

"No, I meant—"

"Right." Lincoln sat up and swung his legs off the bed. He bent for his jeans, crammed one leg into the pants then the other, forgoing underwear. "You know this can't happen again, right?"

Jay got up and searched for his clothes. "Yeah." He yanked his briefs out of the pants. Why had he said anything at all?

Lincoln stood and watched Jay zip up his jeans. "Do you?"

"This wasn't a great idea to begin with." Quieter, Jay added, "Just couldn't stop myself." Couldn't pretend what he felt wasn't powerful. Consuming. Dangerous?

"Yeah. Not a lot of options for gay guys in Edgefield."

"It's not that. It's—"

"We can't forget for the sake of our dicks."

What could he say to that? Jay would never forget. His wife would always be with him. "It was an accident." What was he hoping for? To make Lincoln feel better? Or did he think they could have something?

They watched each other, neither speaking until Lincoln lowered his gaze to the rings on Jay's chest. "I can't let you get involved with me."

Jay laughed and pulled on his shirt. "So noble."

"I try," Lincoln said with a smirk.

It was odd, how easy it was to spend time together, how comfortable it was to be around Lincoln McCaw. Even with the conversation they were having. Time for Jay to get going. "About the threats—"

"I won't let anyone hurt my family."

Jay scrubbed his hands over his face. "I can't imagine whoever's doing this wants to hurt anyone."

"I'm not taking that chance. If it was just me—"

"I know. I don't want anything to happen to your family either."

Lincoln went to the dresser and opened a drawer. He yanked out a T-shirt and tugged it over his head. Jay righted the lamp he'd knocked over and clicked the switch. It didn't turn on. Must have damaged the bulb. The nightstand drawer was open a crack. He went to close it, but the typed page inside stopped him. A match to the one he had in his jacket pocket, except for the message.

> *Ever wonder if she cried out in pain? If she felt the snap of bone? The crush of her chest?*

"Oh God." He sank to the bed and stared at the paper in his hands.

"You weren't supposed to see that one." Lincoln sat next to him.

The printed words read like something Jay's mom would say. Or Stuart. He had to stop this. This wasn't anything Katie would want.

A silence built between them until Lincoln finally spoke. "I looked away from the road for a second. I must have turned the wheel—I don't know."

Jay closed his eyes. "You don't have to say this."

Lincoln came back quick with, "I do. You and I both know I do." His voice lowered with his next words. "I was trying not to drive too fast, trying to stay calm, but I was worried about Nance, about the kids. When I realized I'd crossed over, I freaked, pulled back, and lost control of the truck." He leaned forward, his elbows on his knees, and stared at the *G.I. Joe* poster across the room. "All those years on the track and my instincts flew right out the window."

Jay fought the tears building. A hint of anger sparked inside him. An emotion he thought he'd gotten past, crippled by meeting Lincoln, by talking to him, by having sex with him. He looked at the broken man beside him. Lincoln had held on to his guilt in much the same way Jay had held on to his grief, and it was time for both men to be free of that day.

How could they, though, with someone wanting Lincoln never to forget? "This can't be from my family. They wouldn't—"

"Say something like this?"

"Oh, they'd say this. My mom would say this, but if she wanted to hurt you, she'd come after you, not your niece, not a little girl. I can't believe she'd go that far. I can't..."

"What?"

Lose her too. Lose another person from my life. "Nothing."

"All right. But let's start there. I have to find out for sure. Just think of it like you're clearing her if that helps."

"What do we do?"

"Search their house, see if we can find evidence the notes are from her. This paper looks kinda special."

"Okay. They play cards every week at a friend's house. They won't be home tonight."

"It'd be all right to look. Wouldn't it? They wouldn't find anything.

* * * *

"Is this a Sportster?"

Lincoln let go of the doorknob and found Jay lifting the dust-covered tarp off the bike in the far corner of the garage. They had sneaked out the back of the house to avoid the cartoon slumber party in the living room and were heading through the garage when Jay spotted the Harley.

"Yeah." Lincoln hadn't given any thought to his old bike except when Nancy mentioned it on the phone a few weeks before he left the jail. Just one more thing he'd had to give up. He barely recognized his new life. Especially considering whom he'd spent the night with.

Jay had the tarp peeled back. He ran his fingers over the orange tribal flames on the tank. Lincoln had paid good money for the custom paint job. The flames weren't a big deal, but the detailed bald eagle on the top had been. He'd met with several shops before he found someone he trusted to do it right.

"Nice-looking bike." Jay swept his fingers over the eagle. "Minus the dust and tarp."

"Used to be mine." He moved to stand beside Jay. He wanted to head outside. Get out of the garage. He hated hanging out there, hated the stack of boxes from his old life piled next to the kids' bikes and sporting equipment.

"Used to be?" Jay asked.

"Gave it to my sister when I left. Told her to sell it. She needs the money. But my asshole brother-in-law kept it until he finally left."

"Doesn't look like he took care of it."

Lincoln grunted.

"He was the one who—"

"Yeah." Lincoln clenched his fist around the handlebar. "A lot after I left."

"Sorry."

"Took all her goddamn money when he finally ran off."

"Why didn't she leave him?"

"She needed the insurance for Jessica. Her asthma gets bad sometimes. Her medications aren't cheap."

"You should do something with it." Jay covered the bike with the tarp.

Lincoln shrugged. "It's Nancy's now." He went for the front door again. He'd already lost so much. Why did that one bike matter?

Jay followed this time. "Ask her about it."

"You want to buy it?"

"Nah. You should fix it up."

"Don't have the money." Lincoln opened the garage door and stepped outside.

"Does it run?" Jay had stopped walking when Lincoln had. Apparently he needed an escort to the curb.

Lincoln started for Jay's Jeep. "She had a guy here a couple of weeks ago who had it running, but he backed out on the deal." Too bad too. Nancy would've had some cash before he got home.

"If it's still able to start, it might not be that bad off. A tune-up and a dust off, and you'd have her on the road. Wouldn't take much money."

He stood next to Jay's Jeep and stared at the door handle. "Can't drive it."

"Oh." Jay opened the driver's-side door and got in without another word. He gripped the steering wheel, but made no move to start the Jeep.

Fuck. Lincoln shoved his hands into his pockets. He'd left his jacket inside and the cold tore through him. Or maybe it was Jay's abrupt silence. Lincoln shouldn't have said anything that would remind Jay of the night his wife died. The man had just gotten a piece of ass after months without. Even if it was Lincoln's ass, he should've been enjoying the morning after. Lincoln tapped on the Jeep's window, and Jay cranked it down.

"Yeah?"

"Meet me at Sonny's after work tonight. We'll head out from there."

"Sure." Jay started his Jeep and checked the street behind him in the rearview mirror.

"Put your seat belt on."

"Right." Jay reached behind him for the belt and snapped it in place. Only then did he glance Lincoln's way. "Thanks for last night."

"You too." Lincoln stepped back.

Jay gave a slight nod and drove away from the curb. Lincoln hadn't known Jay for long, but he already knew one thing. When Jay stopped talking, something was wrong. The man's first night with another guy. Was he freaked about that? Or about whom he'd spent the night with?

The Jeep turned a corner, and Lincoln kept staring at the stretch of empty street. He shouldn't have slept with Jay Miller. He had let his lust get the better of his good judgment and crossed a line neither of them could handle.

Hope I didn't fuck him up more than I already have.

Chapter Thirteen

"Watch out!"

Jay swerved the Jeep to the left, avoiding the stray dog by mere inches. He let off the gas and jerked the wheel back before the Jeep made it into the other lane. Sucking in a ragged breath, he gripped the steering wheel.

"You all right?" Lincoln asked from the passenger seat.

Jay couldn't take his eyes off the dark asphalt visible in the Jeep's headlights. Was he okay? He pulled to the side of the street and put the Jeep in park. "Fuck!" His voice trembled.

"It's okay." Lincoln laid a hand on the back of his neck.

Jay wanted to shrug off the touch, but at the same time, he longed for more.

"You didn't hit it."

Yeah. If he had hit the damn dog, he'd be throwing up on the side of the road. "I know. I just—"

"It's okay, Jay. Don't make it more than it was. You didn't hit anything."

Jay rested his temple against the glass of the driver's-side window. The dog was gone. Could he drive the rest of the way to his parents' house? Or were they going to be stuck there all night, stranded along the road, just the two of them in his Jeep? Lincoln rubbed his neck with an open palm. No one had touched him like that in months. He closed his eyes and breathed deep.

When the shaking in his hands lessened, he shifted the Jeep into drive and eased away from the curb. Lincoln hadn't removed the hand from his neck. The rubbing helped calm his pounding heart. Why was that? They were thinking the same thing—about the same moment in time. It should've been complicated. Tense. It wasn't. If anyone understood what almost hitting that dog meant to Jay, it was Lincoln.

Ten minutes later, they turned into his parents' drive. He could barely uncurl his fingers from the steering wheel.

Lincoln opened the passenger door and said, "You ready?"

No. What if they found something that proved his parents were the ones fucking with Lincoln? What would he do then? "I guess."

When he didn't make a move, Lincoln spoke again. "Want me to go in alone?"

"No." Jay got out of the Jeep, and they made their way to the house. He used the key he'd had on his ring since he'd moved out. The house was dark, the ticking of a grandfather clock all that broke the subtle rhythm of their deep breaths.

"You gonna turn on a light?" Lincoln asked.

"Sure." Jay fumbled for the light switch. Which was stupid. He'd lived at their house his entire childhood. He knew where the damn switch was. He flicked on the light in the entryway, and the brightness had them both frozen in place as they blinked away the shock of light.

Lincoln glanced up at the ornate glass chandelier, then moved to the doorway of the formal dining room. "Why is the table set?"

Jay stopped beside Lincoln. China place settings, silverware, linen napkins, and crystal stemware decorated the long mahogany table. "It's always like that."

"What? On the off chance six of their closest friends drop by without notice for a formal affair?"

He laughed. There was no explaining his mom's way of thinking.

Lincoln stepped farther inside the house and headed for a hall table. Hanging on the wall above it was a plaque. He leaned in as if reading the engraved message. Jay didn't need to look. It was from the nursing school where Katie had planned to go.

Thank you for your generous donation in memory of Katherine Miller.

Lincoln stared at it for several deep breaths. Finally he looked back at Jay and said, "This where you grew up?"

"Yeah."

"Nice house." Lincoln picked up an empty glass bowl sitting on the hall table and examined it. Waterford crystal. No one touched her crystal pieces. What would she do if she knew Lincoln McCaw had his hands on one of them? Jay smirked.

Lincoln lifted the bowl up in the air. "What's this for?"

"I have no idea. It's always sitting there. Nothing's ever in it."

"They always have a lot of money?"

"They don't. They just like to make it look as if they do."

"Ah." Lincoln went into the living room and walked the perimeter, eyeing the ceramic figurines and crystal vases as if he was casing the joint. He came to a stop in front of the fireplace. His face paled, and a low gasp left him, like no sound the man had made the night before.

It startled Jay, but he didn't want to look or ask what Lincoln saw. Didn't want to know what could cause that reaction.

Lincoln turned toward him and opened his mouth to speak, but Jay shook his head and took a step backward into the hall. "Let's check out my dad's office first."

Lincoln didn't move.

"It's this way."

When the man finally turned and crossed the room, his gaze was fixated on the carpeted floor before him. He didn't acknowledge Jay as he moved past him into the hall.

Should he ask what was wrong? No. This trip wasn't easy on either of them. They didn't need to talk about it as if they were at a counseling session. Would any therapist in the world tell Jay he was doing the right thing sleeping with the man who caused his wife's accident? He didn't want to think about what it meant that he was glad he hadn't bothered with therapy.

They proceeded down the dark hall to the last door on the left. The room hadn't changed since Jay lived there. As an owner of an office supply store, his dad often worked at home to take care of orders, accounting, and payroll. Stacks of papers covered the desk, each sorted into trays with typed labels. Accounts receivable. Accounts payable. Employee records. Nothing labeled *Threats to Lincoln McCaw*. Too bad it couldn't be that easy. Although, that wouldn't be easy at all, would it?

Jay sat at the desk and removed the note from his pocket. He combed through the items on top of the desk first. Nothing resembled the paper he held. He opened one drawer after another and came up empty on papers of any kind.

A noise echoed down the hall. Like someone had dropped a metal pan. He held still and waited for footsteps. Nothing. The quiet continued. Maybe it had come from outside.

Lincoln hadn't moved away from the door.

Jay said, "This will go faster if you help."

Seconds ticked off on the wooden clock on his dad's desk before Lincoln slowly stepped away from the door.

"You okay?" Jay asked.

"Not sure I want to find anything."

"I thought you wanted this over?"

Lincoln stared at him, the shock evident on his face. Right. Like this would ever be over. For either of them.

"Just don't want it to be your parents. You've been through enough."

Jay tried to say thanks or smile or nod. Something. When his voice finally returned, he said, "My parents or the Shaws. I don't think—"

"They'd hurt anyone. Yeah, you said that. We had to take Jessica to the hospital, Jay. They're already hurting me. Hurting my family."

There was nothing Jay could say. He continued the search.

"Hey, is this you?" Lincoln was holding up a framed photo of Jay—ten years old, wearing his weight in padding, a football tucked under his arm.

"Yeah. I can't believe he still has that."

"Bet your father-in-law liked that you played ball."

"I only played the one year. I think the coach told my dad not to send me back. My brother was on the same team, and he had to pick me up off the ground a lot."

Lincoln examined the picture and laughed. "You do look like you're about to fall over."

"You should've seen me try to run in all that gear."

Lincoln laughed again and set the frame on the desk.

"Did you play sports?" Jay asked.

"Wrestling. In junior high school."

"Then what? You figured out you were gay, and you didn't think the close-minded kids of the Edgefield high school would appreciate you rolling around on the floor with them?"

"Nah. I had to work. By then my mom was pretty sick. Hospital bills ate up all the money my grandpa had left us."

"And your dad?"

"Gone long before then. Ran off for something better."

"Sorry." It sucked that sometimes parents didn't love their kids enough to stick around for their lives.

"No big." Lincoln opened a nearby file cabinet.

"Still sucks." Jay glanced at the frame on his dad's desk. Or maybe...sometimes parents loved their kids too much. Were his parents behind the threats? Or his brother? Was one of them—or all of them—doing this for him?

He finished searching the desk and moved to a filing cabinet next to the one Lincoln was going through.

Lincoln stopped, a computer printout in his hand.

"What?" Jay asked. "What did you find?"

"Did your parents donate all the money they got from the settlement?"

Jay scoffed. "Hardly. Why?"

"It doesn't look like your dad's business is doing all that well."

"What?"

"See here." Lincoln handed over the papers and pointed. "If these figures are accurate, he's losing a lot of money at his store."

Hard to believe. His dad's business had always been successful—maybe not successful enough for his mom, but enough for his parents to continue to live the way they always had. How much longer could his dad keep the store open? And where had all the money from the lawsuit gone? Did they invest it? Somewhere his dad couldn't access to save the store?

Lincoln took the papers back, and they finished searching the cabinets. "Nothing in here," he said as he shut the last file drawer.

Jay wanted to believe that meant something. But if there was nothing to find in the house, it didn't mean his parents hadn't sent the notes. Perhaps they'd been either smart enough to hide the paper they'd used, or his dad kept it at the store. Searching the store would take hours. And even if the type of paper used to harass Lincoln was there, it didn't mean his parents had anything to do with the notes. Someone else could've purchased it. Did his dad keep detailed customer records? They'd have to check at the store to find out. "Let's try upstairs. My mom has a sewing room with a desk."

They made their way through the dark house, walking close but saying nothing. The room upstairs had far fewer places where his mom could've hidden anything, but there were several boxes full of odds and ends in addition to the desk. After they came up empty on the desk, Jay picked up a box and started in on it. Lincoln followed suit.

Three boxes later, a car door closed somewhere outside.

Lincoln dropped the papers he held back into the box. "You said they'd be gone until—" The sound of the front door opening and closing downstairs interrupted him. "Fuck." Lincoln strode to the window. "Can I get out here?"

"No." Jay rushed to Lincoln's side. "It's too far, and there's nothing for you to climb out on. You'll get hurt."

Footsteps thumped below them. The kitchen.

"Better than the alternative." Lincoln reached for the lower window sash.

Jay stilled his hands. "No."

"What then? They can't find me here."

"I know." Jay ran a hand through his hair. "My old room. There's a ledge. You can reach the tree out back and climb down."

Jay went to the door and peeked out. The hallway was still dark, but a sliver of light filtered up from downstairs. He stepped into the hall, and Lincoln followed. They crept along the wall toward Jay's old room. Jay twisted the doorknob, pushed in, and winced when the door squeaked. Same way it did when he slipped in after missing curfew all those times his senior year. He'd never once regretted it, though. He'd only been late on the nights when he and Katie had sneaked into the County Cooler, the boarded up ice-cream stand where they sometimes went to have sex.

And he didn't regret sneaking around now. He had to know what was going on—who was tormenting Lincoln and his family. Had to stop all this shit before someone got hurt.

He entered the bedroom, but apparently he didn't move fast enough. Lincoln crowded him inside and pulled the door shut behind him. It took a moment for Jay's eyes to adjust to the low light of the streetlamp seeping in between the curtains. Lincoln grabbed his arm and hauled him toward the window. Having Lincoln touch him in the dark, Jay nearly forgot what they were doing there and why. He wanted to feel Lincoln's body against his own, to repeat everything they'd done the night before. And maybe a few things they hadn't.

The echoing of footsteps ascending the stairs yanked him back into the moment.

"They got any security?" Lincoln asked.

Jay shook his head, too focused on the footsteps to verbally answer. The solid steps couldn't be from his mom. His dad, then. Better?

Lincoln either caught the head shake or didn't care. He lifted the window and then the screen and sat on the windowsill. "What're you going to tell them about why you're here?"

"I don't know."

"You'll be okay?"

"Yeah." The footsteps halted, then started down the hall, heading toward them. "Go."

Lincoln didn't. He settled a hand at the back of Jay's neck. The quick kiss said more than Jay wanted to admit. Too bad there could never be more. Not for them.

Lincoln released him and crawled out on the ledge. Jay watched for a second, then closed the window and rushed to sit on the bed. The footsteps in the hall ended with the opening of a door. Not the one to his old room, though. Jay sighed. They had to know he was there. His Jeep was in the driveway. It wouldn't be long before they found him.

He'd been in his old room before, several times since the funeral. His parents would let him sit there until he returned to the living room on his own. They never once came to collect him. Whether they knew it or not, he'd needed those times alone. Not just to get away from his parents' anger, but to fill himself with the memories of the first night he and Katie had made love. It was their junior year, and his parents had gone on a business trip to an office supply expo in Chicago. He and Katie spent the weekend in his room, laughing, making love, talking about their plans to elope and get their own place.

It was in that room Jay sometimes needed to be.

His dad wouldn't be surprised to find him there. Eventually, he'd head out. He just needed a minute to forget that kiss. Forget how Lincoln had touched him. Should be easy to forget while sitting on the bed where he and his wife had first discovered each other's bodies. It wasn't. No matter how hard he tried, he couldn't shake the affection in the kiss Lincoln had given him at the window. Jay fell to his back and rolled to the side, tucking his legs up, and curled his arms under his head. She was everywhere around him.

Then why couldn't he get Lincoln out of his head?

The bottom drawer of his old dresser caught his eye. The drawer was open a crack. He had taken everything when he'd moved out. His parents must be using it for storage. He pushed off the bed, turned on the bedside lamp, and knelt before the dresser. Inside the bottom drawer was a large manila envelope. Typed on the front: his mom's name and address. No return address. A postmark from the local post office.

He unfastened the clasp and opened the envelope. A typed note slid out. Same style paper he and Lincoln had searched for all night.

> I hired a private investigator. Thought you might like
> to see what he's been up to.

Jay reached into the envelope and removed several eight-by-ten photographs.

He flipped through them. Lincoln at night with a woman in a waitress uniform. Another of him walking with a small child, her hand tucked in Lincoln's. His niece? One through a window with Lincoln standing at a kitchen table, two children writing with pencil and crayon. The same little girl and a boy. Jay set the photos on the floor before him. He didn't want to touch them any longer.

Who had sent his mom the pictures? Todd? The Shaws? Stuart? Emily?

Down the hall, a toilet flushed and a door opened. The footsteps started toward Jay's room. He stuffed the letter and photos into the envelope and tucked it inside the back of his jeans, using his shirt to cover the top half. He dropped to the bed and kicked the drawer shut with his foot as the bedroom door opened.

Todd stood in the doorway. "Hey. Wondered where you were. Saw your Jeep out front." He leaned against the doorjamb. "What're you doing here?"

"Could ask you the same thing."

"I had to pick something up."

"What?" Jay asked.

"Just stuff."

"Stuff?"

Todd tapped the bottom of the doorjamb with the tip of his boot. "A new rifle Dad bought for me. I wanted to try it out tomorrow morning."

"When did you start hunting?"

"A couple of years ago. Dad and I started going"—he paused and kicked at the wood trim again—"after you guys eloped."

"Oh." Why hadn't they told him? Because they knew Jay. No way would he want to have anything to do with killing something. Didn't think he could be the one to do it even if he was starving to death. And that was before the accident. He'd tried vegetarianism for a month when he was eight years old and first found out where hamburgers came from. Todd had made fun of him until Jay finally gave in, and they begged their mom to take them to McDonald's.

Jay stared at the closed drawer where he'd found the pictures and said, "Sorry I didn't call you back the other day."

Todd waved him off. "No problem. I just wanted to make sure you knew where I was, see if you'd keep an eye on Marge for me."

"You weren't home?"

"No. I left on Monday to fill in for the first responder training in Chicago. I told Mom to let you know." He shook his head. "I knew she'd forget."

The tightness in Jay's chest eased. Todd hadn't been home. He couldn't have stolen the inhalers the other day. Jay squeezed his eyes shut and tried to fend off the guilt. No luck. Thinking his entire family were crazed vigilantes was killing him. How fucked-up could his life get? And what was even more fucked-up: the only time he'd been able to forget all of it was in Lincoln McCaw's arms.

Todd sat on the bed and nudged Jay's shoulder with his. "What's going on? You haven't been up here in a while. Thought you were doing better."

"I am."

"You look like shit."

"Thanks."

"Jay." The exasperated sound of his name wasn't anything he'd heard from Todd before. "You need to get on with your life. Get past this. Go out. Get laid."

Jay smiled. He couldn't help it.

"Hey," Todd said. "That's the first real smile I've seen from you in over a year. Meet someone?"

"Yeah, but..." The smile vanished. There would be no telling Todd about Lincoln like he was dating someone. What had Lincoln said? *A fuck. Nothing more.*

"But what?"

"It's not someone I can keep seeing."

"Why?"

"Too complicated."

"Don't let it be. You need to live again."

Jay stood. He was trying to live. He was doing better than his parents. Than the Shaws. "I'm gonna head home." He quickly crossed the room so Todd wouldn't ask him what he had hidden under his shirt. Not until he had a chance to question the Shaws, find out who had sent his mom the pictures. He stopped at the door. Todd was straightening the bedcovers Jay had mussed when he'd lain down. When the bed was arranged, Todd turned off the lamp. His brother was cleaning up after him. Like he had for the past year.

Not anymore. Time for Jay to take care of things for a change. To find out what was going on. Time for his wife's memory to be what she deserved.

Time to end all the lies. The hatred. The threats.

* * * *

Sparky jumped onto Lincoln's lap and crushed his groin with a huge paw.

"Dammit. Get off me." Stupid thing thought he was a lapdog—all eighty pounds of him. He pushed at the dog's face before Sparky could slobber on his chin and added tugging on the collar until the dog jumped down.

"Don't you like dogs no more?" Jessica climbed onto the couch and sat next to him. It must suck to be so tiny. She had to work just to get on the damn couch. Nancy said she was the smallest kid in the kindergarten class at Edgefield Elementary.

"I like dogs fine," he said. Sparky wagged his tail and paced the length of the couch, probably trying to figure out if he should jump on him again. Lincoln sighed. "I miss mine."

Jessica sprang to her knees. "Uncle Paul brought him over before you came home. He's gotten soooo big. You gotta see him. He's taller than me!"

Lincoln laughed. "I knew with the size of those paws he'd be huge."

"The paws are the same. The rest of him just grew and grew and grew." She held her hands out and moved them apart as far as she could to demonstrate.

Davy gave up on the movie he'd been watching from the living room floor and rolled to his side. "He is big. Almost knocked me over when he ran into me."

Sparky jumped onto the couch on the other side of Jessica, a safe distance from Lincoln. Jessica wrapped her arms around the dog's neck and kissed his snout.

"Ewww," Davy said. "Don't kiss the dog. That's gross."

"Not gross." Jessica stuck her tongue out at Davy. "He's family. He's not a dog."

Davy went back to watching the movie and said, "He's a dog."

Jessica giggled and kissed Sparky again.

Lincoln reached across her and patted Sparky's head. He definitely missed Duke. He missed a lot of stuff. And the only time he'd forgotten any of it was during the night he'd spent showing Jay Miller the joys of gay sex. Lincoln hadn't slept that well without being drunk off his ass since he'd gotten home.

Jessica leaned into his side and whispered, "Your wolf's not running no more."

"Oh." Davy jumped to his feet. "Forgot to tell you. A man dropped off a check for you. It's huge. Mom told me to make sure you got it." Davy ran to the kitchen and returned with a check in hand. He gave it to Lincoln.

"Is that a lot of money?" Jessica asked, leaning into Lincoln's side as they both stared at the piece of paper.

"Of course." Davy pointed to the typed numbers. "See all those zeros. Was your car really worth all that?"

"Yeah."

Jessica jumped to her feet on the couch. She hopped and did a dance. "Uncle Lincoln's rich!"

Lincoln read the sticky note stuck to the back of the check. From his attorney.

*I know it's not what you were hoping, but it's the
only offer in the past year.*

He ripped off the note and crushed it into a ball.
"What are you gonna do with it?" Davy asked.
"It's for your mom." Lincoln got up and went to the kitchen. He
signed the back of the check and wrote a note for Nancy.

Put it toward the bills.

He stuck the note to the check and hesitated. Someone was going
to be driving his car. He could live with that. Right?
It wouldn't kill him.
But it did sting. He smacked the check onto the table, grabbed his
jacket, and headed for the door. "Kids, I'm going out for a while.
Adam's in his room."
"Okay," Jessica said. She stroked Sparky's ear while she watched
the movie.
Lincoln stepped out the front door, then leaned back inside.
"Jessica?"
"Yeah."
"Remember, no Kitty or Sparky in your bedroom."
She smiled as she kept rubbing the dog's floppy ear. "I know."
He wanted to lecture her about pet hair and allergies, how letting
them in her room made it a little harder for her to breathe when she
slept, and that she had to stop sneaking the animals in there at night or
else Nancy might finally give in to her motherly fears and get rid of
the pets, but Jessica's sweet smile had him holding back.
It also had him almost forgetting his pity party. He glanced at the
check on the table. Almost.

* * * *

*The dead don't cry at night. But I do. And someday,
you will too.*

*Ever wonder if she cried out in pain? If she felt the
snap of bone? The crush of her chest? I do. Every
night. Now I hope you will too.*

Jay read the words again. He'd handwritten the line from the note
in Lincoln's bedside table onto the paper with the first one Paul had

given him. Was it the Shaws who had sent them to Lincoln? Did they hire the PI? Did they send his mom the photos?

Who would go so far as to contact Lincoln and hire an investigator to follow him? It had to be someone in Jay's family. Or Katie's. Nothing else made sense. Lots of people loved her, but losing her hadn't hurt anyone as much as them. No one else would want to make Lincoln pay. Well, Jay had. But that was before they'd met. Before he'd spent the night pressed against the man's naked body. Before Jay had given in to desire and let his dick run his life.

Everything was spinning out of control. And he hadn't yet come up with what to say when he approached the Shaws. How do you ask two parents who'd lost their only child what their grief had forced them to do?

He stuffed the letter into the glove compartment and went into Sonny's. He found Lincoln at a table in the back by the restrooms. The old whiskey sipper was still sitting nearby, sipping away. Did the man ever go home? Or did they just leave him sitting there at closing time with a full bottle to get him through the night, then dust him and the bottle off the next morning?

Jay sat across from Lincoln. "Hey."

Lincoln stared at the beer in front of him. He held on with one hand, twisting the bottle in circles, only stopping the action when he took a long pull. Finally he said, "If you came for more talking—or more sex—you can forget it. Not in much of a talking—or a fucking—mood today."

Had anyone heard that? Possibly the old man with the whiskey. Hopefully he was too far gone into the bottle to care about the fags sitting at the next table.

Jay leaned forward. The scent of beer clung to Lincoln. Had he bathed in the stuff? What happened since he'd sneaked out of Jay's old bedroom window? Since that kiss? Was it the threats eating away at Lincoln? Or the accident? Or something else?

Another cigarette lit and Lincoln took a drag. The puff of smoke as he exhaled hit Jay in the face.

"Why don't we go take a look at your bike?"

"Not mine." Lincoln swallowed more of the beer.

"Did you ask Nancy about it?"

"She said I could have it back. Said it wasn't right for her to sell it."

"Let's go check it out, then."

"Jay—"

"What?"

"Don't need the company today. Got some shit on my mind."

"About the threats?"

No answer.

"Because we didn't find anything at my parents' house?" Jay didn't want to mention what he had found, and he wasn't sure why.

No response.

"Something else?"

"Yeah, something else." Lincoln slammed the beer bottle onto the table and gripped it tighter. "Like how some other goddamn motherfucker is driving my car. *My* car."

The anger startled Jay. He had seen Lincoln like this when someone had stolen his niece's inhalers, right before Jay had sucked the man's cock. "Your race car?"

"Just leave, okay? Don't want to talk about this. Not with you."

"Fine." Jay leaned in. "Wanna fuck?"

The other man's eyes widened, then softened with the grin. The laugh that came next had Lincoln letting go of the beer and sitting back in his chair. "Yeah, you're gay."

"Just know what I want."

Lincoln stared at his beer bottle, the smile fading. "We shouldn't."

"It doesn't have to mean anything. Like you said. No strings."

Except there were strings. Huge strings. Strings they could wrap into a ball so big the people from the Guinness World Records would come calling. Who were they kidding?

Lincoln rolled his eyes and smiled again. "How about we check out the bike first?"

Jay stood. "I'm good. Before or after. Or we could go for before *and* after."

"Must be nice to be twenty." Lincoln got up from the table and headed for the door.

"Twenty-two," Jay said and waited until they were outside and no one was around before he added, "And with gay sex I'm hitting puberty again. I can probably get it up a third time if you want."

That stopped Lincoln in his tracks, just in time to notice the truck driving by. He didn't need a second look to spot who was inside. *Mel.*

"What?" Jay asked. He stepped closer to Lincoln. "What is it?"

"That was my sister's jackass husband."

"Here?"

"In that truck that drove by. I wasn't sure if he was still in town. Guess so." He needed to tell Nancy. *No.* She had enough to worry about, and he didn't want her to have any reason to talk to the man again.

"Do you need to call her?"

Lincoln shook his head and continued to stare down the street toward where Mel had driven off.

"So"—Jay nudged Lincoln with his shoulder—"before *and* after?"

Lincoln laughed. "You're going to be the death of me."

Chapter Fourteen

"Doesn't sound too great." Lincoln kicked at the tarp he'd tossed onto the floor. He shouldn't be doing this. It wasn't like he'd be able to drive the damn bike. Wasn't like he wanted to either. Right?

"It's not in bad shape," Jay said over the roar of the bike. He was sitting on the Harley inside the garage. They had started it as soon as they'd gotten to Nancy's. The bike seemed to fascinate Jay. Maybe Lincoln had to try harder to keep the man interested in sex.

No. He should be trying to figure out how to get Jay uninterested. That'd be the best thing. For both of them.

"At least it's running," Jay added.

It had been a great bike at one time. Different than Lincoln's car. He liked the sound, the speed, the power of it between his legs.

"Let's make a list of what we'll need." Jay cut the engine and got off the bike. "For a basic tune-up. Then we'll take her out and see what else needs work." He wandered around the garage, peeking in boxes and on shelves. "Got anything to write with?"

Were they really going to do this? Work on a motorcycle together after the way Jay's wife had died? Pretend Lincoln had any right to drive for pleasure? He hit the close button on the garage door and handed Jay a pencil from the can on the workbench. Jay watched the door close and seemed to relax as it fell shut. Made sense. Lincoln wasn't crazy about anyone seeing them together either.

"Paper?" Jay asked.

Lincoln hunted around and didn't come up with anything. Jay muttered on about spark plugs, air filters, lubricant—and not the fun kind. Lincoln smirked and reached into the pocket of his leather jacket. The good kind of lube was in there and so was the latest envelope. He tugged out the note and stuffed it into his pocket. He handed the empty envelope with the typed name and address to Jay.

The other man stared at it. His brow furrowed. "Another one?"

"Yeah."

"Can I see it?"

"You don't want to." It had come in the mail and described how she had looked when she'd died. From someone who had obviously seen her that night—at the hospital maybe. Which still pointed to her family. The anger it took to describe the woman's broken, bloody body could've only come from someone destroyed by her death. Her parents. Or her husband.

He didn't want to consider the idea again it might be Jay. Not because that would hurt—although it would, like a bitch—but because Jay simply wasn't capable of the threats, the horrible descriptions, of hurting a little girl. The man didn't have a hateful bone in his body. What had his wife been like? Probably a lot like him.

"I need to talk to the Shaws," Jay said. "I think it's them."

"I've been thinking about that. If it's not your parents, then I think we need to let the police handle this."

"Maybe you're right." Jay turned over the envelope and scribbled with the pencil, adding the bike supplies he'd muttered about.

Good idea. Focus on the Harley. Anything but what that note had said. Jay should never hear those words.

Lincoln crouched and examined the bike more closely. It wasn't as bad off as he'd thought when Jay had first uncovered it. His asshole brother-in-law hadn't been as rough with the Harley as he'd been with Nancy.

The bike's exterior was in okay shape. No rust. No damage on the custom paint job. He ran his fingers over the spread wings of the eagle on the tank. The same eagle that graced his race car.

No. Not his car any longer. The new driver had probably already painted over the eagle. Already raced in the car.

Lincoln's last race had been such a rush. The best news of all had come after his win. The sponsorship with Performance Motors would mean better venues, a bigger budget for repairs, a real crew, and larger cash-outs when he won. That was the news he and Paul were celebrating before the call that sent him out on the road and into the path of Jay's wife.

The quiet reached him, and Lincoln stood. Jay stared at the list scrawled across the back of the envelope, biting the pencil between his teeth.

There were far better things for those teeth to gnaw on. He pulled Jay by the waist. "Come here."

Jay came to him easily and parted his lips, leaning in, inviting the kiss Lincoln had craved since he'd crawled out the window at Jay's parents' house the other night.

Hell, kissing Jay was something Lincoln had craved since he'd first seen the man. Those lips were irresistible. Even watching him smile got Lincoln's heartbeat going faster. He wanted to help the man smile more, to know what would make Jay happy. Wished he could be someone who filled the void. Did the universe know how to play a cruel joke or what?

Jay dropped the pencil and envelope. He wrapped his arms around Lincoln, clinging to him. And Lincoln didn't mind one damn bit. If they had been any other two people, he'd admit what he was feeling was more than a crazy need to fuck Jay, admit that he was feeling anything at all.

He backed Jay to the workbench behind them, running his hands up and down Jay's body as they kissed, wanting so desperately to fuck the man, to yank off their clothes and bury himself in Jay until balls met ass, until all other thoughts were gone and all that was left was the two of them—their bodies, their need, their skin, their breath. He couldn't ask Jay, though, couldn't assume Jay would want that— would want his first time accepting another man into his body to be with Lincoln of all people.

Jay removed his shirt, and Lincoln followed suit with his own, then opened Jay's jeans. They kissed again, and the intense urgency of Jay's desire slammed into Lincoln. Or was there something more to it? More to the way Jay clutched and caressed, the way he devoured Lincoln's kisses?

Forcing himself to focus on their bodies, pushing everything else aside, Lincoln tugged Jay's jeans and underwear past the man's hips. Jay boosted himself to sit on the bench, and Lincoln helped him get his pants off. Getting Jay naked was fast becoming a favorite pastime. He leaned in and added kissing a naked Jay to his favorites list.

So much of what they were doing went on that list.

Jay raised his legs and hooked them around Lincoln's hips. Lincoln wanted to get his pants off, but the kiss, those legs tight around him, drove him crazy, distracted him. He didn't want to let go. No one had ever been as sexually raw, as sensual as Jay.

"Need to touch your skin," Jay said. He unzipped Lincoln's pants and slowly caressed the length of cock to balls. Lincoln shoved his pants lower while Jay bent and kissed with lips and tongue from the tattoo on Lincoln's arm to his neck, to his ear.

The man's mouth, his tongue, drove Lincoln crazy. He couldn't wait any longer. He pulled back, gripped Jay's cock in one hand, and bent over the man, wandering his tongue over cock and balls in an openmouthed kiss that had Jay groaning, his eyes closed, his head tilted back to the wall behind him.

Lincoln opened his mouth wider and stroked Jay's prick with his lips, wanting nothing more than to taste the man, to help Jay let go, to give him a moment of pleasure.

Jay worked his hands through Lincoln's hair and slowly rocked his hips. The sweet, sensual way he fucked Lincoln's mouth and ran his fingers through his hair, the low purrs Jay couldn't seem to control—it was unlike any other blowjob Lincoln had been a part of. He wanted to keep it going, but before long Jay cried out.

"Yes. God, yes. Linc!"

With those shouted words, Lincoln took his own cock in hand. Two quick thrusts into his palm, and he came with Jay. He swallowed and sucked until Jay's body was so limp, the man could barely sit up. Lincoln straightened. He had a stupid smile on his face. He knew it, but he didn't care.

Jay licked his lips and gave a lazy grin in return. "You are very good at that." He caressed Lincoln's arm, stopping to pet the wolf.

"I do believe that was a combined effort. I haven't come that fast in a long time."

"You came?" Jay's eyes widened.

"I did."

"But…"

"But what?"

"I wanted to, uh…I wanted to return the favor."

Lincoln laughed. "It's not a favor, Jay. I like sucking."

"Oh." Jay's cheeks pinked.

So goddamn cute. Lincoln stroked the heated flesh of Jay's cheek with an open palm. "I like sucking you."

Jay ducked his head. He trailed his fingers along the edge of the tattoo on Lincoln's arm and said, "The eagle is a symbol of courage."

The touch. The words. Something made Lincoln shiver as Jay traced the feather that decorated the widest part of his biceps. Jay knew just when to use a soft hand and when to get more intense.

"My grandfather was Iroquois." Lincoln hadn't talked about the old man to anyone since his death. "I like the freedom of the eagle."

Jay nodded. "The Iroquois believe the eagle can see the past, present, and future with one look. The eagle can alert you to coming changes." He kept stroking the skin with the tips of his fingers, moving in a slow caress.

"You sound like my grandpa."

"You get along with him?"

"I did. He died when I was in high school. Best man I ever knew. Worked his ass off to help my mom take care of us. And he was my dad's father, not hers."

"Sounds like a good man." Jay glided his fingers across Lincoln's chest. "Sounds like you."

"Nah. Grandpa wasn't the kind of man who ended up in jail." Lincoln drew in a sharp breath as Jay scraped a fingernail over one nipple. "And he never cheated."

"Cheated?"

"I got the tattoo the week after I cheated on the first serious boyfriend I had." Lincoln pulled back and wrenched on his briefs and jeans. "Some stranger I met at a bar hits his knees, and I let him suck me off just like that. I hated myself for it, for putting sex above something more. My boyfriend tried to tell me it was okay. Turns out he'd had his own share of strangers sucking him off in back alleys. Didn't sit right with me, though. A week later, I'd broken it off with him and my mom had died. I got the tattoo an hour after the funeral."

"How old were you?" Jay asked, naked and still sitting on the workbench.

Lincoln leaned into him again and kissed his neck. He didn't want to give up the touches. Not yet. "Nineteen." Jay smelled like the fresh, woodsy cologne he wore lately and like the bike oil and sweat, like the adrenaline of race night.

With his hand, Jay burned a path down Lincoln's body, fingers sliding over skin, over the tattoo, petting the image of the running wolf. "The wolf symbolizes loyalty and fidelity."

"How do you know all this?"

"I've read a lot. Native American history, symbolism. I was studying to be a history teacher before—" He removed his hand from Lincoln's arm. "I had to drop out."

Stupid. Jay was too smart not to do something more with his life. Lincoln traced Jay's jaw with the palm of his hand. "I got the tat to remind me of what I had done. I told myself I'd never cheat again. That wasn't the kind of man I wanted to be." He forced Jay to look at him. "And I expect the same from someone I'm seeing." The words could scare Jay off, but Lincoln needed to say them, needed Jay to know what was happening between them—whether they wanted to admit it or not. Make sure Jay understood where this was headed if they kept things going the way they'd been.

Jay dropped his head to Lincoln's shoulder. "What are we doing?"

"I don't know, but the idea of stopping this bothers the hell out of me."

Neither man spoke for several breaths.

"I'm sorry about your mom," Jay finally said.

"Thanks." Lincoln ran a hand over Jay's back. A slight shiver in response didn't mean anything, did it? "It was just Nance and me after that. She was fifteen. I promised my mom I'd always take care of her."

Jay lifted his head. "She's lucky to have you."

"Not lucky enough." Lincoln backed up. Jay reached for him and held him close. Another long, deep kiss and Jay raised his legs and wrapped them around Lincoln again.

"Ow." Jay dropped a leg to the table.

"What is it?" Lincoln twisted him sideways and looked for the cause of the pain.

Jay slid a hammer out from under his ass. "Fucking around in a garage is dangerous."

Lincoln laughed. "You okay?"

"You need a room with a normal bed."

"So quit your bitching and take me to your place."

In unison, they froze, eyes wide. Jay tensed beneath Lincoln's hands.

Shit. He needed to shut up. There was no way they could walk into Jay's house and—

Jay jumped off the table and pointed to the ceiling. "What's the room upstairs for?"

"Storage."

"Is it livable?" He picked up his clothes and dressed.

"It's got heat and plumbing. It was built to be a living space before Nancy and the asshole bought the house. They never finished it. Didn't have the money."

"You could do the work yourself. Then you'd have your own room."

Lincoln leaned against the workbench. If he did, he could give Davy his room back. "It'll need drywall. The electrical isn't finished."

"That's doable. Then you can stay with your sister but have some privacy."

"It'd be a lot of work." Lincoln stared at the steps leading to the second floor. "Not sure I'm up for that." It would mean moving on. He didn't deserve that. Not yet. Then what was he doing with Jay?

"I'll help," Jay said. "With the bike. And the room. We can take a look tonight."

Lincoln kept staring at the steps for a moment more, then said, "All right."

Jay smiled as he tucked the wedding bands beneath his T-shirt.

Lincoln's gut churned. He hadn't noticed the rings that time. "But not tonight," he said. "I've got something to take care of first."

* * * *

Jay's tennis shoe caught on the windowsill, and he scraped his ankle on the wooden frame.

"Fuck."

His shoe slipped half off. He freed it from the windowsill before it fell to the ground, and he crawled inside, landing with both feet on the toilet lid. Too bad his shoe still hung from his foot. He tripped and fell forward, bracing himself with the towel rack until his feet found the floor. He stuffed his foot into the shoe and waited for any sign of the Shaws.

His deep breaths echoed off the flower-stenciled walls in the small pink bath.

Same bath he'd sneaked into at the age of nineteen, on the night he and Katie ran off to Vegas. She had packed all her clothes and belongings so she wouldn't have to return if her parents took the news of their marriage how she had expected them to. She and Jay lugged her bags into the guest bath and out the window.

He had wanted to use another entrance, both then and now, but the bath's first floor window was the only one sheltered by shrubs and trees in a way none of the neighbors would see the activity. It was also the only window where movement in and out wouldn't kick on the outdoor motion lights. It worked as well as it had when he'd come for Katie.

Jay slowly opened the bathroom door and crept through the house and into the living room. He didn't need to turn on any lights to find his way around that part of the house. He'd been there enough times he could manage not to run into any furniture. Once he moved on to other areas, he'd need the flashlight he had tucked in his back pocket. He'd also need it to search for what he hoped not to find: evidence the Shaws were threatening Lincoln.

The plan: search as much of the house as possible in three hours and leave a full half hour before the Shaws returned home. He didn't want to chance getting caught. Retired pro baller Stuart Shaw would pummel any intruder first, ask questions later. Better to leave plenty of time to go over every room if need be and get out long before tackling commenced.

But where to start? The offices? Stuart and Emily each had offices on the first floor.

Jay hurried toward the back hallway. Two steps down the hall and the slight creak of footsteps echoed above him. Jay clicked on the flashlight and pointed it toward the ceiling. Like that would give him a clue. He cursed at himself and flipped off the light, holding his breathing in check as he waited to hear more. Maybe he had imagined it.

Nope. Another creak. Someone was walking around upstairs. The house was dark, and the Shaws should have left twenty minutes earlier.

He padded to the staircase. Had he somehow missed their return? Or maybe one of them had stayed home. He'd assumed both of them would go to their Wednesday night church meeting. Like they always did a year ago.

He should turn around and head out the bathroom window. But something about the slow way the steps progressed above told him it wasn't either of the Shaws walking around in their own home.

He ascended the first step of the carpeted stairs, trying to gauge where the intruder had gone in relation to where he'd arrive at the top of the staircase. There were no more sounds anywhere in the house. Shouldn't there be something? The tick of a clock, the hum of an appliance—something. The silence faded as Jay's heavy breaths increased in volume with each step. It was as if he wore headphones that only allowed him to hear his own heartbeat, his own deep breaths and nothing else around him. The top of the stairs ended in the middle of a hall. Once there, he'd have to decide which way to go. He wanted the flashlight back on. The moonlight seeping in through the window of the front door behind him offered no hope he'd be able to see who lurked in the house.

Jay climbed the last step, and the dark figure of a man crept by the top of the staircase.

"Jesus." Jay stepped back, and only then did he remember it was a step down. His foot twisted on the riser, and he pitched backward. He flung his arms out, grasping for the banister before he could topple down the flight of stairs ass-first.

A hand clutched the front of his shirt and hauled him forward. Jay swung his arms, grabbing for something, anything, the flashlight in his right hand impeding the process.

"Don't hit me with that thing."

"Lincoln?"

"Yes."

Jay gripped the other man's biceps.

"Don't fall either. I don't want to have to call 9-1-1 and explain what the hell I'm doing here." Despite the annoyed tone of Lincoln's words, the man slipped his arms around Jay's waist and tugged him close.

"What *are* you doing here?" Jay asked as he steadied himself.

"Same as you, I suspect." Lincoln hadn't let go of him. The warm body against Jay's had his heart easing, the fear subsiding. The touch was more intimate in the dark, easier to let another person hold him, calm him. He pushed away from Lincoln. No one was supposed to be that for him. Not again. "You broke in here?"

"So did you if the dark clothes and flashlight are anything to go by."

Standing close, Jay made out the smirk on Lincoln's face. "This is my in-laws' house."

Lincoln grabbed the flashlight, flicked it on, and shone it in Jay's face. "Do they know you're here?"

"Shut up." Jay snatched the flashlight back and started down the steps, this time walking instead of falling. He had more of a right to be there. Stuart would do more than tackle Lincoln if he found the man in his home.

"So where do we look first?" Lincoln asked as he followed Jay. "I tried the upstairs but couldn't find anything. Unless you count a kinky bondage porn DVD in a bottom dresser drawer."

"God!" Jay halted halfway down the stairs. "Don't tell me that."

Lincoln laughed as he joined him on the same step. "You know, heteros do have sex lives."

"I know that." Or he had known it at one time.

"Shit." Lincoln gripped Jay's elbow. "I'm sorry. I—"

Jay shrugged him off and strode down the remaining steps. "They each have an office. I was going to try there first. You might as well help since you're here." He used the flashlight to guide their way to the back of the house. Lincoln was quiet as he followed. Jay paused outside the first office door, and Lincoln smacked into his back. Their heads collided.

"Ouch." Jay rubbed his head and faced Lincoln.

"Sorry. Was thinking."

"About what?"

"Nothing." Lincoln stared at the floor, looking more like he did the first night Jay had seen him at Sonny's Tavern. "It's just weird."

"What? Being in their house?"

"Yeah. And..."

Jay raised the flashlight until the beam lit Lincoln's face. "What?"

"She lived here. She grew up here." He kept staring at his feet.

Jay ached to pull the other man into his arms. Not only to comfort Lincoln, but for Lincoln to comfort him. Why was he the only person Jay wanted to hear talk about her? The only person he wanted to touch him? To ease his pain?

"I need to shut my goddamn mouth," Lincoln said.

"No. It just shows."

"What?"

"How much you care about what happened. How bad you feel."

"God, did you doubt that?"

"Not since I met you."

"Good."

Jay wasn't sure what else they could say. He entered Stuart's office, and Lincoln followed, pausing briefly at the door, then walking around the room. Jay stood in the center and shone the flashlight on the walls and shelves where Lincoln browsed. Jay had seen it all before. Photos of Stuart with his famous teammates before the injury had forced him into early retirement. A signed ball encased in glass. Framed awards. Metal trophies and wooden plaques. Winners and champs all around. Did any of Stuart's teams ever lose?

"Let me see the paper," Lincoln said.

Jay handed it over along with the flashlight.

Lincoln shone the light through the back of the paper. "That's a college seal."

"What? Which college?"

Lincoln pointed the flashlight beam to a plaque on the wall. From the college where Stuart coached.

Runner-Up, NCAA Division II National Football Championship—Stuart Shaw, Head Coach.

Above that: the same college seal as the watermark. Even if Jay couldn't make out the words around the outer edge of the seal, it was obvious the two were identical.

"Wanna know the funny part?" Jay said. "That was his first year coaching. The way he tells the story, they won the championship game. He never gets the facts right."

Lincoln's eyes widened, lips parted.

Right. None of this was funny. "Why would he use paper from his job?"

"Maybe," Lincoln said, "he wasn't the one to select the paper. It's hard to see the watermark without good lighting. I wouldn't have known what it was without seeing the same one on that plaque."

Did that mean Emily sent the threats? "Should we keep looking?"

"I guess. Maybe we can find some of the paper to match up."

The search of Stuart's office took a half hour and yielded nothing more except the usual office supplies and file after file of team records and football play diagrams. Who knew coaching a local college team involved so much damn paperwork. Did anyone from his parents' generation store their files electronically?

Without a word, they made their way to Emily's room. Lincoln went to the large desk first. He flipped on the desk lamp. The glow shining through the rose-colored glass shade was dim but offered enough light for their search. Lincoln opened the top drawer and combed through the contents.

Jay stayed by the doorway and watched him, captivated by the intent way Lincoln concentrated on the task. He searched drawer after drawer, careful with the items inside, neatly putting everything back. He wasn't overly muscular, but he was toned, fit, strong. He moved with precision, each muscle of his body focused on the activity at hand. Serious. Determined. Beautiful. There was not one inch of the man's skin Jay didn't want to touch, to lick, to feel against his own body again.

Lincoln shut the bottom desk drawer and stood. "What are you doing?"

"Nothing."

"I noticed. Something more you're afraid of finding?"

"No. I don't know. Yes."

"Which is it? You can leave if you don't want to be a part of this."

"It's not that."

Lincoln walked around the desk. "What then?"

"Nothing." Jay sidestepped him and opened a nearby cabinet. No way he'd admit how the man got to him. *A fuck. Nothing more.*

Together they searched the cabinet drawers. When they came up empty-handed, Jay continued on to the next and found it locked.

"There were keys in a drawer." Lincoln returned to the desk and retrieved a ring with ten keys.

Jay tried three before the cabinet unlocked, and five hanging folders into the first drawer, he discovered a thin box of blank cream-colored paper. He held a sheet in the air alongside the note someone had sent to Lincoln's old home. Same color. Same thickness. Same watermark.

"That's it," Lincoln said over Jay's shoulder. His breath came in heavy pants and deep lines crossed his forehead.

"What are you going to do?"

"Come on." He snatched the paper from Jay's hand. "You think I'm just going to let this go?"

"They won't hurt anyone. This must be—"

"They took her fucking inhalers."

"I can't believe that."

"You read the note."

"I know. I just... Let me talk to them. I can make them see what they're doing is wrong." Maybe he could convince them tormenting McCaw wouldn't do them any good, wasn't how they should honor their daughter.

Lincoln's stare didn't falter. Finally, he said, "For you. Because I owe you."

"You don't owe me anything."

"Right." Lincoln returned the paper to the box and shoved the cabinet door shut. "One more note, and I'm going to the cops."

Jay nodded. It was a fair deal. More than the Shaws deserved. Lincoln was putting a lot of trust in him, and Jay intended to live up to it. No one else was going to get hurt.

Solid footsteps thudded out in the hall. Jay spun toward the closed office door.

"Shit. Not again." Lincoln eyed the window behind the desk.

The steps grew louder, sounding angry as they thudded against the hardwood floor. No one would miss the light seeping out from under the office door.

Lincoln went to the window and cursed in a low hiss as he tried to work the lock.

Jay gripped his hand. "They have security lights."

"I know. I triggered one earlier when I came in through the garage window, but since the cops didn't come I figured there wasn't an alarm."

"Well, they'll see now. You have to go out the small bath by the kitchen." Without hesitation Jay held Lincoln's face in his hands and kissed him, a press of lips hard enough they'd both feel it minutes later. Had the panic in Jay's chest short-circuited his brain? He let go, grabbed a notepad and a pen from the desk, and flipped off the office light, leaving Lincoln in the darkness behind him. The Shaws could not find Lincoln in their house. Things would get even more fucked-up than they were. Jay stepped into the hall. He barely had the door shut when Stuart Shaw appeared out of the darkness.

"Jay?" He flicked on the overhead lights. "What are you doing here?"

"I stopped by to… I thought I'd…" Jay huffed out a breath. "I wanted to sit in her room."

"Emily's?"

"Katie's. Her bedroom." The guilt slammed into Jay, and his stomach clenched as if Stuart had taken a punch at him. Jay had been lusting after Lincoln and had just kissed the man. Now he was using his wife's memory as cover.

Stuart glanced at the office door.

Jay held up the paper and pen. "I was going to leave a note. I didn't want you to think someone had broken in." *Like I had done by coming through your bathroom window.* How was he going to explain getting inside the house?

Stuart didn't ask. He said, "Come have a drink with me."

The two men walked through the house in silence. Stuart didn't bother switching on any other lights until they were in the kitchen. The bright glare of the overhead light and the stark white walls blinded Jay for a moment. He helped himself to a seat at the table, choosing a spot that would keep Stuart's back to the doorway. How long would Jay have to sit and shoot the shit with his father-in-law before Lincoln had a chance to get away? He wouldn't need to pass by the kitchen doorway to get to the bathroom, but Lincoln didn't know the house layout like Jay. Hopefully he had sense to pick up the flashlight Jay had left in the office and even more sense not to use it.

"Emily's at a meeting," Stuart said. "Then dinner with friends from church." He fished out a couple of beers from the fridge, handed one to Jay, and sat. "That woman refuses to drive anywhere since the accident. I used to believe it was because she didn't want to get hurt." He took a long swallow of his beer, his huge hand engulfing the bottle. If it hadn't been for the beer in Jay's hand, he would've assumed Stuart held one of those miniature bottles of liquor from a hotel minibar.

Stuart stared at the neck of his beer bottle. "But the more I think about it, I've come to understand why." He laughed and set the bottle on the table. "Almost thirty years together, and I'm still learning about my wife."

That stung. What hadn't Jay had a chance to learn about Katie?

What did he have left to learn about Lincoln?

"I'm glad we have a chance to talk," Stuart said. "Just the two of us. We don't get to much anymore."

Jay tried for a smile. Who was Stuart kidding? There'd never been a time when the two of them had sat alone with each other. Too bad the first time had to be the night Jay broke into the man's house and found out he and his wife had put the life of a five-year-old girl in jeopardy. Or had Emily acted on her own? Was Stuart involved? Was he clueless?

"Emily and I are leaving on a trip for three weeks. I've got recruiting to take care of, and then we're staying in Chicago for a vacation."

"Sounds nice," Jay said. Should he mention the paper? Ask about the photos, the threats? If he waited, he could see if the notes stopped while the Shaws were gone. Although they could've hired someone to deliver the threats. Hired the investigator to take the photos. That's how people like the Shaws did things, after all. Never getting their hands dirty.

Perhaps whoever they'd hired had taken liberties. Perhaps the Shaws weren't specific in how they expected Lincoln McCaw dealt with. Perhaps they knew nothing about the inhalers.

As much as Jay wanted them to pay for what they'd done, he also wanted to keep Katie's parents from getting into trouble.

Stuart took another drink and then spoke again. "I think Emily doesn't want to drive because she's afraid of hurting someone. She doesn't want anyone else to go through losing a child."

Jay stared at the man. How far would Emily Shaw go to keep that from happening?

Chapter Fifteen

"I don't know, Jay." Lincoln finished tightening the brake fittings, needing something to do with his hands as he thought over Jay's words. It was the same thing Jay had suggested every day they'd gotten together. A week working on the bike, and they were just about done. Nothing more to distract them. "It doesn't sit right with me."

"I think it'll be okay." Jay squatted next to him.

Lincoln wanted to argue, demand Jay confront the Shaws before they left, but he buried the words. Jay didn't deserve the anger.

"It should stop now that they're leaving," Jay added. "And maybe they'll let it go when they get back."

"We'll see." Lincoln stood and went for his smokes on the storage shelf.

Jay wrapped a hand around his wrist and whispered in his ear, "You should quit those."

Lincoln turned his head and eyed the man pressing in close behind him. Jay had lubricant on his cheek and more lube in his hair—and not the good kind. "Thought you smoked."

"When I was sixteen." Jay smiled and pulled Lincoln by the hips until ass met groin. "And whenever I want to get into a guy's pants."

"How cliché of you."

"Worked, didn't it?" Jay rotated his groin and rubbed his dick along the seam of Lincoln's jeans.

The press of the firm erection against Lincoln's ass got his attention. Jay rotated his hips again, and that did a bit more than get Lincoln's attention. It had him ready to rip his damn pants off and get Jay's dick inside him. "Are you always hard?"

"Around you that seems to be a common affliction." Jay spun them until they faced the bike and shoved Lincoln forward.

Lincoln gripped the seat and stuck his ass out, loving Jay taking the lead, loving the thrill of giving himself over to someone—to Jay.

Jay ran a hand down one jean-covered ass cheek, then into the space between. *Damn, stupid pants.* Lincoln went for the top button, but Jay slapped his hand away.

When did the kid get so confident? And bossy?

Hell, who was he kidding? From the first night they'd met, Jay was the perfect blend of sensual innocence and erotic strength. It was a turn-on, and Lincoln wanted more, wanted to do everything they hadn't done yet. Wanted to sit on the bike and let Jay ride him. But was Jay ready?

Better to let the other man lead. For now.

Jay bent over Lincoln's back and spoke against his ear. "You need to quit the smokes. Okay?"

Lincoln gasped with his words. "I will."

"Promise me."

"I promise." He loved Jay's weight on his back. Loved the heat and pressure, the feel of Jay's hands as he unbuttoned Lincoln's shirt. Then Jay was gone, taking the shirt with him. Lincoln clasped the bike's seat in both fists. He wanted to turn around and grab Jay, pull the man to him, get his tongue in Jay's mouth. He didn't have time for any of it.

Jay pressed a hand to his back and said, "Stay there. Don't move."

Fucking hell. He loved the man's commands, the way Jay leaned forward and licked along the base of his neck. Jay's shirt was off, and the bare chest to his back gave Lincoln some of what he craved. He reached around with one hand and grasped Jay's jean-covered thigh.

He didn't get to touch the man for long. Jay seized Lincoln's hands and stretched his arms out in front of them. "Lean forward against the bike. Grab the edge of the workbench."

Lincoln did as instructed, and the action shifted them so Jay's body forced Lincoln's groin against the bike's seat.

"I want you." Jay rolled his hips, putting all the right pressure against Lincoln's ass. "Can't stop wanting you."

Yes. Can't stop. Even if they should?

It felt so damn good, though. Lincoln wanted Jay inside him, needed to feel the man's cock pushing in. He wanted Jay to take him—show him the desire was as strong for Jay as it was for him.

Jay enveloped Lincoln, one arm around his shoulder, and with the other hand, he lowered Lincoln's zipper. "Kick off your pants."

Lincoln breathed deep, trying to get his desire in check. He had every intention of making this last.

But it couldn't last. No matter how much he'd enjoyed the past week working on the bike together. No matter how much fun he had hanging out with Jay, how much he'd laughed and relaxed. No matter how much they deluded themselves. Sex was all they'd ever have. His stomach churned. Like he'd just downed too much whiskey. Why? Because he liked Jay. More than he should admit. A hard swallow, and he forced away the unease. He'd enjoy this for what it was.

Jay stood, and Lincoln heard him undressing. "Linc, get your pants off."

Why couldn't he move?

Desire?

Fear?

Or something more?

Jay covered his back again, the man's naked body warm and close and so right against his. Jay swept a hand across his chest, plucking at his nipples, tilting his world like the time his car had spun out on the last curve at the Tri-State Raceway.

"Need your pants off so I can fuck you, really give this bike a test run."

Lincoln nodded, but he still couldn't move.

"You okay?"

"Yeah. Just give me a sec." He sucked in a long breath and reached for his pants. He needed to snap out of it, get undressed, and let Jay screw him into oblivion. Forget all the bullshit about what he wanted and what he could never have. Too bad he couldn't hide the shaking of his hands.

"Want you so much," Jay said as he helped work Lincoln's pants past his hips. "Want you to know how much. Want to show you."

Lincoln froze, his pants stuck around his thighs. Jay had to quit talking. He was always talking too much. "Just fuck me. Now. Please, Jay."

Apparently Jay didn't need any more encouragement than that. He grabbed Lincoln's pants and yanked them the rest of the way off. Then he had on a condom, applied lube, and was pushing inside Lincoln in no time. He loved that part—the slow, sweet burn as Jay entered him. The way his own breath hitched when they came together. The smell of Jay's cologne overwhelming his senses. His own dick rubbing against the leather of the bike seat with each shove as Jay thrust into him over and over. The bike rocked with their movements, the kickstand scraping along the concrete floor.

"You like it, don't you?" Jay asked, his words punctuated by low grunts. "You like getting fucked?"

"Yes! Like that it's you. Just you."

Everything stopped. Jay. Him. Time.

Lincoln needed to shut the hell up. If he didn't, he'd say something he'd regret—they'd both regret.

Too late for that?

Jay grasped Lincoln's hips tighter, the pinch almost painful. They stood immobile, body to body, the pounding of Lincoln's heart the only sound he could hear until Jay finally moved. They both groaned as he pulled back and they came together, hips to ass, with the next slow thrust. Lincoln wanted Jay to stay buried inside him, wanted the moment to last as long as they could stand it. Jay must have felt the same. He stayed still for several deep breaths, then finally rocked his body again, speeding up more with each movement. Lincoln eased his hand between the bike and himself and wrapped it around his cock.

It was unlike any sex he'd had with Jay yet.

And it wasn't just the sex that had changed between them. Lincoln was falling for Jay. Hard.

With that thought, he jerked forward, driving his cock into the grip of his hand. He slammed his hips against the bike seat and came, his skin more alive and on fire than the flames on the Harley.

Jay held Lincoln and drew him close until they touched along the length of their bodies again. The angle had Jay's thrusts shallow, but the contact of chest to back was nothing Lincoln wanted to change. He'd never have all of Jay, but he'd take all he could get.

Jay thrust one last time, his hips snug against Lincoln, his cock buried deep. He pinned Lincoln to him and shivered through spasm after spasm. Lincoln gripped the arm Jay still had pressed across his chest. He wasn't ready to let go.

"Oh God," Jay said between deep gulps for air.

They stayed like that, breathing heavily, sweat and cum drying in the air. They should have withdrawn, gotten rid of the condom, but Lincoln didn't care about anything but touching Jay, feeling the man against his back.

Then he felt more: the two bands on the chain around Jay's neck smashed between them. Lincoln leaned forward against the bike.

Neither man spoke. What could they say? Lincoln didn't need to ask any questions. The experience had been as intense for Jay as it had been for him. There was no way either of them could pretend differently—pretend they weren't feeling something for each other.

The bike rocked as he pushed off the seat. "She held up okay."

Jay laughed. "She did." He put his shirt on, covering the rings that had dug into Lincoln's back only moments before. "We'll have to get her on the road to see what else she'll need."

Nope. Not going to happen. Lincoln reached for his pants and underwear.

Jay beat him to the pants and handed them over. "That was incredible."

There Jay went again, talking too much.

"You like it a lot?" Jay asked, his gaze on the flames of the bike.

"What? Sex?" Lincoln never had a lover want to talk about it after. Should've known Jay was the kind of guy who'd need that.

"Yeah. But…I mean, bottoming." He blushed.

Another new one. None of Lincoln's lover's ever blushed.

"Getting fucked," Jay added.

Lincoln chuckled as he tugged on his shirt. "Sure, I like it. Did you miss me coming all over the bike seat?" Time to distract the man. Since testing the bike was out of the question, he pulled him forward. "I liked it a lot."

This kiss was as passionate as those before the sex, Jay grabbing and clutching as much as Lincoln. Jay tilted his head back, and Lincoln licked down the man's neck, working up marks and earning little hums from Jay.

Before long, Jay shifted his hips. "Never in my life been ready for round two so fast." He glanced away and bit his lower lip. No avoiding the sadness in his eyes.

What could Lincoln say to the man? Maybe he would've had the right response if he hadn't been the one who had taken Jay's wife from him.

"It's okay." He cupped Jay's chin and forced his head up until the man looked his way. "You need to let yourself feel. I'm sure she'd—" What the hell was he doing? Putting words in her mouth. He had no right.

Jay nodded. "She'd understand. She'd never blame me for how I feel."

Would she blame you for being with me? Lincoln swallowed around the lump in his throat.

Jay ran a hand along Lincoln's cheek to his chin. Why was that one touch more important to him than the ones Jay had given him when he was bent over the Harley?

He waited. The next move had to be Jay's.

The kiss Jay offered was soft and slow, and Lincoln heard what the other man didn't say.

If they weren't careful, they were going to back themselves into a corner where the only way out would wound them both. Jay didn't deserve more pain.

Not from Lincoln.

He should pull away, walk out, and never look back. It'd be best. For both of them. If only the kiss weren't so good, so full of the passion Lincoln had been missing for the last year. If only he didn't like Jay so goddamn much.

Jay's next words melted all Lincoln's resolve. The husky whisper had his desire flaming to life. Or maybe it was Jay's request.

"I want you to fuck me."

Lincoln sucked in an uneven breath, pressed his forehead against Jay's temple, and said, "Not here. Not in the goddamn garage."

Chapter Sixteen

The Jeep sputtered and jerked forward. Lincoln put a hand on the dashboard to keep from jostling into it. The silence continued between them. Neither he nor Jay had spoken since they'd left Nancy's house.

They had rushed through a cleanup of the garage and made sandwiches they ate standing at the kitchen counter. Nancy and the kids would be home in less than a half hour. Their only option: Jay's house. Without discussing where they were going, or why, they'd climbed into Jay's Jeep.

Lincoln couldn't stand the silence any longer. "You need a new car."

Jay laughed. "I need a lot of things."

What did that mean? Sex? Booze? Love? Why hadn't the man bought himself a new vehicle? He certainly had the money. Too bad there were questions Lincoln could never ask. How did that saying go...curiosity killed the cat?

Five minutes later, they pulled into Jay's driveway, and Jay stopped the Jeep in front of the ranch-style house. Lincoln had been there once before, but he'd been so pissed at finding out someone had stolen Jessica's inhalers he hadn't taken note of the place. The neighborhood wasn't the worst in Edgefield, but it wasn't anywhere close to the respectable, middle-class part of town where Jay's parents lived. There was no denying Jay's house was the cheapest of the block. That could've been the lack of upkeep alone: the chipping paint, the loose shutters covering the windows, the overgrown bushes with branches poking out on all sides, like the tentacles of a beast from a science fiction movie. Would the long vines attack Lincoln when he tried to enter Katie Miller's home again?

Jay climbed out of the Jeep, and Lincoln followed. They walked to the front of the vehicle and stopped three feet apart. Lincoln had the urge to grip Jay's hand in his and haul the man toward the house. Not the best move. He stuffed his hands into the pockets of his jeans and waited.

This had to be Jay's choice.

Jay looked toward the house for a moment. His gaze finally swung back to Lincoln, and the smile that hit his lips was nervous, but real. He wasn't the type to play games, or to lie. He wanted this. He wanted Lincoln.

"Come on," Jay said with a tilt of his head toward the house. He didn't look at Lincoln as he slid the key into the lock and stepped inside. Lincoln followed him in and froze.

Had it looked like this the last time? Take-out food containers everywhere. Clothes strewn about. Empty bottles of beer lying on their sides on the coffee table.

"Your house is a disaster."

"At least I don't live with my sister." That smile was less nervous, more genuine, more like Jay.

Lincoln laughed and closed the door behind him. "You got me there."

Jay wandered through the house and stood in the middle of the living room as if examining it for the first time. "We were barely out of high school. Couldn't afford much, so we went for a fixer-upper."

That didn't really explain it all. Unless fixer-upper meant *I don't give a shit and no longer bother to clean my house.*

"You sure you want to do this?" Lincoln had to ask. Had to hear the words again.

Jay spun around. "Yes!" His eyes wide, his mouth open, he nodded and licked his lips. "I want you here."

Lincoln let it go and joined Jay in the living room. Jay was a grown man. It was up to him to speak up if they were taking things too far. Besides, Lincoln wasn't leaving unless Jay physically tossed him out. Sex was something they needed. It could be that simple, couldn't it? It had to be. No matter what else they wanted, no matter what else he'd been crazy enough to feel back in the garage, there couldn't be—shouldn't be—anything more between them. They both knew it.

Didn't mean they couldn't enjoy the sex. They were damn good at that part.

The interior of the house would've been nice had Jay cleaned up, dusted, swept, or even taken out the trash. The furniture looked secondhand, but it worked with the curtains and the shelves stocked full of books to give the place a comfortable charm. Lincoln pointed to the wall of bookshelves. "You read a lot, huh?"

"Used to. Before. When I was in school." The reply came out choppy, jittery. Best to relax Jay before he shook apart.

Lincoln reached for his hand. "Which way?"

"Last room down the hall," Jay whispered. Maybe he thought no one would ever know he was about to get it up the ass if he didn't speak any louder.

What would his family say if they found out? Would they be okay knowing Jay was with another man? Maybe until they found out which man.

They moved toward the room, Jay's hand in his. He didn't tug or force; he let Jay set the pace. The door to the last room was open.

A double bed. Two dressers. Two nightstands. Everything set up for two people—for a couple. The room was cheerful in a way the living room wasn't. Less cluttered, less unkempt. Filled with signs of a thoughtful touch. An arrangement of candles lined the shelf on one wall. Matching sheets and a bed skirt outlined the bed. A collection of photo frames sat on a table under the window.

Either back out now or get things started. Lincoln couldn't think about where he was for another second, couldn't let her into the moment, or it would all be over. He didn't want it over, didn't want to leave Jay. Not yet.

He shed his coat, strode to Jay, and buried his face in the man's neck. "You smell good."

"I smell like the bike and your garage." Jay held him close and shivered. "I'm, uh, kinda nervous."

He rubbed Jay's back and tried to remember his first time, tried to remember what had sucked about it, so he could avoid that for Jay. "Wanna shower first?"

"Together?"

"Yeah, together."

"Oh. Okay. Just...give me a sec." Jay stepped away and pointed toward the bedroom door. "The bath's across the hall."

Lincoln stopped at the door to tell Jay to take his time. No matter how much Jay wanted this, it couldn't be easy. Jay was staring at the picture frames on the table. Lincoln didn't want to see whose face filled the frames. He left the room. He should've left the house, but his dick was leading the show, and it wasn't going anywhere. Except, it was more than his cock, more than his body that desired Jay.

Better not to think about that. He had to keep what they were doing in the realm of fuck buddies.

Could they be buddies? Friends?

Probably too late to avoid that—too late to avoid so many things.

The tension eased when he got to the bathroom door. There was no door handle. A screwdriver was wedged in the hole where the knob should have been. Lincoln used it to open the door. He laughed as he stripped off his clothes and turned on the shower. The top of the shower curtain drooped in the middle and eight broken plastic rings were still looped around the curtain rod. He tried not to laugh again. Easy to do when he thought about the reasons Jay probably lived the way he did.

Steam filled the bathroom by the time he heard Jay enter. The rustle of sliding clothes had Lincoln's dick firming. For once, he wished his cock didn't look long and thick when he was hard. He wasn't freakishly big, but the sight of him would make anyone nervous about getting fucked for the first time. He wanted Jay to enjoy it.

Hell, who was he kidding? He hoped Jay would crave it—crave him.

Jay slid the shower curtain aside and stepped in. The sight of his naked body wiped away all Lincoln's concerns. Jay was as ready as he.

Lincoln moved closer and ran both palms over the front of Jay's chest, and Jay pushed into the touch. So sensual. So damn sexy. Lincoln grabbed a bar of soap and worked lather between his hands. He washed Jay's arms and back, easing tension out of every muscle, moving his hands lower and lower, loving Jay's firm grip on his shoulders.

Jay rocked into the contact of Lincoln's fingers up and down the space between his ass cheeks. Lincoln had to force his hands away before he lost control and gave in to the primal desire thundering through his veins. He lathered extra soap between his palms, turned Jay around, and pressed in close, cock to ass. Jay jumped.

"Relax." Lincoln licked and nipped at the flesh of Jay's neck, and Jay's muscles loosened under his hands. "Not going to fuck you standing up. Not the first time." He reached around Jay and washed chest, abs, groin, and let his fingers linger at the firm nipples. He cupped and caressed Jay's balls and the skin behind them. By the time he had washed Jay all over, they were both breathing heavily, their cocks red and swollen, Lincoln's dick sensitive to every touch of Jay's body brushing against it. They rinsed, dried off, and made their way to the bedroom, kissing and touching as they went. The urgency evident. Need driving them on.

It all ended when they stood side by side before the bed, both staring at it.

Jay had to make the first move. It had to be his decision to go forward. With each breath that blew out of Lincoln's chest, the anxiety built. Was he asking too much? Were they taking this too far?

Without saying a word, Jay crawled onto the bed, his ass in the air. When he flipped onto his back, his cock was still hard and moist at the tip.

The tension flew out the window along with all his unease. Jay wanted him. No more evidence needed. No need to change the scenery. No grief or guilt to get in the way. Not then. Lincoln lowered himself to Jay, and Jay raised his hips, bringing their bodies together. So eager.

Too eager?

They had to take this slow. Lincoln looked down at Jay. "Have you had anal sex? I mean, did you and...did you do...toys? Fingers? Anything?"

"I haven't—No, nothing."

"Oh." Lincoln sucked in a sharp breath. He was going to go slow, make this good for Jay. "I'll take it easy, use a lot of lube, but it'll still hurt some." He ran a hand over Jay's chest. "But it isn't completely unpleasant." He toyed with one nipple, then the other.

Jay arched and said, "I trust you."

Lincoln stilled his hand and looked away, staring at the bed beside Jay. "Are you sure?"

Jay cupped Lincoln's face in his hand. "I want this."

They held the stare until Lincoln finally nodded. "I'll go slow. It's going to burn some."

"It's okay. I want to feel it. Want to know." Jay bucked up, demonstrating his impatience without restraint. So damn sexy.

"I remember," Lincoln said. "First time you bottom, you kinda want to get it over with fast. To know. To see if you like it."

"No." Jay met his stare. He stroked Lincoln's cheek with his thumb. "Want to know how you feel." He entwined his right hand with Lincoln's, their fingers clasped together. "Don't want this over fast. Want to feel all of you."

Did he mean that? Lincoln lowered his eyelids and tried to remember how to breathe.

JAY RAN THE thumb of his free hand over Lincoln's cheek again. What was that look on his face? Nervousness? Desire? Fear? Jay wasn't about to ask. He wanted—needed—Lincoln to be with him. He wasn't going to let anything derail that. "Do you still have that handy tube of lube in your jacket?"

A surge of air huffed out of Lincoln as he laughed. He rolled off Jay and rummaged in his jacket pocket. He threw the lube and rubbers on the nightstand. A strip of condoms. Five of them.

"Uh, I was kidding about getting it up that many times."

Lincoln laughed again as he lay down. "I'm not getting out of this bed until morning." He flattened the length of his body against Jay.

"Sounds good." Jay spread his legs and gripped Lincoln's hips with his thighs. He'd always associated that position with femininity and submission. As much as he dreamed of getting fucked, he had never imagined he'd find himself pinned beneath another man, spreading himself wide open, offering his body to someone.

Lincoln rocked, and his cock slipped between Jay's ass cheeks. The next slow thrust put pressure where Jay wanted it, but he wanted more. He gave Lincoln one last kiss, lowered his legs, and rolled to his stomach. He stuck his ass in the air, his elbows on the bed, his head down. Vulnerable. Exposed. Natural. "Is this okay?"

"Jesus." Lincoln's breath hitched. "You're gonna kill me." He rubbed a hand along Jay's spine and reached for the lube on the nightstand. He stroked Jay's balls and cock, working the slick lubricant all over Jay. Except the one place they needed it most.

Every one of Lincoln's touches had Jay panting harder, writhing more. Lincoln kissed his lower back and pushed his fingers into him, slowly, gently thrusting. So new. Foreign. Hot.

The stretch, the fullness didn't diminish Jay's desire. It had him wanting more. Everywhere. His cock. His ass. Pleasure spiked in his balls. "You're gonna make me come."

"No." Lincoln pulled back. "Not yet. Not until I'm inside you." He opened a condom and rolled it on himself, adding more lube. "Last chance."

"Linc!" Jay startled himself with his own impatient scream. The whimper that followed didn't sound like him. When had he gotten so desperate? So wanton? So turned on by another person he had no thoughts of sex with anyone else? Could Lincoln see that? See how crazy with need he was?

Lincoln pressed his cock against Jay's ass. Who knew that pressure would be so erotic? Such a turn-on? Jay clenched the sheet in his fists, trying to focus on breathing. In. Out. Lincoln nudged his cock in, so gradually it had to be killing him, stopping every other second and waiting a moment before continuing.

Jay dug his fingers into the sheet more and groaned. Despite the care in Lincoln's movements, the stretch burned as the head of his cock nestled inside. Jay panicked, and his body seemed to tighten of its own accord. Then Lincoln's hand was on his lower back, caressing, rubbing. Jay could breathe again. He relaxed...everywhere. Lincoln moved, shifting farther inside, and the burn eased.

"Okay?" Lincoln asked, the one word grunted out.

"Yeah. It's better now." So much better than anything he'd felt before.

"It gets even better." But Lincoln held still, his hands digging into Jay's hips.

The burn was gone. Jay wanted something, anything. He'd never felt like this before. Aching. Out of control. Like he'd explode if Lincoln didn't move.

"Touch yourself," Lincoln said.

"Huh?"

"Touch your own dick, Jay."

He did. He wasn't as hard as in the bathroom, but the slide of his hand on his lubed cock had him barreling toward release with just a few strokes. Before he knew what he was doing, he began to rock, his movements timed with his grasp on his dick. But his own touch wasn't what thrilled him. It was the slide of Lincoln's cock in and out of his ass—no, more like the slide of his body on Lincoln's cock.

The more he moved, the more he craved.

Fucking Lincoln had been amazing. He understood the appeal of topping, but now that he'd experienced the flip side...why wasn't every gay man begging to be on the catching end of sex? Something about every team needing a pitcher sped through his mind, but it was gone when Lincoln thrust for the first time. Every nerve in Jay's ass felt connected to his own dick, the flesh more sensitive than ever before.

"Fuck." He let go of his cock and gripped the sheet again.

Lincoln's movements halted. He released his firm hold on Jay's hips and massaged instead. "Fuck good? Or fuck it hurts?"

"Fuck, would you please fuck me."

"Yeah. You're gay." Lincoln grabbed Jay again and pulled him back with each thrust, grunting with the drive of their bodies coming together.

Jay clutched a pillow with one fist and his own cock with the other. The slap of their bodies, the smell of their sweat, the grunts and moans that filled the small room—it was intense, electric, hotter than any moment they'd shared. Jay loved all of it. He either never wanted it to end or wanted to repeat it all as soon as humanly possible. A tingle spread across his lower back. He quickened the erratic movement of his hand over his cock. "Yes. Yes!"

"Jay." Lincoln snapped his hips faster, slamming into Jay.

That was all he needed. Jay fell forward and gave a couple of quick jerks of his hips, his hand not even moving, and he came against the mattress.

Lincoln pressed Jay to the bed and kept pumping into him.

So this is what it's like to get fucked into the mattress.

"Jay!" Lincoln shouted. He came, his balls slapping against Jay's ass as he jerked and rode out his orgasm. He dropped forward, his entire body covering Jay's.

"Damn." Jay had no other words and no breath left to speak with.

"Yeah. Damn." Lincoln shifted and fell onto the bed, his hand still on Jay's hip, his palm gliding over the man's skin. Jay rolled to his side and ran his fingers over Lincoln's tattoo. He traced around the feather first, then the wolf. He loved how the wolf looked. In motion. Always running. Strong, powerful, like nothing could catch it.

"You should get one," Lincoln said.

"What? A tattoo?"

"You're so fascinated with mine."

"Nah. I promised—" Jay clamped his mouth shut. They couldn't talk about her. *Not now.* But no one else eased his thoughts, made it seem okay to remember and not have it be about pain and heartache. And that was crazy. Not only would it be weird for him. It'd be a shitty thing to do to Lincoln.

"She didn't like tats?"

"Nah."

"Why not?" Lincoln settled his opposite arm behind his head.

"A buddy of mine from college has a ton. She was afraid I'd end up drunk with him some night and come home with 'Mama' tattooed across my chest. She said—" God, he needed to shut up.

"What?"

"She said they were trashy looking."

Lincoln laughed. He rolled to his side and faced Jay. "What would she think of me? If I wasn't me, just a guy you were seeing, you know?"

Jay stared at Lincoln. Why would he ask that? No one else talked about Katie like she still existed, like death didn't mean the end of her. The Shaws were Christian, active in their church, and they never mentioned Katie's soul or where she was. He got off the bed, slipped on his jeans, and stood before the table of frames. His parents. The Shaws. Katie's younger cousin. His childhood dog. The last picture was gone. Tucked away while Lincoln had left for the shower.

Jay cleared his throat as he focused on the empty spot on the table.

"She was the kindest person I'd ever met. She had a smile and a laugh for everyone. She wanted to be a nurse. The plan was for me to finish college first, and then she was going to go. She cared about people, and she never got to use that gift."

He heard Lincoln sit up.

God, please do something. Anything. Hold me.

No. Too much.

So he kept talking. "She'd want me to go on living." Another long silence. He faced Lincoln. "She'd like you. Like that you make me feel good for the first time in a year."

Lincoln smiled at him, his dark eyes a little sad, but the smile widened as he made eye contact with Jay.

"I think…" Jay walked to the bed but didn't sit. "She'd want me to go back to school."

"That's a good idea. You should get on with your life."

But how could he do that when everyone else he cared about couldn't move on?

"Come here." Lincoln tugged on Jay's hand until they sat side by side, their combined hands resting on Lincoln's knee.

They didn't say anything more.

Hearing about her had to have hurt Lincoln. Jay had never wanted to ease someone else's pain as much as he did right then. It was the first time anyone had listened to him—really listened. And their hands clasped one in the other on Lincoln's knee felt like the first loving embrace Jay'd had since he'd lost her.

* * * *

Warm air blew over the back of Lincoln's neck. He smiled. Jay's bed was not only larger than the one they'd shared at Nancy's, but was also more comfortable. The weight of Jay's arm lounging over his back and the man's body pressed against his hip were a welcome reminder of what he and Jay had shared the night before.

He missed the mornings the most. The ease of waking up with someone, lying in bed, talking, making love, kissing, caressing. Those memories with Paul were fading. He had hurt him, but the man was moving on. Was it time for Lincoln to do the same?

He turned to Jay. Sleeping on his side, his mouth partially open, Jay's eyes were closed, but scanning side to side. Dreaming?

Twenty-two years old. A widower. He had his whole life ahead of him. He deserved to be happy. Lincoln wasn't the right choice. He couldn't be. He should leave, and let Jay find someone else. Let Jay move past the accident. Have a lover who wouldn't remind him of the pain and loss and heartache every time they were together. Lincoln rolled to his back and flung an arm over his eyes. He should get up, get dressed, head out the front door, and never think about Jay Miller again.

He had left Paul to keep him away from the pile of shit his life had turned into. How could he invite Jay in?

How could he not?

He turned back and ran his thumb along the length of Jay's nose, over his parted lips to his chin. He was falling for the man. He'd give almost anything to make Jay happy. Even if it meant he had to walk away from the best thing he'd found in a long time.

Jay slowly opened his eyes and stretched. "I haven't slept that good in forever."

"Yeah? Me neither."

"That could have something to do with the size of this bed. Or maybe it's the lack of robots on my sheets."

Lincoln buried his face in the pillow. "Fuck off," he mumbled with a laugh. He faced Jay again. "Maybe I'll redo that room over the garage."

Jay smiled and leaned into him. The kiss was slow and sensual and unlike any kiss they'd shared yet. Less tongue, more lips. Each breathing the other in. Lincoln slid closer and brought their bodies together, needing to feel more of Jay. They tightened the embrace, and together they rocked, a slow, steady sway of their bodies.

A gasp came from the doorway behind Lincoln.

"Jesus." A male voice. "What the fuck?"

Jay's eyes widened. "Todd!"

Lincoln flipped over as the fierce close of the bedroom door rattled the walls. Whoever Todd was, the stomping down the hall said it all. He was not pleased to find Jay in bed with another man.

Was Jay getting more action than he'd led Lincoln to believe?

Jay shot out of the bed and fumbled for his jeans. "Shit. Shit."

Lincoln threw back the blankets and sat up. "Todd is?"

"My brother." Jay fumbled with the zipper on his jeans.

"Ah." *Thank God.* Lincoln reclined against the headboard and let out the breath he'd been holding. He didn't have to consider punching Jay's lights out—or Todd's.

"Shit. What do I say to him?" Jay worked a T-shirt over his head.

"He doesn't know—"

"That I'm gay?" Jay froze, his hands still clutching the bottom of his shirt. He sank to the other side of the bed, his back to Lincoln.

"Shit. I'm... I mean... I've never said that before."

"It's who you are."

"Yeah. I just... This isn't where I expected to be. Never expected to have to explain to my brother, my parents."

Lincoln shifted to sit beside him.

Jay jumped up. "I have to go talk to Todd. I don't think he saw who..."

"Who you were kissing?"

"Should I tell him? I don't know if I can."

"Don't." Jay looked about ready to fall apart as it was. No need to add to it. "No one needs to know that part."

"Okay." Jay walked to the door. "Thanks, Linc."

"Hey." Lincoln went to him and kissed Jay hard, backing him to the door, unsure what he was doing. Reassuring? Staking claim? "I like that."

"What?"

"You calling me Linc." He kissed Jay again and said, "It's no one's business but your own."

Jay's gaze drifted to the doorknob and back to Lincoln. He nodded once and left the room.

Lincoln got dressed and made the bed to keep busy. The screaming didn't take long to start.

"You're a fag? Is that what you're saying?"

"Don't say it like that!" Jay yelled.

Lincoln stepped into the hall. Every instinct told him to march into the kitchen and punch Todd out, brother or no brother, accident or no accident.

He went to shut the door and give them privacy, but the next words stopped him.

"What about your wife? What was she? Your beard?"

A long pause followed. Then Jay spoke in a low whisper. "She was my..." Lincoln couldn't make out the rest. Did he want to hear it?

"And what's he?" Todd asked. "Whoever that is in your bed, what is he to you?"

"I don't know." There was a scrape of a chair and a *thud* as someone dropped into it. "I wanted to know. To make sure."

Lincoln backed up into the bedroom and swung the door shut. He pressed his forehead to the cool wood and held the doorknob in the tight grip of his fist. A dull ache formed between his eyes. What the hell was he doing? All he was to Jay was some goddamn experiment.

* * * *

The bedroom door opened slowly with a *creak*.

Lincoln didn't look away from the ceiling as he said, "How'd it go?" He should get off the bed and make for the front door, but his legs weren't helping him out.

"Like I expected," Jay said. "He's always afraid of what our mom will say about everything. She's not easy to please."

"Maybe this isn't a good idea."

"What?" Jay asked, the edge of the door still in his grip. "Why?"

"I don't want to fuck up your life any more than I have."

"You're not fucking up my life. Complicating it, maybe." Jay gave a slight grin and moved toward the bed.

Lincoln sat up. "This isn't just a fuck-buddy thing for me. Not anymore."

Jay froze, the grin gone.

Great, scare the man to death.

Lincoln stood, grabbed his leather jacket, and stormed through the house. He didn't go for the front door, though. He pulled on his coat and stopped in the middle of the living room. How had he ended up in her goddamn house? Fucking her husband? Falling for—No. He couldn't go there.

Jay's low, husky whisper from across the room surprised him. "Don't go."

Lincoln slowly turned around. Several feet separated them. It didn't take long for Jay's deep breaths to match his.

The doorbell rang, but neither man made a move for it. Jay touched the front of his T-shirt, gripping the wedding bands through the fabric. His gaze darted between Lincoln and the door.

"You're shaking." Lincoln went to him. He couldn't stop himself. He caressed Jay's biceps, trying to calm him, to ease the nerves, trying not to think about why Jay didn't want him to leave.

"Jay, let me in!"

Todd was an ass. No more evidence needed.

He added pounding when he got no response. Three pounds later, the door swung open. Todd entered, took one look at Lincoln, and said, "No way in hell."

Chapter Seventeen

Todd narrowed his eyes until the whites were no longer visible. But the scowl sure was. The same look he'd given Lincoln in the courtroom months earlier, and the same guilt settled in Lincoln's gut like a boulder.

He stood his ground, though. No matter what Jay's family thought of him or what he'd done that night on State Road 91, he wasn't about to leave Jay to deal with this alone.

Todd looked to Jay. "Is this who you're fucking?"

"Yes," Lincoln said. "And he's damn good at it."

Todd ignored him and spoke to his brother again. "I hope you're screwing with him. I hope you've got a reason for this."

Jay moved in front of Lincoln and said, "I need to speak with my brother."

Lincoln met his gaze. "Are you sure?"

"Yes. It's fine." Fine? The frightened look on Jay's face didn't say fine.

Lincoln didn't want to go, but he also wanted to give Jay what he needed. "Great to meet you, Todd."

Todd stepped around Jay and came at Lincoln until they stood a mere foot apart. It took all his resolve to hold back the urge to lay into Todd.

Jay slid in between them. "I'll call you later, Linc."

"Yeah. Okay."

In four quick strides, Todd was at the door. He held it open. *So helpful.*

Lincoln glared at the man as he crossed the room. The door slammed shut behind him, almost hitting his ass. The fucker better not hurt Jay. No matter what Jay had done and with whom, he didn't deserve more pain in his life.

* * * *

Todd hadn't moved. His hand was still pressed against the door like he had to hold it there to keep Lincoln out. Finally, he faced Jay. "What's going on? Why is he here? And why the fuck were you in bed with him?"

Jay headed for the kitchen. Lincoln didn't deserve to hear the verbal shit Todd was about to spew. He opened the fridge and remembered too late he didn't have any beers left.

Todd stormed after him. "Goddammit, Jay! Say something."

"I didn't know it was him when I met him."

"When? Last night?" The surprise in Todd's voice hit home for Jay how crazy it would sound to hear about him and Lincoln together.

"I just wanted to know."

"Know what?"

"About men."

"About whether you like getting fucked by one?"

Jay slammed the fridge shut. "Don't be an ass."

"What the hell? I'm trying to understand."

"I'm…I'm bisexual."

Todd rolled his eyes. "I don't give a shit about that. Fuck whoever you want to. Just not him."

"He's not who you think he is."

Todd stared from across the kitchen, his mouth open, his tongue hanging out as if he was about to speak. Or sneeze. Was it too much to hope for the latter? Todd took a step toward Jay and then, as if he thought better of it, moved back and leaned against the countertop. "Little brother, this is all too goddamn impossible to believe. You better tell me what is going on here. You met him?"

Jay nodded.

"And you didn't know it was him. Did he know who you were?"

"Not at first."

"He knows now?"

"Yes."

"Last time we talked about McCaw, you made it seem like you might go looking for him, to have it out with him, make sure he understood what he did."

Jay breathed deep. He smelled like sex and sweat; he smelled like Lincoln. He pulled out a chair from the table and leaned his weight on the seat back. He had no intention of sitting, but he needed something to help him stand. "He does understand. He doesn't take what happened lightly."

"You mean what he did. He doesn't take what he did lightly? That's what you're saying?" Todd looked away and glanced out the kitchen doorway into the living room. Did he notice the missing pictures? Jay had put them in a drawer the morning after he'd first slept with Lincoln. He couldn't face her smile, her eyes, but he also couldn't get rid of her image. He kept the photo of her in the bedroom. Until the night before, that was. Until he'd invited Lincoln into his bed.

"Are you fucking with him?" Todd asked without looking back. "Is that what this is? Tell me you're getting even with him. That this isn't—"

"Getting even with him? Why? You think he deserves to pay more than he has?" Jay glared at Todd. "Are you involved with the threats?"

"Threats?" Todd shook his head. "What the hell are you talking about?"

"Someone's been sending him notes about the accident—saying he deserves to suffer."

"He told you this?"

"I've seen the notes. They threaten his family. His little niece."

"Shit." Todd dropped into a chair. "Who are they from? You don't think Mom would..." He stared at the chair Jay held in his hands. "It would be just like her to do something that crazy for you." A sadness Jay had seen too often washed over his brother. He hunched in the seat.

"I don't know. I think it might be the Shaws." Jay sighed and gripped the chair in his fists. "I don't want it to be anyone. I just want it to be over."

"Should we talk to Dad?"

"Lincoln and I are trying to find out for sure who it is. If the notes start up again, I'll talk to Stuart."

Todd jumped out of the chair and ran a hand through his hair. "*Lincoln and you?* What the fuck are you doing, Jay? He killed your wife, and you're fucking him?"

"You don't understand."

"No, I don't. I don't understand any of this."

Jay shoved the chair in, and it smacked the edge of the table. "I think you need to leave."

Todd's eyes widened. The wounded look on his brother's face stung. Was Jay going to hurt everyone by being with Lincoln?

"Right," Todd said. He moved to the kitchen doorway and stopped. "Don't talk to Stuart alone. He lost his only child. If he's pissed enough to send threats, he's not going to like you siding with McCaw." He held still a moment more, then walked out.

Did he think Stuart would actually hurt Jay?

Siding with McCaw? Would Stuart Shaw see it that way?

Yes. There were two sides to every game, and Jay had chosen the wrong team in so many ways as far as Stuart would be concerned.

Would Todd tell anyone about Lincoln? Their mom?

It didn't matter. The answers would come soon enough. Too soon. Jay couldn't avoid his family. He couldn't avoid the Shaws either. He had to talk to them. When the Shaws got home from their trip, he had to make sure the threats stopped.

* * * *

Lincoln kicked at the tarp. It was the third time he'd tripped over the damn thing, and it was starting to piss him off. He should drape it back over the bike. It didn't make sense to keep working on the Harley. So why did he? Was it because it gave him a reason to hang out with Jay? Or because he really hoped to ride the bike again?

He'd been doing final adjustments on it all morning, but nothing held his attention. All he could focus on was the fear in Jay's eyes the day before. Damn man had been through enough in life. He didn't need his family treating him like shit for whom he chose to sleep with, even if no one would understand how he and Lincoln had gotten as far as they had. Hell, Lincoln couldn't understand it.

But if Jay was okay spending time with him, then the asshole brother could shut his mouth about it.

He kicked the tarp into the corner of the garage. Might as well clean up. He wasn't going to make any progress at this rate. He bent to pick up a grease-covered rag. A small silver gift-wrapped box sitting on the workbench stopped him. An all-too-familiar paper with typed lettering was tucked under the edge of the red ribbon.

So much for the hope that the Shaws leaving town for three weeks would mean the end of it.

When had they been in the garage? He hadn't seen the note when he'd come in to work on the bike that morning, but he'd been distracted.

He went for the items on the workbench. His hand shook as he lifted them. Even if he deserved the torment, they had no right to come into his sister's home. He read the note.

Don't forget what you are.

He dropped the paper and tore open the wrapped box. A red die-cast car. Not the same make or model, but it looked as close as one could come with a toy to represent Katie Miller's car.

Someone had beaten the hell out of the tiny car. The top was collapsed in on the seats, the front window cracked, and the side doors crushed in. The most disturbing part was the lone handwritten word in black lettering on each side.

Murderer

He tossed the car and box onto the workbench, grabbed a hammer, and threw it at the back wall of the garage. "Motherfucker." The resulting *clank* as the hammer hit the wall full of tools and the *crash* when the lot of them fell to the floor was satisfying.

"You keep that up, and we'll be fixing the entire garage." Jay stood at the side door. With both the overhead door shut and the side entrance closed behind him, Lincoln barely saw the man's face in the shadows of the garage. Was he upset? Pissed? Why had he come? Lincoln stepped sideways to block Jay's view of the box and prize inside. Jay didn't need to see the smashed car. "You okay?"

"Sure. Sorry my brother's an ass."

Lincoln waved a hand through the air. It didn't matter what Todd had said about him. It was Jay who didn't deserve any more shit. "How did he take it?"

"He was surprised."

Understatement of the year? Lincoln wouldn't have handled it too well if he'd found Nancy with one of the assholes who had hurt her.

Jay laughed. "*I'm* surprised most of the time."

"I remember that feeling."

"How old were you when you knew?"

Were they really going to pretend this was about Jay being gay? And not who Lincoln was? Pretend this wasn't the world's worst coming-out story?

He could if that's what Jay needed. "Fourteen. The first high school dance came along, and I had no interest in the girls. Just wanted to see inside Tommy Vanderline's pants."

"Did you get to?"

"Yeah. Up close and personal the next year. He was the first boy I fucked."

Jay's eyebrows rose. "Really? I was a junior my first time."

"Yeah, but she was a girl. It takes more finesse, I'm sure."

Jay laughed again and picked up a screwdriver from the top of the open toolbox. He scraped the metal tip along a crack in the workbench as if he carved a message.

When it seemed like Jay would keep working the screwdriver until he split the table in two, Lincoln spoke. "You can talk about her more. If you want. I know it'd be weird, but I don't want you to hold back because of me."

"I don't need to talk about her." Jay chucked the screwdriver into the toolbox.

"I didn't say you need to. Just thought you might like to."

Jay met his gaze, the inner battle evident on the man's face, like he wanted to remember her, but couldn't figure out how or why Lincoln would be asking. Or maybe Jay could never share more with Lincoln, not about her.

Someday Jay would find someone he could talk with. Someone to love again. Lincoln wanted to be strong enough to walk away. He just couldn't. Not yet. He gripped Jay's shoulder, tugged him forward, and kissed him, putting enough tongue into it to entice Jay. "I want to keep seeing you."

Jay's eyes searched his. "Yeah?"

"I know this isn't going to be anything long-term. I also know I'm not ready for this to end."

Jay leaned against the workbench. "I am getting good at the gay sex stuff."

"Yeah." Lincoln shook his head and laughed. "You are." He paused, then said, "Sorry if your brother doesn't understand."

"He's not always like that. He's not a homophobe or anything. He's just confused about…the rest."

Weren't they all?

Maybe talking wasn't a good idea. There were better ways of making Jay forget his brother, forget what the Shaws were up to, forget the pain. It was the least Lincoln could do for him. He stepped closer, wrapped his arms around Jay's middle, and kissed him again, taking his mouth in a fierce touch of lips and tongue, wanting to make the reality of that small box on the workbench disappear.

Jay held nothing back as they came together. The sensual kiss deepened with every second. Jay ran his hands all over him, and Lincoln returned the touches, massaging every tense muscle he came across until he was certain Jay would've slumped to the floor if he let go of him.

With one hand supporting Jay, he reached for the sleeping bag on the storage shelf and spread it out on the floor. He lowered Jay, falling to the makeshift bed with him. They kissed and undressed each other,

Jay still pliable, the kisses tender and sloppy and sweeter than any Lincoln had ever known.

Once naked, Jay rolled to his stomach. Maybe fucking face-to-face was something he could never do. And Lincoln could never ask. He accepted the invitation, and in no time, he retrieved a condom and lube and was inside Jay. The slow way they moved could never be described as a fuck, but he had no other word to use.

After, they lay beside each other, breathing heavily, and Lincoln pulled Jay close, chest to back, unable to stop himself from keeping contact with the man—the second person in his life he'd felt the urge to hold like that.

Jay clutched Lincoln's forearms like he never wanted to let go. "I want to keep seeing you too."

Lincoln closed his eyes and breathed deep. Jay smelled of sweat and sex. Amid the grease and oil of the garage, Jay smelled alive.

"Jesus." Jay laughed. "When we're not having sex, lying on concrete hurts like hell." He rolled over and kissed Lincoln. "You need to get a bed."

"I have one. In the house."

"A real bed." Jay smacked his arm. "Big enough for both of us."

"I started working on the room upstairs."

"Yeah?"

"I've been thinking about it since you first suggested it. Did some of the walls last night."

Jay sat up. "Can I see it?"

"Sure." Lincoln stood and reached for his pants, taking his time. Jay finished dressing and shifted on his feet while Lincoln slipped his T-shirt over his head. He picked up the sleeping bag and made like he was folding it. "Go on up. I'll be right there."

Jay took off for the stairs at the back of the room.

Lincoln wadded up the sleeping bag and threw it on the shelf. He grabbed the car, note, and empty box from the workbench. He didn't want Jay to see them, but he also needed to figure out what to do. The Shaws were done invading his life, his sister's house, all of it.

"You coming?" Jay called down.

Lincoln stashed the items out of view behind the toolbox and ran up the stairs.

Jay was leaning against the fresh drywall on the opposite end of the room. "I think the bed should go here."

The teasing smile on Jay's lips forced a bit of the anger away. Lincoln would deal with the gift-giving asshole soon enough. In the meantime, he wasn't giving Jay any other reasons for his life to suck. "Great idea."

He'd meant for the kiss to be a gentle touch, a thank-you for Jay's encouragement on the room. But Jay turned the kiss into more, adding tongue and hands and body. He rotated them and slammed Lincoln against the new wall. Drywall dust rained down from the exposed board over their heads, most of it landing on Lincoln's hair and clothes.

"Uh-oh." Jay backed up, chuckling. "Sorry." More dust fell on Lincoln, and Jay laughed harder. It sounded nice. Jay definitely needed to laugh more.

Lincoln tried to work off the dust like a wet dog shaking water from his coat. "You don't sound sorry."

The grin lingered on Jay's lips even after his mouth met Lincoln's. "I'm glad you started the room."

"It was a good idea. I'm not going to be another asshole who runs out on them."

"That's not you." Jay brushed the drywall dust from Lincoln's shirt and jeans.

Lincoln gripped his wrist and stilled the cleaning effort. "I'd like you to meet them."

Jay opened his mouth but didn't speak.

Panic welled in Lincoln's chest. He was pushing Jay too far, asking for too much. They weren't going to move in together and live like a goddamn married couple. This was about a need fulfilled. For both of them. He released Jay's arm. "I just thought... Nancy said she wanted to meet you. She knows I've been—" What? Dating? Fucking? "With someone."

Jay stepped forward and laid a chaste kiss on Lincoln's lips. "I'd love to meet her and the kids. When do they get home?"

"I heard them pull in a few minutes ago."

"Yeah? Come on." Jay crossed the room and headed down the stairs.

No matter what Jay had said to his brother, he felt something for Lincoln. It was obvious there was more between them. Lincoln longed to figure out what, but why bother? Once he finally turned his Secret Santa over to the cops, it would all be over. No matter how Jay's conversation went with the Shaws, Lincoln was planning to have one of his own.

One way or the other, whatever was building between him and Jay would be over soon—too soon.

Chapter Eighteen

"You're good for him," Nancy said from where she stood at the stove.

Jay smiled. "Think so?" Smiling was starting to feel natural. It had felt good to laugh with Lincoln. Hell, everything with Lincoln was good. Jay hadn't dared hope he'd be with someone again the way he'd been with Lincoln on the garage floor a half hour earlier.

Nancy lifted the wooden spoon from the chili and pointed it toward Jay as if it were a magic wand. "I do." She went back to stirring and said quietly, "He's been drinking less."

Jay's smile widened.

Lincoln joined them in the kitchen, carrying three bottles of soda from the garage. He deposited the two-liters on the countertop next to Nancy. "Where are the kids? I want them to meet Jay."

"Adam isn't home yet. Jessica and Davy are supposed to be setting the table." She leaned into the hallway. "Kids! Hurry up. Uncle Lincoln's ready to eat."

One door then another banged against the wall in rapid succession. The scampering of two kids down the hall was followed by a *thud.*

"Ow. Don't push me."

"Davy!" Nancy yelled from the stove. "Stop pushing your sister."

A young boy with hair as dark as Lincoln's sprinted into the kitchen. "I didn't push her. She tripped."

Lincoln hugged him from behind in a playful grip. "Be nice to her." Quieter he added, "Small things affect her breathing." He tousled the boy's hair.

"I know." The kid squirmed in Lincoln's arms, turning the grip into a wrestling match.

Lincoln stilled him and pointed toward Jay. "I want you to meet someone. This is Jay. Jay, my nephew Davy."

"Hi," Davy said. "Are you his new boyfriend?"

The appearance of a little girl wearing bright red pants and a pink and white Hello Kitty T-shirt saved Jay from answering. Small for the age Lincoln had mentioned. She sported a fierce scowl for her brother and was clearly out of breath, but she still raced forward toward her uncle when she caught sight of Lincoln. Jay stopped her with an arm across her chest. She stared up at him, clearly unsure why a stranger was touching her.

He removed his arm but crouched next to her, ready to stop her again if need be. "Just don't want you to get too close. He's covered in dust."

Lincoln stared at him. Nancy too. Both had their mouths hanging open, their eyes wide.

Jay gave the girl a smile. "You're Jessica?"

She nodded.

"My name's Jay. I'm a friend of your uncle's."

"Hi," she said, her head tilted to the side, her brown eyes looking so familiar—like Lincoln's.

Lincoln finally spoke. "Jay's eating with us. I better take a shower first. Come on." Lincoln gestured toward the hall. "I'll loan you something to wear." Jay wasn't as covered in dust as Lincoln, but he shouldn't have been close to Jessica either. He stood.

Jessica tapped the back of his hand. "Have you seen his wolf?"

Davy snorted out a laugh. "I think he's seen it."

Nancy dropped the spoon to the stove top. "Davy!"

"I didn't say nothing bad. It's on his *arm*. We've all seen it."

The heat rose in Jay's face. How had a couple of kids managed to embarrass him?

"Come on," Lincoln said with a laugh. "We'll make it quick," he told Nancy. Jay followed him down the hall, and Lincoln asked, "You're not used to kids?"

"Not really around many."

"You'd make a great dad."

Jay's next step faltered, and the breath trapped in his chest. He reached for the wall.

"You okay?" Lincoln moved to his side.

"Yeah. Just…"

"You don't have to say anything." Lincoln's voice was low. "I'm guessing your life isn't what you imagined on your wedding day."

Jay leaned against the wall, his head falling back. His life was nothing like what he'd pictured then. A part of him would always grieve that loss. But now, another part of him wanted to move on, wanted much more than he'd even known possible.

Lincoln released his arm and leaned against the opposite wall. "You still want kids?"

"I don't know. You?"

"Not sure," Lincoln said. "Never pictured myself as a dad. I'm not much of a positive influence on these kids. Probably wouldn't be with my own."

"Why do you say that?"

No answer. Finally, Lincoln shrugged but wouldn't look at him.

Jay seized Lincoln's hand, led him to the bathroom, and shut the door behind them. "Let's not talk about kids or the future or anything else." He slipped his arms around Lincoln's neck. "I want to feel you."

Lincoln returned the embrace. They said nothing as they held each other, as they undressed and stepped in the shower, as Jay washed Lincoln the way Lincoln had done for him the night before. They didn't talk or kiss or linger in the shower, but the sensual way Jay slid his hands over Lincoln said more than he should've let on. He rinsed the shampoo from Lincoln's hair, and let his fingers trace the lone wolf on the man's arm before turning off the water.

They made quick work of drying off. Lincoln wore a towel around his waist and sneaked into Davy's room to hunt for clothes. Thirty minutes later, they were seated at the kitchen table with Nancy and the kids, finishing off the last of the chili and corn bread.

"Sorry it wasn't fancier than canned chili," Nancy said as she stacked Jessica's empty bowl inside her own. "If Lincoln had told me you'd be by, I would've planned something else."

"It was delicious." And the first time he'd relaxed during a meal in a long time.

"You could serve him seaweed soup," Lincoln said, "and he'd eat it. He's been surviving on takeout. You should see his place."

Jay playfully elbowed the man in the side.

"Ow." Lincoln smacked his arm in return and threw a crumpled napkin that bounced off Jay's forehead before he could react.

The kids laughed and smacked one another's arms, tossing their own napkins around.

Nancy stood. "Everyone, stop it." She looked at her brother. "You're as bad as the kids." She cleared dishes, and Jay got up to help. "Sit," she said. "The kids'll help."

With no more encouragement than that, Davy and Jessica carried plates and glasses to the sink.

"They're good kids," Jay said.

"Yeah." Lincoln gripped Jay's thigh under the table. "Too bad their dad and stepdad couldn't appreciate what they had. Some men should never get a chance to be a father."

The chili in Jay's gut churned. He'd lost his chance at being a dad. Hadn't he? He grabbed the hand Lincoln had on his thigh and forced himself to focus on the other man. "They're lucky to have you."

"I hope you like chocolate fudge." Nancy carried a half-gallon box of ice cream and a metal scoop to the table. Jessica and Davy followed with bowls and spoons for everyone.

Jay didn't bother moving his chair back, and his abdomen hit the edge of the table as he stood. The table skidded six inches, rattling the bowls and silverware. "Sorry. I—"

Lincoln steadied a teetering bottle of soda.

"I have to go. I'm sorry. I can't stay for..." He sounded like an idiot, but he couldn't hold back the jittery start and stop of his words.

Lincoln got up and grasped his arm. "You okay?"

Jay forced a breath in and spoke to Nancy. "Thanks for dinner." He couldn't look away from the carton of ice cream in her hands.

"You're welcome," she said. "You'll have to stop over for ice cream another time." The kids cheered. For the ice cream or to see Jay? It didn't matter. He'd probably never see them again. Too bad. They were cute kids.

Nancy set the box of chilled dessert on the table.

Jay stepped back as she pushed it closer to him. "I have to leave."

"Okay." Lincoln rubbed his arm before letting go and moving to the front door. He held it open for Jay and went outside after him. "What's up?"

Jay wanted to explain, to admit he couldn't eat ice cream if someone shoved it down his throat, couldn't look at it for anything in the world.

What was he doing at Lincoln's house? Meeting his family?

How could either of them move on when it stared them in the face every day, each reminding the other with their existence?

How could they ever let go of the past?

With the truth. It was the best place to start.

"I need to talk to my brother. And my parents."

Lincoln watched Jay. "Okay."

"I want to tell them the truth. About me. About everything." Before the Shaws returned home. Before anything more happened to Lincoln. And most importantly, before Jay ended up falling for the one man he could never have a life with.

* * * *

Lincoln closed the front door, but kept his hand flat against the wood panel.

Jay's freak-out at the table had to have been about his wife. The man had grieved deeply for her—was still grieving. Every time Jay pulled away from him, it had to be about her, about what Lincoln had done to her.

How had they let themselves get this far? Meeting his family? What a fucked-up idea.

A hand pressed against his lower back. "Everything okay?" Nancy asked.

Lincoln faced her. "Yeah. I think he feels guilty about moving on." She knew Jay had lost his previous lover, but Lincoln wasn't explaining more right then.

"Do *you* feel guilty?"

"I know I gave up a good thing with Paul but—"

"I'm not talking about Paul. What about your guilt over the accident? Are you letting go of that?"

"I'm trying to."

"Even with stuff like this?" She held out the typed note and box with the destroyed toy car tucked inside. "I found them when I went to get the ice cream from the garage freezer."

Lincoln snatched the items and held them in a tight fist before her face. "This isn't your business." He marched past the kitchen where the kids were digging into the half-gallon for extra chocolate fudge.

Nancy followed and slipped her hand along the inside of the bathroom door before he forced it shut. "This is my business. You are my business."

He released the door, dropped the toilet lid, and sat.

She stepped into the small room. "How many things like this have you gotten?"

"A few."

"Since when?"

"Since the funeral."

"Lincoln!"

"What? They're just words." No need to mention Jessica's inhalers. He wouldn't frighten her.

She swiped the car from the box in his hand and held it up as he had done to her. "This is not just a word. What do the rest say?"

"Stuff to make sure I don't forget. That's all this is about." Or so Jay kept saying.

She stared at the car and spoke softer. "Are you sure?"

"I took another person's life. If someone hurt you or the kids"—or Jay—"I'd want to make them pay."

"Pay?" She sat on the edge of the bathtub. "Linc, you've paid over and over for this. You made a mistake that led to a huge tragedy, you served the time the judge gave you, you paid the fines, you paid your lawyer. And what about that outrageous settlement they got?"

"That wasn't all my money."

"It came from your insurance. You lost all the money you earned from your racing. You lost your home, your partner, your career. You've paid enough. You need to call the police and report this. Tonight."

Jay's dust-covered jeans and T-shirt were lying in the laundry basket beside Lincoln. The same clothes Jay wore when they'd made love in the garage. Made love—that was the description he'd been searching for. "I can't. Not yet."

She stared at Lincoln until he offered more.

"I know who they're from now, and I'm handling it."

"He might be dangerous." Of course she'd assume they were from the widower. It's what he had thought until he met Jay.

"I won't let anything happen to you. Or the kids."

"I'm not talking about us."

Even though it would scare her, she deserved the truth. "Someone's been in the house, the garage. That's where I found some of the notes."

"Here?" She glanced out the door of the bathroom. Giggles floated down the hall. The kids would probably keep eating ice cream until they reached the bottom of the half gallon or their mom told them to stop. She turned back to Lincoln.

He nodded.

"How are you handling this? Saying you're sorry? You've said that. You can't make her family not hate you. That's something they have to want to do. And frankly…" She looked out the door again, biting her bottom lip. Listening to her kids? Their chatter had grown softer. Kids should be able to enjoy an ice-cream treat and not have to worry about threats and guilt and revenge. "With that kind of pain, they might need to hate you. They might not be able to ever let it go."

He wanted to tell her the truth about Jay, about the forgiving person he'd been lucky enough to meet. Why bother? As soon as he worked up the nerve, Lincoln would confess about the latest note and then tell him he was going to the cops. Jay might not be happy with Lincoln for turning the Shaws in, might not want to speak to him—let alone more. Despite all the Shaws had done, no one had gotten hurt.

"Okay. I trust you know what you're doing," Nancy said. "And I know you are trying to do the right things." She flipped the car over and over in her hands. The word *murderer* resurfaced with every flip. When she spoke again, her voice cracked. "You didn't have to do it. You've already done enough."

"Do what?"

"Pay the electric bill. And the insurance and the mortgage. Not after all the money you give me every week. Not after all that money from the sale of your car."

"Nance, I didn't pay those bills. I've been giving you the money."

She lifted her head. "I called to get the balance. They were prepaid for six months. Who else—" She sucked in a gulp of air and covered her mouth with her hand.

"Mel." Lincoln had hoped he'd never have to say that name again.

"Why would he do that?" she asked.

"Maybe the bastard actually feels guilty for leaving you and the kids." Lincoln stood and kissed the top of her head. "He's still not allowed in the damn house, Nance."

"He can't buy me back. I'm not that stupid."

"I know." But Lincoln was glad he'd changed the locks. No one was hurting his family. Not ever again.

Chapter Nineteen

Jay parked in front of his parents' house. The street was quiet, not a single car lining it in either direction. Every vehicle was parked behind garage doors. There were no people visible in the yards, no neighborhood football games, no dads playing catch with their kids, no one riding bikes or skateboards. No signs of life. Maybe spring never reached middle-class Edgefield.

How had he ever felt at home there?

He turned his Jeep off and sat behind the wheel for a moment more before getting out. He should've called Todd. He hadn't seen or heard from his brother since Todd met Lincoln. What would his parents say? Had Todd told them? A message from his mom on Jay's answering machine, asking him over for dinner was the only contact from any of his family.

Like a lone sheep entering the wolf's den, there'd be no escape. He slid out of the Jeep and trudged toward the house.

"Jacob!" his mom exclaimed with a smile when she opened the front door.

He stepped inside and moved toward the archway of the living room. His dad was seated in a chair by the window, reading the financial section of *USA Today*. All the lights were on in the room, and it was brighter than usual, like they'd upped the wattage of every possible bulb. A fire was blazing in the fireplace, the air thick and stifling. The sweat would be rolling off Jay before long. He shed his coat. Hadn't his parents gotten the memo that winter was over?

His dad lowered the newspaper to his lap and searched Jay's face for a minute before speaking. "I'm glad you didn't skip out on us this week. It's been too long since you've been over for dinner."

He'd been a little busy. Not that he could force the truth out yet about whom he'd been busy with. Was it harder to tell his parents he was gay? Or harder to admit he was sleeping with Lincoln McCaw? His dad leaned forward, rested his forearms on his knees, and opened his mouth. He didn't have time to say whatever he was planning to before Jay's mom came into the room. His dad picked up the newspaper again.

"Do you want a cup of coffee?" she asked. Her pleasant tone and the light bounce of her steps told him all he needed to know. Todd hadn't talked to her. Not yet. Maybe Jay needed to give his brother more credit.

"No, I'm fine."

"Todd is running late," she said. "He won't be here until six."

Jay went farther into the room, exhaling as he took each step. At least he could break the news on his terms. He had to explain to his parents, and to Todd, before the Shaws' homecoming. If talking the Shaws out of their threats didn't work, Jay's relationship with Lincoln might be impossible to keep quiet. And Jay didn't want it to be a secret. Not anymore.

Could he do this? Telling his parents he was sleeping with another man would be hard enough. Add in the fact that it was Lincoln, and he might not survive the resulting battle.

His mom gripped his forearm and steered him to a chair facing the fireplace. He hated that creaky wooden chair, hated the fireplace. He shook off her touch and sat on the couch.

She sighed and left the room, heading toward the kitchen.

Jay smelled pot roast finishing off in the oven. *Odd.* She never made roast. He hated it.

"Jacob," she said as she returned carrying a tray of coffees. She set a cup on the table in front of him and sat on the love seat across the way. Hadn't he said no on the coffee? She sipped her own and said, "I heard that lumber company of yours is doing well. I saw in the paper they handed out raises last week."

His dad turned a page of the newspaper, then another. The slap of pages startled her. She glared at her husband and then focused on Jay again.

"Yeah, I got a raise."

She smiled at him before sipping more of her coffee. She knew nothing of his life with Lincoln.

Jay checked his watch. Five thirty. Half an hour until Todd showed up. Plenty of time to get the words out. He shifted on the couch, placed his hands on his lap, then on the couch cushion on either side of him. Did all gay men become completely aware of their bodies the moment they tried to tell their parents they liked to fuck guys? Why hadn't he planned out what to say? How to say it? His mom watched him. Any minute she'd say something critical. Better to cut her off and just say it.

Or maybe he'd take a couple of minutes to plan the words. He stood. "I'm going to the bathroom." He walked past the too-frilly first-floor bath and headed up the stairs. Maybe he'd hide out in his old room until Todd got there. *No.* Better to get it over with before then. For all he knew, Todd was planning a big reveal over appetizers.

Jay went into the upstairs bathroom, the one his parents used. He splashed cool water on his face and held the edge of the sink in both hands. *Start with the gay thing.* But how?

He stared at himself in the mirror. Funny how the further from his teen years he got, the more he looked like his dad. *They're your parents. They love you. They might listen.*

Oh, who the hell was he kidding? They were going to yell, say they were disappointed, and demand he stop seeing Lincoln.

At least they would have gotten the truth from Jay. He was man enough to do that. He was man enough to do a lot of things as far as Lincoln was concerned. That had him smiling.

The happy, relaxed face staring back at him couldn't be Jay Miller. He hadn't seen that look on his own face in the mirror in a long time. Not the expression to wear downstairs for such a serious discussion. Too bad he couldn't force it away. Thoughts about what had him smiling in the first place—thoughts about him and Lincoln on the garage floor—had the smile widening. He could give himself all sorts of reasons about why he wanted to come out to his parents, but the real reason was he wanted to keep seeing Lincoln, wanted more with him, would give almost anything to have it, to remove every obstacle from that outcome.

If only that were possible.

He turned away from the mirror and sat on the edge of the sink. He didn't want to see his own doubts, his disappointment.

Half-full makeup jars and glass perfume bottles lined the counter on either side of him. "*War paint*," he and Todd had called it when they were kids.

Funny how little had changed since he'd lived there. The chipped tile on the floor in the corner. The dull stainless steel faucet with grit and gunk caked around the handles. The flaking caulk outlining the shower enclosure. Why did his parents go out of their way to make the downstairs as extravagant as possible while the upstairs looked like any other middle-class home in Edgefield? Average. Lived-in. Why did they try to hide that? Hide the truth?

Because that's what they always did. The truth was never good enough.

Like the time he and Todd had found a sex education book under their parents' bed while searching for hidden Christmas presents. *How to Talk to Your Kids about Sex.* When their mom had come home and discovered them sitting on Todd's bed flipping through the diagram section of the book, she turned a deep shade of red and snatched the book from their hands. Todd didn't say a word, but Jay had wanted to know more.

At dinner that night he'd asked his mom what oral sex was.

She choked on a mouthful of ambrosia salad, pressing her cloth napkin to her lips to keep bits of marshmallow and mandarin orange from falling out of her mouth.

His dad chuckled around a swallow of food and explained married people sometimes touched their spouses in private places with their mouths.

Jay gasped. "My wife is going to put her mouth on my penis?"

His mom slammed her napkin to the table. "No! Decent people do not do those sorts of things."

His dad tried to say something, but she cut him off.

"No more talking during dinner."

Jay never asked about sex again. He knew she'd never tell him the truth.

He and Todd had spent the next day searching for that book. They had found it too.

Shit.

How had he forgotten? He pushed off the bathroom counter and crept down the hall to his parents' bedroom. He opened their closet door and tugged the string overhead to turn on the lone uncovered lightbulb. He knelt on the floor and jerked aside the hanging dresses and slacks, most still in dry-cleaning bags or with store tags pinned to the sleeves. He flinched with the scrape of hangers and the rustle of plastic bags and waited to see if anyone came to investigate the noise. When the silence carried on, he moved the clothes aside the rest of the way.

There in the corner, near the bottom of the closet, was a two-by-two-foot square opening covered by a thin piece of board painted the same cream color as the closet walls. Jay needed to look. He just didn't want to. He tapped the board in on one side, and the opposite end popped away from the wall.

He worked his fingers into the opening and pulled the board away. Three feet in from the opening was another wall. There was nothing visible inside—just as he and Todd had found it when they'd first uncovered the secret hiding place all those years ago. Just as they'd found it every year after when they went hunting for their Christmas presents. Only it was never as empty as it seemed.

Jay reached in, dropping his body to the floor so he could work his arm in up to his shoulder. The open space between walls continued along the full length of the closet and was just as tall. When he was little, he'd crawl inside. He'd hand the hidden unwrapped gifts from "Santa" out to Todd who'd stack them on the closet floor. After they had looked through everything and decided which gifts were for each of them, Jay crawled back into the empty space and stacked the hidden treasures inside. How their parents had gotten the gifts in and out he'd never know. He and Todd had never confessed their discovery. Still hadn't.

He pressed his cheek against the wall and groped around with his right hand, finding nothing but the wood floor and bare walls. Until his index finger came across a metal object small enough to fit in his hand with a finger-sized hole. He slipped a finger through it and dragged the item forward. He got a better grip and didn't need to see it to know he held a handgun.

Once he sat upright, he laid the gun on the closet floor. He shifted around and sat with his legs crossed under him, his eyes wide as he stared at his discovery, the same as he and Todd had done as kids. Only they had never discovered Santa had bought them a gun. Not even the pellet gun Todd had begged for every year.

How long had their parents owned a handgun?

And why had they hidden it away? If it was for security, there were easier-to-reach locations for a weapon.

Jay left the gun on the floor and resumed his earlier search position. When he had his arm as far into the opening as before, he groped around where he'd discovered the handgun. His search produced a plastic bag. He dragged it out of the hole, set it on the closet floor, and hesitated before looking at it. It couldn't be worse than a gun, could it?

Stupid question.

Considering he sat on the floor of his parents' bedroom closet staring at a bag full of inhalers, two still in their boxes, the name "Jessica Connell" printed on the prescription labels.

His mom was crazier than he thought.

What had anger and grief driven her to do?

"Jacob?" his mom called from downstairs.

He scooped up the gun and inhalers and shoved them inside the small opening. He stood and tugged the light cord, but remained inside the darkness of the closet. *What now?* Could he really turn his own mother in to the police?

Chapter Twenty

Jay entered the living room.

"There you are," his mom said. "What took you so long?"

"How could you?"

His dad looked up from the paper, his eyes narrowing. Confusion? Anger?

"How could I what?" she asked, the coffee cup resting in both hands on her lap.

"Threaten him."

"Who?" Her eyebrows rose.

"Lincoln McCaw." Jay's breath sped as the anger worked its way through him. He wanted to shake the truth from her. "What do you want? To hurt him? To harm his family? How far are you planning to take this?"

His dad stood, the newspaper still in his hand. "Jay, your mother's said some things in anger and grief, but she wouldn't hurt anyone."

Jay took a step back. He'd get the inhalers, force her to admit what she'd done. He should have brought the bag and gun with him into the living room, taken the inhalers to the police, but he hoped it wouldn't come to that.

The front door opened, and Todd stepped inside. "Hey, something smells great."

Their mom turned to Todd as he came into the living room. "I made pot roast."

"Really? My favorite."

"I know. We never have it enough."

Todd hugged her and gave a nod to Jay over her shoulder.

Jay wanted to march across the room and drag her out of Todd's arms, force her to explain. But the anger kept him planted where he was. He didn't want to physically hurt her, no matter what she had done.

His dad shoved the newspaper into a basket beside his chair.

"Now, can we finally talk to our son?" He remained standing and did not make eye contact with Jay.

They know.

A shrewd woman, his mom had waited days to confront Jay. Waiting a few more minutes while chatting casually over coffee had been nothing she couldn't handle. She knew to wait for the perfect moment. Of course, for Jay that time would never come. They'd never understand what he did, or why he had done it.

That was okay. He'd never understand what she had done either.

She crossed the room, followed by Todd. As mad as Jay was at Todd for spilling his secrets, he also felt sorry for his brother, still a small child who never had his parents' approval. Sometimes parents didn't love their kids enough.

Neither Todd nor their mom made a move to take a seat. They stood beside his dad, their arms folded over their chests, their expressions stern. All so similar it was like they each wore the same Halloween mask.

Jay's back was to the staircase. They literally surrounded him.

"Well, your brother's clued us in," his dad said, the tone of his voice softer and more kind than his words implied.

"My God, Jay," his mom said. "What were you thinking? You're having relations with that man?"

What was *he* thinking? Better to threaten Lincoln? Better to put the life of a little girl in jeopardy?

His dad stepped forward, his gaze finally level with Jay's. "Are you gay?"

"Howard!" His mom screeched the name.

"What? I want to know. He's our son. We should know these things about him."

She shook her head, the force of it likely to cause a headache. "That's not the issue." She pointed a finger at Jay, the appendage shaking. "Him having anything to do with that bastard McCaw is."

"Shut up!" Jay strode forward. "All this time you've talked like you know what he deserves. How can you? When you don't know what happened that day? When you don't know what he went through? How he feels about it? You don't know him."

"And you do?"

"Yes, I do."

She came at him. "And you have no idea why that disturbs us? Do you?" She searched his eyes. "How can you let this man into your life? How can you betray her? Anyone else. Not him." She paused and more softly said, "Not even *she* would forgive that."

Her words tore at Jay. A truth he had closed himself off to. He stumbled to the couch and sat. What had he thought? That he could keep pretending sleeping with Lincoln was okay because Katie was gone, because she would've liked Lincoln, because Lincoln feeling bad about the accident was enough? Jay held his head in his hands and tried to remember how to breathe.

Sitting in the home he had grown up in, surrounded by the only family he seemed destined to have, he fought to cling to the truth he had seen that first night in Sonny's Tavern when he'd met Lincoln. The man's despair, the anguish so like Jay's own had called to him.

Had it all been a mistake?

"Are you the one threatening him? His family?"

"What are you talking about?" she asked.

He stared at his mom, trying to read the stern look on her face. For the first time in his life, he understood her. Cunning. Conniving. Whatever she had done, she had done on her own. She didn't want either her husband or her new favorite son to know.

She sat on the couch next to Jay. "Even if you believe this man is sorry, the truth is your wife isn't here, and he's to blame. Do you think about the future you were supposed to have together? About the children you were planning to have? Do you think about her?"

Yeah. His mom was crazy. He felt like the only one who thought about Katie. Until he met Lincoln.

His mom stood and pulled him off the couch. He fought her on it at first, but she held firm and led him to the fireplace. He kept his back to the burning flames. She glanced behind him and tears filled her eyes. He wanted to know what she was staring at, but something told him not to turn around. *There's nothing to see.*

He tugged his hand free from her grip.

She said, "She'll never be twenty-five. Or thirty. Or fifty. She'll never be a nurse. She'll never be a mother. She was so good at taking care of people. She would've been a wonderful mother to your children."

The tears pooled in Jay's eyes. He squeezed them shut, tilted his head back—anything to make it all stop.

"You never say her name."

He said her name. He was the only one who did.

"You never talk about her."

He talked about her. To Lincoln. The one person who had really listened.

"You never look at that picture." She stared behind him. "She was so lovely. I bet your daughter would have looked like her."

He pictured Katie when he'd first met her. She had moved to town halfway through the third grade. On her first day of school, she wore a green dress, her long red hair in braids, which she told him she hated but her mother wouldn't let her cut her hair. He envisioned the smile she had given him when she sat next to him during their history class and the laugh she had carried with her from that day until the day she died. Would their daughter have had that same laugh? Would her hair have been as long? Her smile as sweet?

"Look at her, Jacob." His mom shoved at his shoulder.

He let her turn him, and the gasp tore out of him—nothing he wanted them to hear.

On the fireplace mantel sat a framed photograph. The last one.

He had seen it there the day of the funeral and had looked away, never wanting to see the last picture of her again, never wanting to see how happy they'd been that day, never wanting to remember any part of her final hours. Somehow he'd let himself forget the photo existed.

Too late to forget again. The flood of memories burst through the dam.

The moments leading up to the flash of the camera slammed into him. Lunch with his parents at Manichello's, Katie's favorite restaurant. He and Katie had just announced they were planning to try for a baby. His mom had hugged them both, clinging to them as she cried and squealed and cried more. His dad signaled to the waitress. That's when Jay had teased Katie as he spotted the ice cream the waitress brought with the cake. He and Katie were smiling when his mom snapped the photo, Jay's arm around Katie, her hand on his knee.

Eight hours later, he sat beside a hospital gurney holding his dead wife's hand.

The guilt crashed into him. He had failed her in so many ways. Letting her leave that night. Having sex with Lincoln, developing feelings for him. Jay stared at the photo over the fireplace. Her smile wide, her eyes crinkling at the corners. The joke was several years old. He shouldn't have teased, shouldn't have said those words that he could never take back. It was late, and still he let her go. He never even said good-bye. Hadn't kissed her. Hadn't hugged her. Hadn't been there with her when she took her last breath.

But Lincoln had.

Jay sank to the chair where his mom had tried to force him earlier. He was betraying his wife—in the worst possible way.

His mom knelt beside him and gripped the wooden arm of the chair he sat in. He ignored her and kept staring at the picture. Even if he wanted to stand, to leave, he couldn't. Denial was no longer possible. The blinders were off, and he was too startled to make his escape.

When his mom finally spoke again, she said, "She would never have let your life be what it is now. Don't you see what he's taken from you? You've got nothing."

"Mom!" Todd stepped forward.

She looked up at him. "Look at what your brother's life is like. They were going to have a baby."

"She wasn't pregnant," Todd said.

Jay threw him a grateful look. The talking had to stop. He wanted to go home, crawl into bed, and forget the last two hours. Forget what he had learned about his mom. Forget what she had forced him to see.

"It doesn't matter," she said. "That would've been our first grandchild."

Jay bounded out of the chair, his legs unsteady. "You're still going to have a grandchild. Todd's baby—"

"One can't replace the other." The expression on her face demonstrated, for her, there'd be no comparisons between his and Todd's kids. Maybe Todd hadn't become the favored son after all.

The disappointment all too clear on Todd's face, he backed away from her, turned, and left the room.

"Susan," his dad said, "don't you hurt Todd over this."

Too little too late?

His dad sighed, and he went after Todd.

How much could she prove her craziness in a single day? "You're talking like a baby died with her." Jay squeezed his eyes shut, trying to clear the grief, the misery. Was there any hope of stopping her from hurting Lincoln or the man's family? Jay had one way to end this.

"I'll..." The words were harder to say than he expected. "I'll stop seeing him if you leave him alone, if you stop talking about him like he's a killer."

He could do this to protect Lincoln. Although, it was more than that. He and Lincoln had been kidding themselves spending time together, jumping into bed, pretending they'd ever be anything more than who they were, who they'd always be to each other—a widower and the man who had caused his wife's accident. They couldn't avoid that. Jay had finally opened his eyes to the reality surrounding them.

His mom stared at him, her eyebrows drawn in. She opened her mouth as if she wanted to speak and then clamped it shut again. Finally, she nodded. "I think the best thing for you is not to have that man in your life."

Jay walked away from the fireplace and his mom still kneeling on the floor, the crackling and pops of burning wood growing softer behind him. Without looking at her, he said, "It all stops, Mom. No one in this family will have anything more to do with Lincoln McCaw."

He left their house without a good-bye. He couldn't say anything else, not another word, and when he stopped off at the Late Night Paradise Plaza convenience store, he didn't speak to the clerk as he paid for the beers.

Yet, no matter how many of the beers he drank, he couldn't work up the words he'd need next. He hoped they'd come to him in the morning.

One way or the other, he had to end it with Lincoln. Time to bury the past and let them all be free.

* * * *

"I can't make it to Sonny's tonight." Jay sank farther into the couch, switched the cell to his other ear, and added, "I'm sick."

"What's wrong?" Why did Lincoln have to sound so damn good? That throaty whisper did shit to Jay, even when he hoped to avoid any sexual thoughts.

"Just a headache. Had it all day. Sorry about tonight."

"How did it go with your folks?"

"Fine."

"Fine? That's it?"

"I just called to cancel for tonight and to tell you..." *What? That my mom's a crazy psycho?*

"What?" Lincoln asked.

"No one will bother you anymore."

"How do you mean?"

"There won't be any more threats. It's over." Jay paused. "Listen, I'll give you the details later. I'm a little out of it right now. I just wanted you to know you don't have to worry."

"I understand."

Did he? How could Lincoln really? He knew nothing of the darkness Jay had fallen into since he'd recalled the last moments he'd spent with Katie. "I'll talk to you later."

"Sure," Lincoln said. "Give me a call if you need something to get you feeling good again." No missing the innuendo in the tone.

"Will do." Jay pressed the power button on his cell, flung it onto the coffee table, and draped his forearm over his eyes. There was no one else he needed to hear from.

How do you break up with someone? There were more words he needed to share with Lincoln than, "it's been fun." The man deserved to hear the truth about the threats. To hear Jay's part in the day Katie died.

Maybe he should make his mom break it off with Lincoln for him. It was her fault he'd been unable to face the man, too afraid he'd look at Lincoln differently than he had since their first night in the bar—too afraid he'd hate him even after all they'd shared.

But Lincoln didn't deserve to deal with her. And if Jay's mom kept to the bargain, he wouldn't have to again.

Hopefully, it was over. For all of them.

* * * *

"Can I come by tonight?" Lincoln asked. He squeezed the cell phone until the volume button dug into his palm. He let up. He'd just gotten the damn phone. He didn't need to bust it.

He hadn't seen Jay in a week. He longed to touch him, to kiss him, to come inside the man without a rubber like he'd been dreaming of every night. Lincoln shifted on the small bed and adjusted his cock. Blood had begun pooling south as soon as he'd dialed the number. Five days back, he had planned to ask Jay if he wanted to get tested and forgo the condoms. Lincoln was sick of dealing with the rubbers. He and Jay had been celibate for a year after both coming off monogamous relationships. It didn't pose a huge risk.

He silently laughed at that. Maybe for any other two guys things could be that simple. Not for Jay and him. Yet since the idea had crossed Lincoln's mind, he couldn't let it go.

And in the meantime, Jay had disappeared. So had the notes and threats. Maybe Jay was right when he said it was all over. Lincoln wanted to know why. He wanted to see Jay again.

"I was about to head over to Todd's," Jay said. "He's helping me work on my Jeep's brakes."

"And that's more fun than spending the night fucking?" The tone was shitty, but Lincoln couldn't control it. His sexual frustration had reached the point it'd been at when he stepped out of the jail.

No. It was worse than that. Then he didn't want sex. The release wasn't something he deserved. Now, he craved being with Jay. He ached for it.

Jay didn't respond.

"I can help you with your brakes."

"Todd said he'd do it."

"And we wouldn't want to what? Hurt Todd's feelings?"

"Don't be an ass about it."

Lincoln scoffed. He calmed himself and tried a different tack. "I miss you."

Jay's deep breath came across the line loud and clear.

"Jay?"

"I have to go, Linc."

"Jay?"

Nothing. The line went dead.

Fuck that bullshit.

"Nance," he called out and stormed into the kitchen where she worked with the kids on their homework. "Can I get a ride?"

Chapter Twenty-One

Jay tossed the empty beer bottle across the room. It bounced off the bookshelf and dropped to the floor, knocking down a couple of the books with it.

He laughed as the hardcover books hit the carpet and splayed open, pages bending here and there.

Those stupid books used to mean something to him. Most of them Katie had bought for him, scouring used bookstores, library sales, and auctions. She supported and listened to every silly idea he had about continuing on to get his master's degree and what he'd write his thesis on. He laughed again. He was a community college dropout, and those books didn't mean shit to him now. He'd keep them forever, though. Gifts from another life he'd never be able to part with.

The sound of a vehicle pulling into the driveway forced Jay to drag himself off the couch and to the window. Lincoln got out of the passenger side of a compact car that looked older than Jay and waved to Nancy as she backed out of the drive.

Great. Jay turned away from the window. He ran a hand over the two-day-old stubble on his chin. He grabbed his T-shirt off the arm of the couch and slid it on, tucking the rings underneath. The shirt smelled funky. Stains from the frozen burrito he'd forced down the night before covered the front. Better than going without a shirt. At least in front of Lincoln.

Time to get everything out in the open.

He lunged for the front door and onto the porch before Lincoln got more than a few feet up the sidewalk.

"Hey," Lincoln said.

Looking in those dark eyes, Jay lost all his resolve. He wanted to go to the man. Hold him. Kiss him. Get them naked and sink into Lincoln until everything else fell away. But he couldn't. All Jay could give Lincoln was the truth. He stepped off the porch onto the sidewalk and kicked at a pebble with the toe of his shoe. "Hey."

Lincoln joined him, both men kicking at stray stones as if there was an immediate need to clear every last inch of the concrete.

"You feeling better?" Lincoln asked.

"I think so." Jay couldn't find more stones to boot off the sidewalk. He wanted to ask Lincoln why he'd come, but he couldn't bring himself to say the question aloud. Instead he said, "It wasn't the Shaws sending you the notes. I know who it was now. They promised me they're done with it. I think they were just trying to scare you—make you sorry."

"I *am* sorry."

"I know that." One look at the man in the courtroom video recording, at the man Jay had first met in the bar, and there was no doubt about that.

Lincoln stared at Jay. "And taking Jessica's medicine? That was more than an empty threat."

"I know. It's done, though."

"How'd you manage that?"

"Doesn't matter."

Lincoln took a step closer. "You pissed at me?"

"Nah. Just got all this stuff going on with my family."

"Okay. You busy right now?"

"Told you, I'm heading over to my brother's. We're working on my Jeep."

"Tomorrow?"

"Todd's moving soon. He needs help packing up his house."

Lincoln glanced off toward the street. "I'd offer to help, but hanging out with your family doesn't seem like something we'll be doing anytime in the near future."

Yeah. That was an understatement. If Lincoln went there to help, they'd be lucky if Todd didn't call their mom over to let her have at him. Jay tried to speak. How was he supposed to tell Lincoln they were over—that whatever they were becoming had to end—for both their sakes? How could he explain that in exchange for keeping Lincoln and his family away from his mom's torture, Jay had given him up? Or that his mom had helped him see the real reason why this had to end?

"Are you done with me?" Lincoln asked.

Jay lifted his gaze "What?"

"I'm getting the impression your little gay experiment is over."

"My what?"

"You heard me." Lincoln crossed his arms, his biceps flexing, the wolf tattoo jumping with the movement. "What am I to you?"

Jay couldn't answer. He wasn't sure himself.

"I get it," Lincoln said. "No sweat, okay? I knew it was coming. We knew this could never be anything." Lincoln pulled several folded pieces of paper from his back pocket. "Thought you might want to take a look at these." He waved his other hand through the air as if the papers were no big deal.

Jay reached for them. Their hands didn't meet, but Lincoln kept his grip on his end of the pages as if he wanted to force Jay to look at him.

When Jay didn't, Lincoln released his hold, turned, and walked to the curb. Jay waited until the man was out of sight before he went into the house. He shut the door and leaned against it. Alone. Again.

The seconds ticked off on the clock above the entertainment center. The only clock in the house that ran on batteries. How long would it keep on chugging away until it finally died without Katie there to tend to it?

His stomach in knots, Jay wandered across the living room. The lack of breakfast and the beers he'd drank made vomiting a possibility. Was it always this shitty to break up with someone? No. This was about more than that. This was about losing his first chance at happiness in a year—his first chance at more than he imagined he'd have again.

He stared at the books he'd knocked to the floor. He picked one up and set it on the shelf. Only then did he remember the papers in his other hand. Information on the history and education programs at Indiana University's Fort Wayne campus. He read several lines from the history brochure. The pages blurred, and the small type jumped on the page. He tossed the materials onto the coffee table.

The glasses he needed for reading and hadn't used in months were in his nightstand drawer. He held them under the light of the bedside lamp and grimaced at the dust and fingerprints covering the lenses. He wiped them on his shirttail, and when that proved no help, he rinsed them in the bathroom sink and used a towel to dry them. He went back into the living room, flicked on the lamp, and fetched the papers.

A half hour later, he had read and reread every word. Lincoln had marked three Native American history courses, and Jay liked what he read.

He scooped up the pages he'd scattered across the coffee table and headed for the office in the back of the house. He turned on the computer. There'd be no hope of reading anything through the one-quarter-inch layer of dust on the monitor's screen, so he went in search of something to dust with. He hadn't done much cleaning in the past year, and when he had cleaned, it was to sweep the visible dirt and crumbs from the floor and throw the dirty dishes into the dishwasher. Dusting was a bit fancier than he got. Didn't he have one of those feather things that sucked up the dust like a magnet picks up paper clips? Todd had used it once when he said Jay's TV was too dust-covered to watch football. Todd hadn't stopped with the TV. He'd proceeded to dust the entire house.

Jay found the blue feather duster under the sink in the kitchen and used it to clean the computer screen. By the time he finished, the system had booted. Good thing he hadn't canceled his cable bill. Included in the monthly package was his Internet access.

When he'd been in school over a year ago, he planned to transfer to a four-year college after completing his associate's degree. Three universities within driving distance offered teaching programs. The Fort Wayne campus was the closest. At the time of the accident, Jay had been a year away from transferring and hadn't checked into the specifics of each school. Once Katie was gone, he didn't give a shit about any of it.

After reading the papers Lincoln had brought, he craved more information. He searched the university's Web site for course catalogs, application materials, and student financial aid programs.

He read a detailed description for a Native American course titled Family Units. It reminded Jay of something he'd read in high school. He opened another browser window and did a search for Iroquois customs and myths. When he came across a list sorted by category, he clicked on the heading "The Importance of Uncle." He read the page.

Just as he thought. There was more of his grandfather in Lincoln than the man realized.

* * * *

"No more smoking, Adam. None!"

Lincoln stepped into the house and winced at Nancy's shouted words. He folded over the top of the paper sack with the bottle of Jack inside. The television set was on but the living room was empty. The voices carried down the hall.

"Why?" Adam screamed. "Uncle Lincoln smokes, and you don't say nothing to him."

He knew that was coming. Might as well face the music. She'd have at him later anyway, and he needed to have a talk with Adam.

"It doesn't matter what your uncle does," she said. "You're my son."

Lincoln dropped off the paper sack in Davy's room and went to stand in front of Adam's open door. The kid was sitting on his bed, his thumbs moving over the buttons on his cell phone. Did the kid text twenty-four/seven? Lincoln hadn't known enough people in his entire life to message so damn much.

"You have to think before you act," Nancy said. "Your little brother looks up to you."

Adam rolled his eyes and went back to his typing. "Jeez, Mom. It's not my fault. You cram him in my room like I'm some sort of kid. I can't be responsible for what Davy's gonna do."

"Yeah, you are," Lincoln said as he entered the room. "That's how life works."

Adam looked at him for a moment, then shut the phone and flung it onto the bed beside him.

Nancy returned her attention to her son. "Your actions have consequences. It's not healthy for you. It's not healthy for your family."

The cell phone beeped. Adam rolled his eyes at his mom's words and picked up the phone. A quick read of the screen and he tapped buttons again. "I get it. Cigarettes kill. Nicotine is addictive. Blah blah blah." He spoke the words in a singsong mock of every public service announcement on the subject. His thumbs never stopped the texting.

Lincoln marched across the room and yanked the cell out of Adam's clutches.

"Hey!" Adam whirled onto his knees and grabbed for the phone.

Lincoln kept it out of reach. "Show some respect. Do you know how hard your mom works? How much she sacrifices for you kids?"

"Right. Her life sucks 'cause she got pregnant when she was eighteen. I got the message."

Nancy stepped closer to the bed. "I never said my life sucks. I wouldn't trade you kids for anything."

"Mom, I'm not going to mess up." Adam gave her a pleading look. "I hung out with the guys and tried a smoke. No big deal." He glared at Lincoln. "I listened to the lecture. Can I have my phone back?"

Lincoln shoved the cell into his pocket and folded his arms over his chest. "Not a chance. I haven't given *my* lecture."

Adam's eyes widened, and he sank onto his heels.

"Your sister has trouble breathing as it is. She doesn't need you smoking around here."

Adam opened his mouth to speak, but Lincoln held up a hand to stop him.

"Yeah, I've been smoking since I got back, but I'm damn careful about it. I never smoke in the house, and I always change and wash up when I get home. It's a bad habit, and I'm quitting. I haven't smoked in days. You don't need to start something that isn't healthy for you, something you'll have to watch yourself with around Jessica. It's reckless. It's stupid—"

"I'm not stupid." Adam jumped off the bed and went to the door. He held it open as if the action would give the adults a clue about leaving him alone.

Lincoln didn't budge. "I didn't mean you're stupid."

"Can't you trust me?"

Lincoln moved to stand in front of him. "This isn't about trust. This is about expecting you to start acting like a grown man. To think before you make a mistake that'll hurt your sister." Lincoln clenched his jaw. He needed to shut the hell up. He was not the person Adam needed to hear shit like that from.

Adam met his gaze. "I wouldn't hurt her."

"I know. I just don't want you to make a mistake and regret it later."

The words seemed to penetrate. Adam's posture eased, and he nodded. "Can I have my cell now?"

Lincoln handed over the phone and stepped into the hall with Nancy. Had he made a mistake? He'd never been that hard on the kid. Smoking wasn't the worst thing in the world. There were a lot bigger mistakes the kid could make.

Adam shut his door without another word, and Nancy glared at Lincoln. "I was handling it."

"He needs a father." He needed someone whose advice wouldn't sound like a hypocrite talking.

"Well, there's nothing I can do about that."

"I didn't say it was your fault." Lincoln headed for the living room. "It just pisses me off."

She followed. "He doesn't need a father. It would've been nice, yeah, but he has me. And you. Even when you move out, you're still his uncle, and no one is a better role model for him."

Lincoln plopped onto the couch. "Jail. Smoking. Booze. Unprotected sex. Explain how I'm a good role model?"

"You're a great uncle, a great brother. You take care of us better than anyone. We wouldn't have a place to live without you."

"Kids don't see that shit. He sees an uncle who served six months." Lincoln hated feeling sorry for himself, but it kept pouring out of him. Nancy always drew out the raw truth. Nancy and Jay.

"We're back to this? Why don't you—wait!" She sat beside him. "Unprotected sex? It's that serious?"

Not likely. "We're through. He doesn't want me."

"Bullshit." She lowered her tone. "I've never seen anyone want you more. Not even Paul looked at you the way Jay does."

Lincoln snorted.

"You don't believe me? You may have been with Paul for seven years, but he didn't once do for you what Jay's done in a couple of months."

"Leave it alone." He pushed off the couch and went to the kitchen. He got a beer out of the fridge, opened it, and played with the bottle's label under his thumb.

"Lincoln?" she called out from the next room.

"Dammit, Nance." He slammed the refrigerator door shut. "It's over."

Silence. A minute later she stood at the kitchen doorway. "Why don't you call him?"

"I can't lose anything else." He gripped the refrigerator handle. "If I let him in, and he walks for good..." He didn't want to explain all the reasons they'd never last. He went to Nancy and tucked a stray strand of hair behind her ear. "Thanks for trying. I'm quitting the smokes for good, okay? I'll make sure Adam knows that. And Davy can have his room back. Give Adam space to be a teenager."

She looked ready to argue.

"I'm not going anywhere," he said.

She gave a reluctant smile and said, "Okay."

He kissed her forehead and handed over his opened beer before heading down the hall. He slid the duffel bag out from under the bed and crammed in two days' worth of clothes and the bottle of Jack he'd stopped off for after leaving Jay's house.

He checked the windows and locked all the doors in the house. The sleeping bag from the garage tucked under his arm, he climbed the stairs to the unfinished room above. There were worse places to sleep. He spread the sleeping bag out on the floor and opened the whiskey. And better ways to keep his thoughts at bay.

Jay had been one of those ways.

Now that he was gone, the dreams would return. Better to hold them off.

Lincoln stretched out on the sleeping bag and tilted back the Jack. Better to keep everything and everyone at bay. It's what he should have done all along.

Chapter Twenty-Two

"How long have you known you wanted to sleep with men?"

Jay choked on the green beans he'd managed to force into his mouth. He hadn't been able to eat much of the chicken and stuffing on his plate. His stomach had been in knots since his dad had called three hours earlier and asked to meet.

When was the last time Jay and his dad had done anything alone? Nothing came to mind.

His dad had chosen a diner one town north of Edgefield. They sat in a booth in the back, and his dad had talked about his plans for a summer blowout sale at the store between bites of food while the waitress came by with refills for their coffees. His dad had flashed her a wide grin and offered a thank-you, bantering with her in a way Jay had never witnessed his father do before. Maybe his mom sucked all the life out of the man. Must have been how his dad had success running his business for all those years. By not letting his wife in the door.

Eating the beans was supposed to be safe. They couldn't make Jay too sick to his stomach. They could, however, get stuck in his throat. He swallowed and a coughing fit ensued.

His dad half stood, leaned over the table, and smacked him on the back.

Jay held up a hand and reached for his glass of water. His dad sat and didn't say anything more on the topic of Jay's sexuality. The vinyl of the booth's bench squeaked as Jay shifted his weight. How had he picked the squeaky side and his dad's seat didn't make a sound when the man moved? Would Jay ever make another decision in his life that wasn't fucked-up?

The cool water eased his throat with each swallow. He kept at it. What was he supposed to say? *I always knew I wanted dick, Dad, but I loved my wife so I held it in check?*

Not the best response. He kept downing the water. Maybe

something else would come to him before he got to the bottom of the glass.

The waitress came by the table again and filled his dad's coffee cup to the brim. "Need anything else?"

His dad glanced at Jay. "More water for my son. He's going to need it." He leaned forward and whispered, "I have more questions."

Jay sputtered out a laugh and almost dropped his glass to the table. The water failed to escape his nose, but it was close.

His dad smirked at him as the waitress made quick work refilling Jay's water. "So?" he said when she'd left the table.

"I guess I always knew." Jay reached for the water glass, and the seat squeaked again. He set the glass on the table without taking a drink. "I loved her."

"I never suggested you didn't. She's not here and you are. You have to move on with your life. You're not even twenty-three. You deserve a future. A family."

"I know."

"And this man—"

"He's not...we're not together."

"Not because of your mother, I hope." His dad glanced around the diner, then said, "Because of what he did? Because of the accident?"

Jay didn't respond. He didn't want to think about the reasons again, didn't want to give Lincoln much thought at all. If he did, he might not be able to convince himself to stay away.

His dad took a long sip of his coffee and sat back. "Your mother doesn't know I called you." He paused as if searching for the precise words to say something Jay wouldn't want to hear. "It haunts her, what your life might have been."

No secrets there.

"She was so excited that day. All the way home talking about being a grandma, about babysitting, and buying a stroller. She was specific on the stroller. She wanted one with a detachable car seat so it'd be easy for you to bring the baby to see us."

"Todd—"

"Yes. But for some reason it's different for her, and you know it. You're her baby. And even though we didn't want you to get married so young, she loved your wife. She saw this perfect future for you. The accident destroyed that dream."

Jay stared into his dad's eyes and saw a man he didn't recognize. Softer, more understanding than before, or more so than Jay had ever noticed.

His dad continued. "She just doesn't understand. Hell, I didn't understand. I've given it thought, though. A lot of thought, actually. That you could befriend that man, have a relationship with him—" He shook his head. "You're a good man, Jay. And I'm okay with you being gay. The rest of it...well, if you keep seeing him, it might take time on my part, but I want you to be happy."

"I don't know if—"

"He's good for you."

"What?"

"You've been different."

Nancy had said the same thing about him being good for Lincoln. They were both right. "He is."

"I'm afraid your mother will never understand that."

"I can't live for her."

"No one is asking you to."

But the deal Jay had made with his mom couldn't be undone, could it?

His dad drank his coffee and didn't offer anything else. Maybe he had said all he could. It was miles from where Jay imagined the man to be.

Jay wanted to talk more, to ask his dad if he knew about the threats, if he knew what she'd been doing, but he couldn't bring himself to ask that question. Instead, he chose another.

"Dad, what did you do with your share of the money from the lawsuit?"

His dad sighed and sat back, the vinyl finally squeaking under his shifting weight. "The store's been losing a lot of money over the past few years. We used most of it to pay off some debts and a second mortgage we had to take out on the house. The store doesn't carry any computer equipment, and there just isn't the same demand for office supplies as there used to be. I haven't wanted to admit it, but the store isn't going to survive unless I change my way of thinking—change what I envisioned for the place."

"Sorry. I hope it works out."

His dad leaned forward and said, "I hope the same for you, Jay."

Jay nodded and stood. "Thanks for dinner. And for the rest." He took a couple of steps from the table, then stopped, and added, "I won't visit the cemetery next time. It's not how I want to remember her. I can't go there..." He wanted to say "ever again," but he couldn't bring himself to admit that.

His dad rose and laid a tip on the table. "It's okay." He came to Jay and placed a hand on his shoulder. "I'll talk to her."

Would she listen? Had she ever?

What would his mom do if Jay didn't keep his end of the bargain? What would she do if he saw Lincoln again?

It didn't matter. Despite the conversation with his dad and how much Jay still wanted Lincoln, he couldn't take a chance. All he could do was offer Lincoln the truth. Tell him about the threats, about the night of the accident, about the real reasons they couldn't be together. He owed Lincoln that.

* * * *

"Are you the new boyfriend?" the teenager holding the door open asked.

Not as easy a question as it sounded. "I'm Jay."

The kid gave a nod and said, "Adam."

"It's nice to finally meet you."

"Same here."

"Your uncle has a lot of good things to say about you."

Adam let go of the door and looked down at the floor, but he couldn't hide the smile.

"Adam, who is it?" Nancy stepped up behind the kid and spotted Jay. "Oh. I've got this. Go on to your room."

The kid walked away, and Jay asked, "Is he home?" His low, timid voice unnerved him. The truth had always come easily to him. Why was facing Lincoln so hard?

"He's in the garage working on the room upstairs." Nancy moved aside and held the door open for Jay.

He entered and headed for the kitchen.

"Please don't hurt him. He's been through enough."

Jay faced her. "I'm not trying to hurt him." *I'm trying to help him. Trying to do the right thing.*

"But if you think you might, maybe you can just go." She brushed a strand of hair out of her eyes. She wouldn't look at Jay. "Before he falls for you more than he already has."

He wanted her to understand he didn't have a choice. He didn't want to lose someone else, but he couldn't betray his wife anymore. Wasn't that what he'd been doing?

Katie would not want Lincoln to suffer. And she wouldn't want Jay to be alone. Yet, even with those truths, Jay owed her something. He owed her respect for the life they had shared, respect for the future they'd lost.

"I'm not sure we can... I have to talk to him."

Nancy met his stare and nodded.

Jay thanked her, and took off for the garage. Someone had picked up the place. No stray tools. No rags they'd used on the bike. The Harley was under the tarp again, hidden away. He climbed the steps two at a time and found Lincoln hammering a piece of drywall in place. One look at the lines of Lincoln's bare back, the curves of muscles accentuating his arms, the determined focus on the man's body as he worked to secure the board, and all Jay's concerns and the words so important a moment ago vanished.

He couldn't let go of Lincoln. The man who eased him with a single look, who made him feel safe and alive, who had listened and cared when it had to have killed him to hear about her. Lincoln was the best man Jay had ever known. There had to be a way to make what they had last.

Lincoln hefted another drywall sheet to the wall, a hole already cut for an electrical outlet. He positioned the board, and held it in place with one hand, while tapping hammer to nail with the other.

The drywall panel slipped. Jay crossed the room and held up the opposite end of the board. Lincoln stared at him, his eyebrows drawn in, several nails sticking out between his lips. Jay's heart raced; he longed to step closer. To touch Lincoln. Hold him. Anything.

Without a word, Lincoln looked away, slid a nail out of his mouth, and pounded it into the wall. He hammered in several more nails until the board was secured. They each took a step back and watched the wall, as if they had to give it a few minutes to make certain the board wouldn't slip.

Jay couldn't glance away from it. As soon as he'd left the diner, he knew he had to talk to Lincoln. He owed the man an explanation. Now, all he wanted was a kiss, a touch, a look. Would Lincoln still want anything with him? Could they manage it with everything between them? He gave up on the board and watched Lincoln out of the corner of his eye. "It's looking good in here."

Lincoln grunted, but still wouldn't so much as glance at Jay again.

"Thanks for the college information. It was fascinating."

"You should go back to school." Lincoln walked to the other side of the room and dropped the hammer into the toolbox sitting near the door. "You're too smart not to." He breathed deep, and his back tensed. He finally faced Jay.

It was Jay's turn not to make eye contact. Across the room, the sleeping bag lay spread open on the floor. Next to it: a duffel bag with clothes sticking out the top, and a half-empty bottle of Jack Daniel's lying on its side. "You're sleeping up here?"

"Adam deserved to have some space." Lincoln wiped sweat from his brow with the side of a fist and added, "He's in high school," as if he'd just figured that out.

"I owe you an explanation."

Lincoln scoffed and said, "You don't. I knew from the moment you told me your name this would never last."

"I want it to."

"Christ." Lincoln strode to where he'd been working and picked up a box of nails. "Don't say that shit to me." He crossed the room again and jammed the box on top of the tools. Any more force and he'd have rammed the nails through the thin cardboard and into his palm.

"I have to." Jay stepped closer.

"Why are you here?"

"I need to explain. About everything." Another step. "It was my mom."

Lincoln nodded. He returned to the half-finished wall, grabbed a utility knife off the floor, and slammed it on top of the nails in the toolbox. "I'm not going to the cops. You say she's done, I believe you." Lincoln lifted his head and looked at Jay, those dark eyes serious. Frustrated. Hurt.

Jay advanced. For the second time in his life, he didn't give a shit what anyone else said about his choice in a lover. He seized Lincoln by the waist and crushed his mouth to the other man's. Lincoln spread his lips and grabbed hold of Jay. No hesitation. No delay. Everything faded but the strength of that kiss, the power, the depth, the drive of man against man.

The clutching, the clawing at clothes, the rocking of bodies, the heat of tongue on tongue—it was gloriously distracting. Jay wasn't aware they were moving until Lincoln lowered him to the sleeping bag. The slight separation of their bodies as they lay down was too much.

Jay tugged Lincoln closer. "I need you."

Lincoln pressed his body against Jay in all the right places, but they still had their clothes on. Jay would've done something about it. But he couldn't stop the kissing, the touching, for anything.

Good thing Lincoln had better ideas. He pulled back and ripped open his own jeans then Jay's. He shoved his hands down the front of their pants and released their pricks. Draping his body over Jay's, he planted a hand on either side of Jay's head, and thrust his hips forward as he came in for another kiss.

The slide of their shafts, the taste of Lincoln, the touch, the smell of him—more intense, better than any fuck they'd had so far.

Yet, right then, Jay wanted to give Lincoln more. "Wait."

Maybe Lincoln didn't hear him. He kept driving forward.

Jay arched his back and pushed his pelvis against Lincoln's, a contrast to his next word. "Stop."

Lincoln stilled. Their bodies still fused together, he dropped his forehead to Jay's shoulder and exhaled, the warm breath hitting the sensitive skin of Jay's neck. "We have to stop?" he asked in a low whisper.

"God, no. I want more. I want you naked. Want you to make love to me."

Lincoln's breath hitched. He rose up. "Get your clothes off. I've got lube in my bag." He rolled away and worked his jeans off.

Jay did the same and lay naked on the sleeping bag while Lincoln searched through his duffel bag full of possessions. He came back with a condom and lube. Jay didn't have to give it thought. As easy as breathing. He stole the condom and flung it like a Frisbee across the room. The small package ricocheted off the newly constructed wall.

The *smack* of it hitting the floor pierced the silence that had fallen over them. Lincoln stared where it had landed. When he finally moved, he rolled slowly atop Jay, their legs, hips, groins touching. He held Jay's face in his hand, swiping a thumb over his lower lip. "Are you sure?"

"Yes." Jay ducked his head and sucked on the tip of Lincoln's thumb. "Want to feel you like that. No one else but you."

The kiss came fast and hard, and Jay couldn't breathe by the time it ended. Good thing Lincoln wanted him too much to wait for long. The man sat back on his heels. He slathered lube on his cock and more between Jay's spread ass cheeks, penetrating him with those thick, strong fingers. Jay would never tire of Lincoln's hands, the strength of his touch. He spread his legs and lifted them as he scooted toward Lincoln, offering himself in what should have felt like a ridiculously blatant, wanton move, but didn't. It felt like the truest thing he'd ever done. He wanted to see Lincoln while they made love, wanted to watch the man's face as he came inside Jay with nothing in the way for the first time.

The only time?

No. Jay wouldn't think about that, couldn't think about anything but feeling Lincoln—all of him.

Lincoln stared at Jay's spread thighs then slowly raised his head. "This is what you want?"

"Yes." Jay stroked the side of Lincoln's face. A loving gesture. One he couldn't explain to either of them. "I'm scared."

"We don't have to. Just let me get the rubber and you can roll over."

"Not that."

"Oh." Lincoln's gaze fell to the rings on Jay's chest. "Of feeling something for the man who destroyed your life?"

Jay sat up and cupped Lincoln's cheek in his hand. "Don't say that. I don't want to hurt anymore. What if this doesn't work? What if it can't work?"

"All we can do is try." Lincoln kissed the palm of his hand. "If you can take a chance, I can."

"I think I have to."

Lincoln surged forward until they lay back on the floor again. He kissed Jay, a sweet slide of tongue over lips and said, "You're the bravest person I've ever known." He shifted his hips, lifting Jay's legs higher with the change, and entered him.

He began a slow, sensual rock, and Jay moved with him, loving the slide of body to body with nothing between them any longer.

If only there were nothing else between them in every other way.

* * * *

Lincoln's ass was cold, and his hip tender where he'd lain on his side all night. He had to hurry and get a bed. He couldn't keep sleeping on the floor. Then it came to him. He'd done more than sleep on the floor. And that had him smiling.

They'd had sex twice the night before. Once before falling asleep. Again when Lincoln had awakened from an erotic dream full of Jay-flavored blowjobs. He hadn't bothered to wake Jay. He straddled the man and drew cock into mouth. A few pulls of his lips and one long suck of the crown, and Jay woke up. The words, "Oh. My. God," were all Lincoln understood before Jay started moaning.

It urged him on. He sucked Jay to climax, then stroked himself until he came on Jay's abdomen. Jay lazily ran his fingers through the cum and smeared it over the tattoo on Lincoln's arm. Lincoln joined him, spreading the cum around Jay's nipples, then collapsed on Jay, both men laughing until the sated drowsiness claimed them.

The best night of his life.

Lincoln opened his eyes and smiled again. Jay still lay next to him on the unzipped sleeping bag, a sheet Lincoln had been using as a blanket spread across them. Jay was lying on his stomach, facing away from him. The sheet barely covered the top of Jay's ass. Lincoln reached out and caressed his bare back. The flesh jumped at his touch, and a low moan from Jay had Lincoln's morning hard-on stiffening more.

"I miss the robots," Jay said, then laughed as he turned his head to face Lincoln. He rested a cheek on his forearm. "At least the bed was softer than this sleeping bag."

"Won't take much more to get the room done."

"It'll be great." Jay rolled onto his side and glanced around. "Not much space, though."

"Yeah, but it's private." Lincoln wound his arm around Jay and pulled him close. "I've got to start over. Get my life back on track."

"I'd like to help."

Lincoln buried his nose in Jay's hair, taking in the scent of shampoo, sweat, and cum. His fingers had been damp with it when he'd run them through Jay's hair as they fell asleep.

He'd been so easily distracted. One kiss from Jay, and Lincoln would do anything to keep seeing him. But was it the right thing to do? "You shouldn't want to help me. It doesn't make sense."

Jay took Lincoln's face in his hands and kissed him. "We'll figure it out."

He wanted to protest, wanted to be strong for Jay, pull away if it was what was best, but most of all, he wanted Jay.

He was losing his mind. Sex and attraction and laughter and friendship—it was all making him comfortable. Happy. Delusional?

Jay smiled. And Lincoln didn't give a shit about delusions. He wanted more of that smile, of Jay's laugh.

And he got it. After Jay's stomach growled, he laughed again.

"Hungry?"

"Uh, maybe." Then Jay's face grew serious. "I haven't been eating much."

Lincoln rubbed a hand over Jay's abs, and the man shivered.

He'd never get used to Jay's reactions. No one had ever been so open, so there in every moment. "I'll see what we have to eat." He kissed Jay's forehead and sat up. "Wait here."

"No. Come here." Jay tugged him to the sleeping bag. "Let's go to my place. We'll lounge around all day. Eat. Sex. Sleep. TV. Repeat."

"Sounds good. But I've seen your house. You have no food. Or dishes. Or a clean place to eat."

"But we'll be alone. Your clean dishes and food come with three children and a sister."

"Good point. I love those kids, but they do cramp a guy's love life."

Love life?

He was going to scare Jay. But the man didn't look scared as he ran his thumb over Lincoln's mouth. He caressed lower, moving his fingers down Lincoln's neck, past his shoulder to the tattoo, tracing the lines of the eagle feather. "You're a great uncle." He kept moving his fingers over and around the inked skin.

Lincoln wasn't sure the way Jay touched him was a good thing. They were moving far beyond "let's try to make this work" and were slamming headfirst into a love affair he didn't think he'd ever want to give up. He picked up his underwear and stood to dress.

Jay asked, "Did you know the Iroquois used to value the uncle more than the father?"

Lincoln zipped his jeans closed, then spread out on his stomach beside Jay. "What are you talking about?"

"A lot of times, the father didn't live with his children. Extended families on the mother's side lived together. The uncle filled the role of father and was more important to the kids than their biological father. The term 'uncle' held great respect."

"Is that true?"

"Uh-huh. I looked it up."

"You—when?"

"The other day. I remembered a book of Native American customs and myths I'd read in high school that mentioned it. It reminded me of you and the kids."

Lincoln tried to pretend moisture wasn't building in his eyes.

Yeah. There was no way to avoid it. He was in love with Jay Miller.

Chapter Twenty-Three

"Beer?"

Jay shook his head. "I don't need any. You?" He held his breath as he waited.

Lincoln replaced the six-pack in the cooler and readjusted his armload of chips and hot dogs. "Me neither."

A wave of relief crashed into Jay. He didn't like thinking of Lincoln drinking alone in the room above the garage for the past week. The man had been through enough.

Hadn't they all?

Lincoln stepped up to him. "I don't suppose you have ketchup or mustard for the dogs?" The tone he used to ask the question didn't fit the words. More like he asked for a blowjob right there in aisle five of the Edgefield Super Value.

Jay laughed. It felt good, so he did it again. They were alone in the aisle. He shifted the hot dog buns and corn chips to his left arm and reached out to swipe his thumb over Lincoln's bottom lip, a promise for later. "If I have any in the fridge, we wouldn't want to use it. I'll go grab some."

It required all his willpower to turn and step away from Lincoln. Silly. But a year of misery had him craving the company, craving the relaxed ease of being with Lincoln. Jay forced himself to move and hustled down the aisle. He thought he heard his name behind him, but not in Lincoln's low voice, so he kept moving. Funny how familiar that sound was to him now. He made quick work of grabbing the condiments, stopped off for a basket to carry their load, and headed to the aisle where he'd left Lincoln. He rounded the corner and almost dropped the basket full of groceries.

At the other end of the aisle was Emily Shaw, standing motionless, staring up at Lincoln.

Jay took a shaky step, then another. Lincoln spotted him first. The look on the man's face was pure panic. Of course he knew who she was. He'd seen her at the courthouse for the arraignment and sentencing, neither of which Jay had gone to.

Jay quickened his pace. "Emily?"

She turned to him. "Jay." There was no anger in her voice. "I tried to catch you, but you were running in the other direction. I figured I'd wait with your..." She gestured to Lincoln but didn't look at him. "I didn't know the two of you were friends."

The basket slipped from Jay's hand and fell to the floor, tipping over, the ketchup bottle smashing the buns, the chips crunching underneath.

Emily held out a hand to Lincoln. "Emily Shaw."

Lincoln looked at her hand but didn't move. He raised his gaze to Jay, his eyes asking for something. For help? For permission?

Jay nodded, and Lincoln shook her hand.

"Lincoln McCaw."

The name hung in the air, like a new melody for an old song. Jay didn't want to hear the hatred and disgust of the original. Not any longer. That was written for a man who didn't exist.

Emily watched Lincoln. Her eyes moved rapidly, scanning his face. Jay wanted to demand she stop. She'd never find what she looked for, not in Lincoln.

The silence continued on. Oddly, Jay couldn't break it. Finally, she faced him. Without speaking, he pleaded his case, pleaded for her understanding. She broke her stare and glimpsed the items in the basket at his feet.

"You're off to have lunch. I won't keep you. It was nice to see you, Jay." She stared at Lincoln again, and her mouth curved up at the corners. Jay had never seen her smile like that. Her smiles were usually poised, perfect, contrived. This one was sad, with a hint of something else. Confusion? Resignation?

She dropped her head and rounded the corner for the next aisle.

"She knew." Lincoln slumped and sat on the edge of the beer cooler.

"Yeah. Before you said your name, I think. After, for sure."

"I recognized her right off. She just walked up to me after you left."

"What did she say?"

"Nothing. Until you got here." Lincoln glanced at the stack of beers inside the cooler beside him. "I expected... I don't know. More."

"Me too." Jay didn't want to think on what that meant or what

Emily had thought about seeing him and Lincoln together. The time for truths was long overdue.

How could he explain to everyone what he wanted? How was he supposed to convince his mom to leave Lincoln alone? How could he tell her he had no intention of keeping their deal?

* * * *

"Uncle Linc."

"Yeah?"

Adam stood in the hallway between the living room and the kitchen. "Can I ask you a question?"

Lincoln tossed the newspaper he'd been reading onto the coffee table. "Of course."

"When did you know you were gay?"

So much for reading the sports section. Lincoln gathered the rest of the paper from the couch and tossed it onto the table. "About your age." Talking to the kids about sex wasn't something he wanted to do, but he wouldn't lie to them. There was too much important shit for them to know. If they wouldn't ask Nancy, then he'd give them the facts. He just wished he had more knowledge on the sex-with-women thing. Then again, Adam wasn't asking him about women, was he?

Adam sat beside Lincoln and said, "Did you get beat up?"

"Once or twice."

"They must have been big guys."

Lincoln laughed. "Sometimes it's not about size. It's about how many. There something you want to talk about, kid?"

Adam pulled his cell out of his back pocket, scrolled through a couple of messages, then flipped it shut and tossed it onto the coffee table. Lincoln had all day. He'd just wait until Adam could work up the nerve to get out whatever he wanted to say.

"Yeah, I guess." Adam crossed his arms over his chest and sank farther into the couch. "The other day I was arguing with this guy Troy after gym class about dirt track racing. He said the rules for each series—weight limits, the engine, the tires—are all the same. And that's bullshit. They're all different. Everyone knows that." He bit the side of his thumbnail.

"You had it right."

"I knew it, and he kept arguing with me. Then this scrawny kid I've never talked to before backed me up, said my uncle was a driver, and I'd know what I was talking about. Troy and his friends got pissed. They pushed the kid down and kicked at him. Bloodied him up good."

"Not just because he agreed with you?"

"No."

"'Cause he's gay?"

"I don't know. They called him a fag. Everybody calls him a fag."

"What'd you do?"

Adam sat taller. "Nothing! Honest!"

"But maybe you should have?"

He was quiet for a minute. "You mean, I should've helped him? But then they'd think I was a..."

"Fag?"

"Sorry." Adam slouched onto the couch again, his arms folded in a pissed-off pose Lincoln had used plenty of times. The kid wasn't pissed at anyone but himself. He shook his head. "I guess I did the wrong thing."

"Only you can answer that."

"I guess...someone wanted to help me, and when he needed me, all I thought about was myself." He threw his arms in the air, and his hands landed on his thighs with a smack. "I just didn't want to get suspended again. Mom would've killed me. They might've expelled me if I got into another fight."

"I understand that. But sometimes you have to do what you know is right, despite the consequences."

"Yeah, I get it."

"You never said what that first fight was about."

He shrugged and sank back to the couch again. "It wasn't a big deal."

"Must have been important enough to fight about."

"Someone just said some shit to me." He looked away.

Just as Lincoln had guessed. Maybe Adam hadn't changed all that much after all. "About me?"

Adam nodded. "He said since you raced and knew what you were doing, they should've sent you to prison for the rest of your life." He faced Lincoln. "Which is bullshit. I looked it up online. Most people don't serve any time at all. It's only 'cause you raced."

"Yeah. But I don't want you fighting over me, no matter what."

"Thought you said some things are worth fighting for? Isn't family one of them?"

The kid was also smarter than he let most people know. Lincoln nodded and tapped the kid's knee with the side of his fist. "Anyone who means something to you is worth it."

Adam rose and crossed the room. He stopped beside the couch. "Jay seems cool."

Lincoln laughed. "He is."

"He's uh, kinda young."

"Yeah?"

"Uh…duh. He's closer to my age than yours."

"Hey!" Lincoln grabbed the sports section off the coffee table and tossed it at Adam who successfully dodged the newspaper.

"I'm just sayin'." Adam laughed as he headed for the hall again.

"Adam."

He stopped. "Yeah?"

"It's good you see your mistake. Mistakes help you figure out what kind of man you want to be."

Lincoln almost missed the next words as Adam turned away. "I want to be like you."

Damn, if that didn't hit him in the heart. He'd never been more thankful he'd agreed to live there. Maybe Nancy was right. Maybe the kids didn't need a father. Maybe Jay had been right too. Maybe Lincoln could be what they needed.

But Adam had said something that hit a nerve too. Lincoln should be more like the kid. Not vice versa.

Time to face the truth.

Chapter Twenty-Four

Jay sat in the living room of the Shaws' home, Stuart Shaw on the sofa opposite him. Neither man spoke.

Magazines and newspapers were piled into a large, uneven stack beside the couch. A sewing basket sat on a table beside a chair. Several blouses were wadded up next to the basket. The room no longer smelled of lemon furniture polish. It reeked of dust. And sweat? A binder lay on the coffee table. A football playbook open to a printed diagram of a play. Maybe Stuart's entire college team had sweated on the pages while they huddled around the notebook, memorizing the play for their next game. Funny how the book was sitting out even though Jay had called ahead for the visit.

Not funny was what else was sitting out. A framed photo of Katie at her high school graduation. Jay hadn't seen that picture in over a year.

"Sorry about the house," Stuart said. "She's finally grieving. Really grieving."

Was that a good turn of events? Jay was doing his best to move on, and Emily Shaw had decided it was time to lose it. How could Jay explain what she'd seen the other day?

She entered the room with a tray of coffee cups and gave a slight smile as she passed one to Jay, but the smile faded with a deep breath as she sat on the couch beside her husband. They looked battered. Wrinkled. Hard. When had they aged? Emily had crow's-feet forming at the corners of her eyes. She wore dress slacks and a blouse, both wrinkled like she'd worn the same clothes all week. Stuart had fared worse. His eyes were squinted to slits and deep lines crossed his forehead. There were also signs of a thinning hairline. How had Jay not noticed the changes in them before?

Silence filled the room as they drank their coffee. Jay didn't know what to say, and the Shaws, it seemed, didn't either.

But Jay had to speak. For them. For himself. For Lincoln.

"I feel bad I haven't visited more. By myself."

"We're glad you're here now," Emily said. "Aren't we?"

Stuart didn't answer but gave a slight nod.

"I was surprised to meet your friend at the grocery store," she added. "I wasn't aware you knew him."

"I imagine not." The words left Jay's mouth harsher than he intended. He didn't want to be angry anymore, didn't want there to be only grief that held them together. A part of him didn't want to lose the Shaws in his life. They had given him Katie. He owed them something.

"Does he know who you are?" Emily asked.

"He does."

"It seemed... Well, you were touching him. And the way he looked at you... It seemed you were more than—"

"What?" Stuart's eyes shot open wide.

She didn't answer him.

"Emily?"

She swung her gaze to her husband, then back to Jay. "It seemed like you were intimate. Like lovers."

"What?" Stuart's eyes widened as he glared at Jay. "You're gay?"

Jay opened his mouth to explain, and the other man cut him off.

"What was our daughter to you?"

"I loved her. I'll always love her."

"But you're sleeping with this man?" Stuart teetered on the edge of the sofa, his body looming large before Jay. Even with Todd's warning, he hadn't believed that Stuart Shaw might actually hit him. Stupid. The man spent his career slamming into people for money and now trained the next generation to do the same.

"It's more than that," Jay said.

Emily set her cup and saucer on the table. The loud clink of porcelain to wood didn't match the graceful movement of her hands. "It looked like it might be."

Odd how the delicate pink and white fine china hadn't broken with the force she'd used to set it down. Even stranger how Jay's life seemed more fragile than the china. Was he going to lose everything to be with Lincoln? "I want to keep seeing him. I want a future with him."

Her jaw dropped. Stuart stood and strode across the room to the large picture window. A flock of birds sitting in the bush outside took flight as he drew near. Jay stared at the man's tense back. He had expected anger, yelling, disappointment.

Not the silence.

Emily's calm whisper startled him.

"It's that serious?"

Jay looked her way. "I'd like it to be."

"I'm not sure—" She breathed deep and picked up the coffee cup and saucer. She raised the cup in front of her, but didn't take a sip. "I'm not sure what to say, Jay. I want to understand, but—"

Stuart scoffed, his back still to the room.

Emily set the cup onto the saucer and lowered them to the table, the move more refined than earlier. She spun the cup until the handle stuck out at a perfect right angle. The precise gesture combined with the thin layer of dust on the coffee table underneath disturbed Jay. Was everyone around him losing their minds? Maybe Emily finally reaching the stage of grief Jay had been at before he'd met Lincoln was a good thing. Maybe she'd understand his actions one day.

"He's sorry," Jay said.

"Yes. We heard what he said at the courthouse."

Stuart spun around, his hands clenched into fists. "It's what any decent human being would've said."

"He is decent," Jay said. "The guilt—the accident almost destroyed him."

"I can't hear this." Stuart stalked out of the room.

"It destroyed all of us," Emily said, her voice so low maybe her words weren't meant for anyone else.

Jay couldn't ignore them. "It doesn't have to." He paused. "She'd want us all to live again."

Emily nodded. It was more than he had expected he'd get from her, or her husband.

"I have something else to tell you."

Her eyes widened. Perhaps she had heard all she could handle, but he had to say the rest.

"I'm not keeping the money. I never wanted it."

Tears filled her eyes. "I didn't either."

"I'm giving it to the nursing school for a scholarship in her name."

More tears fell, and she swiped at them. "Will you come see us again?"

Would Stuart Shaw appreciate that?

Emily smiled with a sweetness reminiscent of her daughter. She needed something from Jay.

For the first time in over a year, he felt as though he could give it. "I promise I'll keep in touch."

He could give a lot more than he thought he'd have left in him to give.

* * * *

Lincoln stopped on the sidewalk in front of the house. The walk had taken him longer than he planned, but not long enough for him to figure out what to say.

He wasn't a coward, though.

He climbed the porch steps and knocked on the front door. He couldn't recall ever having knocked before entering the house. He had lived there for five years. Then, he'd parked his truck in the garage and entered through the side door.

Not today. Today, he waited with his hands shoved deep inside his pockets.

The door finally opened. Only it wasn't whom he expected standing inside. The man had blond hair, a tall, lean body, and a crooked smile. Cute guy.

A dog barked and came barreling out the door.

"Duke." Lincoln dropped to his knee and let the dog lick his face. "Remember me, buddy? You are huge." He stroked the dog's fur.

"Lincoln?" The blond guy sounded pissed.

Lincoln stood. "Yeah. Is Paul home?"

"He is." Blond Guy didn't make a move to let Lincoln in, or to call out for Paul.

"Can I talk to him?"

Blond Guy shifted on his feet, his gaze darting from the ground to Lincoln's face to the ground again. "Are you here to take him back?"

"No."

"Good." Blond Guy opened the door and stepped aside. "Why don't you have a seat. You know your way around. I'll get Paul." He took off up the stairs. Duke ran after him, tail wagging. Why wouldn't he? The dog was just a pup when Lincoln had lived there. This guy had obviously been around for a while.

Lincoln closed the door behind him, holding on to the doorknob a little too long. He gathered his nerves and moved away from the escape route. This wasn't going to be easy, but he wouldn't chicken out.

The house hadn't changed much. Same living room furniture they'd bought after his first big win. Same recliner with the built-in massager. Same entertainment center and huge-ass TV. Same table in the hallway that still held stacks of junk mail, pizza flyers, and bills.

Lincoln made for the couch and then stopped short of sitting. Paul and he had spent too many hours there. Kissing, touching, fucking. He headed for the kitchen. The table wasn't a much better choice. There really was nowhere in the house he and Paul hadn't made love. The hallway, the stairs, the living room floor, the kitchen counters. Several years together meant a lot of memories. A lot of shared moments, intimacies. What would he be remembering seven years from now? Would he be looking back on the time he'd had with Jay? A year together? Two? Seven?

He sank into a chair at the table and waited.

Footsteps started down the staircase. He stood as Paul came into the room. They stared at each other, but said nothing.

Paul looked the same. A touch thinner. Nothing anyone would notice except a mother or a former lover. He wore his old high school state wrestling finals T-shirt with the tear on the right sleeve, and a pair of new jeans. The mix of old and new mocked Lincoln. The past wasn't forgotten, but life had continued on. He'd missed a Christmas, a birthday, an anniversary.

Blond Guy walked into the kitchen wearing a coat and carrying a set of keys. He kissed Paul on the cheek, said, "I'll call you later," and left out the side door to the garage.

Lincoln had missed a lot. "Does he live here?"

"Not yet." Paul went to the sink and filled a glass with tap water. "You want something to drink?"

Lincoln inspected the tabletop. Same long scratch on the edge. They had dinged the table when they'd moved it into the house from his apartment.

Paul was watching him. "Why did you come? I gave Nancy the last of your stuff."

"I got it. Thanks."

"Sit down, Lincoln." Paul carried his water to the table and sat.

Lincoln joined him. Words were really failing him. This wasn't supposed to be easy, but hell, it could go a little better. He cleared his throat.

"Just say it," Paul said and took a short sip of his water. He pursed his lips with the swallow as if he hadn't wanted any of it in the first place. He set the glass on the table and skated his fingers over the side of the smooth surface. A nervous gesture he couldn't hide. The unease of Paul's movements hit home what Lincoln had done to the man.

Lincoln leaned forward and ran his thumb along the crack in the wood table. "I'm sorry. I never should have left like that."

"You don't have to say this now."

"I do. I only thought of myself, of what I wanted for everyone. You. Nancy. Me. I thought I was going to ruin your life, drag you through shit you didn't deserve because of me and what I'd done. I didn't listen when you tried to tell me what you wanted. You wanted to be there for me."

Paul clutched the glass in his hand again as if the contact was all that held back the emotion. Anger? Sadness? Relief? "I did," he said. "That's what family does. Of all people, I thought you'd get that. You'd never let Nancy push you away."

He was right. Lincoln said, "What happened that night—it's the hardest thing I've lived through."

"You made it worse on yourself."

"I get that now. At the time I figured I deserved all the pain. But you didn't." Lincoln paused. "We had a good life."

Paul finally looked at him. "We did."

"I'm sorry I threw it away."

They held the stare for a moment, and then Paul let out a long sigh, like he'd been holding his breath since he'd entered the room. He nodded.

Lincoln sat back in the chair and asked, "Are you happy?"

"Yeah."

"He's good for you?"

"He is." Paul smiled and gave Lincoln a playful look. He was about to tease. "Mom loves him."

Lincoln shook his head and laughed. "How'd he manage that?"

"He's a doctor."

"Ah. A mother's dream. And not a race car driver."

Paul leaned forward and rested his forearms on the table. "Lincoln, I hope you coming here means you're trying to move past what happened. It was an accident."

"I'm starting to accept that."

"You should. How are Nancy and the kids? I tried to check in with her, but she wouldn't talk to me, wouldn't say if anything was—"

"It's okay. She's stubborn as hell."

Paul bit his lip, but he couldn't hold back the smile. "Must run in the family."

Lincoln laughed again. He never thought he'd be able to sit with Paul and laugh, or smile, or talk. "I appreciate you trying. He's gone now and won't hurt them anymore. That's what matters."

"Did he hurt the kids?"

"Not with his fists."

"I'm sorry. I wish I'd been able to help."

"I didn't make that easy for you to do. You're a good man for trying."

They were quiet as Paul drank more of his water. His body had relaxed, and he looked calm, peaceful. He glanced Lincoln's way and asked, "Do you love him?"

"What?"

"You heard me."

"How—"

"He came by here. Told me he was an old friend, but he didn't fool me. He had a taste, and he wanted more. Did he get it?"

The smirk that hit Lincoln's lips wasn't anything he could've prevented. "He did."

"And it's serious?"

"I'd like it to be. But—"

"Don't."

"What?"

Paul reached out and laid his hand over Lincoln's. "Don't push him away. Let someone in this time. Let yourself be happy." Paul removed his hand. Lincoln's own was flat to the tabletop. The crack in the surface had disappeared under his palm.

Lincoln blinked away the moisture forming in his eyes. He wished there was more he could say to Paul, but sometimes words weren't enough.

They stood, and together they moved in silence through the house they once shared. Paul opened the front door and asked, "You walked here?"

"Yeah."

"The suspension was up last week."

"Just haven't—not yet." Lincoln stepped onto the porch and faced Paul. "You tell your doctor he's a lucky man."

"I will. You tell your guy he is too."

Was Jay lucky? The man had lost the life he thought he'd have. Was Lincoln the right future for Jay? And could they ever look at each other and not see a red-haired woman between them?

Chapter Twenty-Five

Finding Jay proved more difficult than it should have in a town the size of Edgefield. Of course Lincoln was walking around like a man without so much as a dime to his name. He headed back to Nancy's.

He stopped at the end of the driveway and stared at his truck. Nancy had driven it once or twice when she needed it, but other than that, it had sat parked in the driveway since he'd been released from the jail. He hadn't so much as gotten behind the wheel since the day he tried to drive Jessica to school. Was he ready?

Would he ever be?

He passed by the truck and went into the house. The kids weren't home and neither was Nancy. She'd had the night off, so he had expected her to be there by now. He took note of the missing bikes on his way through the garage. Probably at the park. There were bike paths with benches along the way for Jessica to rest. Nancy would let Jessica ride in short spurts, but only when they could go together.

Lincoln climbed the stairs and opened the door to his room. A bright pink child's bike helmet sat on top of his sleeping bag. He crossed the room in three strides, dropped to his knees, and grabbed the helmet. A note was taped inside. He tore it open.

She forgot her helmet. I hope a truck doesn't cross over onto the sidewalk.

The helmet hit the floor, and he sped out the door and down the steps. He ran through the house and swept the keys off the kitchen counter.

It was all too much like that night. Rushing to his truck. Someone he loved in trouble, and he wasn't there to protect them. The fear. The agonizing wait to find out what had happened. To find out if someone he loved was hurt.

Lincoln tugged open the driver's-side door of his truck and got in.

His hands shook as he gripped the wheel and turned the key in the ignition.

He thrust the gearshift into reverse, flung his arm over the back of the seat, and turned to look behind him. He couldn't do it. He couldn't let off the brake. Never mind give the truck gas.

He took a deep breath. He would not let anyone hurt his family. He lifted the foot pressing on the brake.

Davy came into view first. The kid pedaled like mad along the sidewalk twenty feet in front of his mom and sister. He wore a helmet. Jessica did not.

Lincoln threw the truck into park and shoved open the door with his shoulder.

"Uncle Linc!" Jessica's scream wasn't one of fear or pain. She was always so damn happy to see him.

Lincoln went straight for her. She pulled to a stop as he approached, and Davy spun around and circled them, pedaling as fast as before. Lincoln crouched on one knee next to Jessica's bike and shook her shoulders. "Don't ride without your helmet again. In fact, no more goddamn bike riding."

"Lincoln!" Nancy stopped her bike beside Jessica's. "She couldn't find it. I told her it was okay this time. We stayed on the sidewalk."

"I'm sorry, Uncle Lincoln." Tears streamed down Jessica's face.

He let go of her shoulders. "Shit." He held her in his arms. "I didn't mean to yell. I was just worried." He released her and wiped the tears from her face.

"You worry too much," Nancy said.

"I wasn't sick at all today." Jessica's brown eyes widened. She bobbed her head.

He smiled at her as the tension left him.

She returned the smile with a giggle. "Oh." She did a wiggle and reached into her jacket pocket. "Here."

A typed envelope with his name on the front.

"Where did you get this?"

"It was in my backpack."

He tore open the envelope.

Leave Jay, or you'll know what it is to grieve.

Lincoln rose and said, "Get the kids inside and stay there until I get back." He started toward his truck.

"Where are you going?" Nancy called after him.

"To the cops."

He didn't give a fuck whose mom she was. This ended. Tonight.

He stormed past the truck and kept on going down the sidewalk. First he had to talk to Jay. The man deserved to know what he was doing. Lincoln just hoped Jay wouldn't blame him. Or worse.

* * * *

Lincoln twisted the knob on the front door. Locked. He'd been waiting on Jay's porch for ten minutes. Might as well wait inside. He had no idea where Jay was or what time he'd be home, but Lincoln wasn't leaving until he talked to Jay. Then the police.

He wandered around the house and found the back door unlocked. He walked through the laundry room to an office. He'd never been in this part of Jay's house before.

The office was small with a fiberboard writing desk, computer, and bulky monitor that looked so old it might not display in color. Next to the desk were a file drawer and a plant stand that held a printer. Several planters sat on the file cabinet and more hung from hooks by the window. Each container held only long brown vines, and scattered along the baseboard were piles of dried leaves, the remnants of houseplants long dead.

Lincoln felt the need to do a cleanup. And he hated doing housework.

Maybe it was the day for putting things to rights.

What would Jay think if he came home and found Lincoln sweeping and dusting his house? Lincoln smirked as he stepped closer to the window to peek inside a planter with mold growing up the interior walls.

If he moved in there, they'd definitely need to do some cleaning. He couldn't have Jessica over with the house the way it was.

Wait.

He plopped into the chair at the desk.

Move in?

Was he ready for that?

Best not to evaluate that line of thinking. Not before he had a chance to tell Jay what he was about to do. Not until they could stop Jay's mom from hurting his family.

Lincoln straightened a pile of envelopes that looked like they'd been thrown on the desk whenever Jay got the mail over the past six months. Junk mail. Pizza coupons. Utility bills. The latter all several months overdue. Where had all the money from the settlement gone? Lincoln never could bring himself to ask.

He tossed the bills onto the pile, and cleaned up more of the desk. Tape, pencils, an empty checkbook register, and an old datebook. The book was two years old. He laughed at that. Jay really hadn't cleaned his house in forever, probably since...

He flipped open the datebook. The month-at-a-glance entries didn't have much written in them. A few scribbled lines in the neat swoops of a female's handwriting. Lincoln ran his index finger over the words.

> *Drop the car off for repair at 8.*
> *Pick up Jay from school tonight.*
> *Mom and Dad's anniversary.*
> *Jay's final exams.*

Lincoln turned to the beginning of the book and stared at the month of January. The date one year to the day before the accident was marked with a single line.

> *Jay's 20th birthday.*

Under that, in a more masculine scrawl:

> *Don't forget the ice cream.*

Lincoln dropped the book. "No." *She died on his birthday.* An ache built in Lincoln's chest. Jay lived with so much pain and never talked about it. At least not to Lincoln. Not as much as Jay needed to. Did he have anyone else to share his thoughts with, his feelings, his pain? Lincoln wanted to be that person. But could Jay talk to him like that?

A piece of paper sticking out of the bottom drawer of the desk caught Lincoln's attention. Fancier than the loose papers piled on top of the desk. And also too familiar for his taste. He threw open the drawer and lifted the pages.

Same stationery.

Same watermark.

The room around him blurred, the cream-colored pages the only point of his focus, all that mattered to him right then. His hands shook, rattling the papers. The coming change loomed as inevitable as...well, death. The phrase "no turning back" ridiculed him.

He jumped with the hum of the refrigerator kicking on behind the wall in front of the desk. He snapped out of the trance, stood, and rifled through the stack of mail. He had no idea what he looked for. Confirmation? Explanation?

He found nothing.

He clutched the blank pages and marched into the kitchen. The room had been cleaned. No dirty dishes in the sink, no empty pizza boxes stacked beside the trash, no burger wrappers wadded up on the counter. Lincoln didn't want to face what it meant that Jay had cleaned. He went into the living room. The side table next to the couch had a drawer. He sank to his knees and opened it. Newspapers, pens, and a pad of paper with the words *history teaches us the mistakes of the past and how to make them again with more style* printed across the top of each blank page. And at the front of the drawer—a strip of condoms and a bottle of lube. New additions to the junk drawer?

He scoffed and slammed the drawer shut. He moved to the second table on the far end of the couch. More junk. TV remote, deck of cards, rubber bands, two picture frames tucked in the back of the drawer, a large manila envelope, and a plastic bag. He pulled out the bag and sank to his heels. Jessica's inhalers.

He gripped the bag to his chest and reached for the envelope and frames. Inside the envelope were photos. Him. Nancy. Jessica. Davy. Walking outside. Inside the house. He threw the photos on the table. He didn't want to see any more, but he had to look. He flipped over one of the frames.

The red hair caught his eye first. Same hair. Same smile. Same beautiful eyes as the woman in the picture he carried in his wallet.

He set the frame on the table and turned over the second. Her again. And standing next to her was Jay. Lincoln held up the picture for a better look. Jay was smiling. As happy and alive as he'd been when he last lay in Lincoln's arms.

With the image of that young, in-love couple, Lincoln accepted the truth. Even if it hurt like hell to admit it, he and Jay Miller were through.

The front door crashed open, and before Lincoln turned, a jolt of pain and fire ripped through his upper arm.

Only then did he hear the bang—like the backfire of a car.

Weren't you supposed to hear the gunshot first?

Chapter Twenty-Six

Lincoln plunged forward with the force of the blow to his arm. The table lamp crashed to the floor, and the picture frame in his hand broke as it connected with the corner of the table. He landed sprawled over the end table, and a shard of glass punctured his lower abdomen. That hurt like a bitch. Almost worse than his arm. Almost.

He slumped to the floor, warm blood pooling over his stomach, more running down his arm inside the leather jacket. Every instinct in him told him to pull the piece of glass out, but that didn't sound right. He rolled to his back and looked up at Jay's dingy living room ceiling. A crack ran the length. Was the ceiling about to split apart and the whole building crash down around him? Maybe.

Funny how we never bother to notice the broken parts of our lives. Was it because we didn't see them, or because we didn't *want* to see them?

Lincoln didn't need to see his arm, though, to know he'd been shot. Just below the shoulder. Damn close to his wolf. He almost laughed at that. Silly to laugh when the person who wanted you dead would, at any moment, finish the job.

He waited.

He needed to get his ass off the floor and get out of the house, but he didn't hold much faith he could get up, what with his legs made of jelly and the dizziness.

Was there anything he could use for a weapon? He couldn't reach far. Something under the couch? The end table? The paper of choice for sending threats and the broken picture frame with a young smiling couple stared back at Lincoln.

He had to get up. Had to get his cell phone out of his pocket. The shooter would certainly fire again before long. Too much time had already passed. Or maybe Lincoln had lost all sense of time. Maybe blood loss slowed the world around you. Or maybe not. Katie Miller had lost a lot of blood, and time had simply stopped for her.

Lincoln forced himself to sit, pulling himself up with the help of the couch and his uninjured arm. The front door of the house was open, but no one else was in the room. He strained to hear any movement. Nothing except an occasional car passing by the house. Had anyone heard the shot? This was small-town America. Gunshots weren't commonplace unless you were on hunting grounds. Jay's property wasn't zoned for hunting. Apparently, someone didn't care.

Blood kept seeping out around the glass still protruding from his stomach, soaking his T-shirt. But his arm worried him more. He hefted his hand into his lap and worked on stripping his jacket off that side. A hole was torn in the T-shirt, directly over his tattoo.

Blood had dripped out from under the cuff of the shirt and formed deep red lines like veins running the length of his arm, but the blood flow from the wound seemed to have slowed. A good thing?

He had to lie back in order to get to the phone in his jacket pocket with his uninjured arm. He lowered himself to the floor.

"Lincoln!"

Jay.

Lincoln squeezed his eyes shut at the threat of tears and pain that had nothing to do with the injuries.

"Linc!" Jay's voice increased in volume as he came in close and shook Lincoln by the shoulders. "Lincoln, wake up."

He tried to open his eyes, but the moving around he'd done had worn him out. And the blood he'd seen had made him queasy.

Jay's hands disappeared.

"I need help... He's been hurt... Hurry. There's a lot of blood." Jay's voice hitched as he spoke. Fear? Concern? "Please, hurry."

Something landed with a *thud* beside Lincoln's head, and then Jay tightened his hands over the wound on his arm.

Jay's hands. His Jay.

No.

Not his. Katie Miller's Jay. Her husband. First and foremost.

Lincoln gave up on opening his eyes. The darkness felt safe, peaceful. But the press of warm lips to his neck kept him from falling further away.

The words whispered in his ear startled him even more. "Stay. Please. I love you."

Too bad they were a lie.

Too bad it had all been a lie.

JAY FOUGHT OFF the tears, but he could do nothing about the fear.

Blood spread across the part of Lincoln's tattoo not covered by Jay's hand. A bullet wound. Jay was certain of that. The entrance wound had ripped through the face of the wolf.

The stomach wound worried Jay just as much. So much blood. Where had the protruding glass come from? How deep was the cut?

Focusing on anything was becoming difficult. Someone had shot Lincoln. In Jay's own home. He pressed harder against the injured arm and waited for the sirens.

He had never heard the sirens for Katie. He hadn't seen the blood either. By the time he saw her, they had cleaned her up, stitched closed the wounds.

This wasn't ending the same way. No one was taking Lincoln from him. No matter whom he had to go up against. Even if it was his own mother.

"I'm sorry."

Lincoln's face was pale, his breathing rapid, his chest rising and falling with each ragged breath. Jay stared at that movement, clinging to it, willing Lincoln to keep breathing. To stay alive.

Sirens screeched in the distance. Not an ambulance. An ice-cream truck. Playful music enticing children to run for a sweet treat. Jay wanted to vomit. He swallowed it down. What was taking them so long?

Louder sirens blasted through the open door, drowning out the tinny music of the ice-cream truck.

"Please, Linc. Stay with me."

Lincoln's eyes fluttered but didn't open.

"Don't leave me. I can't lose you. Not you too." He kissed Lincoln's forehead.

A woman dropped to her knees on Lincoln's other side, and a man knelt beside Jay. He pulled at Jay's arm. "Sir, move back. Let us take a look."

Jay let the man pull his hands off Lincoln. "He's been shot."

"Is the shooter still here?"

"I don't know." Jay shrank back from Lincoln and let the two work. They had to save him.

Someone tapped Jay's shoulder. "Sir, what happened here?" A police officer. The man's mouth kept moving, but Jay couldn't hear the rest. He turned to Lincoln. The EMTs had cut away his shirt and packed dressings on his wounds. No sounds or words reached Jay. A bubble had surrounded him, muted the world, causing the pain to implode on him. Time had lost all meaning. He'd felt like this once before.

The EMTs lifted Lincoln onto a gurney, and Jay tried to stand and follow, but the officer stopped him. Jay wanted to punch the cop, hit him until the man stepped aside. Which wasn't fair. The stranger standing before him didn't deserve the rage.

Jay sank to his knees again and stared at the blood covering his palms. A large envelope and photos lay on the floor next to the couch. The ones someone had sent to his mom. Jay had left them in his desk. How had they gotten in the living room? Beside the pictures were the bag of inhalers and a sheet of blood-soaked paper with the familiar watermark.

Oh God.

Had Lincoln brought those with him? Or had he found them in Jay's house? Jay reached for the paper.

"Sir, don't touch anything."

Jay stilled his hands at the officer's request. He couldn't focus on anything but the drops of blood that had landed on the picture of his own smiling face in the broken frame beside the table. So much blood.

"Sir, I need you to explain what happened here."

Clarity opened a thought to Jay. He'd been the one who discovered Lincoln shot in his home. He had been there before the EMTs.

He was going to be the number one suspect. For many reasons.

* * * *

"He has to be okay," Nancy said.

Jay agreed with a nod. He'd already told her he hoped for the same outcome numerous times while they sat waiting in the hospital's surgical corridor. He also told her all he could about what had happened to Lincoln, but he couldn't force himself to tell her the rest—tell her all he'd said to the police officer at his house earlier. He had talked fast then, explaining to the cop about the accident, the threats to Lincoln, that he hadn't seen who had shot Lincoln. What he didn't say was who he was or that he still held out hope his mom had nothing to do with it.

A door down the long hospital corridor swung open. Jay jumped out of the chair as a man and woman in scrubs exited. They passed by him and Nancy in a rush, their shoes squeaking on the scratched vinyl floor. Jay settled in his seat and watched the quick clip of their shoes until they passed by the two police officers at the other end of the hall.

The bald officer who had interviewed Jay talked with another cop, a taller man also in uniform.

"Someone's been leaving him notes," Nancy said. She gripped her cell phone in her hand. She had called her kids earlier and hadn't let go of the phone since.

"I know." Jay patted her knee. "It'll be okay. Nothing's going to happen to him."

She faced Jay and the flimsy plastic chair creaked with her movement. Hopefully the hospital spent more money on their doctors and surgical equipment than the waiting areas. That's if he could call fifteen green plastic chairs lined along one wall a waiting area. It wasn't like anyone even called the Grant County Medical Center a hospital. Bandage Station was the more common term.

"Something already happened," Nancy said. "I need to talk to the police." She looked down the hall at the two officers. "I need to tell them about the threats. About the accident."

"I told them." Jay did not want to come clean to Nancy right then.

"I think it's the widower. There was a smashed toy car. Whoever sent it wrote *murderer* on the sides."

"What?"

"A murderer?" she said. "Lincoln? I know he made a mistake, but he doesn't deserve this." She clutched her cell phone to her chest. An intercom behind the nurses' station several doors to their left squeaked as it came to life. Nancy jumped in her seat and clasped the phone tighter.

"Do you have someone to stay with the kids?" Jay asked.

"I called Paul. I'm sorry. I didn't have anyone else to call. All my friends have to work. I didn't want Adam to have to deal with this alone. They're scared."

"I understand." Jay did. He just wished that man didn't have to be a part of Lincoln's life any longer. But maybe Lincoln needed him— needed a friend. Jay couldn't ignore the flare of jealousy. He tilted his head back to the wall behind him. What must it be like for Lincoln? To compete against a memory? Was that worse than his jealousy over a living Paul?

It had to be.

The officers down the hall eyed Jay. Did they think he had something to do with the shooting? They didn't even know the whole truth yet—didn't know who he was. Even Nancy thought he had sent Lincoln the threats, not that she knew Jay was the widower. He wished the damn doctor would come out and tell them what was going on. He needed to see that Lincoln was okay before the cops hauled him in for questioning.

The door at the end of the hall opened again, and a woman in scrubs stepped forward. "Nancy Connell?"

Nancy jumped out of her chair "Yes. How is he?"

"He's doing well." She gestured for them to sit and took a chair next to Nancy. "He lost a lot of blood, but there was no major damage from the puncture wound in his stomach. The gunshot wound to his arm was more serious. We were able to repair the artery, and it looks good. There was some extensive nerve damage to his upper arm. He'll most likely need physical therapy." She paused. "But even with that, he might not regain the full use of his hand. All we can do is wait and see how he heals. He's lucky the bullet entered where it did, and that he got help so quickly. It could've been much worse."

The words "full use of his hand" had Jay's gut churning like the queasiness he used to get when he ate anything the month after the accident. The memory of Lincoln's hands on his body didn't calm Jay like usual. He ached to feel the confidence, the strength only Lincoln had shown him.

"Do you have any questions?" the doctor asked.

"Is he in a lot of pain?" Jay's voice was barely a whisper. Nancy turned to him and clasped his hand. She held it firm in hers.

"He'll be on pain medication, and that should help. The first few days and the physical therapy will be the worst of it. We'll give it several weeks to see how everything heals on its own."

"Can we see him?" Nancy asked.

The doctor rose. "When he's awake I'll have someone come get you. I believe the police are waiting to talk to him too. Then I'd like him to rest."

"Thank you." Nancy stood and shook the doctor's hand.

Jay couldn't move, the reality of it all penetrating past the fear. *Someone had shot Lincoln.*

Had his mom used the gun from her secret hiding spot? Was that why the bullet hadn't done more damage? She wouldn't know how to shoot all that well. Or maybe it had been a warning. Lincoln was in Jay's house. Maybe that was her way of saying, *Stay away from my son.*

* * * *

A nurse led Nancy and Jay into a room with two beds, each cordoned off with a floor-to-ceiling curtain. The curtains were a dull shade of pink. Like someone had accidentally washed them with a red sock, and the hospital was too cheap to replace them. Was the color supposed to be cheerful? It reminded Jay of mistakes that could never be undone.

The room smelled of antiseptic and a metallic odor as if the entire place was covered in metal surfaces, which it wasn't, and that had Jay's stomach flopping around again. If he saw one more ounce of Lincoln's blood, it'd be too much.

Several people surrounded the first bed, their feet visible under the pink curtains. The nurse proceeded to the far side of the room. She peeled back the curtain at the second bed and said, "Visitors," in a voice too lively for anyone in the hospital, let alone a gunshot victim coming out of anesthesia.

Lincoln lay in the bed, his head propped on two pillows, eyes shut, his left arm draped across his chest, loose bandages covering the wound on the upper arm. His skin was as pale as in the video recording of him in the courtroom months ago. At the nurse's hail, his eyes fluttered twice and opened. He spotted Nancy and gave a slight smile. She reached out and ran her fingers over his cheek. He closed his eyes again as Nancy caressed the side of his face. Lincoln had to have noticed Jay, but he hadn't looked his way.

"Just a few minutes," the nurse said. She pulled the curtain around the bed as she left, giving them a semblance of privacy. With Nancy there and Lincoln refusing to look at Jay, it would never be private enough for Jay to do what he ached for—to hold Lincoln and let the world around them disappear.

"You're going to be okay." Nancy kissed Lincoln's forehead. "Jay and I are here."

Lincoln nodded and opened his eyes, but he kept his gaze on the foot of the bed. His dark eyes held a sadness beyond what Jay had seen when he first saw Lincoln at Sonny's Tavern. If Lincoln would just look at him.

Nancy's hand hovered over Lincoln's injured arm. "Oh, Linc. Does it hurt?"

Lincoln licked his lips and spoke in a slow drawl. "Not feeling much of anything."

"I'm sorry about your tattoo," she said. "We'll get you home where you can rest. I'll take care of you. The kids'll help too. You'll be fine, you'll see."

The bald officer from the hall opened the curtain. "Excuse me. Mr. McCaw, if you're up to it, we'd like to get a statement. Your family can step out for a moment."

Nancy gave Lincoln another kiss and said, "You tell them everything, okay?" She stepped away from the bed toward the opening the cop had made in the fabric enclosure. She stopped and looked to Jay.

He hadn't moved since the nurse had left, hadn't said a word. And Lincoln still hadn't acknowledged him. *Why?* Did he think Jay had anything to do with the threats?

The taller cop pulled aside the curtain more and rounded the foot of the bed to stand near Jay. He didn't speak, leaving that to his partner.

Baldy pointed toward the exit. "If you could wait outside."

"He can stay." It was the clearest and loudest Lincoln had spoken yet.

"Are you family?" Baldy asked.

Jay opened his mouth to answer, but Lincoln beat him to it. "He's my boyfriend."

Tall and Silent groaned and rocked backward on his feet, his leather boots squeaking in the silence following Lincoln's declaration. Jay wanted to tell the cop what he could do with his homophobia. Not the best idea when you were going to be the lead suspect in a shooting.

Nancy patted Jay's arm on her way by him.

"Mr. McCaw," Baldy said, "tell us what you can about what happened today."

Lincoln stared at the blanket covering his feet as he talked. "I was waiting inside Jay's, facing away from the door. I didn't see it open and didn't hear anyone come in. Felt the pain in my arm and fell forward. That's about it."

Baldy watched Lincoln as he asked, "You didn't see the shooter?"

"No."

"Any idea who might want to hurt you?"

Lincoln didn't answer.

"The young man here said there were some threats. Related to the crash on 91 last year. Do you think it might be someone in the woman's family?"

Silence. Lincoln shifted on the bed, wincing as he tried to sit up more. Jay reached out to help him, tripping over Tall and Silent's boot. Lincoln stilled and looked at Jay's hands as if he'd just figured out who he was. He met Jay's stare, then looked away.

Baldy wrote in his spiral-bound notebook as Lincoln explained about the notes, Jessica's inhalers, their informal searches of Jay's parents' house and the Shaws' place, all of it.

The cop jotted another note and then said, "Sounds to me like the threats might have come from the widower."

Lincoln stared at Jay again.

He thinks I did this.

The last of the air in Jay's lungs left him, and he couldn't breathe. Like the hospital room was a spacecraft in a science fiction movie, and all the oxygen had escaped with the truth.

The silence continued until Jay finally managed to suck in a ragged gulp of air.

"Have you talked to him?" Baldy asked. "Do you know who he is?"

"No." Lincoln met Jay's gaze again. "I don't know him at all."

Jay couldn't take it any longer. He stepped closer to the bed, not caring that he had to squirm past Tall and Silent. "I did not leave those notes. I did not shoot you."

Lincoln scoffed and stared at the foot of the bed again.

"I would never hurt you."

Tall and Silent glanced between Jay and Lincoln. "You're the widower?"

Baldy flipped his notebook shut. "Let's step outside and have a talk."

When Jay didn't move, Tall and Silent inched closer and gestured toward the door with a wave of his arm.

Jay looked at one cop, then the other. "I did not shoot him." He focused on Lincoln again. "Lincoln? You can't believe it was me."

"You had the papers in your office. Pictures of me. The kids. Her inhalers were in your house." Lincoln's jaw twitched as he clamped his mouth shut.

"The Shaws had the paper. You saw that. I found the pictures at my parents' house. The inhalers were hidden in their closet. I left them there. I have no idea how they got in my house."

"Sir, I'm going to have to ask you to step out into the hall." Baldy moved toward the door. "This way." Apparently these two cops thought Jay was a moron.

"I did not shoot him." But he did know who had, didn't he? Had it really been his mom? He wanted to tell the cops about the gun in his parents' closet. He wanted to tell them everything, but he didn't know everything, did he? First he had to talk to Todd, to his dad. If either of them knew anything they'd tell Jay. Wouldn't they? They wouldn't cover for her? Or were they already?

"Sure you didn't," Tall and Silent said. He looked ready to grab Jay by the neck and drag him into the hall.

Jay looked to Lincoln again before they forced him out.

"Now," Baldy said, "I'm asking you one more time to come with us."

"I'd never hurt you." Jay pleaded with a single look, his words, his heart.

Lincoln closed his eyes again. Maybe the anesthesia was still in his system. Maybe all the talking had been too much and the meds made him tired. Maybe he had had enough of Jay.

How could he believe Jay had shot him? Had threatened his family? Had stolen Jessica's inhalers? Anger flooded Jay. He glared at Lincoln. After everything they had done, everything they had shared? Maybe it hadn't meant to Lincoln what it had to him. Maybe it had all been a way for Lincoln to get a piece of ass.

Jay had never had a casual relationship before. Had he seen things that weren't there? How naive and stupid and sappy could he be?

Maybe this had all been so Lincoln could get Jay's help in finding out who sent the threats.

No. It was more than that. And that's why the pain in Lincoln's eyes was worse than before. He thought Jay had betrayed him.

"Sir, now!" Baldy said.

Jay forced himself to concentrate on the officer. He couldn't get arrested. He had to find a way to show Lincoln the truth. To keep him safe. To find out who had shot Lincoln, even if it was his mom. He would not lose out on love for the second time in his life. He took one last look at Lincoln and left with the officer.

The hall outside the room was empty. Baldy tapped his notebook on the back of his other hand. "I'd like you to come to the station so we can get your statement on record. Clear things up."

"Okay." They weren't arresting him. That was something. "Are you leaving him alone? I didn't shoot him, but whoever did might come back."

Neither cop answered.

Did they think he had shot Lincoln and stuck around to call 9-1-1 while he tried to stanch the blood pouring out of Lincoln's wounds and then had come to the hospital to wait?

Maybe that's how criminals did things—to draw suspicion away from themselves. Maybe that's what the Shaws were doing. He had just told them about Lincoln. They were the ones who had the same paper used in the threats. The stationery with the seal from the college where Stuart coached. They had hated Lincoln for a long time.

Maybe they were hiding the evidence linking them to the threats. In his house, at his parents'. After Emily Shaw had seen him with

Lincoln, she'd been pleasant to Jay, understanding even. Could it have been an act?

Was it any better if she or Stuart had pulled the trigger?

Would they try again to kill the person who took away their only child?

"If we get more evidence he's in danger," Baldy said, "we'll have someone watch him."

Jay eased toward Lincoln's room. "I'm not leaving him by himself. Let me find his sister first."

Tall and Silent rolled his eyes. "Fags. Such drama queens." He turned and walked away, leaving Jay with the bald cop.

"I'm not leaving him like this," Jay said.

Baldy tilted his head toward the hall behind Jay.

Nancy rounded the corner, carrying two cups of coffee. "Is everything okay? Is Lincoln—"

"He's fine. I need to go to the police station to answer more questions. Can you stay with him? He shouldn't be alone."

She glanced at the door to Lincoln's hospital room. "You think he'll be back? The man who shot him?"

"Maybe."

Chapter Twenty-Seven

"Nancy, sit down," Lincoln said.

"Huh?" She stopped playing with the edge of the thin blue blanket draped over his hospital bed. "Oh, okay." She spun around and dropped onto the edge of the bed. He groaned with the jostling.

She didn't seem to notice. "Jay is Jacob Miller?" She faced Lincoln, swinging her leg to rest her upper thigh on the bed. "Are you sure?" Her knee smacked into his thigh. He moved over, and a stabbing pain exploded through his gut and up his arm.

"Fuck!" He clutched his side and groaned again. "I'm sure."

She stood. "I'm sorry." She patted his leg before stepping backward and falling into the chair beside the bed. "And you knew? The entire time?"

"Not the first time."

"He *fucked* you before he told you?" She glanced at the curtain behind her as if she could tell through the material if the guy in the next bed heard her words. More quietly she said, "What was he thinking?"

"He didn't know then either. And it wasn't like that. We'd just met."

"Why did you keep seeing him?"

"We were trying to figure out who was sending the threats."

"You said that was all taken care of."

"I guess I wasn't clear on a lot of things."

She shook her head, several strands of her hair falling from her ponytail. "You really think it was Jay?"

"No." He'd seen the inhalers in that drawer, and he'd been furious. At first he had let himself believe it might have been Jay, but deep down he knew Jay wouldn't do that to him—to anyone. When Lincoln had awakened in the hospital, he'd accepted that he and Jay had to be finished. Better to give Jay a push in the right direction: away from him. Lincoln collapsed back onto the pillow and breathed deep. He ached all over—his head, his stomach, his arm. His heart. The pain medication was making him foggy. He wanted to sleep. Forever. "Jay doesn't have it in him."

"But you let him believe you thought he did it?"

"Jesus, Nance. Don't you think I feel bad enough about all this?"

"I know you do. I just want this all over for you. I want you to move on. To put this behind you."

Sounded like a good plan, but how could he put it behind him—how could he forget—when someone wanted him dead?

* * * *

"I need you to leave me alone."

Jay entered the confines of Lincoln's hospital room. The curtain around the bed was drawn back, revealing a healthier-looking man than the day before. One pissed-off, red-faced, healthier man.

The sparse well-wishes on the bedside table spoke of how few people Lincoln could count on. Did it matter how many people a man had in his life? Or did it matter more how much those he did have loved him? The colorful page torn from a coloring book with *Love love love you, Uncle Lincoln* sprawled across the top in purple crayon said a lot.

"I'm not going anywhere." Jay moved to the edge of the bed and wheeled aside a silver tray with its pitcher of water, plastic cup, and TV remote. "I need to talk to you."

"It's been a long couple of days, Jay." Lincoln gripped his left wrist with his other hand as he sat taller.

Jay reached for the man's shoulder. "You need to sit still."

Lincoln shrugged away from him. "I need you to go."

As much as Jay wanted to grab Lincoln and shake the stupidity out of him, he gave in and backed away. He wasn't about to leave, but he also wasn't coming up with the right words. The ringing of a phone down the hall and the low chatter of visitors in nearby rooms did nothing to break the silence between them. Jay sat in the chair beside the bed, and the scrape of the metal legs on the floor hid the clearing of his throat. "You can't believe I'd hurt you."

Lincoln finally looked his way. "I don't."

Jay searched his face and found truth. In the expression. In the dark eyes. Truth and despair and something more. What was it? "But you think I sent the notes."

"Did you?"

"No! They're interviewing my parents, and the Shaws. My mom

said it wasn't her. She just wanted me to stop seeing you. She said she didn't send the notes or do anything else. It has to be the Shaws. I think they might've planted all the evidence."

"Has to be, huh?"

"Yes. Someone sent my mom those pictures of you. Of the kids. Someone's been watching you."

"When did you find this out?"

"When we searched my parents' house."

"Figures." Lincoln shifted again, wincing. "What an idiot."

"Me?"

"Me! For trusting you. For thinking this—whatever the hell we are—would not somehow end up destroying us both."

"You were the one thing that hasn't—that doesn't suck about my life." Quieter Jay added, "I want to keep seeing you."

Lincoln laughed, the howl surging out of him until he doubled over, the pain visible on his strained face. Jay ached to touch the man, but he held back.

When Lincoln could speak, he said, "This can't go on. You have to see that." He reached into the drawer of the bedside table.

Jay stood. "What do you need?"

"I got it." Lincoln opened a wallet and pulled out a newspaper clipping. He unfolded it, the creases as worn as an old love letter he'd read many times throughout the years. "At night, in bed, when you're not there, she's all I see." Lincoln laid the piece of paper across the blanket over his thigh, spreading out the curling edges with his fingers in a careful caress. "She's all I see. Bloody. Broken. Dead."

Jay took a step back. He didn't want to see what was printed on the newspaper. He stared at the pitcher of water on the tray, watching the slight ripples on the surface. What caused the water to move? His movements? The flurry of nursing activity in the room across the hall? The gurney a hospital employee pushed by the open door? Funny how you couldn't sense the ground shift under your feet.

Lincoln removed something else from his wallet. Probably wasn't anything else Jay wanted to see.

"I know you don't want to look," Lincoln said, "but I need you to."

The pleading of Lincoln's voice broke Jay's resolve. He looked at what Lincoln held out. A photograph, folded in half, and crushed in at the corner. Jay closed his fingers around it, brushing the tip of Lincoln's thumb with his own. With that contact, Lincoln jerked his hand away.

Everything in Jay told him not to look. Not to unfold the photo. If it was enough to keep them apart, it had to be bad.

But he owed this to Lincoln.

He unfolded the photograph. *Katie.* She looked as she did when Jay had last seen her. Pale. Lifeless. Dead. The blood rushed to his head and a sudden dizziness swept over him.

Lincoln was talking, but all sound muted as if Jay had sunk into a pool of water where all was still and quiet, where Lincoln was a far-off distorted vision above the surface, in a different world, and so far from Jay's reach.

"Listen, Jay. You have to listen to this." Lincoln read the note in his hand. The words "gash from her temple to her chin," "blood stuck to her red hair," "her left leg twisted the wrong way," were all Jay could comprehend.

"Wh-where did you get this?"

"Look at me."

Jay couldn't tear his gaze from the photo, couldn't let go of it.

"You know where it came from." Lincoln leaned toward him and seized the picture.

Jay grabbed the photo back, and his hands trembled as he looked at the image again. "She's dead."

Lincoln yanked off the thin hospital blanket, swung his legs off the edge, and stood. "Was I some sort of sick game for you?"

"What?"

Lincoln invaded his space in an instant, pushing him backward until Jay's calves smacked into the plastic chair. "What were you playing at?"

"Playing?" He shoved at Lincoln, ignoring the part of him worried over hitting any injured body part. "You think this wasn't real for me? You think I'd actually go to bed with the man who caused the accident that resulted in this"—Jay held up the picture—"if I wasn't seriously interested? Fuck you!"

It was the first punch Jay had handed out since the time he'd tangled with Todd for stealing a video game from his room and the hardest ever, and it hit Lincoln square in the jaw, thrusting him backward into the bedside tray. The tray skidded and rammed into the bed frame. The pitcher of water flew through the air, raining droplets of room temperature liquid onto Jay's face. Lincoln toppled over. His uninjured arm smacked the floor, his head just missing the same outcome. The newsprint floated in the air between them, and the picture of Katie landed on Lincoln's chest. The man's breath came in heavy pants, his brow furrowed and his face scrunched up. Pain.

"Oh God. Are you okay?" Jay looped an arm around Lincoln's waist. What the hell had he been thinking?

Lincoln tried to push him away, but Jay wouldn't let go. He helped Lincoln stand and eased him onto the bed. "I shouldn't have—"

"Leave me alone."

"What's going on?" Nancy rushed to Lincoln's other side. "Are you okay? What happened?"

"Nothing. I'm fine." Lincoln's breathing had calmed, but he still held the look of a man in serious pain.

How had Jay gotten to a place where he punched his injured lover?

"I think you should go," Nancy said. "You've hurt him enough."

Lincoln shook his head. "Don't, Nance."

Jay stepped back. She was right. He wasn't good for Lincoln. Had he ever been? "Whoever shot you might not be finished yet. Please be careful." He left without another word. They'd either believe him that Lincoln wasn't safe, or they wouldn't. Jay couldn't do much more than state the truth.

Chapter Twenty-Eight

"So we're back to the no talking thing?" Todd asked as he entered the garage.

Jay took another swig of his second beer since the tour of Todd's new home had begun an hour earlier. He'd finally managed to sneak off to the garage while his parents carried on about the brass bathroom fixtures, precise tile work, and ceramic soap dispensers. If he had to hear Todd ask their mom if she liked something one more time, Jay would've lost it.

He set the beer on a storage shelf. Todd already had the garage stuffed with a riding mower, a two-person motorboat, fishing poles, boxes of tackle, and a new Kawasaki motorcycle Jay didn't know Todd had bought. With one look at that bike, Jay was back in Lincoln's garage, the two of them naked, Lincoln bent over the Harley's seat, the orange flames on the tank visible with each shift of his hips.

Jay forced the image aside. "Mom and Dad still here?"

"Yeah. We're grilling steaks for dinner. I told them you promised to help me unload the pickup. We've got a little time before they come looking for us."

"Thanks." Jay finished off the beer while Todd untied the boxes, tossing the red nylon rope aside. It coiled on the floor beside Jay, looking oddly like a pool of blood. Or maybe that was all he could see anymore. Blood. Death. Pain.

They worked in silence, unloading boxes from Todd's truck.

"I don't mind the no talking," Todd said when they neared the end of the load, "but I do mind you letting your life turn to shit." He dropped a box onto the floor near the entrance to the house and added, "He isn't worth it."

"Don't."

"Don't what?"

"Don't talk about him like that."

Todd's voice was low when he spoke again, and Jay had to strain to hear him. "I hate that he hurt you."

Jay picked up the third beer he'd brought with him. The bottle was warm. He didn't care. He twisted the cap and downed half before speaking. "I don't want to talk to you about him."

"Why not?"

"You won't like what I have to say."

Todd wrenched the last box off the truck. "I'll never understand how you—"

"Stop. It was an accident that destroyed him as much as it did me." Jay swallowed the last of the warm beer, wishing he had brought out another. He set the empty bottle on the wooden workbench that stretched the length of the back wall. The bench was covered with various handheld electric tools, spools of the red nylon rope, a gas can, and more boxes of fishing tackle. A crossbow and a large foam deer sat beside the bench.

Jay bent and stared into the fake deer's dark eyes. He wanted to ask the deer what it felt like to get shot with an arrow. He'd officially had too much to drink.

He straightened and said, "It's a real nice house, Todd."

"Thanks." Todd glanced around the garage. "Didn't realize how much shit we had at the old place. I'm going to mount plastic storage units on the ceiling." He kicked at a couple of the boxes they'd unloaded. "Put this crap up there." Another fishing pole and gas can sat beside the boxes. Todd didn't glance at Jay as he said, "I just have to know, did you go after him to make him see what he did, like you said you wanted to? Was that why you kept seeing him?"

"No. I fell in love with him."

"Do you know how crazy that sounds?"

"I think the Shaws might have done it. The threats. Shooting Lincoln. I think they planted all the evidence. I told the police so."

Todd lifted his head. "That's not possible, Jay. You're making this more complicated than it is. He was in jail. Who knows what people he pissed off there. A man like him probably has a lot of enemies."

"He doesn't. He's not like that."

"You fuck a man, and you think that means you know him? You're such a kid sometimes."

"I do know him." Jay snatched the empty beer bottle off the bench, needing something to hold on to. "I want to get him back."

Todd ripped the bottle from Jay's hand. "He killed your wife."

"It was an accident." How many times would Jay have to say those words before people understood them?

"God, you're a fucking idiot."

Why should he expect Todd to get it? From an outside perspective, what he and Lincoln had been doing didn't look healthy. For either of them. Jay leaned against a metal shelving unit. It scraped along the concrete floor as it shifted with his weight; the gas in a can beside him sloshed. Not one gas can. Two more. No. Three. "What're you doing with all the gas cans?"

"You wouldn't believe me if I told you."

"What?"

Todd set the empty beer bottle on the bench, then picked it up again and moved it closer to the door leading inside.

"Todd…"

"We had to get a generator. Marge is scared we'll lose power after the baby comes, and we won't be able to feed him."

"It's a baby. It doesn't need filet mignon."

"Yeah. I tried to tell her. I'm guessing it's a woman thing."

Jay nodded. Katie had been the same, wanting to make the house perfect, wanting to make sure every part of their lives was ready for a baby they hadn't conceived yet.

"I hate this," Todd said as he finally faced Jay. "I hate talking to you about the baby. I feel like a shit for having a kid when you—"

"Don't. It's a good thing. You shouldn't feel like you have to hide that from me. Not anymore."

"Things are just so fucked-up." Todd sighed. "It's not how it should be."

"It's not fucked-up. We all have to move on."

"How can you?" The pity visible on his brother's face, in his eyes, was worse than it had been months before. Todd didn't get it.

Would anyone in Jay's life ever understand?

It didn't matter. "I have to get him back."

Todd walked to his truck and slammed the tailgate shut. He threw the last coil of the red rope onto the workbench. "I have to pick up Marge from the hospital. She's off in ten minutes. Tell Mom and Dad I'll be right back." He yanked open the driver's-side door, but stopped short of getting in. "No way a man is going to date the widower of someone he killed. You need to let this go." Todd climbed into the truck and drove off.

Was he right? Was there any way Jay would ever have Lincoln in his life?

* * * *

"Well, you're working and not drinking." Nancy leaned against the doorjamb. "I'll take that as a good sign."

Lincoln bent and added paint to the brush from the open can on the floor, ignoring his sister.

She reached around him and grabbed the brush. "Let me do some of this." She pointed toward the new box spring and mattress in the corner of the room. "You, take a break."

He hadn't bought a bed frame yet, but the mattresses on the floor worked well enough. He eased himself onto the makeshift bed, keeping his weight on his right arm. Every muscle ached. Probably had done too much work. His body was healing. He just wasn't sure about the rest of him.

The police hadn't made an arrest, and fear for his family's safety weighed heavily on him. Despite searching the Shaws' house, the Millers', and Jay's, as well as questioning everyone, the cops hadn't found evidence any of them had shot Lincoln. The major suspect? Jay. Which made sense. What with the inhalers, papers, and photos all found at his house. But all that had warranted was a couple of rounds of questions by a detective. Since Lincoln had been the one to find those items—and hadn't handed over the earlier threats before the shooting—the matching stationery and the medications weren't much proof of anything. To the local cops, the case was a dead end.

Nancy continued painting. She hadn't come to Lincoln's room to help him with the walls. She'd come to say something. Probably nothing he wanted to hear. He wouldn't help her get started.

He was grateful for the assist on the room, though. He was still limited in the use of his hand. Even with the additional surgery, it might never be the same again. Now driving a race car wasn't just something he was legally banned from. It was something he physically couldn't do. So much of his old life—of who he was—had disappeared. Was he sorry?

For the accident? For the death of Katie Miller? Hell, yes.

For meeting Jay? Nothing could make him regret the time they'd had together. Nothing.

But his career, his love of the sport, the thrill of the ride—all had been ripped away from him, and it killed him to know he'd done it to himself.

Blame. That's what it all came down to. He blamed himself for the accident—had since the moment his truck collided with the little red car.

But did Jay blame him? How could he have been with Lincoln

knowing he was responsible for the death of his wife? How had they fooled themselves into continuing along a path that had no future?

It didn't matter.

It was over.

Jay would never be his. Not his lover. Not his friend or partner. He'd always be the person Lincoln had hurt most in the world. That's why he'd said what he did to Jay in the hospital. Why he had pushed away the man he loved.

He wouldn't deny something had sparked between them, hidden under their passion, the touches, the kisses. But no matter how hard he tried, he couldn't escape the past, couldn't put aside the one thing keeping them apart.

After a few more round trips of paint to wall, Nancy spoke. "Mitch called. He said they are okay with your request for half days."

Great. He had hoped to keep that news from her a little longer.

She stilled the paintbrush in the middle of an upstroke. "Why are you going back to work so soon?"

"We need the money."

"I can pick up some extra shifts. Your arm is still healing, and you need to start physical therapy. They can't expect you to work."

"Mitch said I could do paperwork and inspections."

"No lifting?"

"None."

"I want you to take it easy. You're doing too much around the house. You don't have to finish this room. You can sleep on the couch. Or I can move Davy back into Adam's—"

"No." He eased off the bed, cradling his left arm in his other hand. She dropped the brush and moved to help him up, but he shrugged her off. He could get off a goddamn bed. "I'm not letting you down again."

She stared at him, her forehead scrunched up, her mouth hanging open. "You have never let me down." She pulled him into an embrace, her arms tight around his neck. "Never. Even when you were gone. You are the one person I can count on to love me. And that means everything to me."

He squashed the tears before they formed. He would not feel sorry for himself any longer. He had a lot to be grateful for—more than some men. He was going to live up to it. Live up to the Iroquois legend of an uncle Jay had told him about. Be the father figure Nancy's kids deserved.

She let go of him. "Do you think there'll be more trouble?"

"Not sure. I'm not seeing Jay anymore. Maybe that'll help." He didn't want to tell her about the note in his pocket, didn't want her to know that despite the police getting involved, despite being shot and the two surgeries on his arm, despite losing Jay, whoever wanted him to pay wasn't done with Lincoln yet.

"All right," she said. "I'm going to check on the kids and go to bed. You'll be okay?"

"Yeah." He sank to the bed again.

She didn't move to leave. "You were happy? For a while?"

"I was." He couldn't stop the smile. "He changed me."

"I know. Maybe—"

He rubbed a hand over the back of his neck. "It's over."

"I believe you said that once before."

"It's different this time."

"Really?" She kept staring at him.

"What?"

"You're an idiot." She put her hands on her hips. That stance more than any other made her look like their mom, like the time he'd gotten in trouble for stealing a pack of smokes. *Never take what isn't yours,* his mom had told him. He should've remembered that when he met Jay.

Nancy also looked angrier than their mom had. "If you're lucky enough to find someone who loves you, someone who'll stand by you and care for you, then you should be on your knees thanking God or the universe or the damn tooth fairy. You've found that twice, Lincoln McCaw. That's twice more than a lot of people get."

What could he say? She deserved better than the men she'd believed had loved her.

"When I picked you up at the bus station, I saw it. You were lost. If you let him walk away, then you are choosing to stay lost."

Then he'd have to be lost. A relationship with Jay Miller would be his second biggest mistake. The worst risk of his life.

Nancy ran a hand over his cheek and left the room. He pulled the typed note from his pocket.

Meet me at the cemetery. You know the one. 4:00 a.m.

It had to be over with Jay. Because tonight Lincoln planned on making sure his shooter was finished sending threats or stealing medicine. Finished hurting anyone.

And Jay would lose another person he cared about.

Chapter Twenty-Nine

Lincoln sucked in a sharp breath. The swirl of a tongue over the crown of his dick had him moaning and writhing.

Remarkably, Jay was getting even better at giving head. He worked his heated mouth down Lincoln's shaft, pulling slowly, massaging the length with lips and tongue. Then he pulled away; the heat of his body disappeared.

Lincoln lifted his head. "Jay?"

A sliver of light from the garage below streamed across the bed, but the rest of the room was too dark to see where Jay had gone. Lincoln reached out, and the heat of Jay's body pressed in close again as he slid alongside Lincoln.

Only it wasn't Jay.

The body was smaller, the flesh more silky, the legs more feminine against Lincoln's. A small hand glided over his abdomen, pausing briefly at the new scar tissue where the glass of the picture frame had punctured him. The mysterious woman ran her hand higher, spreading feathery touches all over him, drawing out goose bumps across his chest. She touched his left arm, running her fingers over the scar and the ruined tattoo.

"Wake up, Lincoln."

That voice. Definitely a woman's.

She caressed his chest again, plucking his nipples. Lincoln couldn't recall ever having an erotic dream about a woman. Not even when he was a teenager and just about anything got him off. He arched into her touch, wanting more, and for once in his life, not knowing how the hell to ask or what to do about it.

He couldn't see her face, but the tips of her red hair were visible in the low light as the strands swept across his chest, tickling him as she made her way up his body.

"Linc, wake up." Her voice was insistent in his ear as her fingers

twisted his nipple harder, pulling his flesh past arousal into pain.
"They need you. Wake! Up!"

Lincoln shot straight up, his eyes wide, his breath pouring out in heavy pants. The room was dark and he was alone, lying on the mattress in his room over the garage, wearing jeans and nothing else, the sleeping bag draped over his lower half.

What time was it? He couldn't have slept long. He had set his alarm for 3:00 a.m. Plenty of time for him to walk to the cemetery.

His body was warm despite the chill of the air. The erotic dream disturbed him. He had always known he was gay. He never went through moments of doubt. Never dated women. Never wanted one before.

He touched his chest, his nipples sensitive, his body aching in a delicious way. He moved his hand lower and froze when the sweet scent of flowers reached him. Just as quickly, the stench of smoke replaced it.

Smoke.

He scrambled out of the bed. His feet caught in the bottom of the sleeping bag, and he plunged forward. He flung his hands out to stop his face from smacking into the floor, only to realize too late his left arm shouldn't take part in such activity.

Pain raced up the appendage. He rolled onto his back and cradled his arm. Screw the pain. He had to get moving. He kicked off the sleeping bag, shot to his feet, and grabbed a shirt from the top of his bag. The shirt barely on, he sprinted down the stairs, skipping every other one, his side slamming into the wall as he lost his balance on the last step. The garage was clear of smoke, but the scent was stronger. The handle on the door leading to the house was warm, but it didn't slow him. He burst into the kitchen.

"Nancy!"

Flames worked up the wall toward the ceiling over the refrigerator. He ran through the kitchen and shouted again for Nancy and the kids.

Down the hall, he found Adam pulling Sparky by the collar. Lincoln pointed toward the front door. "Get outside. Now!"

"Lincoln." Nancy was at the end of the hall pushing Davy toward him.

"Get out of the house."

"Jessica!" she screamed.

Lincoln charged into Jessica's room. "I've got her. Go!"

Jessica sat on her bed, fully awake, her eyes as big as the round black orbs on Mr. Wuzzie's face, the stuffed animal clutched in her hand, the kitten on her lap.

Lincoln went to her. She kicked off the blankets, gripped the kitten behind the neck like a mother cat carrying her young, and held out her arms. He scooped her up, wincing and shifting her to his right side when her weight hit his healing wounds. She wheezed and clutched at his shoulder as he hurried toward the front door.

Her soft voice whispered in his ear. "I dropped Mr. Wuzzie."

"We can't go back."

The fire had spread throughout the kitchen but hadn't blocked the front door yet. The plume of smoke wasn't going to do anything for Jessica's airway. Why hadn't he climbed out her damn window?

Nancy and the boys waited just outside the door and followed him away from the house. He knelt on one knee and laid Jessica across his other leg. Her eyes were closed, and the kitten slipped from her slack grip. She didn't notice.

He bent his head to her chest and mouth. The breath was soft, but there.

"Baby?" Nancy fell to her knees on the ground beside them. "She's breathing. Did you call?"

Nancy didn't say anything.

"Nance! Did you call for help?"

"I did," Adam said. He held his phone in one hand, the kitten in the other. Damn good teenager, attached to his cell at all times. "They're sending the fire department. And an ambulance."

Lincoln held Jessica and watched her chest rise and fall as they waited. Sirens rang out in the distance. Still a couple of streets over. He stood and carried Jessica to the curb. Her eyes fluttered open, and she coughed, a tiny sound, but it opened a floodgate. She wiggled in his arms, trying to sit up.

He knelt again and helped her up. "Inhaler?"

Nancy was on Jessica's other side. "In the house. Wait—there's one in my car."

"I'll get it." Adam ran off.

"The glove compartment," Nancy called after him. "And stay back from the house."

Jessica wiggled more. "I can breathe." Another small cough followed. "Kitty?"

Adam handed over the inhaler. "I've got the cat."

"Take this," Lincoln said and raised the inhaler to her mouth.

She huffed on it twice, and when she was done, she looked at him with her large brown eyes, then at her mom. "I'm okay." Air slammed into Lincoln's lungs with her smile.

"The garage," Davy said. "It's on fire now too."

"Here, take her." Lincoln handed Jessica to Nancy and sprinted for the garage.

"Lincoln!" Nancy shouted after him.

Fuck if he was losing everything. The bike was all he'd have left to remember Jay.

Flames climbed the exterior wall of the garage nearest the house. He placed an open palm on the side door. Warm, but not too bad. He gave the knob a twist and pushed in. Heat and smoke rushed toward him.

* * * *

The glow from the muted television zipped across the ceiling of Jay's living room, creating an eerie light show.

If only he could sleep. But sleep brought the dreams. And waiting in those dreams was Lincoln, the second person Jay could never have again. He'd been so close to that magic—that blend of physical attraction and emotional connection few were lucky to find. To lose it again sucked more than the first time.

The dance of lights across the ceiling changed from white to yellow to orange. Jay raised his head. The blaze of a house fire filled the TV screen. Amid the smoke and flames, the red trucks and television crews, the firefighters and reporters, was a house with a one-car attached garage. Nancy's house.

Jay leaped for the coffee table and fumbled until his hand met the remote. He turned up the volume.

"*These shots were taken not long ago as firefighters battled this Edgefield house fire. Officials have not made a statement on any injuries or fatalities, but we've learned there were several young children inside the home at the time of the fire. An ambulance was on the scene and left with at least one occupant of the house. As you can see behind me now the fire is out, leaving behind what looks to be a completely destroyed home.*"

The news returned to the anchorwoman at a desk signing off for the late-night news broadcast. Jay checked the time on his watch. 3:00 a.m. Not a live broadcast. The second airing of the late news. He threw the remote on the couch and sprinted for his Jeep, trying not to think about the conclusions he was drawing. About who had written the threats. Who had stolen Jessica's inhalers. Who had shot Lincoln. Who had taken a photo of Katie in the hospital morgue, had seen her, and could describe exactly how she had looked that night.

He'd deal with what that meant later. He had to know if Lincoln and his family were safe. And if they were, he had to make certain they stayed that way.

He knew now this was never going to end, not until Lincoln suffered more. Maybe not until Lincoln McCaw was dead and buried.

Wasn't that what she had said? *Someone should kill him.*

* * * *

Jessica raised her tiny hands and pulled the oxygen mask away from her face.

"Leave that on." Lincoln lifted the mask and settled it into place. He was sitting in a chair beside her gurney in the emergency room.

She furrowed her brow. The look almost had him laughing. Almost.

Nancy returned from where she'd been talking with a doctor outside the exam room. She held Jessica's hand and said, "Just a bit longer, hon."

"She doesn't have to stay?" Lincoln asked.

"No. They don't think she breathed in much smoke. All the excitement probably triggered the attack."

Lincoln smothered the scream that wanted out. "I'm sorry about your house, Nance."

"This wasn't your fault." She removed the hand she had on Jessica's arm and gripped Lincoln's fingers in hers.

Sure it wasn't.

Jessica removed the mask again. "Can we go home? I'll be good and rest in bed. I promise."

"Oh, hon. I think most of our stuff is gone. The house is—" A sob tore through Nancy.

Lincoln rounded the hospital bed and drew her into his arms. "It'll be okay." She cried as she held on to him, and he said, "You're not alone in this."

Jessica tugged on his pant leg. "Mr. Wuzzie?"

What was so hard about breaking the news of a stuffed animal's demise? When it was a five-year-old's best friend—everything. "In the house," was all he could say.

Her lower lip quivered. "I'm sorry."

Nancy let go of Lincoln and went to her daughter. "Sorry for what?"

"I wasn't supposed to have Kitty in my room."

"It's okay."

"You saved her life," Lincoln said.

"I did?" Jessica stared at him. "I saved her?"

"Sure," Nancy said. "We wouldn't have had time to find Kitty if you hadn't had her with you. And you held on tight until you got out of the house."

Lincoln patted Jessica's knee. "You did great, kid."

A tear slid down her face. "Maybe when the fire's over, we can find Mr. Wuzzie."

"Maybe," Nancy said. "We'll see what's left later, okay? Just please keep the mask on."

Jessica stopped her mom's hand from moving the oxygen back over her mouth and nose. "It wasn't his fault. He didn't do anything wrong." More tears streamed down her cheeks. "I didn't mean to drop him."

"It wasn't your fault either." Lincoln stroked her hair and buried another scream.

"I didn't mean it." She coughed and cried, and Nancy held her.

"He knows you didn't mean it. You still have me. Your brothers. Uncle Lincoln. Kitty and Sparky. Think about what you still have, baby."

Tears filled Lincoln's eyes. He still had his family. And he was going to make sure nothing happened to them. He checked the clock on the wall. 3:00 a.m.

Plenty of time.

Chapter Thirty

"Adam! Adam!"

The kid turned around with the scream of his name. Jay waved his arms in the air to get Adam's attention. Damn cops wouldn't let him any closer to the house. The fire was long out, but the fire department was still on the scene. Both the garage and the house were destroyed. What was left behind would probably be torn down when all was said and done.

It had taken Jay twice as long as usual to get to Nancy's. His Jeep kept stalling, finally dying two streets over. He'd sprinted the rest of the way.

Adam spotted Jay and jogged over. A small black-and-white kitten lay inside the crook of his arm, and Sparky ran alongside them.

"Are you okay?" Jay asked.

"Yeah. The house isn't."

"What about everyone else? Your uncle?"

"Fine. Jessica had trouble breathing. They took her to the hospital, but she's okay. Davy went with them."

Jay bent and gripped his thighs, letting in the deep breaths he'd been denying himself. He stood upright. "She's okay?"

"Yeah. Mom called. They said it wasn't bad at all."

"What happened?"

"I don't know. I woke up when I heard Uncle Lincoln screaming. The place smelled like smoke. Like someone was burning something outside but stronger than that. The whole kitchen was on fire when we ran out. The smoke alarms didn't even go off. Mom's always bitching at us not to steal the batteries, and they didn't even work."

"I need to talk to your uncle. Are they still at the hospital?"

Adam glanced at Jay, then at the kitten, then at the destroyed house behind him. "Someone started the fire, didn't they?"

"Yes."

"You know who?"

"Yeah. And I know who shot him. He's not safe. I guess none of you are."

Adam swung his gaze back to Jay. "What should I do?"

"I'll take you with me to the hospital."

"Mom told me to stay here with Sparky and the cat."

"We'll drop them at my house."

"Okay." Adam pulled on Sparky's collar and walked toward Jay. "Shit. My Jeep won't start."

"You could borrow Uncle Lincoln's pickup. He never drives it."

The large black truck sat in the driveway, unharmed by the fire. It looked enormous, a monster Jay didn't think he'd be able to approach, let alone climb inside and drive. "I suppose the keys were in the house?"

"Yeah," Adam said. "But there's a spare set in a magnet thing by the front tire."

Okay. He could do this. He could drive a couple of miles in that truck—he had to.

* * * *

"I need to find him," Jay said to Nancy as he tried to ignore Paul, but the man stared at him from farther down the emergency room corridor where he sat with Adam and Davy.

Nancy shook her head. "I don't believe you had anything to do with all this, but I promised him I wouldn't say anything. Not to the police. Not to you."

"He's not safe. Adam said the smoke alarms didn't go off. You know this was on purpose. Someone wants him dead, and apparently they don't care if you or your kids get in the way."

Nancy gasped and clasped a hand over her mouth. When she'd regained her composure, she spoke. "He said he could handle this. He promised me he'd call the police when he figured out who it is."

"Nancy, he's not planning to call the police."

"He said as soon as he saw who, he'd call for help."

"Did he even have his cell with him?"

She shook her head again.

"The police couldn't help last time," Jay said. "And Lincoln doesn't believe they'll do anything based on his word."

"What are you saying?"

"He isn't taking another chance with your lives. I'm guessing that's why Paul's here—to make sure you're safe while Lincoln's gone."

"What…" She glanced toward Paul and the kids. "What is he going to do?"

"Whatever he has to. This time he's protecting you."

She looked at Jay, searching his eyes. "He said there was another note. I don't know where—"

"He's at the Pleasant Valley Cemetery."

Paul's voice startled Jay. "How do you know that?"

"I asked him where he was going. I don't think he wanted to lie to me. He said he had to meet someone. I thought he meant you. I thought he wanted to tell you what happened that night."

Jay took off for the exit. Goddamn motherfucking stubborn man was going to get himself killed. And in the process, Jay might also lose another person he cared about.

Screw that. He knew who was behind it all. No matter how the night ended, he'd already lost too much.

* * * *

Lincoln paced behind the headstone. He couldn't bring himself to face the front, to look at the name etched in stone.

Birds chirped in the tree overhead. Didn't they sleep? Weren't they used to disruptions at four in the morning? Not if a cemetery was their home.

He'd been at Pleasant Valley many times during the weeks leading up to his time at the jail, and more since he'd been back. The vast expanse of green grass, the occasional tree, the sweet scent of flowers always hanging in the air—even in the winter months, even at four o'clock in the morning—gave the place a peaceful vibe. Serene. Tranquil. Had Jay picked out her final resting place?

Lincoln stopped pacing and stared at the back of the stone.

Where would he have been buried if he'd died in the accident? Nancy would've done the best with what she could've afforded, but it wouldn't have been Pleasant Valley. And that made sense—at least Katie Miller wouldn't have had to share space with the man who'd taken her life.

A slight breeze cooled the air but not enough to chill him. The next breeze that blew through his hair was warmer, like the caress of a palm over his cheek.

"You come here a lot."

The female voice shouldn't have surprised him, but it did. The only thing he'd been sure of was that whoever showed, it wouldn't be Jay. Despite all Lincoln had said, Jay wasn't vindictive, wasn't a liar, wasn't a man who did anything but love. He wore the truth and compassion like a tailored suit. Whoever hated Lincoln—it wasn't Jay.

Emily Shaw stood in the darkness on the opposite side of the headstone. She wore a skirt and jacket, a silk blouse underneath, her posture straight, her hands clasped in front of her. Her hair was styled into loose curls that framed her face but didn't move with the wind. Odd, how proper she looked at four in the morning, as if she were on her way to a prayer meeting. Did her fellow churchgoers know she tried to kill little kids in her spare time?

Moonlight lit her face. The uneasy look didn't mesh with the reason she'd come, with the notes she'd left, with the way she wanted to kill Lincoln.

Why? Didn't she like seeing him at her daughter's grave?

Fuck it. This was her choice. "This isn't your private property."

"No. I've just never seen you here at night." She crept closer to her daughter's grave marker. Without taking her gaze off the front of the stone, she said, "I may not have always understood my daughter, but I knew her well enough to know she'd be touched that you took the time."

This was what she wanted to say? She was better at letter writing. If she hadn't been a woman in her late forties, dressed like she was heading to church, he would've already punched her out. But things were more complicated than that. Always had been.

"I get what you think of me," he said. "I get how much pain you're in. But—"

"I'm not sure you do." She stared at him and cocked her head to the side, her hair moving in a single stiff block like a helmet she wore for protection. Funny how she had come alone to face him. Or maybe she hadn't.

Many of the headstones surrounding them were like monuments. They could easily hide a full-grown man crouched behind them. Lincoln forced himself to look at her again as she spoke.

"I may not be able to let this go. I may not be able to forgive you, but there are things you should hear." She dropped a hand to the corner of her daughter's headstone and didn't look at him as she continued. "She wouldn't want everyone's lives destroyed because of her death. My daughter would want you to forgive yourself. That's who she was." Emily let go of the stone and stepped around it. Lincoln wouldn't have let her get so close to him if he weren't so damn confused, if he didn't want to believe her so badly.

She stopped a foot from him. "If she were able to say it, she'd tell you she forgives you." Emily Shaw laughed. It sounded joyful and sad at the same time.

Was this woman crazy?

He shivered. Wasn't it supposed to get warmer as the morning approached?

"Don't ask me how she got that way," she said and laughed again. "Not from her father. Not from me. I'd say she learned to be so accepting, so forgiving from Jay, but she was like that before she met him, since she was a little girl. For a long time I let myself forget that about her. I know now, she'd never blame you for her death."

He scoffed.

"You don't believe me?"

"I'm not believing much of what you're saying."

She nodded and walked to the front of the grave. "I didn't want Jay and her to get married. I thought they were too young. That he was too naive to appreciate my baby, to take care of her." She played with the wedding band on her finger, and then touched the stone again. Was this some sort of therapy for her?

"I didn't think he was good enough for her. Not until the day I saw you with him at the grocery store. Then I knew. He's just like her. I may not understand how or why, but I know what he's doing with you isn't something she'd be angry over." Emily looked up at Lincoln. "He doesn't blame you, doesn't hate you. He's letting it go, moving on with his life, not letting the grief destroy him. He's honoring the spirit of who she was." Her eyes filled with tears. "He's the best of us."

Lincoln swallowed down the anger. She wasn't deserving of it. She never had been. "You didn't ask me to meet you here, did you?"

"No. I come when I can't sleep. To be close to her. To be alone with her. My husband doesn't even know." She paused. "I've seen you here sometimes, but...I wasn't ready to talk to you before now."

That had been his fear every time he had made the visit. He didn't want anyone to see him, didn't want her family faced with him at her grave. "Why now?" he asked.

"I'm not sure I can understand—not sure I can see the two of you together—but I don't want him to think he has to be ashamed of it, that he has to hide who he loves."

"He doesn't love me."

She let go of the stone. The sound of an approaching car broke the silence between them. It faded as the car drove past the cemetery.

"I used to watch my daughter with him. From the time they were seven years old they always had their heads together, talking, laughing. Like girlfriends. I'd never been that close to any boys, not even Stuart. At first, I was afraid Jay would break her heart. After they were married, I finally accepted there was something special there. Even if I didn't want to admit it, their connection was obvious. She loved him with everything she was. It was in the way she looked at him." Emily paused. "The same way I saw him look at you."

Lincoln shook his head and stared into the darkness toward the cemetery's lone exit.

"I know what I saw. He couldn't have gotten there without forgiving you first. There's not one ounce of hate in that man. Never has been."

She was right. Jay was the best of all of them.

"I don't mind you being here," she said. "It means something to me that you've come so often. I used to watch you from my car. I saw the shame, the sorrow." She raised her hand as if she wanted to reach over the tombstone and touch him. She didn't. She dropped her hand to her side. "My daughter wouldn't want you to live with that."

The glow of headlights spilled over them, blinding Lincoln. He held up a hand to shield his eyes. The light dimmed and swept away as the vehicle turned a corner in the distance, but not before he caught sight of the powder blue Honda parked along the cemetery road.

"Is that your car?" he asked her.

"Yes."

"Do you know the time?"

She checked her watch. "Four fifteen."

"You should leave." Whoever drove the vehicle through the winding road of Pleasant Valley Cemetery would be back. "It isn't safe here."

"Why?" She glanced to where the lights had come from. "Why did you ask if I wanted to meet you here?"

"You need to go." He gestured to her car. He had the urge to tug on her arm to get her moving but couldn't bring himself to approach her with any harshness.

She started for her car, and he followed a step behind.

"Do you have a cell phone?" he asked.

"I left it at home." She unlocked her car doors but didn't move to get in. "Is this about the shooting? The police said there were threats. Why?" She closed her eyes for a moment. She didn't need to ask, and he didn't need to answer. "Come with me," she said.

He opened the driver's-side door for her. "I have to end this."

She didn't move.

"I'm going to the police as soon as I see who it is."

She glanced around the dark cemetery and then at him before finally getting into the car. He shut the door behind her, and she started the engine, but didn't pull away. Instead she rolled down the window and spoke in a low whisper he couldn't hear. He leaned forward and rested a hand on the edge of the window frame.

"Things were easier then," she said. "Simpler for all of us. I think he needs you more than he ever needed her."

Lincoln squeezed his eyes shut. He couldn't let himself believe her. "I'm sorry," he said when he met her gaze. "I'm sorry for taking her from you—from him."

"I know you are." She patted his hand but didn't let the touch linger. He understood. "I want him to be happy, but I'm not certain I can watch—"

"No one expects you to be okay with seeing us together."

"Do you have to stay?"

"Yes." He straightened and stepped back from her car.

"If he loses someone again… I think this time, losing you will destroy him." She drove off without rolling up her car window. Her helmet hair still didn't blow in the breeze. It seemed more fitting than before.

She was a strong woman. Lincoln hoped he could be as strong.

* * * *

"Lincoln!" Jay waved his arm out the truck's open window as he pressed on the gas harder. Was there a speed limit in the cemetery? Probably nothing official. Most people knew to drive at a snail's pace. He would too, had he not been trying to save Lincoln's life.

The beam of the truck's headlights had revealed Lincoln standing at Katie's grave, staring at her headstone. Jay had to turn a corner on the lone road through Pleasant Valley, and he lost Lincoln to the darkness.

Another turn, and he slammed on the brakes. He was as close as he was going to get. He threw the truck in park, shoved open the door, and ran through the rows of headstones. "Lincoln!" he yelled again even though he couldn't see the man. He was out of breath fast. He had to be close. His foot caught on the edge of a flat grave marker, and he tripped. He landed on his belly, the heels of his hands scraping across the ground.

"Jay?" Lincoln was close, but Jay still couldn't see him in the darkness.

"Yeah." He pushed onto his hands and knees. Lincoln gripped him around the waist and helped him up. He winced as he put weight on his right ankle.

"Are you okay?" Lincoln's breath brushed over Jay's cheek. The moonlight offered enough light for Jay to see those dark eyes studying him. "What are you doing here?" Lincoln asked.

"Nancy said there was another note. What do you think you're doing coming here alone?"

"I need to take care of this. My way this time." Lincoln turned and walked away, the darkness enveloping him.

Jay followed, hobbling on his twisted ankle, keeping Lincoln in his sight. "I know who shot you."

Lincoln halted, and Jay did the same. His ankle throbbed more than when he'd walked on it. He leaned on the edge of the tombstone next to him. Something rustled above them. A flock of birds fluttered out from the black oak tree overhead.

"Oh God." Jay jerked his hand away from the headstone. His legs shook as he took a step back and looked down at the face of the stone. Thanks to the moon behind him, he saw the words. The headstones surrounding him were gone. He'd never see the rest of them again. Only that one.

"It's pretty," Lincoln said to the ground before them. "A good fit for her. She was beautiful."

Lilies adorned the top of the headstone and continued down the length of the sides, leafy stems and petals growing smaller until one lone lily sat near the bottom corner on each side. Etched into the granite above the dates were three simple lines:

Our Beloved
Katherine Anne Miller
Forever Young, Forever in Our Hearts

Nowhere did it mention she'd been a wife. A standard Stuart Shaw rewrite of history.

Jay dropped to his knees. He raised a hand and followed the stem of a lily toward the words. He traced her first name, and tears blurred his vision. There was no stopping them this time.

Lincoln knelt beside him and laid a hand on his back. "You never looked?"

"I couldn't." He swiped at the tears.

Lincoln grasped Jay's hands and lowered them from his face. "Don't. You have to let yourself grieve." He slid an arm around Jay's chest and pulled him sideways until he was cradled in Lincoln's arms, half across the man's lap. "So you can live."

With those words, Jay let the walls fall. He could barely breathe between the gasps. The tears fell from his face and dripped onto Lincoln's forearm, those strong arms never letting go of him.

"Breathe," Lincoln said in a low whisper to the hair above Jay's ear. "Just breathe."

Jay focused in on the low, deep voice.

"Let yourself miss her. Talk about her. Be angry. Or lonely. Or even happy. Whatever you need to feel. It's all okay, Jay. Just feel it. Keep remembering Katie, and it'll get easier to keep close to her."

Katie.

Jay pushed himself up. He wiped the tears from his eyes and met Lincoln's stare. "At first, I thought you and she were nothing alike. I know better now." He touched the side of Lincoln's face and ran the pad of his thumb over the man's lips. "You're the only one who made the pain go away. Who made me feel alive. Who listened. Who talked about her. The only one who's said her name since the funeral."

Lincoln pressed his forehead to Jay's. "No matter what, no one can take her from you."

Jay fell into Lincoln's arms again, holding as much as being held, taking in the warmth and scent of the man he loved. He wanted Lincoln in his life. They had to find a way. They had to take a chance.

Lincoln's hand around Jay's neck tightened, then went slack, and the man slumped in his arms. Jay caught him. "Lincoln?" He lowered him to the ground, and Lincoln sprawled out on the grass. "Lincoln!"

A sharp prick struck Jay's left arm, like a bee sting. Dizziness overwhelmed him. He fell backward and landed on the ground, his right arm draped over Lincoln's chest, his left foot touching the lower corner of the headstone, a lone lily visible over the tip of his shoe as his vision slowly darkened.

Chapter Thirty-One

Jay groaned and stretched. His left arm and hip ached, both feeling the throbbing pain of lying on a solid surface for far too long. The stubble of trimmed grass tickled his nose, and the smell of earth and flowers surrounded him.

The cemetery.

He opened his eyes. He was on the ground under the oak tree near Katie's grave. He tried to sit up but could barely move. His arms were restrained behind him and his ankles tied with rope.

Red nylon rope.

It stung to know he'd guessed right when he'd seen the fire on the news. All those gas cans in the garage had nothing to do with a generator. Would he ever stop losing people he loved?

More of the cemetery was visible around Jay. Dawn was fast approaching. A dark figure sat slumped against the headstone ten feet in front of him. Lincoln. Restrained similarly.

Jay gathered his strength and forced himself to a sitting position, his legs out in front of him. He leaned his shoulder against the tree. More dizziness. He'd been shot full of some kind of drug, and whatever it was, it was still in his system. He blinked and tried to force his feet under him.

His right ankle throbbed with each movement, the tight ropes keeping his legs pinned together. There was no way he'd make it to standing. "Lincoln! Wake up."

"Don't talk to him."

Despite Jay's earlier acceptance of who he'd find at the cemetery, his stomach churned at the ring of the familiar voice.

Todd sat perched on a headstone four rows away. The sun was rising behind him, and Jay didn't miss the gun Todd had aimed at Lincoln.

She had said, *"Someone should kill him."* How far would Todd go to please their mom?

Jay gasped. "What are you doing?" A low rumble came from Lincoln. He shifted in his restraints, but he didn't open his eyes. "What did you do to him?"

"He's fine. Just something to keep him out for a while."

Jay turned to get a better look at his brother. "Why are you doing this?"

Todd laughed, but the sound wasn't joyful or happy. He jumped off the tombstone without lowering the gun, and stepped closer. Jay saw his brother's face more clearly. The frustration and disappointment weren't a new expression.

What would it take to stop him?

"You're a real great brother, you know that?" Lincoln's words slurred.

The air rushed to Jay's lungs. "Linc, are you okay?"

Lincoln lifted his head. "Drugging him? Tying him up? Who does that to his own brother?"

"Shut up!" Todd moved a step toward Lincoln. "You take a man's world away, and you don't have the decency to stay clear of him? You should have walked away the minute you figured out who he was."

"Linc?" Jay squirmed in his restraints.

"It's okay, Jay. I'm all right."

"Todd, get over here and untie me." Jay struggled to wrangle his feet under him again.

Todd took another step closer to the headstone, the gun aimed at Lincoln's chest. "Stop talking to my brother."

"Fucking untie me!" Jay screamed.

"I'm sorry, Jay. Not yet. You weren't supposed to be here."

"*I'm* not supposed to be here? Why are you doing all this? For mom?"

Todd gave up on staring Lincoln down. The confused look he threw Jay's way was almost amusing. Did he think what he was doing made sense?

"Yes, for Mom." The gun shook in his grip. "And for you. For everyone." The warmth and compassion on Todd's face unnerved Jay. "I thought if I tortured him enough, he'd figure out he shouldn't live around here. Or maybe he'd figure out he shouldn't be alive at all."

Lincoln pushed his shoulder against the stone and sat taller. "So you tried to kill me to get your mommy's attention?"

"Fuck you! I shot at you to scare you. Once I found out you were fucking my brother, I knew the notes and the empty threats had to end. This all had to end."

Jay twisted his wrists in the ropes. "You hurt his family." How far would Todd go? He wouldn't actually kill Lincoln, would he? He had to know he'd never be able to claim credit for this. He'd never be able to tell their mom he'd done what she'd said she wanted.

Jay wasn't waiting to find out. The scraping of the ropes against his skin burned. They dug into his raw flesh. He kept at it. Soon it'd be bright enough out for anyone driving by the cemetery to see them. How long would Todd wait? "You can't believe she meant for someone to really kill him?" Jay asked, his voice more broken than he'd ever heard it.

"If he's gone then she can move on, enjoy being a grandma to my son. We can all move on. I have to end this." He looked at Jay. "End your suffering."

"End it? No matter what you do, she's still gone. You can't take that away from me." Moisture pooled at his wrists. He was bleeding. The physical pain crashed into him, blending with the emotional heartache. His chest felt heavy, like his lungs were full of blood, not air. He couldn't breathe.

"You'll never be free of this so long as he's in your life. He stole your future." Todd looked to Lincoln again. "Did you know they were trying to have a baby? Hell, she may have been pregnant already."

Lincoln's eyes widened, all dark pupils in the low light. Like the fake deer in Todd's garage. The fates of both man and deer were in Todd's hands now. Lincoln turned his head toward Jay in a slow sweep, like he couldn't bring himself to ask, but not knowing would be worse.

Jay shook his head. "No. She would've told me."

A long sigh and Lincoln lowered his eyelids. He rested his temple on the headstone. His head covered the words *Forever Young*. His closed eyes lined up with *Forever in Our Hearts.*

Todd strode closer, the hand with the gun steady.

Jay had to do something. He'd been right when he'd put all the clues together. Todd would not stop. He had spent his life vying for their mom's attention, and it was never enough. Jay had to get Todd to see he'd gone too far. He had to reach through Todd's pain and find his brother—the one who'd spent his life looking after Jay. Of course that was probably how this had started. Todd had driven Jay home from the funeral. Stayed with him for the first week. Without asking or offering, he'd slept on the couch every night. Had cleaned up the vomit when Jay first tried to eat. Had cleared the bathroom counter of Katie's makeup and body lotions.

"How could you hurt a little girl?" Jay asked.

"He wasn't getting the hint. I had to try something else. I'm so sick of this, Jay. Sick of worrying about you all the time. Of hearing Mom go on and on. I figured if he thought his niece was in danger, he'd leave town. I told everyone I went to training so I could follow her that day. If it had gotten serious, I'd have stepped in."

"They had to take her to the hospital." Had Todd lost his mind? Couldn't he see what he was doing was only going to make it worse— for so many people? "This *is* serious."

"You think I don't know that? This is your life, Jay. I care about your future."

"Right. Then why did you plant evidence to frame me? The Shaws?"

"Not to frame you. I didn't want him or the police to have clear answers if they looked into it. I figured he'd let it drop. But no. He kept on fucking you." Todd pointed the gun toward the headstone behind Lincoln. "Get on your knees and turn around. Face her grave."

Jay struggled against the ropes more. "What are you doing?"

"Ending this." Todd moved to Lincoln's side and pressed the gun to his temple. "Move!"

THE TIP OF the gun's barrel dug into Lincoln's skin. He had no doubt this guy would shoot him. Again. He should run. Attack. Something. If only his hands weren't cuffed behind him, and his legs tied together with rope.

Todd forced the gun harder against his skin.

Lincoln shifted onto his knees and did as instructed. Was there a part of him that wanted it over?

"Stay like that." Todd reached into Lincoln's back pocket and removed his wallet. Out came the newspaper clipping. It landed in front of Lincoln. Todd dropped a letter next to it and said, "Dear Nancy. I cannot go on. Not after what I've done. Please forgive me."

"You're not going to kill me."

"You don't think I'll do it? I saw her. Lying on the highway. That beautiful woman…her body broken, the life sucked out of her because of you."

"They'll know I didn't pull the trigger."

Jay still squirmed against his restraints. "Especially when I tell everyone."

"You won't want to put Mom and Dad through anything else."

"You think I'll cover for you? Are you crazy?" Jay's voice cracked on the last word.

Lincoln ached to comfort him. Was Todd really going to put his brother through losing someone else? Even if Lincoln didn't mean the same to Jay as she had, it would still hurt Jay to lose him. Wouldn't it? What had Emily said? *Losing you will destroy him.* Was she right?

"No one will believe I did anything," Todd said. "Suicide, plain and simple. I'm an EMT. My poker buddies are cops. I tell them what I found at my sister-in-law's grave, they aren't going to bother with much of an investigation." He thrust the gun at Lincoln. "Not for someone like you."

"Someone like him?" Jay screamed. "You don't know him."

Todd turned to Jay, his mouth hanging open. "Sometimes, little brother, you're so naive, so trusting. No wonder I'm always having to bail you out of trouble. No wonder you don't have a cent of the lawsuit money left. Did you give it all to some good-looking guy so you could get in his pants?" Todd stepped in front of Lincoln and looked him in the eye. "I'm going to do what you should have—what you couldn't." He raised the gun to Lincoln's head again.

"Todd!" Jay screamed. He stilled and the life drained from his face. "Don't do this."

Lincoln wanted to go to Jay, but the restraints held him back, never mind the asshole brother with the gun.

"I'm not doing anything. He is."

"Todd."

Jay's plea broke Lincoln's heart. "You're going to force your brother to watch this? What kind of sick fuck are you?"

Todd kept his focus locked on Lincoln.

Jay said, "You won't get away with this. You tried to kill his family. I saw all the damn gas cans in your garage. They're going to figure out it was arson."

"That wasn't me." Todd turned his attention on Jay. With a little more distraction, Lincoln might be able to knock the gun away. Then what? He was restrained. Todd wasn't.

Todd added, "What do you think I am?"

"A no-good bastard," Lincoln said. "A sick fuck who can't let his brother be happy."

"Shut up." Todd directed his next words to Jay. "I wouldn't do that. I wouldn't hurt little kids."

A chill raced up Lincoln's spine. He sat back on his haunches. *No.* "You left the note asking me to meet you here before the fire started."

"You're just catching up?"

Lincoln twisted his wrists in the cuffs. How had he not seen it before? Todd wouldn't have left a note if he was planning to kill

Lincoln in the fire. Someone else started it. *Mel.* "He tried to kill them. To collect the insurance money on the house."

"I did not."

"Insurance money?" Jay sat up, no longer fighting the restraints.

"Nancy doesn't own the house alone. Her husband's been paying her bills, making the insurance payments. So she wouldn't lose the place, and he'd collect the goddamn insurance after he burned it down. After he killed them."

Jay's mouth gaped open. "He removed the batteries from the smoke detectors."

Lincoln nodded. What would Mel do with Nancy now that she was still alive? Finish what he started? He'd have to get rid of her to keep the money for himself. Or at least convince her to give him all of it. No doubt with his fists.

"I won't see Jay anymore." Lincoln blurted out the words without thought. He had to get to Nancy and the kids.

"That's right," Jay said. "That's why I was trying to find him, to tell him it was over."

Over? Jay had to be playing along, but it didn't matter. They could never be together.

Why had he tried to convince himself of anything else? They had one path to follow, like a lone, dark highway with no crossroads and no way to turn around. It would never lead them to a place where they'd have a future with each other.

Todd raised the gun to his temple again and said, "Jay, don't watch."

Chapter Thirty-Two

Lincoln forced himself not to flinch as Todd pressed the cool steel of the gun's barrel against the side of his head. He'd be bruised from the force of it. That's if the bastard didn't kill him first.

The orange glow in the east spilled more light over the gravestones before Lincoln. If Todd had half a brain he wouldn't wait much longer. Of course the half a brain was debatable. Did he really think he'd get away with this?

Maybe.

Lincoln wrenched his wrists, trying to free his arms. Scenarios raced through his mind. Ram his shoulder into Todd's gut. Flip to his ass and swing his bound legs at Todd. Head butt the man in the groin. But even with the gun at Lincoln's temple, Todd had been smart enough to keep his body as far away as possible. Maybe a quarter of a brain, then. Lincoln would have to throw all his weight at the man.

So he did.

They twisted in midair, and Todd fell to his palms with Lincoln sprawled across his lower limbs. The gun landed three feet to their left. Now what?

Todd squirmed out from under Lincoln. Without the use of his hands, Lincoln had no hope of keeping the man down. Brilliant plan. He fought anyway, and they rolled with the struggle. Todd swung a heel at his chest, then jumped to his feet and kicked Lincoln in the gut. The force sent Lincoln rolling sideways. His shoulder with the gunshot wound slammed into the nearest headstone. The asshole kicked once more, and Lincoln's head smacked the stone. His vision blurred. Pain blasted through his skull like vibrations after the ring of a bell.

"Lincoln!" Jay's voice. Farther away than before. How far had they rolled?

Pain shot down Lincoln's healing arm and threatened to pull him into the dark fog rolling up around his consciousness. Todd manhandled him to his side, grabbed his ankles, and dragged him.

He needed to stay awake. He focused in on the only thing in his sight—the tombstone he'd smacked into. He read the epitaph:

The acts of this life are the destiny of the next.

Hardly. He didn't have to wait that long for destiny to do her thing.

The words blurred as the distance increased. Todd dropped Lincoln's legs. They were back in front of Katie Miller's grave again. Todd bent, picked up the gun, and dug in his pocket for another section of rope. He wound it around Lincoln's legs above the knees and left him lying there, his forehead mashed against Katie's headstone.

"Lincoln." Jay sounded as miserable as he had when he'd first looked at his wife's tombstone.

Losing you will destroy him.

He met the man's stare. "Jay." The desperation in his voice should've made him feel weak. It didn't. He needed Jay.

Jay was on his knees five feet from the tree. That's as close as he'd be able to get to standing. He locked gazes with Lincoln and said, "I'm tired of grieving. Tired of being lost. Todd…please."

The asshole didn't acknowledge his brother.

"Todd, look at me."

Nothing.

"I never had a chance to say good-bye to her. You can't do that to me again."

Todd's jaw twitched. He bent to where Lincoln lay on the ground and tapped the barrel of the gun to his head. "Don't move."

Funny. Like he had a choice. There'd be no running or fighting with the way his legs were bound. He had to wait for Jay.

Todd held the gun on Lincoln, stepped to the side, and removed the restraints from Jay's ankles.

Jay rose, wobbling when he put weight on his right foot. "Untie my hands."

"Someday you'll thank me for this." Todd left Jay's arms bound and helped him shift into a kneeling position in front of Lincoln. "Say your good-bye. And hurry before someone sees us." He backed up, giving them a semblance of privacy. Oddly polite for a guy about to blow someone's brains out.

Fucker. As soon as Lincoln got out of the restraints, he'd show

Todd that when you wanted to take someone down, you didn't hesitate.

Jay bent and pushed at Lincoln with his shoulder and arm. Lincoln took the cue and tried to help get off the ground so he could kneel with Jay.

It wasn't working. Todd sighed. He gripped Lincoln by the upper arm and hefted him until Lincoln knelt facing Jay, then Todd moved away again. Could this guy really go through with killing him? Most people didn't have it in them to take another life. But Lincoln couldn't take a chance. He had to get to Nancy and the kids—had to protect them this time.

He saw the fear in Jay's eyes. No matter what had happened, no matter what Lincoln had done to hurt Jay, he could count on him. "You have to help my sister. You have to stop Mel from hurting her or the kids. Not for me. For them. Please, Jay."

"Shut the hell up." Jay kissed him, the touch of lips soft, as sweet as Lincoln had ever known. "You talk too much. I'm not letting him kill you."

"Get up." Todd tugged on Jay's arm.

It went down fast. Jay lunged at his brother, and both men toppled over. Lincoln twisted his wrists in the restraints again, trying to slip out of the cuffs. No way would Jay win with his hands tied behind his back. Stupid man would be joining his wife if he wasn't careful.

A shot rang out.

Lincoln stilled, and so did the wrestling men ten feet away. Todd wriggled out from under Jay and got to his feet, but Jay remained on the ground, his back to Lincoln.

"Jay?" Lincoln tried to stand and fell forward to his knees. "Jay!"

Time seemed to slow. Finally, Jay rolled and pulled his legs up underneath him. He sat up. "I'm okay."

Air rushed into Lincoln's lungs. He could breathe again.

Todd had the gun aimed at Jay. "You're choosing him over your family?"

"Todd!" A deep voice rang out from somewhere near veteran Victor Donnelly's grave. Howard Miller was running in their direction. "Point that gun somewhere else." Howard rushed toward his sons, followed by his wife. Both parents were dressed in pajamas, overcoats, and dress shoes. Susan Miller was having difficulty running in her heels. Or perhaps it was the sight of her sons—one tied up on the ground, the other aiming a gun at the first—that had her every step faltering.

Todd stared at the gun then followed its path to Jay like he'd just realized where he had it aimed. He lowered the barrel until it pointed at the ground.

"What the hell is going on here?" Howard stepped between his sons and stole the gun from Todd's hand.

Susan approached Jay and dropped to the ground. She hugged her son, the grip so tight Jay grunted. She let go of him and untied his arms, tears streaming down her face. Jay's eyes were wide as he watched her, like she was a crazy person in the middle of a fit, and he wasn't ready to trust her.

"Someone explain!" Howard shouted. "First we get a call at four thirty in the morning from Emily asking us where Jay is, then some guy knocks on our door and makes all kinds of horrible accusations. When we finally convinced him it wasn't us, he tells us to come here and talk to Jay before someone gets hurt."

Lincoln sank back to his heels and sighed. He owed Paul a thank-you.

"Todd tried to kill Lincoln." Jay staggered to his feet, his gaze on his brother. "Dad, do you have your cell?"

Howard pulled out his phone and handed it to Jay.

Susan gasped. "What are you doing?"

"Calling the cops."

"No. You can't do this to your brother."

"Me? He did this to himself."

"No! Let's talk about this first." She grabbed the phone and yanked it away from Jay. It slipped out of her grip and smashed against the tombstone beside her. The phone broke into pieces that rained onto the grass-covered grave. She stared at the busted phone and said, "That man did this to all of us."

They could discuss Lincoln all they wanted. He had other priorities. "Jay, I have to get to Nancy."

"I know." Jay limped to him and untied his legs. He reached for Lincoln's hands but stopped when he found the locked cuffs. "Dad, find the key on Todd." Jay got off the ground and faced his mom. "Lincoln made a mistake. We have all made mistakes. We'll all make more. You want to know why she was out driving that night? Because of me. Because I wanted fucking ice cream to go with the cake she'd baked. It was a stupid joke I made every year. That night she really did forget, and I couldn't keep my goddamn mouth shut. I told her we were really ready for kids if the honeymoon was over. You should have seen the crushed look on her face. She grabbed her purse and keys and said she was going to the store for the ice cream. She was gone before I could tell her to forget it, that it was too late at night, to tell her to stay home. Before I could apologize for being a selfish prick."

Lincoln stood, his arms still bound. "None of this was your fault."

"She would've been home singing 'Happy Birthday' and eating cake if it weren't for me."

How could Jay blame himself? Lincoln stepped in front of him. "What would Katie say about that?"

Jay glanced away.

"You have to know she'd never blame you for any of this."

"He's right." Susan moved closer to her son. "Jacob Miller, no matter what anyone has said or done, you are not to blame." She looked to Todd. "We've all been angry, bitter."

Jay said, "Todd's crossed too many lines. He was going to kill someone!"

Her eyes widened as if what she'd witnessed her son about to do had just sunk in.

"Mom," Todd pleaded. "I can't leave Marge and the baby."

She walked toward him, her shoes giving her no problems as if she fluttered above the ground between her sons. "Jay's right. You went too far."

"I did what you said you wanted. I was making him pay."

"I did want him to pay, but...I never wanted this." She stopped before Todd, and her shoes sank into the earth. She lost several inches and looked small. Frail. "Did I?" Her tears came quickly and everyone stared at her, eyes wide, Lincoln included.

Howard went to her and held her in his arms. She sobbed and clung to her husband.

"You'll see, Mom." Todd snatched the gun from the hand Howard had pressed against his wife's back.

Lincoln barely had time to take a breath. Jay shoved him aside as Todd fired. They fell, Jay's weight thrusting Lincoln backward. His injured arm and the side of his head smacked the ground as Jay landed on top of him.

Lincoln heard the shouts. Howard's. Susan's. Todd's. But all he saw was Jay. All he felt was the blood seeping from Jay's chest onto his own. Using his body and legs, he carefully rolled Jay to the ground.

"Jay?" Howard had the gun in one hand, Todd by the arm in his other. "Is he shot?"

Susan ran to her youngest son and knelt beside him. "Jacob?"

"Get these cuffs off me." Lincoln was on his knees on Jay's other side. "Now!"

Howard tossed Susan a key, and she unlocked the cuffs, silent tears streaming down her face.

His hands free, Lincoln lunged for Jay. He flattened his palms to the blood-soaked shirt. A chest wound, low, over the rib cage.

"Hang on, honey." Susan stroked Jay's brow with a shaking hand. She looked at Lincoln. "Do you have a phone?"

"No."

Jay's breath hissed as he said, "It's bad."

"No." Lincoln shook his head. "Stay still." He pressed harder against the wound and to Susan said, "Get in your car and find the nearest phone. Call for help."

She stared at Lincoln for a shocked moment.

"Go!"

She kissed her son's temple, stood, and took off, the heels of her shoes not even connecting with the grass.

Jay spoke again. "Maybe this was…always supposed to end…like this."

"Don't talk."

"And that's why she's not here…so she didn't have to…lose me…like this."

"Stop. You talk too much. Besides"—Lincoln brushed his lips along Jay's cheek—"she doesn't get you. Not yet."

Ragged breaths hissed in Lincoln's ear.

Howard knelt on Jay's other side. "Too much blood."

Lincoln straightened. Todd sat on the ground where he'd last been standing, his arms folded around his knees. He was rocking, staring at his brother. Lincoln ignored him. If the asshole ran off, he'd find him. No matter where. No matter how long it took. "I have to get him to the hospital. Now."

"Is that your truck?" Howard asked.

With the sun over the horizon, it was hard to miss.

Lincoln's truck sat along the cemetery road two hundred feet away. He grabbed the gun from Howard and threw it on the ground. He pressed Howard's hands to Jay's chest. "Keep pressure here."

He dug in Jay's pocket for the keys and sprinted for the truck, pushing aside any thoughts on what he was doing, pure instinct driving him on. He climbed behind the wheel, started the engine, and slammed on the gas pedal, then raced through the sea of headstones toward where his lover lay bleeding. Nothing would stop him from saving Jay.

From saving Nancy and the kids.

From making it up to all of them.

Chapter Thirty-Three

Lincoln maneuvered his truck around the next corner, a mile from the hospital, and kept his gaze fixed on the road before him. Driving through the early morning traffic with his hand on Jay's bleeding chest wasn't how he wanted to start back on the road, but he could do this.

He had to do this.

He gave the truck more gas and pressed harder against Jay. "Hang on. Please. Just hang on. We're almost there."

Jay's next breath came out as a gurgle.

One more intersection, and Lincoln swung into the Grant County Medical Center's parking lot. He slammed on the brakes in front the emergency room entrance, shoved the gearshift in park, and raced around to the other side. Two women in scrubs stood near the entranceway.

He threw the passenger door open and shouted, "I need help!"

One of the women ran inside the hospital, and the other rushed toward Lincoln.

Jay was still conscious. He stared at Lincoln and reached out with his right hand. Lincoln gripped it in his and pressed his forehead to Jay's. "Don't you dare fucking die on me."

"Sir, step aside." The woman tugged on Lincoln's arm.

"He's been shot." He let go of Jay's hand and moved so she could get closer through the open door.

The other woman returned with a gurney and two more hospital personnel. They lifted Jay from the truck to the gurney and headed in through the ER's sliding doors.

Lincoln ran after them, but one of the women stopped him outside a room marked TRAUMA as they wheeled Jay in. "You need to wait out here while we take a look. Go ahead and wash all that blood off." She pointed toward a nearby sink, then turned and pushed through the double doors.

Lincoln stared down at the blood on his hands. His chest felt heavy. Was he still breathing?

Was Jay?

He wanted to stand there until he knew for sure. But he needed to find Nancy and the kids. Hopefully Jessica had been released a few hours earlier, and they had waited at the hospital with Paul like Lincoln had asked them to do.

He slowly moved to the sink, washed his hands, and watched as the blood ran down the drain, but it would never be gone for him. He'd seen too much of it in his life.

"Lincoln!"

At first it sounded like someone calling him from inside the room with Jay. He took a step toward the closed doors of the trauma room, and then the voice registered.

He spun around. Nancy and the kids were at the far end of the hall, all running toward him, Jessica's hand tucked inside her mom's. He met them halfway.

Without a thought on what he was doing, he scooped Jessica into his arms and held her tight. "Are you okay?" he asked Nancy.

"Yes. Are *you* okay?" She stared at the blood on his sleeve and gripped his arm. "Is this your blood?"

He looked toward the trauma room behind him. He wanted to rush inside and find out what the hell was going on.

"Lincoln!" Nancy shouted. "What happened?"

"I'm fine," he said. "Are you guys alone?"

"Paul's here. He just went to the bathroom. He left to find Jay's parents earlier, but then he came back to stay with us like you wanted."

Lincoln faced Nancy again. "We need to talk to the police."

"Was that Jay? How did he get hurt?"

"He was shot. But he's going to be okay." He couldn't force himself to say anything more than that. "Mel's the one who started the fire."

She stared at him, her mouth hanging open.

"Mel?" Adam asked. "He tried to hurt us?" Tears filled his eyes.

With his free hand, Lincoln gripped Adam by the back of the neck and pulled him in for a fierce embrace. "It's going to be okay. They'll figure out it was arson. He'll be a suspect." He met Nancy's stare. "We stay together until they arrest him. No one goes anywhere alone."

She nodded.

He needed to take them to the police station, tell the cops about

Mel paying for the mortgage and homeowner's insurance, but he couldn't move one step farther away from the trauma room. He had to know if Jay was going to be okay.

So he held on to his family. And he waited.

Chapter Thirty-Four

The woman outside Jay's hospital room continued sobbing. She'd been carrying on for a half hour. Someone needed to find her a private room, so she could let it all out—not that it would be gone anytime soon.

That level of despair and grief was all too familiar, and Jay wanted to put that phase of his life behind him—not forgotten, but not a part of his every day. Katie deserved his memories to be full of better times.

He'd been waiting for the doctor to give the okay on his release for three hours. Hospitals rarely had time estimates correct. Did they get the details of treatments and medications as out of whack as they did how long it took for a doctor to sign release papers? Jay's dad kept walking in and out of the room, giving Jay updates on who was coming their way—the fat nurse, the too-talkative nurse, the creepy guy nurse, the nurse who wore the crooked ponytail. Jay was ready to call a cab all the way from Fort Wayne. Any minute now.

His dad entered the room again. "The one with the tattoo said there's no update. Just sometime today."

"It's okay."

His dad sat in a chair, his hands tapping the metal bar that ran the length of the hospital bed. "You'll feel much better once we get you home, get you in your own bed."

"Yeah. But you don't have to stay with me."

His dad met Jay's stare. "Yes. I do."

Jay nodded.

They were silent for a few moments. Then the tapping sped up. Most likely his dad's irritation had more to do with the news he'd shared with Jay earlier.

Jay's parents were separating. Not officially divorcing. Not moving apart. Sleeping in different rooms. His dad had said, "Your mother and I haven't seen eye to eye for years. It's just going to take time."

Todd had been arrested and pleaded no contest, while Jay had undergone two surgeries and spent more time than he'd ever cared to in a hospital bed. Todd had made a deal in exchange for his plea. His wife would not be charged for her part in the threats against Lincoln. She had helped Todd steal the photo of Katie from the hospital morgue's records, knowing about Todd's threats but not how far he had planned to go with them. Todd was awaiting sentencing at his own home.

Hopefully, he'd get to see his child enter the world before he went to prison. Jay was angrier with his brother than he'd ever been with anyone. He expected Todd to be punished for what he'd done to him, to Lincoln, but Jay also felt sorry for his brother. A part of him understood what had pushed Todd to where his actions seemed logical. A part of him had known their mother's favoritism toward her younger son would reach a boiling point. He just wished he'd seen the depth of his brother's pain sooner.

How many people would he have to learn to live without? Would he ever be at peace again? Ever have a life not full of anger and grief?

He wanted to try. He wanted to move forward.

His dad wasn't defending Todd, but he had hired a lawyer for him. Jay and his parents had a long way to go in figuring out where they stood with one another. And it had to start with a single question.

"I need to know something, Dad."

The tapping stopped. "Okay."

"When I get home, and I'm all healed, are you going to lecture me?"

"About what?"

"I need to know things will be different. I don't want this to be an issue between us."

"What your brother did?"

"No. Lincoln. Can you live with knowing how I felt about him?" Jay pulled the thin blue blanket up higher. He wanted to get out of the hospital gown and get dressed. Wearing what amounted to a nightgown that didn't close in the back made him feel exposed. Vulnerable.

Oh, who was he kidding? It had nothing to do with his attire. "Can you live with how I *feel* about him?"

His dad ran the tips of his fingers along the metal rail. "I won't lie to you." He dropped his hands to his thighs. The resulting slap echoed off the bare walls. "I don't get it. I can't see how you spent time with him, let alone were"—he drew in a long breath—"intimate with him. But I don't need to understand how you got there. I saw him at the cemetery. He was determined. I took one look at him, and I didn't hesitate. I let him lift you into that truck and drive you—*drive my son*—to the hospital. I knew he'd do whatever he had to, to save your life." He sighed. "I want you to be happy."

"I don't think I can be."

His dad let out a snort and smiled.

What was so amusing?

"You're usually so mature. I forget how young you really are. Before you lost your wife, you lived in a comfortable, beautiful, ignorant bubble. You didn't have to look around to find someone to love. She had been there with you since you were seven years old. Life isn't always that easy for everyone else. Happiness takes work. You have to decide to make your life what you want it to be. Then you have to go after it." He paused until Jay met his stare. "Does he want you?"

"He says we can't—"

"That's not what I asked you."

"I think he does."

"Then you know what to do. You always know the right thing to do."

* * * *

The sun warmed Jay's face. The peacefulness in his heart matched his surroundings: the black oak tree full of green leaves, the sparrows chirping from their perches high above, the acres of trimmed grass, the line of trees to the west, the road winding through the array of monuments to the east—it all made for a lovely spot for his wife to rest. He should have told Emily when she'd made the selection. He'd make a point to do so now. Some things were never too late to say.

He slipped his fingers under the collar of his shirt and slid the chain out. He removed it and the rings from around his neck. "I'll always love you." A sweet flowery scent floated up from the ground and surrounded him. Lilies.

Hadn't he read something about lilies once…about symbolizing renewal and rebirth?

"I hope you understand why I have to let these go." He draped the chain over Katie's headstone. The two gold bands clanked as they hit the side of the stone. "You'll always be a part of me."

He took a step back. "I love him. I know you'll love him too."

* * * *

The door to room nineteen was tucked behind the ice machine at the end of the motel's long building. Jay knocked and held his breath as he waited. His healing ribs ached more without the breathing. Funny. He figured the pain would lessen without the forcing of air in and out. Maybe it did hurt worse to hold things inside. He let in a deep breath, and the pain eased.

The door opened a crack, and Jessica stuck her head out. "Jay!" She shoved the door open the rest of the way. It banged on the wall and rattled the room's lone window. So strong for such a little thing.

With the black-and-white kitten tucked under her arm, Jessica charged forward and hugged Jay's legs, the kitten squeezed between them. He patted her head, and she released him.

"Nice cat," he said as he knelt on one knee beside her.

She cupped her hand around her mouth and whispered in his ear. "I'm not supposed to have her in my bedroom, but here the bedroom's all we have."

The room was small with two double beds, one end table between them, and a lone dresser with a thirteen-inch TV sitting on top.

Nancy stepped up behind Jessica and encouraged her daughter into the room where the boys sat watching TV, the dog on the bed between them. Jessica hopped onto the bed and snuggled in between her brothers, her arm around Sparky's neck.

Nancy didn't say anything. She held the door in one hand and raised an eyebrow at Jay.

"Is he staying here?"

"I promised him—"

"I can't lose him."

She let go of the door and glanced back at her kids, then gave Jay a nod. "He's at Sonny's."

"Thank you. I saw on the news your husband was arrested."

She nodded. "My ex, soon."

"That's good. For you. And for Linc. He shouldn't have to live with more guilt."

She sighed and said, "He's more broken than before."

"He saved me. I'd like to return the favor."

A laugh erupted out of her. "Who *are* you? Without that accident, your life would've been chugging along just fine."

"We can't change what happened. We can only go forward."

"Of all the people my brother could have met since that accident, he needed someone who looks at life the way you do. It's crazy he found that in the one person he hurt most."

"He never hurt me."

Jessica giggled from the bed. Jay smiled, then sobered with another glance around the meager room. "Have you been staying here since the fire?"

"Yeah." Nancy glanced at her kids again and gave Jessica a smile when the little girl looked her way.

"Linc too?"

"Yes." She watched Jay, studying him. "He looked for an apartment again today. We can't afford much. There aren't many places that'll rent two rooms to a family with three kids, a dog, and a cat." She shrugged. "I can't get rid of their pets, though. It's all they have left."

"It's hardly all they have."

Tears welled in her eyes. She breathed deep and pressed the heels of her hands to her eyelids. The tears were gone when she lowered her arms, her face losing some of the tension. "It'll be okay. We're both still working."

Jay knew he'd made the right decision as soon as he'd thought of it, and seeing her strength and courage confirmed that. He pulled out the check with Nancy's name on the front and held it out to her. "I want you to have this."

She reached for it, but froze before her fingers touched the paper. "What is that?"

"It's my share of the money from the lawsuit." He placed the check in her palm and gave her hand a squeeze.

"I can't take this."

"I don't want it. I never did. Use it to buy a house. Jessica's medicine. To keep your kids safe. My wife wouldn't have wanted Lincoln to pay this money in the first place. She'd like it if you used it." He pleaded with one look. "I can't keep it."

She held the check to her chest and tears filled her eyes again. "You'll bring my brother home?"

"That's the plan."

* * * *

The Harley was parked two spaces from the front door of Sonny's. Jay stopped beside it and ran his fingers over the tank. He'd assumed it was destroyed in the fire. Damaged at least. The paint job was perfect, the orange flames and eagle brighter than before. The entire bike was in excellent condition. Time and care had gone into making it look as good as it must have when it was new.

Sonny's Tavern was nearly empty. A couple of young guys sat together, laughing as one told the other a story with arm gestures and curse words mixed in, the bartender and waitress stood behind the bar drying the day's glasses, and the old man sipping whiskey was parked at his usual table by the restrooms.

At the end of the bar was Lincoln, both hands on the glass in front of him. He wore a T-shirt with *Edgefield Motel* printed on the back and no leather jacket. He was hunched over his drink, looking more like the old whiskey sipper than the man Jay had come to know.

The bartender stepped up to Lincoln and asked, "You want another soda?"

Lincoln nodded, reached for the bowl of peanuts on the bar in front of him, and slowly crushed one between his fingers while the bartender poured him a refill.

Jay sat on the stool next to Lincoln, gestured for the same from the bartender, and waited, not sure how or where to begin. Each man had several swallows of their drinks, Lincoln never glancing away from the glass in his hands. Words raced through Jay's mind, but none of them were enough.

The silence lingered until Lincoln set his glass on the bar and cleared his throat. "I'd give anything to bring her back to you." He grabbed his glass and took another long gulp. He wiped his mouth with the back of his hand but didn't let go of the glass. "I'd give anything for you to know how sorry I am."

"Jesus, Linc. I know how sorry you are. You're the most decent man I've ever met. The way you care for your sister and her kids. The way you've cared for me. No one helped me through my grief like you did. I think…" He bit his lower lip.

"What?"

"I think, if Katie still exists somewhere, she made sure we found each other. It would bother her how much you were hurting. And she'd want you to have someone. She'd want me to love someone again."

The stare Lincoln gave Jay was intense, those dark eyes unflinching. He finally looked away and clenched his eyes shut. "There are some things in life you can't go back from. They're always there with you, waiting." He shook his head. "No matter what has happened between us or what we've said, there's no going back from what I did. I was responsible for the death of your wife." He faced Jay again. "Why don't you hate me?"

"That night behind the bar when I figured out who you were, I wanted to tell you how much losing her hurt me. I wanted to scream at you, punch you out. I wanted to hate you."

"And when did that instinct change?"

"When I saw you—really saw who you were. You cared about what happened. It destroyed you as much as it did me."

Lincoln stared at the line of whiskey bottles on the shelf behind the bar and clutched the glass in his hand. "I think..." He swallowed and started again. "There are two kinds of forgiveness. The kind you can give to your loved ones who've wronged you, and the kind of forgiveness you can give to people you don't even know—strangers— who've hurt you. Most people can give the first. Few know how to give the second. It's easier to hate a stranger."

"You're not a stranger to me."

"I was when you forgave me." Lincoln spun the glass in his hand, finally letting go. "Seems to me if the one person who lost the most can forgive me, then maybe I can forgive myself. At least let it go like I haven't been able to do."

"I'm glad, Linc." Jay pressed his knee against Lincoln's. The conversation he'd feared since he'd woken up at the hospital had unfolded differently than he'd expected. Perhaps he had never given Lincoln, or himself, enough credit. It could have been over that first night behind the bar, or when Lincoln was shot, or when Jay hit him, with not another word spoken between them.

"She was so beautiful," Lincoln said. "I think about her...a lot. The day after I met you, I went to her grave. I'd been going there since the accident, but that was the first time I talked to her. I told her about you, but I didn't know who you were yet." A smile appeared at the corners of his mouth. "I told her how much I wanted to move past the accident, take care of Nancy and the kids, move on with someone like you, but I didn't want it to seem like I took what I'd done lightly. It's strange. I always sensed she was saying it was okay. That I could move on."

"She'd never have held an accident against you. Not even if it had taken me from her."

"If that's true, then she was perfect for you." Lincoln looked tired and a little unsure, as if something had aged him since Jay had last seen him. What? The fire? The shooting? Their time apart?

The old man who sat alone across the bar, sipping his whiskey, staring off at nothing caught Jay's eye. The man wore an old tattered jean jacket, his gray hair long. He had a full beard, a sad and lonely expression on his weathered face. He clutched his drink with both hands, never letting them stray from the glass with the exception of the time it took his right hand to raise it to his lips for a long, slow sip. Was there anyone in the world who cared about that old man? Would anyone take the time to plan a funeral, pick out a casket or a burial plot when he died?

Jay let his gaze hang on the old man for another moment, and then he looked to Lincoln and said, "She's not the only one who's perfect for me." He stood, leaned in close, and said, "Give it a few minutes, then meet me out back." He held his breath as he stepped away from the bar and the man he was counting on to take a chance with him.

He was betting his entire future on that one sentence.

LINCOLN SUCKED IN a long breath with Jay's words. He watched the other man leave. Jay didn't falter as he made his way through the bar and out the rear entrance. The door closed behind him, and Lincoln faced the line of whiskey bottles.

Could he really do this?

He wanted to believe he owed it to himself. The truth was, he owed it to both of them.

He stood and followed the same path Jay had, passing by the old guy sipping whiskey at a table near the bathrooms. Lincoln didn't hesitate. He shoved open Sonny's back door and exited into the warm night air. The full moon lit the parking lot more than the streetlamps.

Jay waited for him, leaning against the wall near where they'd first kissed, where they'd first touched.

"Come here." Jay tugged him in close.

Lincoln couldn't trust himself to hold Jay. He stared at the man's chest—where the blood had been when he'd lifted Jay into his truck and drove him to the hospital, where he had pressed against the blood-soaked shirt as he raced through the streets, listening to the breaths gurgling out of Jay, feeling the tears stream over his own cheeks. "Are you okay?"

"I am now."

He kept staring at Jay's chest; it moved up and down with each breath. He'd spend forever watching the man breathe if he could.

Jay cupped Lincoln's chin and forced his head up until their gazes locked. "I'll be okay if you say yes. I don't want to live without you."

"This—us—it can't work."

"It has to." Jay brushed his lips over Lincoln's ear. "I don't want to lose you."

The warmth of Jay's body against his made it hard to think. Lincoln gripped Jay's hip in his hand. "Can you promise me every time you look at me she isn't all you'll see? That you won't see everything I took from you?"

Jay kissed along Lincoln's cheek and chin to the corner of his mouth. "Every time I look at you all I see is you. I can't promise it'll be easy, but I don't even want to think what it'll be like if we don't try. She deserves to be remembered, to be talked about. I'd like to share her with you. I know you're strong enough to learn to love her too. Not to hate yourself because we're here and she's not."

"You give me a lot of credit."

"You've earned it." Jay wrapped his arms around Lincoln's neck. The press of Jay's mouth to his melted Lincoln's resolve to think instead of feel. He pulled Jay closer. Their tongues met, like old lovers, tentative, slow at first, relearning each other, remembering what was so good about being together.

Lincoln fell into the sweet oblivion of kissing Jay. His world shrank to that parking lot, to the two of them.

Slowly Jay placed one chaste kiss after another on Lincoln's lips before speaking. "I was thinking..."

"You think too much." Lincoln leaned in. He wanted more of that kiss. More of Jay.

Jay pressed two fingers to Lincoln's lips. "You need somewhere to live. And I could use help fixing up my place."

"You can't seriously—"

"I want you to live with me. If it's too weird to live in my house, I want us to get our own place."

"Jay...my sister needs me."

"She'll have you. She's got the money to buy a new house. To take care of Jessica, the boys. There'll be more than enough."

"What are you talking about?"

"I gave her my share of the settlement. I never wanted it. It was my parents and Stuart who started it all."

Lincoln stared at Jay, then grabbed him by the back of the neck and crushed their mouths together. Jay Miller couldn't possibly be for real.

How the hell had this man, practically a kid, whom Lincoln had hurt so badly, kept from turning into an angry, jaded person? How had Jay learned to love again?

Following his lead was the least Lincoln could do. He wanted a life with Jay. Wanted to believe they could move beyond the past and really live again.

Wanted to believe forgiveness and love were enough.

Jay held Lincoln's face in his hands. "Come home with me, Linc."

Lincoln rested his forehead against Jay's temple. "You're sure?"

"I am." Jay lifted the sleeve of Lincoln's T-shirt and traced his fingers over the destroyed tattoo. "The eagle's a symbol of courage and wisdom. Some believe if you can embrace both, you can fly above all of the shit in your life."

"All of it?"

Jay nodded and rolled up his own shirtsleeve. The outline of an eagle feather crossed his upper arm; two wolves filled the interior of the feather, running side by side.

Lincoln ran the tips of his fingers over one wolf, then the other. "Why?"

"I wanted you to know...to see...we can both live beyond our pasts. Together."

Whether or not he could forget what happened, Lincoln had a chance at a future, a life he thought he'd never have. He reached for Jay, pressed his lips to the man's neck, and held on.

Maybe Jay was meant to be his after all.

Maybe they were meant to fall in love.

To save each other.

Epilogue

Jay glanced up from the open book lying on the kitchen table before him and checked the time on the clock above the stove. Two a.m. He really needed to get some sleep. Tomorrow was set to be a busy day.

Just one more section, and then he'd put the book away.

The next exam for his History of World War II class was in a week, and he didn't want to ruin his A average. If he could keep it up for the rest of the term, he might be able to get more financial assistance next time around. As it stood now, he and Lincoln were working their asses off to pay for his tuition, their rent, and their lingering hospital bills.

Not that Jay wanted it any other way.

They were building a new life for themselves. Together.

He returned to his reading. The next section was titled *D-day: Letters Home.* The first page included a photocopy of a handwritten letter by a young paratrooper from the 508th Parachute Infantry Regiment of the 82nd Airborne Division. The letter to his fiancée was dated June 5, 1944, the day before the Invasion of Normandy.

He told her nothing of the war, where he was located, or for what he was most likely preparing. Instead he wrote about what he wanted their future together to be like. He described buying a home in the rural farmlands of Wisconsin, spending their nights together on a porch swing watching the sun set over the sea of rolling hay fields, dancing under a blanket of stars, growing old together.

Alongside the letter was a colorized portrait of the man in his paratrooper uniform. He had a full head of red hair, trimmed short, a wide smile, and one crooked front tooth. He looked innocent and barely sixteen.

Below the letter was a notation that read *Private Arthur Roberts died on June 6, 1944 during Operation Neptune at the Invasion of*

Normandy. He was killed in midair during the paratroopers' descent into France, having never seen Wisconsin or his fiancée again.

Sadness for the young man who hadn't had a chance to live the life he'd hoped for overcame Jay. He set the book down and removed his glasses, the sadness turning to relief at how very lucky he was in his own life. Not many people got the kind of second chance he'd been given.

He went to the kitchen sink and filled a glass with water. The ancient pipes behind the walls rattled. He switched off the faucet before the clanking woke Lincoln. Their new place was in serious need of work—even more than Jay's old house.

He sipped the water as his thoughts returned to the young paratrooper and the unfulfilled promise of those nights with his fiancée, the Wisconsin house and farm and fields and…

A porch swing.

Jay stared out the window above the sink into the darkness behind the house. That was what he'd suggest for the place once they'd taken care of the basics. A swing overlooking the fenced-in backyard where they could sit alone under the night sky. He'd point out the stars and share what he knew of the Iroquois legends related to the origins of the constellations and see if Lincoln knew the same ones.

God, Jay had never been this romantic in his life. Maybe with the passing of time came a sentimentality that the kid he'd been a few years ago could never comprehend, or maybe it was something else. Maybe whatever time he'd get to spend with Lincoln would always be special—because they'd been so close to not having any more time at all.

An arm came around his waist, and a hand settled over his stomach. A warm, solid body pressed against his back.

"You smell good." Lincoln's voice was low, and the heated air from his breath blew across Jay's neck, sending a shiver throughout Jay's body. He'd never get tired of this man's touch.

Jay tilted his head back. "You feel good."

Lincoln let out a little hum in response and kissed the side of Jay's neck. "You're studying too hard. Come to bed."

Jay leaned into Lincoln's bare chest, grateful he hadn't slipped on his own shirt before heading into the kitchen to read because he'd also never tire of feeling the press of their bare bodies. He reached around behind him and held Lincoln in return—even more grateful Lincoln hadn't put on anything more than a pair of briefs. If only Jay weren't wearing the jeans.

"Did the light wake you?"

Lincoln brushed his lips over Jay's neck again and ran a hand up his arm. "No, the cold bed beside me did." He paused his touch at the tattoo on Jay's upper arm—the outline of the feather and the two wolves running side by side within. He ran the pad of his thumb over the tattoo, gave a stroke to one wolf, then the other, and caressed Jay's neck with his lips at the same time. Ever since Jay had shown Lincoln the tattoo that symbolized the future he wanted for them, Lincoln had been obsessed with touching and kissing and licking Jay's skin over that tattoo.

Those sure, strong hands had Jay forgetting about his coursework. He let his weight settle against Lincoln more. He reached up with his other hand and held the back of Lincoln's neck. "I love it here." He could stand there at that chipped and stained kitchen sink all night, so long as Linc had a hold of him.

Lincoln laughed—that deep rumble in his chest that he only let out when Jay amused him. "You really need to get your head out of those books. Have you even looked at this place? It's definitely gonna need work."

They were renting from an elderly man Lincoln had worked with years ago. The man, who had a gay son living in California, had made a point of telling them he had no problems renting to the two of them. In fact, he'd given them a break on the rent provided they did the repairs themselves, and even offered to let them buy the place as soon as they had the down payment saved up. Which sounded just about perfect to Jay, even with nearly all the kitchen cabinets missing hardware, the living room carpet worn to the stained padding in several places, and the water heater that barely kept the water warm enough for a tepid shower.

None of that mattered, not really. They hadn't been there long, but it already felt like home. Even with the boxes still stacked in the corner of the kitchen, and more boxes with his books along the back wall of the living room.

A new start. For both of them.

"We'll get it fixed up." Jay turned his head and captured Lincoln's mouth in a kiss. Such a simple touch that still surprised Jay, shocking him with its power and the passion sparking between them. Or maybe he shouldn't have been surprised. The physical moments had always been intense for them, from that very first moment in the alley behind Sonny's Tavern.

When they parted, Jay said, "I like that we're paying for the house together, you know?" That was one of the reasons he'd insisted they sell his old house and use the extra cash for some of the hospital bills, not to put toward their rent or a down payment. He wanted this new place, no matter what it looked like, to belong to the two of them.

"Yeah." Lincoln kissed Jay's neck again. "As soon as we get a little cash saved up, we'll work on the repairs."

Jay dropped his hand from Lincoln's head. "We should take the bike back."

Lincoln let go of him in a rush and stepped away. "No way."

Jay kept his back to him. "And I shouldn't be switching to part-time at work."

That didn't even get a response. Jay faced him. Lincoln had his arms folded across his chest, his face held in a tight grimace of frustration.

"Don't." Jay reached up and ran his fingers over Lincoln's furrowed brow.

"Don't what?" Lincoln gripped Jay's hand and kept a hold of him as he dropped their linked hands to his side. "This is not up for discussion. You cannot take all those classes you signed up for next semester, study, and go to work full-time."

"Lots of people do it."

"You're not. You've already put off school long enough. I'm working, and I'll take care of the bills." He eased his grip on Jay's hand and smirked. "We'll have enough money for this place, food, and lube. What more does a man need?"

Jay laughed. "You're right." He leaned into Lincoln. "I've got everything I need."

The next kiss was slow and sweet and full of the promises Jay wanted to share. Yet there was something else he had to say. "You don't always have to be the one to take care of everyone." He kissed Lincoln again. First on the lips, then down along his neck to the sensitive spot between neck and shoulder that always drove Lincoln mad. "You gotta let people take care of you sometimes, Linc."

Lincoln held him by the back of the head and tilted his own head to the side, which encouraged Jay's explorations as Lincoln said, "You took care of me pretty damn good last night."

Jay grinned against Lincoln's skin. "It was a good one?"

"You have no idea. It's like you've been sucking cock all your life."

"Just yours."

Lincoln let out a low rumble. He always liked being reminded that Jay had never been with another man. He gripped Jay by the hips, then swung him around and crowded him against the refrigerator. He planted another deep kiss on his lips, this one more about lust and passion.

Jay wrapped a leg around him and gave himself over to the moment, falling into the sweet sensation of those lips on his, their tongues connecting over and over again, the taut muscles under his fingertips.

Eventually, reluctantly, Jay forced himself to pull back. "When I said you need to let people take care of you, I wasn't talking about sex."

"I know." Lincoln ran a hand down Jay's bare chest, tenderly tracing the scar left behind after the surgery to remove the bullet.

"It's ugly, isn't it?"

"Nah. It's beautiful. Reminds me you're still here." He met Jay's stare with those focused, dark eyes. "A lot of people don't get second chances."

Good to know they were on the same page about that.

Even after Jay's confession that he couldn't bear to lose Lincoln, after packing up his stuff and moving in with him, Jay had worried Lincoln would always have lingering doubts about their pasts—about them. That he would always feel guilty about being too happy.

Jay leaned in, and they kissed again, each caressing and loving with every touch. They had come too close to losing this.

"So..." Jay walked Lincoln backward toward the kitchen table. "We've christened every room in the house but this one." He cleared his books off the table, lowered his jeans and underwear. Lincoln watched him undress and then followed suit with his briefs. Jay lay back across the table's surface, pulling Lincoln with him, and Lincoln slowly lowered his body over Jay's.

They kissed and rubbed and stroked each other in all the right places until they were both begging for more without words.

Lincoln stood, laughing as he unwrapped Jay's limbs from around him. "Gotta get the lube."

Jay pointed over his head to the top box on the pile in the corner. "That box has the shit from my nightstand."

Lincoln went for the box. He returned to the table with the lube. "I vote we either never unpack or we always keep a stash of lube in here."

"It's the kitchen. Where would we put lube?"

"We'll make room in the silverware drawer."

Jay laughed at that. Then he sobered as he watched Lincoln readying himself, slicking the length of his hard shaft.

Staring down at Jay, Lincoln breathed deep and shook his head.

"What?"

"Nothing. Just…" He leaned over Jay and pressed into him as he spoke his next words. "God, what you do to me."

Jay was utterly lost to a reply or thoughts or anything but the intensity passing between them that had very little to do with sex.

Lincoln rocked slowly, angling Jay just right. A few more sweet slides of their bodies coming together and Lincoln pulled out. He gripped Jay by the back of the neck and encouraged him up.

"Ride me." He turned them, taking Jay's place on the table.

Jay nodded and knelt on the surface, straddling him. Lincoln gripped his hips as Jay lowered himself onto Lincoln's cock.

The table creaked and rocked with their combined weight. It sounded like it was about to collapse. They both stilled. Then laughed.

"Shit," Jay said. "We're gonna fall."

Lincoln shook his head. "It'll hold."

"We can't…" Jay lifted up and sank down on Lincoln's cock again, picking up speed each time his body swallowed the thick shaft. "We can't break the table. We'll have nowhere to eat."

"We'll eat in bed." Lincoln surged up into Jay, grunting with each slam of their bodies. The table teetered and squeaked beneath them again. The metal tips of the legs scraped along the linoleum floor.

"Sex on the table and"—Jay kept moving, his thighs flexing as he rode Lincoln—"food in bed? Isn't that a little opposite of how it should be?"

Lincoln's next words were punctuated by low grunts. "Everything…about us…is opposite of how it should be."

No.

Jay stopped. He reached down and laid a hand over Lincoln's chest, over his heart, loving the power and strength of the firm body beneath him. "Don't."

"It's okay." Lincoln gripped Jay's hand and held it in place. "I won't forget, but I don't want to live in the past anymore."

Jay surged forward and kissed him. Letting his body and heart take over, he started moving again, and Lincoln thrust up to meet him. It wasn't long before Lincoln jerked his hips faster and faster. He arched off the table, and a long groan escaped his lips as he came.

They stilled, and the table settled underneath them. Until Lincoln tugged Jay down to him with an urgency that would've had anyone believing he hadn't come yet. He held him close and whispered, "Love you," against the skin of Jay's neck as he stroked his cock.

A shudder worked its way through Jay. A few more strokes mixed in with a repeat of those whispered words, and he came over

Lincoln's hand. His release landed on his chest, then Lincoln's. He collapsed forward, and they lay pressed together, the table swaying underneath them with each deep breath.

Lincoln shifted Jay around until he lay beside him, Jay's head on Lincoln's chest, Lincoln petting the wolf tattoo again.

"I'm proud of you, Jay."

"For what? My finely honed acrobatic skills that kept us on this table?"

Lincoln laughed. His breath blew through Jay's hair. "Yeah, that. And everything else. Going to school, going to therapy with your parents, forgiving your brother. All of it." He wrapped his arms tighter around Jay. "There's not many men in the world like you."

Jay scoffed. *Him?* He sat up and searched Lincoln's face. Didn't he get it?

"Right back at you."

* * * *

Lincoln pressed the up button for the garage door, and the sun's rays poured into the dark garage. Two Harleys sat side by side, one in great shape with flames and an eagle painted across the tank.

The other was the bike they'd just bought for Jay. Older than Lincoln's and in need of some serious bodywork, but at least it ran decently. They'd get it into shape. Like they'd done with the first one.

Lincoln removed the tarp that covered the stacks of boxes along the far side of the garage. He could at least get some of this stuff unpacked before Jay finished in the shower.

Jay needed to spend his free time studying, not lugging shit out of boxes, especially if he was going to stay up half the night reading his schoolbooks. Lincoln's thoughts turned to the night before—and the kitchen-table-christening sex. He couldn't seem to care that every leg on the crappy kitchen table was now loose. He'd tighten them tonight when they got home. And just maybe he'd see if Jay wanted to test out the table again and make sure he had the legs secured well enough.

He laughed to himself and set to work unpacking Jay's tools from the boxes. He almost missed the hand on his ass. He didn't miss the words whispered in his ear, though.

"You gotta stop coming out here if you expect us to get anywhere on time."

Lincoln glanced over his shoulder at Jay. His hair was still damp from the shower. Who knew the scent of cheap-ass soap and aftershave lotion from the local discount store could smell so damn good? Or maybe it was the way those scents mixed with the man underneath that was so tempting.

Lincoln asked, "You got a thing for garages?"

"I got a thing for sex with you on a bike, and we haven't broken mine in yet."

Forget the table. They'd christen the garage and Jay's bike next. Lincoln moved in to kiss him.

Jay took a step back. "Don't you dare start something. We've gotta get going or we'll be late."

"Me? You really going to put an idea like that in a guy's head and not follow through?"

Jay smirked, a playfulness in his expression unlike any he'd worn yet. Then the look grew into something more. Lincoln wasn't sure what. More serious, maybe. Determined. Confident. "I'll follow through. As soon as we get home."

They'd both learned a lot about living in the moment. Lincoln gave a nod of understanding. Some things they got without having to offer more. From day one they'd understood each other's pain and need in a way few others had.

Contentment lingered on Jay's face as he grabbed his helmet from the workbench, got on his bike, and took off through the open garage door into the sunlight. Lincoln started his bike and followed. He loved this—Jay looking free, at peace as they rode through the streets of Edgefield.

A few blocks later they pulled up to a two-story house. There was a realty sign marked with a SOLD banner out front and a car in the driveway that Lincoln didn't recognize. The car was parked behind the moving truck he and Jay had loaded up the day before. Nancy and the kids hadn't accumulated much since the fire—the apartment they'd been renting had been furnished—but they did have a few boxes with new clothes and toys and kitchen crap.

"Jay!" Jessica ran at Jay and threw her arms around his legs as soon as he got off the bike.

"Hey." Lincoln swung off his bike. "Did you forget about me already?"

She ran to him and jumped into his arms. "Uncle Lincoln, you're funny. You don't forget family."

"Good point."

Adam exited the cab of the truck, lugging a cat carrier through the open door. Davy crawled out after him. He had Sparky on a leash, and they all headed to where Jay and Lincoln had parked their bikes off to the side at the end of the driveway. The furniture delivery truck would be there in an hour with the new sofa and dining room set Nancy had picked out the week before.

A man stepped out of the house with Nancy. He handed over the keys, hesitated, then shook her hand, holding on a little longer than necessary. Together they crossed the lawn to gather up the realty sign, and then he and Nancy continued slowly side by side, chatting as they made their way toward his car. He loaded the sign into the trunk. Then he paused again and spoke more to Nancy, both of them smiling and nodding, the guy's gaze lingering on Nancy's face.

He was definitely interested in more than helping her get settled in her new home. Lincoln exchanged a look with Jay. He was thinking the same thing.

Eventually the real estate agent got into his car and began backing out. When he neared the end of the driveway where everyone else stood, he stopped the car. "Enjoy the new home, kids." He waved and pulled out onto the street.

Lincoln smirked at Nancy as she approached. "He was nice."

She nodded. "He is. And really patient. We must've looked at more than thirty houses all across the county."

Davy groaned. "And then you bought the first one we looked at here in town."

Adam bopped his brother on the top of the head. "Leave Mom alone about it." He gave Davy a playful push toward the truck, then said, "He's a nice guy, Mom. If you want to see him again, I think you should. You know...without the lame excuse of looking at houses."

"Adam!"

He rolled his eyes and headed for the truck, calling back, "Like it wasn't obvious."

Lincoln tried to fend off the laughter. He couldn't hold back the relief washing over him, though. More than anything, he wanted Nancy to be safe and happy and...loved. She deserved someone who'd treat her and the kids with respect.

He dropped a kiss on Nancy's forehead, then headed with Jay for the back of the truck to start unloading. Jessica skipped after them. The boys had the back door open, and everyone began sliding boxes to the end of the truck bed.

"Stop!" Nancy called out as she came around the side of the truck. She went to Jay. "I really hope you don't mind." Louder to everyone else, she added, "The first thing in the house is the angel."

"What angel, Mommy?" Jessica asked.

Nancy retrieved a box from the back of the truck and pulled out a large figurine that was over a foot tall. A woman in a green dress with long red hair. She handed it to Jessica. "You can carry it, sweetie, and why don't you keep her in your room so she can look after you."

Jessica wrapped both arms around the angel, the figurine nearly too tall for her to carry. "But she's so pretty. Don't you want to see her all the time?"

"We don't need to see her every day to know she's looking after us." Nancy looked to Jay. "All of us."

Jay nodded, a pleased smile on his lips, the expression one of appreciation, not sadness or grief. "It's perfect."

Lincoln wound an arm around him and pressed his lips to Jay's temple. "She's a part of all of us now." As much as he wanted Jay to move on, to build a new life, he'd never let him think he couldn't remember her, love her.

Leaning into him, Jay offered appreciation that Lincoln got without words. Again that understanding that defied logic—and maybe sanity—passed between them.

Or maybe it was the sanest connection either of them could've found.

Jessica sped off toward the house, the angel in her arms. The boys followed with Sparky and the cat. Nancy hesitated for a moment. Then in a flurry, as if she had to act before she changed her mind, she lunged for Jay and wrapped her arms around his neck. She whispered her next words, but Lincoln heard her clearly.

"Thank you for everything, but mostly, thank you for helping him find his way."

Jay held her in return and met Lincoln's gaze. "He did the same for me."

She stepped back, wiping tears from her eyes. She looked to one, then the other and sighed. No matter what his little sis had been through in life, she believed in love and happy endings. She watched them for another moment, then grabbed a box from the truck and went inside the house.

"Your sister is pretty great."

Lincoln stared after her at the open front door of the house. "She is."

"Runs in the family." Jay stepped in front of him, blocking Lincoln's view until Jay was all he could see. "I think…"

"What?" Lincoln searched Jay's face, for once believing he was exactly what Jay needed in his life. He knew that now with a certainty he hadn't been sure he could ever feel before this moment. He wouldn't let him down. "You can always talk about Katie, whenever you need to."

"Thanks for that, but this isn't about her." Jay reached for him, running his thumb along Lincoln's jaw. "My future is you. And I think I might just be the luckiest guy around. I've been loved by two of the most beautiful people. Inside and out."

Lincoln scoffed. "You talk too much." He paused, grew serious. "You're the one who's beautiful. The best of all of us." And without a doubt he knew she'd agree with him.

Jay stepped closer. He looked toward the street and then back to Lincoln, gesturing between them. "There's not many people who'll understand this."

"Who cares?" Lincoln let out a long breath. He felt more at ease than he had in months, not wanting to be anywhere else in the world. They'd had this discussion before, but maybe they both needed a reminder from time to time. "I think if I owe her anything—if she'd want anything from me—it's for me to love you with everything I am. Fuck what people think."

That had Jay laughing, a huge grin on his face.

Lincoln drew him into an embrace, holding on, letting the certainty wash over him again. He wasn't worried about who saw them or what anyone thought of the two of them together.

Despite all his mistakes, he'd been given a gift, and he planned on being worthy of it for the rest of his life.

ABOUT THE AUTHOR

Sloan Parker writes passionate, dramatic stories about two men (or more) falling in love. She enjoys writing in the fictional world because in fiction you can be anything, do anything—even fall in love for the first time over and over again. Sloan lives in Ohio with her partner and their neurotic cats. Her greatest moments in life are spent with her family, her friends, and her characters.

To contact Sloan, find out about her other books that are available for purchase, and read free stories, visit: www.sloanparker.com. If you'd like to be notified of new releases and get exclusive sneak peeks, be sure to sign up to receive Sloan Parker's newsletter via her website.

www.ingramcontent.com/pod-product-compliance
Lightning Source LLC
Chambersburg PA
CBHW030239200626
46816CB00002BA/430